Praise for April Sinclair's
I LEFT MY BACK DOOR OPEN

"A winner. . . . Dee Dee is a smart, sympathetic character. . . . Sinclair's lively humor and optimism make this book a worthy successor to her other popular novels."
—*Boston Herald*

"April Sinclair's wonderful new book brims with her trademark soul, intelligence, humor, spirit, and life." —Anne Lamott, author of *Travelling Mercies*

"Refreshingly upbeat and robustly spiritual, the novel steers clear of sentimental inspirational writings by means of its frank and funny dialogue, and follows Sinclair's earlier successes admirably." —*Publishers Weekly*

"April Sinclair is an extraordinary storyteller."
—Dorothy Allison, author of *Bastard Out of Carolina*

"Thought-provoking . . . [with] enough energy to keep helpless romantics turning the pages." —*Dallas Morning News*

"Snappy, entertaining. . . . Dee Dee is bright and likeable, with a quick wit and a shrewd, observant eye. . . . Sinclair wants us to see past the familiar stereotypes and recognize our differences. . . . Her heart is in the right place."
—*Washington Post Book World*

*I left
my back
door open*

I left
my back
door open

a
novel

april
sinclair

Perennial
An Imprint of HarperCollins*Publishers*

Grateful acknowledgment is made for the following permission to reprint previously published material: "God Is the Only Power in My Life," a prayer from *Your Needs Met* by Jack and Cornelia Addington. Copyright 1966 and renewed 1973, 1997. Reprinted by permission of DeVorss & Co.

A hardcover edition of this book was published in 1999 by Hyperion.

HarperCollins books may be purchased for educational, business, or sales promotional use. For information please write: Special Markets Department, HarperCollins Publishers Inc., 10 East 53rd Street, New York, NY 10022.

Designed by Christine Weathersbee

First Perennial edition published 2000.

The Library of Congress has catalogued the hardcover edition as follows:

Sinclair, April

I left my back door open : a novel / April Sinclair.—1st ed.

  p. cm.

ISBN: 0-7868-6229-7

  1. Afro-Americans—Illinois—Chicago—Fiction.   I. Title.

PS3569.I5197I16   1999

813'.54—dc21   98-50784

                                                                   CIP

ISBN 0-380-73280-7(pbk.)

00 01 02 03 04 ❖/RRD 10 9 8 7 6 5 4 3 2 1

This book is lovingly dedicated to my niece,
Lyndsey, my siblings, Marcia, Byron and Nina,
and my half sister, Dorothy.

ACKNOWLEDGMENTS

I couldn't have pulled this book off by myself. A million thanks to my main reader and dear friend, Susan Holper, for her valuable input. We discussed the work in progress over many long, delicious lunches of Pakistani food at the Village Restaurant in Berkeley, California. A big thanks also to my other reader and close friend, Judy MacLean, for her helpful feedback. Kudos to everyone at Hyperion, especially my editor, Leslie Wells; she is an author's dream come true. She's always supportive and usually right. My agent, Winifred Golden, now at the Castiglia Agency in Del Mar, California, is way past cool and won't be satisfied until my work is on the big screen. Thanks also to the Margret McBride Literary Agency for their continued support. *Muchas gracias* to Kimberly Rosa, director of the Conflict Resolution Program of the Central Coast in San Luis Obispo, California, for lending her expertise. I also wish to acknowledge two other friends, for introducing me to the East Bay Church of Religious Science in Oakland, California. I have truly been inspired by the choir, congregation and the minister, Reverend Eloise Oliver. I am also grateful for the heartfelt fellowship I have received at St. Andrew Presbyterian Church in Marin City, California. A special thanks to my aunt Allison Gunter, for providing me with a cozy place to chill and write on location in her Chicago home. Thanks also to my aunt Jean Gunter, for our long chats and sharing her stories over the years. And I will always have a special place in my heart for my talented cousin Eric May, for encouraging me since jumpstreet and introducing me to the family of Columbia College in Chicago where he teaches creative writing. Last but not least, a huge thanks to my readers for their warmth, loyalty and support!

one

I am not young, or thin, or white or beautiful. I'm a slightly thick sista, but I know how to fix myself up. And I'm on the radio. My name is Daphne Dupree, and I play the blues.

I liked everything about speaking into a mike. I even enjoyed positioning my mouth in front of one. And I loved the way my voice sounded, so rich and full, when it came out. Maybe I just liked to hear myself talk.

"We opened the set with the incomparable Etta 'Miss Peaches' James doing 'At Last.' That was by special request from Dianne, a blue-eyed soul sister who knows that when you make a potato salad, you don't leave out the mustard.

"Speaking of food, we're gonna be broadcasting live from Taste of Chicago, in Grant Park next Saturday. I hope to see some of my listeners. You know I'm gon' sho' 'nuff be tastin', too. 'Cause, honey, there's no such thang as a black anorexic!" I laughed. "You heard it here first."

I kept right on b.s.in,' 'cause I was on a roll. And I was in control. "Y'all remember, last year, my boyfriend didn't hit me, but he up and quit me? Yeah, he said, 'Dee Dee you too big,' sho' did. The brotha didn't 'preciate my meat. He wasn't no natchel man. Finally had to tell 'im, I was built for comfort, not for speed!"

I paused for air. "You know, it's funny, there was a time when a skinny woman was almost looked at as deformed. She damn near had to run away and join the circus." I sighed. "When I was a child, nobody wanted the woman with the skinny legs And don't let her have the nerve to be flat-chested, with no booty, too. You had to have something to shake back in them days."

I noticed a lighted button. "I got a call coming in on the board. Somebody out there must be feeling my pain."

"Girlfriend, you need to come on back home to the soulful South Side," the voice on the line urged.

"It sounds like my friend, Sarita."

"Yeah, it's me, girl. Anyway, it's plenty of men on the South Side who like full-figured women."

"Sista, you say I'm just dealing on the wrong side of town? You think that's what it is?"

"I know that's what it is. You drive around the South Side, and you see big behinds everywhere. And it ain't keeping nobody from getting no man, or putting on no pair of shorts, either."

"Big behinds are all over the North Side, too," I insisted. "You need to get out more. Big behinds are everywhere now, and they come in all colors. And they're coming to a theater near you."

"Girl, you crazy! We don't have no theaters around here. I'm calling you from the 'hood."

"It was just an expression."

"Anyway, Dee Dee, you need to come on back to church, 'cause, honey, there're plenty of women heavier than you. In fact, they'd run and bring you a plate of food, girlfriend. Try to fatten you up."

"All right, I'll be in your church on Sunday. So save me some pew. And give some sugar to my play nephew. I just can't help but rhyme, almost every time."

"Okay, then, you put on Koko Taylor for your good girlfriend."

"A request for the reigning Queen of the Blues is always good news! But, first, it's time for the tips, and I'll shoot 'em from the hips. If you want your holiday to be a blast, when you barbecue, put your sauce on last. You can baste it with vinegar, you can baste it with beer. But, Koko fixin' to pitch a 'Wang Dang Doodle,' then I'm outta here! That concludes this edition of Deep Dish Blues on WLUV, 98.6 on your FM dial. And I'm your hostess with the mostest, Dee Dee Joy, born in Alabama and raised in Illinois."

I'd taken off my headphones and unglued my hips from the one-size-don't-fit-all swivel chair. Jade was at the mike now. I listened to her sultry voice as I sauntered through the air-conditioned state-of-the-art studio on Chicago's waterfront.

"Welcome to the world of Belly," Jade said mysteriously, in her Chinese accent. "Slip on your finger cymbals. Toreador your veils. Put your camels to bed. We've got two hours of Egyptian pop ahead."

I swayed to the beat as I entered the spacious but deserted reception area. My ears were filled with the moaning of Egyptians, but my eyes were drawn to the view of the cluster of boats navigating the lake. Outside the picture windows, people strolled along the water's edge or sat in open-air cafés. On summer nights like this one, a jazz band played below a Budweiser sign. Navy Pier was a tourist attraction, pure and simple. But I admired the colorful Ferris wheel lit up against the darkening sky.

Suddenly, I felt someone's presence and my body jumped. I turned around. It was Rob, the station manager. He looked like Mike Moore, the guy who made the movie *Roger and Me.*

"I didn't mean to startle you," Rob said, apologetically.

"I didn't know you were still here," I answered.

"Yeah, I'm still pushing papers." Rob sighed. "Anyway, I got your memo," he continued. "But, guess what, you don't have to worry about doing that stinking fund-raiser this year, you're off the damn hook."

"I didn't mind doing it," I answered. "It was for a good cause. Besides, I can think of worse things than emceeing an event at the Four Seasons. Plus, they've always requested me."

"Yeah, and all these years you've been a trouper." Rob patted me on the shoulder.

"Well, what happened?" I asked, confused. "Have they decided not to do it this year? It was always so successful."

"They're still gonna do it, all right," Rob assured me. "But this year they just decided to try a different angle, go after a different crowd."

"A different crowd?" I asked, wrinkling my forehead.

"Yeah, a younger bunch."

"How young?"

"I don't know, I guess twenties and thirties."

"Rob, I'm in that age range, more or less," I said, trying to sound calm.

"How old are you now, Dee Dee, thirty-nine?"

I swallowed. "Close, I just turned forty-one."

"Ouch, I thought we were the same age. Damn, you're getting up there."

I sighed. "It's not that serious."

"You're right. You've got quite a few years left before you'll need dentures. By the way, happy belated birthday."

"Thanks. So, who are you going to get to do the fund-raiser?" I asked, turning and staring out the window again.

"I'm gonna run it by Jennifer."

"Jennifer!" I wheeled back around. "But she's just an intern!"

"Yeah, but she's bright and perky. Really perky," Rob added, making animated gestures. "I think that's the type they're looking for."

"What am I, iron-tired blood?" I asked, rolling my eyes.

"Not at all. You did a great job all these years. Everyone says that. They just want to appeal to the damn yuppies, you know, Wicker Park, Lincoln Park . . ."

"Bucktown," I added.

"Yeah, exactly, those types. You understand."

"Yeah, I guess," I said, trying to sound like a team player.

"Good. By the way, your show was great as always. Now, go home and put your feet up."

That's not what you would tell Jennifer, I thought. *You would tell her to party like it's 1999.*

I pressed the button for the elevator. When I was a child, forty seemed older than God. I could more easily imagine myself dying in a car crash at thirty-nine than living to see forty.

But, somehow, I had managed to reach forty. And as if that hadn't been traumatic enough, last week, I turned forty-one. Nobody told me that forty was just a dress rehearsal for forty-one. Now I was *in* my forties. And a whole decade was harder to deny than a measly year. I stepped into the empty elevator. At least on my last birthday, I still had a boyfriend. Now I was all alone, except for my cat.

I nodded to the security guard in the downstairs lobby. Freddy's chocolate, moon-shaped face greeted me with a smile. His front gold tooth gleamed in the fluorescent light.

Freddy wiped his bald head and leaned against his desk. "Have you met the new dude in management yet?"

Dude. I cringed. Freddy was still stuck in the seventies. "We don't have any new manager," I answered.

"He was wearing a suit," Freddy informed me. "And he was with y'all's station manager. Rob told me he ain't need to sign in, he was working wit' y'all."

"Oh! You must be talking about the mediator."

"You met him yet?"

I shook my head. We'd only exchanged memos. But I'd agreed to meet with him next week. I figured that the mediator just wanted to touch bases with me about Jade's sexual harassment case against one of the engineers. Bill had made a crude pass at her after she performed a belly dance at the Christmas party last year.

When Jade told me about it, I confided that Bill had made a few sexually improper remarks to me about a year ago. Such as, he liked his women the way he liked his coffee—hot and black. When Bill's comments had gotten raunchier, I had put him in his place. And that had been the end of it.

Jade said she had explained to Bill that belly dancers were not sex objects. She had told him that belly dance was a disciplined art form with a spiritual base, that it had originated as a dance of empathy by women, for women in labor. But Bill had refused to be enlightened. He'd continued to hit on Jade, well into the new year.

Last month, Jade had decided it was time to complain to management. She'd asked if I minded her sharing my experience with Bill, in order to strengthen her complaint. I'd told her that would be fine. I'd even offered to go with Jade, so they could hear my story firsthand.

While listening to our accounts with a poker face, Rob had rearranged his chunky frame several times in his desk chair. Finally, he'd pulled down on his Cubs baseball cap and assured us that Bill would be ordered to stop harassing Jade immediately.

Rob had gone on to say that he liked to think of the radio station as a family. "My definition of a dysfunctional family is one in which the important stuff doesn't get talked about," he'd said. He asked us if we'd be open to mediation. Jade said that if Bill agreed, she'd go along with it. Rob had said that Bill wouldn't be given a choice. I'd told Rob that I didn't have a need to mediate with Bill. I'd simply shared my own experience to establish that this guy had a problem with more than one person, so that Jade didn't come off looking like some feminist nut.

"Anyway, I put in a good word for you," Freddy said, interrupting my thoughts.

You really have delusions of grandeur, I thought. *Like management cares what a security guard thinks.* Freddy folded his arms and sat on top of the desk.

"Thanks, but I don't think I'll need it," I answered politely. "Like I told you, he's not a manager. He's a mediator."

Freddy looked like he didn't know what the hell a mediator was. But it was safer for me not to go into an explanation. Freddy had loose lips. I couldn't talk about the sexual harassment case to him, or anyone else at the station. There were even rumors floating around that this conflict resolution guy had been called in to run diversity and tolerance workshops. Some of the white guys at the station were jittery, even the so-called liberal ones.

"Don't be naive," Freddy insisted. "There's always reason to worry. Don't forget, you in a business. You think they hired that Negro for nothing?"

"He's black?"

"Yeah, he's one of your people."

Freddy had recently disowned his race. He was robbed at gunpoint last winter. Two gangbangers were waiting outside his car after he left a church bingo game. They took Freddy's winnings and pistol-whipped him. Freddy was hospitalized for a day. There was even a small write-up in the *Defender,* Chicago's black daily newspaper.

"I forgot, you don't consider yourself one of *us* anymore."

"'Cause y'all don't know how to act. Y'all act right, I might consider coming back into the fold. But I'm still in *your* corner, Dee Dee. 'Cause you a credit to the race."

"A credit to the race," I repeated. "I haven't heard that one in a while."

"Anywho, I ain't saying they gon' go country/western or nothing like that. Although I did put in a word for disco," he said, rubbing his chin.

"Disco! Don't even go there."

"Well, I do smell change in the air." He sniffed. "Mark my words."

"We're such a unique station, though," I protested. "And that's what makes us special. Why would anyone want to mess with that?"

Freddy raised his eyebrows in disbelief. "Money, that's why. Unique and special don't pay no bills." He shook his head. "I just hope you'll be playing the blues instead of sanging 'em."

"Don't worry, I won't quit my day job." Actually, my day job really involved a lot of evening work. I facilitated consumer focus groups for product advertisers. It paid the mortgage, but my heart was in radio.

I ducked under Freddie's arm as he held the heavy glass door open for me and caught a whiff of the masculine odor that seeped through his deodorant. I thanked him as usual and headed for my car.

Even old steady Freddy was taken, I mused. He and his wife were going on a long-saved-for cruise in August. I fantasized about weekend getaways and a cruise on the Love Boat myself. But I was a single occupant in a double occupancy world. And, although I'd mastered eating meals alone in restaurants and going to movie matinees by myself, I certainly wasn't brave enough to sail solo.

I steered my Honda Accord out of the parking garage. My window was halfway down and the radio was on. The warm breeze played with my braids as I headed north on Lake Shore Drive.

Everybody tells single women that there are plenty of decent guys out there. We just have to be willing to compromise.

For example, "Don't judge a man by what he does or how much education he has. Sista, just 'cause you head of the E.P.A. don't mean you should reject the brotha who cleans the toilets. Don't be no snob. Black women have *always* had to marry down."

And how about this one? "You say you a lawyer. Damn, you in the catbird's seat. You must come in contact with a lot of eligible criminals. And don't overlook death row. Hey, most marriages don't last as long as the average condemned inmate's appeal process. You could have a lot of years of matrimony ahead."

And sistas have even said to each other, "Girl, you can *always* get sex." And we nodded our hot-combed, permed, afroed, braided or dreadlocked heads in agreement. Because we believed it was true—a woman *could* always get sex. And although we might take comfort in that knowledge, we made it clear that we would never settle for *just* sex. No self-respecting woman under forty-one would. And I had been no exception. I convinced myself that I had a little black book chock-full of men's names who would gladly answer my "booty calls." That is, if I were to make them, which of course I never would, because I wasn't that kind of girl.

But this morning, when I woke up alone at the age of forty-one on my expensive Swedish mattress, it occurred to me that there wasn't one special man that I could just casually call up and ask if he wanted to have sex. Except nerdy-ass Bill, the engineer, I chuckled grimly. Of course, I did have admirers who called my show and sent me fan mail. But I tried to maintain a separation between my public persona and my private dilemma.

Most of the men who I actually knew were either married, involved or church types who would trip out if I made such a brazen request. In other words, I was too well-respected.

I imagined that even if I phoned my philandering ex-husband, which I never would, he would gloat, "I knew that one day you'd eat humble pie. But it's too late, you know I have two kids to consider. Where are your family values? I'm trying to be faithful in *this* marriage."

Of course, then I'd recall that Wendell cheated on me less than a year after we said, "I do." When I confronted him about his overnight absences and sudden interest in buying new underwear, he came clean, so to speak. Wendell explained that it was easier to cheat on a woman without a uterus, who wasn't a complete woman anymore, as he put it. You see, I had to have a hysterectomy because of fibroid tumors. And six weeks of abstaining from sexual intercourse while I healed from major surgery was more than poor Wendell could manage. I had to grieve the end of my marriage and the loss of my womb at the same time. It wasn't a good year.

If I called Randall, an ex of mine who'd recently moved to Washington, D.C., and asked, "Do you wanna get funky with me?" he would delicately remind me that we were just "good girlfriends now."

We'd broken up when he came out of the closet. But if Randall were straight, I'd be willing to fly to D.C., especially if it were cherry blossom time.

Who else could I call? I imagined dialing my last boyfriend, Cedric. But he would clear his throat and ask, "How much weight have you lost?" After all, he dumped me because fat was a turn-off. I tried to lose weight, even occasionally vomiting for love, but in the end, my five-foot-five-inch frame was still hovering at twenty percent over my ideal weight. And, according to Cedric and the American Medical Association, that qualified me as overweight. Cedric couldn't commit to somebody who couldn't commit to fitness. And as of this morning, my treadmill was still being used as a clothes rack.

I sighed as I zipped past the expensive high-rises along Chicago's Gold Coast. I knew that I could gap my legs open somewhere and get sex. But that's not what I wanted. I wanted a special man in my life. Was that too much to ask? Books and movies always showed women dealing with mess. But they almost never told you that there were lots of women who didn't even have any mess to deal with. Women who can go for a whole year without even being asked on a date. This is not unheard of; I know women like that. They are not ugly or bitchy or stanky with bad table manners. They're just invisible. I know, because I'm afraid I'm becoming one of them. It wasn't always like this. When I was younger, men wouldn't leave me alone.

"Belly dancers at home, here's music to undulate to." Jade's husky voice on the car radio interrupted my thoughts.

I imagined Jade's listeners moving themselves in wavelike motions to the haunting music.

"Open and close your whole bodies," she instructed.

I glanced at the water, lapping sensually against the shores of Lake Michigan in the dark. I pretended that I was rushing home to undulate with my man.

When I opened the door to my artsy-fartsy-rehab condo, my talkative cat greeted me as usual. I imagined that my orange and white fur child was cussing me out for not being there to feed him at the exact moment that he wished to eat. I set his bowl on the glazed countertop.

"Have no fear, your spinster's here," I said, even though technically I wasn't a spinster, because I'd been married before. It didn't matter to Langston, just so long as I was reaching for the cat food.

I sighed, glancing at the copper pots and pans hanging overhead. "Langston, sometimes I envy you. It's hard to be black and female."

My cat's unsympathetic green eyes seemed to say, "I'm not in the mood for a pity party."

After feeding Langston, I checked my voice mail. The first message caused me to drop the bills and birthday cards that I was sorting through. It was Dr. Hamilton's British accent informing me that there was an opening in the incest survivors' support group at my HMO. Would I please give her a ring back?

I felt my body tense up at the mention of the word incest. I didn't want to think about it, let alone sit in a group and discuss it. I'd called the hospital at a weak moment, right before Christmas. I was having nightmares again, and the holidays were harder than usual. My stepfather was in intensive care in a St. Louis hospital. I was debating whether to confront him about what he'd done, before he died.

It was also almost ten years since my mother passed. Last Christmas, my younger sister, Alexis, was busy with her son and new husband in Philadelphia. And my older brother, Wayne, and his family were tucked away in Matteson, a Chicago suburb. Although I was invited to three parties, I still felt very much alone.

I never got the deathbed confession that I fantasized about. My stepfather died the morning that I was scheduled to leave for St. Louis. He left this world without ever admitting to me that he used to come into my bedroom at night, blowing his whiskey breath in my face, whispering that he needed to check my oil.

It gave me a sickening feeling in the pit of my stomach, just thinking about it. But I didn't know why Dr. Hamilton was still bothering me. I told her when she called in March that I was no longer in crisis mode, that I wanted to put the past behind me.

Dr. Hamilton had accused me of being in denial. She insisted there was a time bomb ticking away inside of me and that one day it was going to go off. I told Dr. Hamilton that if and when that happened, I'd give her a call. And hope she could fit me in.

The only other message was from my best friend, Sharon. She was returning home after a sabbatical year. She'd resume her college teaching position here in the fall. But girlfriend had the whole summer to play. Sharon left her flight information on my voice mail, and added that she had something to tell me when she saw me. She hoped I wouldn't wig out. Her voice didn't sound excited, but it didn't sound sad, either. I wondered what it could be. Maybe it had to do with her fifteen-year-old daughter, Tyeesha. But if T were pregnant or something, Sharon would be much more wigged out than I would be.

Maybe Sharon had finally found Mr. Right. But why would I wig out about that? Maybe he was white, or half her age. I wouldn't trip on his color, if he were a nice guy. After all, didn't Sharon say that many of the black men in Seattle went for white women? I'd heard that was generally the case in the western states. What was a sista to do?

I *would* be a tiny bit judgmental if Sharon were dating someone young enough to be her son. I'd just have to wait and find out when I picked her up at the airport next week.

I stared at the stainless-steel refrigerator door, covered with picture magnets, comic strips and my niece's and nephews' artwork. I was determined not to open the refrigerator. It was always a struggle, but nights were the worst. Langston rubbed up against my leg and purred. Cats are very sensitive. They can tune into your emotions, when they want to. I held Langston up in front of me and delivered my speech.

"If I could only stop eating at night, I could lose some of this behind. If I could only stop eating at night, my bra straps wouldn't dig into my shoulders to support my D cups and leave painful marks. If I could only stop eating at night, my thighs wouldn't play patty-cake with each other and stick together on hot days. If I could only stop eating at night, I wouldn't have to attach a rubber band through the buttonhole of last year's pants, so I can still fasten them."

Maybe the day will come when I can even tuck my shirts and blouses inside my pants and skirts, I thought. Naah, that was going too far. I would probably never have a flat stomach again.

"But just maybe I can remove the tire from around my waist." I sighed as Langston wriggled free and jumped to the floor.

These were my dreams. And I knew that they were achievable if I drank my bottled water and went to bed. But, of course, I didn't, because I hadn't forgotten how good cold pizza tasted, especially when you washed it down with leftover birthday cake, potato chips and beer.

two

"Marriage is like flies on a screen!" the preacher shouted, pausing to wipe the sweat from his shiny, brown forehead. "Follow me now," he instructed.

"Break it on down, Reverend," an older man in the large congregation shouted back.

I sat with Sarita, her husband Phil and their nine-year-old son Jason in Glorious Kingdom Baptist Church.

"I said, marriage is like flies on a screen," the minister repeated.

There was a chorus of "Amens" as people fanned themselves in the crowded church.

"I'm gon' say it again," the preacher insisted, raising his eyebrows.

"Yassuh!"

"I said, I'm gonna say it one more time," Reverend Stewart yelled, holding up his index finger. "And this time, I'm gonna say it with feeling."

"Take your time, Reverend!"

"I'm gonna say it like I mean it!" The minister clapped and danced away from the podium in his black robe.

"Preach, Reverend, Preach!"

"Stick with me, now." The pastor gazed at the congregation as if we were on the brink of some important discovery.

"Come on, Reverend. Bring it on home now!"

"Marriage is like flies on a screen! Some can't wait to get out!" The pastor balled his fists and imitated the posture of a runner, twisting his body to one side. "And some can't wait to get in!" he shouted, twisting to the other side. "Now, can I get a witness?"

Several large, gaily dressed sistas leapt out of their seats and waved their hands. Sarita had been right. Almost none of the women in the congregation looked like they'd ever missed a meal, including Sarita.

"When you build a house," Reverend Stewart continued, raising his arms to call for the congregation's attention, "you don't build it outta sand." He shook his balding head. "No, because the first high tide will wash it away. And when you build a house, you don't build it outta straw." Reverend Stewart shook his head again. "No, because fire can easily destroy it. You build your house outta something strong, something durable, something that will stand the test of time." He pounded his fist in the air, then added with a smile, "And, by the same token, you build a marriage on something solid, if you want it to last." Reverend Stewart tucked his lips in and nodded his head solemnly. "You build your marriage on the Rock of Ages."

The minister cupped his hands as if he were holding a large rock.

"Amen, Reverend, Amen!"

"You build a marriage on faith in God. "

"Preach, Reverend, preach!"

"Because, through God, all things are possible!" Reverend Stewart saluted with his fist.

"Yes, Lawd!"

"Hallelujah now!"

"Let the church say amen!"

"Amen!!!!!!!!"

The organist pounded away and a soloist stepped forward and belted out, "Jesus Is All the Man I Need." I scouted the room for husband material, just the same. But after you eliminated the probable gays in the choir, the elderly, the married and the ones too homely for words, there wasn't much to choose from. I turned my attention back to the service.

When visitors were asked to stand, I made the mistake of introducing myself as an ex-member of the church. I didn't think twice about it, until another woman described herself as a *former* member, a minute later. I cringed with embarrassment. I was convinced that the parishioners were thinking that I must really be doing the devil's work, calling myself an *ex*-member, making it sound like they were a cult or something and I'd been deprogrammed.

What made it worse, Sarita told me that last Sunday, when they asked if anyone had somebody that they wanted the church to pray for, her son Jason had jumped up. And to her astonishment, he'd said in a loud, clear voice, "I'd like the church to pray for my play auntie, Daphne Joy Dupree."

Sarita said that Phil whispered loudly, "What's wrong with Dee Dee?" She said that people who knew me shot *her* concerned looks. They probably figured that it must really be hush-hush, if the child was the only one who had the nerve to speak out.

Jason refused to give an explanation for his strange request. I felt it behooved me to be in attendance this Sunday so that at least people could see that I looked healthy and had a smile on my face. But on some level, it made me nervous, having a child asking the church to pray for me. I hoped that it was childhood innocence and not some psychic intuition of Jason's.

Other than worrying about looking happy and healthy, my mind was pretty much at peace. There was a feeling of reverence in the church that I'd grown to appreciate. Especially these days, it felt good to be surrounded by people who purposed right. The singing alone was reason enough to come to church more often. But I was especially moved by the testifying. Folks told their stories before the congregation and I felt a sense of community that I hadn't experienced in a long time. I was all the way home.

After church, back at Sarita's house, Jason asked me to retrieve a ball that had gotten lost in the tall weeds next door. Neither his father nor his mother would be bothered with such a task. But I agreed, because that was what play aunties were for. However, I did wonder why Jason didn't just go over and get the ball himself. I knew the house was abandoned and the weeds were waist-high, but I didn't think there were snakes in the grass.

Sarita and I sat on her plastic-covered sofa, sipping cold lemonade. Phil was draped across one of the chairs. Jason was upstairs, changing out of his church clothes. This living room was so different from mine: full of white, overstuffed furniture, fake marble tables and gaudy art pieces.

"So, Dee Dee, what you driving these days?" Phil asked, standing up. Even though he was past forty, people still mistook him for a basketball player. In actuality, Phil was a barber and Sarita was a dental hygienist. They'd married right after high school. They had two grown daughters who were working and going to college in Atlanta.

"You know, my Honda Accord," I answered.

"She bought it last summer, remember?" Sarita added,

"Well, if I don't see it out there, I'll come back in and let you know," Phil teased, his eyes twinkling.

"It's five years old, I bought it used."

"It might still be out there, then." Phil winked. "Although they say, business is pretty brisk in the chop shops."

"Don't let Phil scare you," Sarita said, straightening a pillow. The house was immaculate, as usual, but Sarita was always straightening things. "Your car will probably be all right," she assured me. At least she was relaxed about *something*.

"Dee Dee!" Jason rushed into the living room, carrying a copy of his *Boy's Life* magazine. "Why did Cinderella get kicked off the Little League team?"

"Kids still like riddles. That's something that hasn't changed." I smiled.

"Guess, Dee Dee, guess," Jason begged.

"We already know the answer," Sarita informed me.

"I don't know. I can't guess. So, tell me, why did Cinderella get kicked off the Little League team?"

"Because she kept running away from the ball!" Jason burst out laughing.

"That's cute," I said, chuckling.

"You made me forget to pick up the paper," Sarita fussed at Phil.

"How did *I* make you forget?" Phil protested.

"Because I was thinking about it when we were in the car, and you started talking about the grass needed watering."

"So, I can't even open my mouth. I'm supposed to be a mind reader." Phil sighed. "I tell you, it's rough being a man," he said, patting Jason's head.

"I thought you were going to cut Jason's hair." Sarita frowned. "You knew I wanted it cut for church. Dee Dee doesn't see him that often. He could at least look presentable."

"Sarita, you trippin'," I said. "I like his little 'fro."

"So, that's what this is really about," Phil said, holding his hands up in the air. "It's not about the newspaper, it's about Jason's hair." Phil pointed both index fingers. "Or is it really about PMS?"

"Don't go there," Sarita warned.

"What's PMS?" Jason asked.

"Never mind."

"It's when a man thinks the conversation is about ABC, but it's really about MNOP," Phil said, rolling his eyes.

"You should learn to have the whole alphabet at your disposal then," Sarita snapped.

"I have a riddle," Phil said to no one in particular. "If a man says something in a forest and a woman doesn't hear it, is he still wrong?"

"That's pretty good." I smiled.

Jason looked puzzled and Sarita cut her eyes.

"Bring back a *Sun-Times*," Sarita yelled as Phil waved good-bye and ducked into the hallway.

"Bring back some ice cream!" Jason added.

I changed into some of Sarita's old clothes and joined her and Jason in the kitchen. Sarita was shaking chicken around in a brown paper bag.

"Dee Dee, if you're gonna go over in that yard, watch out for needles," she cautioned.

"Needles?" I repeated. "*No comprendo.*"

"Syringes," she explained behind a cloud of flour dust. Then I remembered that the house next door had been on the verge of becoming a crack house, until Sarita and Phil got the city to board it up.

I waded gingerly into the tall, sunburned weeds and poked around the discarded forty-ounce malt liquor and cheap wine bottles with a broomstick. I soon spotted the football in the midst of the debris.

"I see it! Come on over and I'll pass it to you, Jace," I yelled at his skinny figure in the next yard.

"No," Jason refused, clutching the other side of the chain-link fence. "I ain't coming over there. I might get kilt!"

I remembered that when I was visiting at Easter, Phil was washing fresh blood off the sidewalk. Unfortunately, sometimes blood came with the territory. Sarita told me that she'd recently become apprehensive about venturing into the business district, even in the daytime. Last month, she and Jason were walking home from the post office, when they heard shooting. They'd instinctively fallen to the ground, like soldiers in a war. I grieved for the childhood Jason would never have. And for all of those like him, who no longer said, "When I grow up..." but, "If I grow up..." I grabbed the ball and hurried out of the yard

This is what Sarita wanted me to come back to. I sighed. She wouldn't even let Jason play in his own backyard unless she had her eye on him. She was afraid he'd get lured away or run off to explore. Jason *should* know the freedom of riding a bike against the wind, I thought. He *should* be out in the alley, playing kick ball, or shooting marbles in the dirt. Jason *should* be able to play the games we used to play, like Captain May I and One-Two-Three, Red Light. He should be ducking behind trees and garbage cans and hiding underneath porches because he's playing Hide-and-Seek, not because bullets are flying around with no names on them.

I felt sorry for Jason, even though he had all the latest electronic games. His childhood was so different from mine. We simply asked, "Mama, can we go out?" And she usually said, "Yeah, just be home for dinner." Or, "Be in when the streetlights come on."

We played Rock School on late summer nights, when Mama said, "Stay on the steps." I wondered if Jason had ever balled up his fists and asked someone to guess which one a rock was hidden in.

I knew that there was still some heart left in this community. I wasn't an ignorant outsider. I was from around here. I knew that the majority of people living in the aging brick two- and three-flat buildings, bungalows and occasional frame houses were decent, hard-working law-abiding people. When somebody died, maybe neighbors no longer filled the family's home with food and kindness like twenty or more years ago, but some people still looked out for each other. Phil shoveled elderly folks' walks and put down salt to melt the snow. And Sarita had coaxed shut-ins to open their windows during last summer's heat wave. Many of the elderly were more afraid of the rising crime rate than soaring temperatures. Too bad people had to live like caged birds. They deserved better, and I remembered better.

Being a loving pretend auntie, I agreed to play electronic Wheel of Fortune with Jason before dinner. I squinted to read a tiny monitor and made my move. *Whatever happened to tic tac toe or Monopoly or checkers?* I wondered.

Sarita's voice rang out. "Jason, bring your butt down here! What is this mess from your school?"

Jason backed away from the game and trembled visibly. I could tell by the sound of Sarita's voice that he was in some kind of trouble. And Sarita was nobody to cross. She could be rough on her son. I'd even spoken to her about it before, but she'd insisted that Jason was the kind of child that you had to let know you were there.

It had been easier for Sarita with her two older daughters. She got lucky with them. They were quicker to mind. And, of course, it was different raising children in the seventies. Yet, it seemed to me that when you named a child Jason, you were asking for trouble.

When I think of the name Jason, a bad boy automatically comes to mind.

"I'm scared of her," Jason whimpered. "I"m scared of her," he repeated.

I put my arm around his narrow shoulders. His body felt tense and small. "What did he do?" I yelled.

"Tell him to come down here and find out!"

We came down the stairs together, Jason clutching my arm.

"He says he's scared of you, Sarita," I volunteered bravely when I saw Sarita holding a belt.

Sarita became visibly angrier. "Don't make me have to curse on a Sunday, especially after I've been to church. If he's so scared of me, why won't he mind?"

For some reason, I identified with Jason more than Sarita at that moment. Maybe because I'd never known how it felt to be a parent, but I'd never forgotten how it felt to be a child. And Sarita's matronly figure looked scary, with her big hair, blazing eyes, flared nostrils and scowling expression.

"What did he do?" I repeated.

"He knows what he did. He wasn't too scared to call the teacher a bitch to his face!" Sarita said, holding up a note. "I found this in his pocket. He's suspended from summer school for three days."

"It's a man teacher?" I swallowed.

Sarita nodded. "He clowned all year in regular school. So, he had to go to summer school, just to pass. And now this. According to Phil, there's a conspiracy against black boys in the public schools."

"There just might be some truth to that," I said, hoping to spark a dialogue.

"Hmmph, Jason, you better make sure you're not *part* of the conspiracy," Sarita said, wrapping the belt menacingly around her hand.

Jason turned toward me.

"We work too hard for you to show out like you do. Now it's *my* turn to clown! Get over here, boy!" Sarita shouted. "I'm part of the conspiracy against black excuses!"

I felt a lump in my throat. I didn't want to see Jason get a whipping, even though he'd done wrong. Sarita reached out and grabbed her son. I was struck by how charged the air felt, as I watched Sarita whip Jason to the floor. When Jason's body cringed against her blows, I felt like I was witnessing a violent act, instead of just a familiar scene from my childhood. Sarita was whipping the boy like he'd stolen something. Jason finally cried out uncontrollably. I instinctively intervened and caught one of the licks on my arm.

"Damn, Sarita, that hurt!" I said, attempting to pull Jason to safety.

"Dee Dee, I don't allow cursing in my house, especially on Sunday."

I feared for a moment that Sarita might try to whip both of us. I was afraid that things could really get ugly then, because I would have to defend myself. I've never liked being hit, and I could still feel the sting.

I blocked Jason with my body. "Sarita, that's enough. You were hurting him."

"I wanted to hurt him," Sarita answered, looking at me incredulously. "I want him to feel it now, so he won't have to feel it later." She stared me in the eyes. "You trying to protect him from me, but you can't protect him from what's out there," Sarita said, pointing toward the street.

"We're the ones who hear the gunshots at night," she continued. "We're the ones who can't even empty garbage or go outside our door after dark." Sarita nodded toward Jason, who was cowering in the corner behind me. "This child has never even played in that alley," she said with a hint of sympathy in her voice. "*You* try raising a child in the 'hood today." She sighed, wearily.

"Your child *better* be scared of you," she added. "Or else you're gonna end up scared of him."

"I understand what you're up against," I said softly. "I know there aren't any easy answers. People like you are trying to raise the next generation under some heavy-duty circumstances. But people like me are going to be affected, whether you succeed or fail." I turned around and put my hand on Jason's shoulder. "We're all in this together."

Sarita draped the belt around her neck, as if to signal that the storm had receded. "Heaven help us all," she said quietly. "Heaven help us all."

When I got home, I hung up the African mask that Sarita had given me as a birthday present. It fit in nicely with my multi cultural decor. At least Sarita knew my taste. I sat down with the *Tribune* and a glass of merlot and leaned back against my distressed leather sofa. I looked up at my fifteen-foot ceiling. I needed to relax.

If I had pointed out to Sarita that she hadn't even asked Jason why he'd called the teacher a bitch, she would've insisted that it didn't matter; Jason was simply wrong. What precipitated Jason's remark was therefore irrelevent. He deserved to get his butt whupped. It was that simple. But was it? Was Sarita saving Jason from the penitentiary or building her own wall between herself and her son?

You see, once upon a time, I told a teacher, "Fuck you," loudly enough for her and the entire class to hear. I'd buried the incident in my own mind until today. I was a few years younger than Jason and it was 1961. I remember feeling embarrassed and angry because the young white teacher nudged me awake after I fell asleep during class. She wasn't a bad teacher; she was just trying to do her job. But I couldn't tell her that I'd been awakened by a nightmare the previous night. I couldn't tell her that the year before my stepfather used to mess with me. I couldn't tell her why suddenly being awakened was still scary for me. I couldn't explain my rage at being laughed at by the other kids, just because I'd felt safe enough to finally catch up on the z's I'd been robbed of the night before. So I said, "Fuck you."

It was before we moved to Morgan Park on the far South Side. I was living in arguably the toughest neighborhood on Chicago's West Side. Anyway, just on the surface, you'd think that a child who said, "Fuck you" to a teacher wasn't any good, wasn't going to amount to anything. Well, I did amount to something. And I wasn't a bad kid. I was a hurt kid. I was confused and angry and I couldn't tell anybody why.

That's why I could relate to Jason. He was in a rough environment. I'd been in a school filled with graffiti and stopped-up toilets and kids looking for fights. And if you accidently stepped on somebody's gym shoes or looked at them the wrong way, you'd better be ready to put up your dukes. But at least in my day, scores were settled with fists and fingernails. Rocks and bottles and even pocketknives were the exception.

Still, you had to be tough in order to be respected. Otherwise you were a target. I could relate to being scared inside, but jumping bad on the outside. Sometimes, you said things in order to save face. So, when I said, "Fuck you," to that teacher, loud enough for the whole class to hear, I gained respect. I was seen as nobody to mess with. And that was worth a whole bunch of woof tickets. Your reputation was everything.

That afternoon as I walked home from school, the toughest girl in the class marveled, "Most kids say shit like that under they breath. But goddamn, you said it loud enough for the whole world to hear!"

I was incredibly lucky that Miss Larson ignored my outburst. It didn't hurt that she was young and white and inexperienced. She could've hit me with a ruler or had me suspended. Looking back, I wonder if she sensed my pain. I heard a teacher say once that sometimes you can look at a kid and tell they're being abused. Maybe Miss Larson saw something in me that made her cut me some slack. Maybe she just felt sorry for me, because I was a Negro on Chicago's tough West Side and at 3:15 she was going home to *What a Jolly Street.* Or maybe she just felt disappointed and defeated after another day of teaching in the trenches. Whatever the reason, I'm eternally grateful. By not sending a note to my mother, Miss Larson saved me from getting one of the worst whippings of my life.

I headed for the refrigerator and stuffed myself with the plate of fried chicken and greens and garlic mashed potatoes and corn bread that Sarita had insisted I bring home. I knew that I wasn't hungry, but I just needed to feel full.

But then I felt guilty. I didn't want to pay the price in calories for my comfort food. Food was my friend, but calories were my enemy. So, I did something that I hadn't done since the holidays. I went into the bathroom, lifted up the toilet seat and stuck two fingers down my throat until the salty, chunky vomit poured down my hand and into the toilet bowl. I repeated the process several times in order to get everything out. I brushed my teeth and washed my face and hands. I looked into the mirror. My eyes were red and puffy and my face looked haggard. But I felt like throwing up was something I had needed to do.

I wasn't bulimic. I just needed to feel in control of my weight tonight, that's all. I hadn't vomited in six months. And I'd done it maybe ten times in my whole life. Maybe eleven, counting tonight. I just needed an outlet, an escape valve, every so often. But I would never make it a habit. I prided myself on my pearly white teeth. I had a smile that could light up a cave. I would never risk ruining my health.

three

I glimpsed my Africanic behind as I hurried past a storefront window near my home. l was headed for Taste of Chicago, where I planned to meet Jade from the radio station. It was Saturday at high noon and already hot. I'd broken out in a pair of shorts. My backfield was definitely in motion, but there was no way I was going back to the girdle-wearing days of my childhood. Especially not on a scorcher like today. Sweat was already pouring down my face.

I felt the warmth of the pavement through my sandals when I stepped off the curb to hail a taxi. A yellow cab pulled right in front of me. That was one of the advantages of living on the North Side. You could get a taxi. You didn't see cabs much on the South Side, except in Hyde Park, near the University of Chicago and the Museum of Science and Industry. If you were black and hailed a cab in the downtown Loop Area and you were lucky enough to get them to stop, the driver would tell you, point-blank, that he didn't want to go South.

Some cabbies have a lot to say to you. This one almost immediately complimented my lipstick.

"I like that color, especially on you," he said, with a foreign accent. The cabbie's sweaty skin was darker than mine. Perhaps he was East Indian, I thought.

"It's Royal Orchid by Fashion Fair. It's my favorite."

"It's nice. Are you married?"

I hesitated. I wasn't in the mood for somebody getting into my business. But then I remembered that I didn't have any business.

"No, I'm not."

"Not yet, huh."

"Who knows."

"Don't wait too long. How old are you?"

Suddenly, I became aware of the lack of air conditioning and began to sweat. "Never mind," I answered. I rolled the window all the way down.

"You're a career woman, huh."

"Yeah."

"That's nice," the cabbie said, navigating through the snarled traffic on Clark Street. "But you know, you're missing out on the most important part of life."

"Yeah, what's that?" I asked skeptically.

"Getting married and having a family, of course."

"I've been married, but I wasn't all that happy."

The driver groaned, shaking his dark, thick, wavy head of hair. "That's what's wrong with this country!" he shouted, slapping the steering wheel and blowing his horn. "Europe's the same way."

"What do you mean?"

"All you think about is your own selfish happiness! That's why Mother Teresa said, 'Loneliness is the leprosy of the West.' "

"Hmmm," I mumbled. "That's deep. Loneliness is the leprosy of the West. Maybe that's true. " I had to agree that there wasn't the emphasis on family and community like there was when I was growing up. There was a time when any adult on the street could correct a child. Now, if you did that, you might be shot. At the least, you'd run the risk of being cussed out. Times were different, all right. In my childhood during the sixties, it wasn't uncommon for a neighbor to borrow a cup of sugar or an egg. Now, I didn't even know most of my neighbors, let alone be able to borrow something from them.

Fran, an older Jewish woman, was the only neighbor who seemed to care that I drew breath. We looked out for each other's packages and she fed my cat and I waterered her plants sometimes. But Fran didn't really count as a neighbor, because we were already friends. She's the one who told me about the top-floor condo for sale in her building. And the first-time buyer program.

"Mother Teresa said there's an old woman in London who writes letters to herself, just so that her neighbors will think that she gets mail. But really, she has no one."

I turned my attention back to the driver. "No family, no friends?"

"No one, I tell you. She's all alone. She stands outside her door and holds the mail up to the sky, so her neighbors will think she has somebody."

"Well, at least the neighbors still care enough to notice," I pointed out. "Most people don't even have real neighbors anymore, just people who happen to live in their building or on their block."

"It's a shame when nobody cares about you," the driver continued. "What are we doing in this world?"

I cringed. The cabbie was pushing my fear button. Although I'd been blessed with two decent siblings and several close friends, I worried that I would end up a bag lady, a bird without any nest, like the women in Tennessee Williams's *The Glass Menagerie*.

"We have the technology to do everything but give people a smile or hug or a friend who cares," I said calmly. "You can't manufacture love."

My mind went back to my mother, who died of bone cancer in a nursing home. When I used to visit her, other patients begged me in the halls and doorways to come talk to them. I did my best to give them a passing greeting or a warm smile, but it was never enough. I always felt sorry for them. And I hoped I wouldn't end up like them, with nobody to come see about me.

The cabbie broke into my thoughts. "Mother Teresa says, 'It's easier to remove the hunger for bread than the hunger for love.'"

"That's powerful," I said.

"She says a beggar is better off in the streets of Calcutta than in New York City."

"How so?" I mumbled, noticing that traffic had slowed to a crawl.

"Because in India the poor are needed. If you give money to a beggar you can better your chances in the next life. You can even improve your karma in this life. So, even the poorest person is part of the fabric. He feels useful and valued. But in America, the poor are looked upon with contempt and resentment. They're blamed for their predicament. In India, if you're at the bottom, it's accepted as simply your lot in life, your karma."

"Yeah, but you're stuck. You don't pass go. You don't collect two hundred dollars. You can never buy Park Place."

"Huh?"

"Monopoly; it's a capitalist game."

"Oh."

"Not to mention the flies around the lip thing that they have in India and some other poor countries," I added. "At least we don't have *that* kind of poverty in America."

"No." The driver paused. "Your kind of poverty goes deeper than that."

I glanced warily at the meter. It said $6.80; so far, so good. But now that we were downtown, things could get ugly.

"Traffic is just going to be impossible, now." I sighed.

"Too bad they blocked off Columbus."

"Yeah, just take Michigan Avenue. I should've ridden the El."

"Yeah, especially on a day like today."

"I just want you to drop me off in front of the Art Institute. I'm meeting my friend in front of the north lion. We're planning to walk to the park from there. If I'd known it was going to be this bad, I would've met her back on Wacker, in front of the Hyatt."

"No, like you said before, if you really wanted to avoid all this madness, you should've taken the El."

"That's true."

"Today is my birthday," the cabbie announced. "I have to contend with all of this traffic on my birthday."

"Happy birthday. I just had a birthday, recently. It was on Father's Day."

"Happy birthday to you, too."

"Thanks," I said and drifted back to my thoughts. Father's Day was always hard for me. My biological father died from a fall he suffered at the mill where he worked. He was only thirty years old. I was almost four and my brother was six. I don't remember much about my father except that he used to swing me in his arms and once he let me taste beer. Anyway, by the time they could find a hospital near Crackville, Alabama, that would treat a *colored* person, it was too late. My father slipped into a coma and never regained consciousness.

After the funeral, Mama packed our bags. She spat on the red Alabama clay and we boarded a Greyhound bus for Chicago. Back then, she didn't know how racist the white folks in Chicago were. She just knew that she wanted something better for her children than the back doors and "Colored" signs that the South had to offer. We had to ride Jim Crow until we crossed the Mason-Dixon line. But Mama woke my brother and me up in the middle of the night and told us, "Hallelujah, we're out of the South!" I'll never forget Mama dragging us to the front of the bus in the wee hours of that April morning, like we were soldiers on a march.

That summer, my mother met my stepfather at the Bud Billiken Parade. The relatives we were staying with told Mama that the parade would cheer everybody up. It was to honor a black newspaperman named Bud Billiken. It was black folks' parade as much as the St. Patrick's Day Parade was for the Irish. Our relatives said it would make us feel proud to be Negroes. Black Chicagoans turned out in force. The South Side practically came to a halt. Negroes like us came all the way from the West Side just to see it

I have vague memories of a tall, maple-syrup-colored man offering to hoist me on his shoulders to get a better view of a marching band. My mother accepted the stranger's offer. And I minded my mother and thanked the nice man. I had no idea he would become my stepfather.

I just remember watching wide-eyed from atop his sturdy shoulders as colorfully attired band members shook their booties down the street.

A jolly looking woman nudged me and asked, "Baby, are you enjoying the parade?"

"Yes, ma'am," I shouted politely, being fresh from the South.

"Being colored can be fun when ain't nobody looking, huh, baby?" The woman chuckled.

"Yes, ma'am," I answered, somehow knowing instinctively what she meant. It's funny what you remember after thirty-seven years.

My mother married my stepfather during the Christmas holidays. I was a flower girl and my brother was the ring bearer. Everybody said how lucky she was to find a hard-working man, willing to take in another man's kids. They told us to color him father. And at first, it seemed like the coloring book was gonna have a happy ending. But less than a year later, when Mama was pregnant with Alexis, my stepfather was occasionally molesting me and regularly whipping my brother for the smallest of infractions.

Mama was a "good mother," but she was especially good at seeing no evil when it was too close to home. In those days, children didn't have a lot of power. Besides, we were brainwashed to believe that when bad things happened, it was our fault.

When bone cancer left my mother an invalid, our family hated to put her in a nursing home. We paid to have someone come in and take care of her at home as long as we could. But when her condition deteriorated, we agreed to put her in a skilled facility.

Even though Mama had lapsed into a coma and her eyes were shut, we still had hope. But looking back, I believe the nursing home staff had already given up on her. That's why nobody told me to leave that chilly November night, even though visiting hours were over. I was the last one who saw Mama alive. I stayed after the others left, partly because I was a night person and partly because I just wanted to be alone with her. Maybe I just wanted some form of closure.

Mama had always taken pride in her smooth coffee-with-cream complexion and her shapely figure. But now the flesh hung away from her frame like the drooping skin around a chicken neckbone. I kissed Mama's slack, ashy jaw and told her I loved her. I insisted that nobody could ever take her place. I touched the gold star she wore around her neck with the inscription, "Turn your scars into stars." I opened the Bible and read the Twenty-First Psalm to her. Suddenly, I noticed that the lamp-lighted room glowed beyond its wattage power.

I should've sensed that Mama was in the process of dying, but I didn't. The mysterious light gave me hope. Still, I was weary and wanted to go home and get some rest so that I could come back refreshed. But when I got up to leave, I heard a low, faint gurgling sound. It was as though Mama's soul was crying out to me, "Don't go!"

I begged Mama to gurgle again, or to squeeze my hand, or raise a finger, if she knew I was there. But she never did anything. So, I kissed Mama's cool forehead and told her lifeless face that I'd be back tomorrow. But our tomorrow never came.

The next morning I called to check on Mama's condition. The woman who answered the phone said, "Mrs. Joseph is dead," without much sympathy in her voice. They didn't know exactly when she died, just that she was dead by seven o'clock in the morning, when they went to check on her. That's how I found out, in a cold, impersonal way.

I will always regret that I left my mother to die alone. I could've stayed. I know that they would've let me stay all night. I could've been there with her at the very end. Nobody should have to die alone, even if they are in a coma.

"I didn't even look at my wife until my wedding day."

"Huh?" I mumbled. The cabbie suddenly brought me back to the present reality. I glanced at the meter; it was just over eight dollars. I looked out the window. We were crawling down Michigan Avenue, just passing the *Tribune* building.

"I said I never saw my wife until my wedding day."

"Oh. It was arranged?"

"Yeah."

"It worked out?"

"Of course."

"You're lucky."

"I am not lucky. That's how it is for everybody in Pakistan."

"There's no divorce rate?"

"It's less than five percent. I tell you why. Because people don't just think of themselves. You couldn't pay me to marry an American or European woman."

"I thought that you were already married."

"I am."

"Well, you couldn't pay *me* to marry a Pakistani man."

"What do you know about Pakistani men!" the driver shouted, swerving around a bus.

I was a little concerned for my safety, but I didn't back down.

"I know that the men have a lot more freedom than the women," I answered firmly.

"My wife has all the freedom she could possibly want. She doesn't even have to work. I work two jobs to support my family. What could she possibly have to complain about? She can buy whatever she wants."

"What if she gets tired of staying at home? What if she wants a career? What if she needs personal satisfaction?"

"There's no reason for her to want that. I told you I work two jobs. I can support my family."

"Yeah, but money and control go hand in hand," I argued. Secretly I wondered if I'd be happier myself in a more traditional role. Maybe it beat being alone. What if the cabbie's wife felt more fulfilled than I did? So what if I was an independent, successful woman? Didn't they say that success means nothing unless you have someone to share it with?

"There's no battle for control," the cabbie insisted. "We understand each other. I'm a man and she's a woman."

"Yeah, right. I mean, stop right here." I'd spotted Jade's graceful, womanly figure sporting a sarong and a KLUV T-shirt heading toward the Art Institute. "There's my friend Jade!" I pointed. "Jade, hold up!" I shouted before she crossed the street. She heard me and stopped and waved.

I paid the tab and added a reasonable tip. A blast of steamy, hot air slapped me in the face as I stepped onto the warm curb.

"Find yourself a man before it's too late," the cabbie called over his shoulder. "You don't want to end up writing letters to yourself, like that old woman in London." He sped away.

I felt like I was in an art film. It seemed so surreal, a philosophical warning from an almost total stranger on a busy street corner. Jade's almond-shaped eyes gave me a puzzled look. I hunched my shoulders as if I hadn't a clue what the lunatic was talking about. It was too hot to go into it.

Later that evening, I was kicking it with Jade on her spacious, screened porch. I still felt stuffed and worn out from being at Taste of Chicago. It was the first time I'd seen Jade and her husband's new home. Yoshi was playing golf and their teenage sons were somewhere doing their own thing. Although I'd known that Yoshi had recently started his own software company and they'd moved to an expensive North Shore suburb, I wasn't prepared for a mansion that took up half a block.

"Girl, you all are really living large! I can't believe you have wall-to-wall mango carpeting in the master bedroom!" I exclaimed. "Which, by the way, is as big as some folks' whole apartments. In fact, you could rent your master bathroom out as a studio."

Jade shook her head of thick, black, stylishly cut hair. "The carpeting was already in there," she explained, scrunching her soft, wide features together like she was asking for forgiveness. "I probably wouldn't've picked it."

"Your kitchen is da bomb!" I exclaimed. "The whole place is dope, as the kids would say. The skylights, the grounds, the marble bathroom, the gold bidets, everything is tight. How does it feel to 'have it all' at thirty-nine?"

Jade sipped her iced latte and frowned. "This stuff has nothing to do with 'having it all.'"

"Now, as the kids would say, *that's* wack," I said, gazing through the screen at the manicured grounds. "Having stuff sure beats struggling. I've been there, done that and got the T-shirt," I said, snapping my fingers.

"That makes two of us. Don't forget, I grew up in a fourth floor walk-up in New York's Chinatown. There were eight of us in a two-bedroom apartment."

"Damn."

"I don't want to go back to that," Jade assured me. "But money in itself doesn't make you happy. " She hunched her shoulders. "I mean, all of this is nice, but ultimately it's just scenery."

"Well, I'm enjoying the scenery. Come on, Jade, you can admit it. After sleeping in the bathtub, this house *has* to be a dream come true for you."

"It wasn't that serious." Jade smiled, borrowing a black expression. "But really, this is Yoshi's dream come true, not mine. To be honest with you, I was actually nervous about you seeing it."

"Why? I can share the fantasy. I'm not bitter. I'm more than a few paychecks away from the streets myself."

"I was afraid that you might not like me anymore."

"Not like you anymore! Why?"

"Well, you know…" Jade looked apologetic again. "Because I'm not down with the people, as you would say."

"Honey, let me clarify something. I wanna help the po', not be po'. You're my new best friend."

"Yeah, right." Jade smiled, giving her face an attractive, mischievous look. "I'm glad you're so accepting."

"Not to change the subject, but, what's up with you and that sexual harassment case? I meet with the mediator on Thursday. Do I need to have a lawyer present or what?"

"The point of mediation is to keep the lawyers out of it. Obviously the station is trying to avoid a lawsuit."

"And to keep from firing Bill."

"Yeah, I noticed that, too," Jade said.

"I don't even know why the mediator wants to talk to me. I told

Rob that doing a mediation with Bill is the last thing I want to be bothered with. I just wanted to support you," I said, giving Jade a caring look.

"I think the mediator just wants to give you an opportunity to reconsider. In case you want to tie up any loose ends. I'm sure management doesn't want any remaining residue."

"Yeah, right. Speak now or forever hold your lawsuit?" I laughed. "Well, I'll just reiterate what I said to Rob," I continued. "As far as I'm concerned, my situation with Bill is history. Unlike with you, he took 'no' for an answer. So my meeting with Skylar Thompson should be pretty short." I yawned and covered my mouth. "By the way, has he actually met with you yet?"

Jade hesitated. "Yes, but he asked me not to discuss it. You know how it is." Jade stifled a yawn. "You made me yawn."

"You know they're contagious." I paused. "Well, can you at least tell me if the brotha's tall, dark and handsome?" I asked, rocking harder in the porch swing. "And more importantly, if he had a wedding ring on his finger?"

"I don't remember seeing a ring, but I wasn't looking for one. And he *was* tall. When he stood up, he towered over me. And *I'd* say he was good looking."

"But not *too* good looking?"

"I don't know what you mean." Jade shrugged. "Besides, I wasn't really focused on his appearance. I wasn't there to hit on him."

"Yeah, that would've really been tacky, under the circumstances. Anyway, I just don't want a man that looks so good that people wonder how I got 'im."

"What do you mean?"

"I don't want it to look like I'm taking care of him, if you know what I mean."

"You're selling yourself short. Not to mention projecting. I mean, you haven't even met the guy yet."

"Yadda yadda yadda, so how old is he, about?"

"I'd guess around our ages."

How angelic of Jade to group me with her, I thought. A lesser being would've pointed out our two-year age difference—Jade was still under forty. "You wonder about men who aren't married after thirty-five," I said. "I hope he's at least divorced."

"Don't you care if he seemed like he was a nice guy or not?"

"Of course. Well?"

"You can imagine that I was disappointed that they sent a *man*, but after I got over that, I liked him all right."

"He didn't seem gay, did he?" I raised my eyebrows. "You didn't pick up any of those tendencies, did you?"

"I don't know. I mean, he didn't show up in a dress or anything."

"You don't understand." I pointed my finger. "I've been burned before. I told you about Randall."

"Oh yeah, I remember."

"Maybe men see me as matronly. I could stand to lose twenty pounds. Thirty would even give me a cushion. If I lost forty, I'd be skinny."

"You have a great body for belly. In a year, you could perform."

"Don't even go there! I will never roll my belly around onstage in public."

"You gotta come to our Annual Student Night in August. It'll be so inspiring."

"I don't mind being a spectator. I'm even open to taking a class or two. I'd love to tighten up my abs."

Jade sat up straight, like she'd received a sudden burst of energy. "You'll take my class?"

"Sure." I nodded. "So long as I don't have a male audience."

Jade jumped out of her seat. "Dee Dee, you're going to stop dwelling on not having a man!" She shook her fists, excitedly. "And you're going to walk like an Egyptian!"

"Maybe so," I mumbled, trying to muster up some enthusiasm.

Jade threw her head back and held her arms high. She strutted, shifting her hips from side to side.

Jade was definitely not a stereotypical, unemotional Asian, I thought. That's why it's good to get to know people as individuals. It makes it harder to put folks in a box.

"Did it ever occur to you that the grass is not always greener on the other side?" Jade asked.

"Yeah, it has. I got a massage last Mother's Day to treat myself, and the masseuse told me that I was the happiest person that she'd worked on all day. I confided to her that I'd be happier if my mother were still alive and I were married. She said that was ironic, because all day she'd heard women do nothing but complain about their mediocre lives and especially their mediocre marriages. I was sort of surprised."

"Well, I'm not. Married women are the most depressed segment of our society."

"Yeah, I heard that on Oprah, too."

Jade paced with her arms folded. "Marriage is an institution. And the purpose of institutions is to keep the wheels turning, not to make individuals happy."

"Does that mean you're not exactly walking on air yourself?"

Jade groaned. "I'm married to a passive aggressive. "

"I thought you said he was a workaholic."

"That, too. Anyway, Yoshi says to me, 'Honey, don't worry about making money, just do what you love to do,'" Jade mimicked in a syrupy sweet voice. "'Besides, with your bachelor's degree in anthropology, you couldn't possibly earn enough money to make a noticeable contribution to our income anyway,'" she added with a fake smile. "Makes it kinda hard not to feel useless."

I stood up and looked at Jade's face. It was etched in sadness. I guess you could feel trapped in a marriage, despite the fact that it had yielded material rewards, an heir and a spare.

"I understand what you're saying," I replied. But there was a time when I *wouldn't* have understood. I would've thought that if a woman like Jade was unhappy, it was her own damn fault. I'd been raised in the black female tradition. And feeling useless was not one of our fears. I didn't know what they told Chinese girls. But nobody told "colored" girls some knight in shining armor was going to ride in on a white horse and save us.

They told us to always have our own money. "Always be

prepared to make it by your dammie—i.e, your damn self," they advised. "The only person your children can *really* depend on is you," they warned. "They" included female relatives and women on buses and in beauty shops, on front stoops and over backyard fences. They put their hands on their hips or pointed their fingers and warned, "Love don't pay the bills." They cut their eyes and asked, "What has he done for you *lately?*" They folded their arms and twisted their necks and declared, "No finance, no romance." They said they could do *bad,* all by themselves. And they sucked their teeth and said, "Only a fool would put her trust in a man."

But maybe a girl is supposed to dream, I thought, watching a tear form in Jade's eye. I suddenly felt burdened by the armor that had been offered to protect me. I found myself pondering what my life would've been like if I'd been encouraged to see the world through more hopeful eyes. A part of me wished that they'd never told me all that stuff. But another part of me understood that all that stuff came with having been born Negro and female in 1955. They were my operating instructions; back then a colored girl couldn't be raised without them.

"If I complain about Yoshi's being a workaholic"—Jade sighed—"he just says he's Japanese, and Japanese feel guilty if they're not working. Yoshi says he plays golf mainly because of the networking opportunities."

Typically, it was unheard of for a sista to complain about a man working too much. Instead, she bragged about her man working on two jobs. "I just wanna man who's got sense enough to work" was a popular expression when I was a child. Work was what a man was 'spozed to do. If the bills were paid and the credit was good, the sista had no reason to complain.

"Yoshi says that the financial burden is all on him," Jade added. "He says, all I do is wiggle my waist." Tears finally spilled out of her eyes and splashed onto her face.

"That's not true," I said, reaching out and hugging her. "You've created a beautiful home. You're an artist and a teacher, besides being a wife and mother. And you're a good friend."

"My self-esteem means more to me than any of this shit!" Jade shouted, her voice choked with emotion.

"I hear you," I said, looking out toward the blooming garden. I understood about self-esteem. I knew that you could look good on the outside and feel bad on the inside. I knew that you could take a bath and still feel dirty. I knew that you could have a belly full of food and still feel empty. I knew that a child could be read a fairy tale and be tucked into her own bed and still not be safe. But I didn't want to think about that, because I didn't want to fall apart. I hadn't forgotten that all the king's horses and all the king's men, couldn't put Humpty-Dumpty back together again.

four

I hadn't seen Freddy on the way into the radio station, but he was all up in my face on the way out.

"Heard you went to Jade's, after y'all left Taste last Saturday," Freddy said when I walked off the elevator.

"I see the grapevine is popping."

"Very little gets past me. Jade said you might start taking a belly dance class." Freddy winked and twisted his shapeless hips.

"Don't quit your day job," I teased. "Boy, you must've really grilled Jade on her way up. It's a wonder she made it to the mike on time."

"I know Jade must have a nice place if she's out there in Lake Forest, huh?" Freddy asked, wide-eyed, like a child peering into a candy store.

"Yeah." I nodded. "It's real nice."

"I'm surprised she let you come out there," Freddy said, folding his arms and leaning against the desk.

"What do you mean? We're friends."

"I just know that if I had money, say if I won the lottery"—Freddy lowered his voice—"I wouldn't let black people know where I lived. Uh-uh." He shook his head. "Not unless they had money, too."

I rolled my eyes and leaned back against the wall. "I don't think she has to worry about me robbing her or anything."

"Maybe not you, personally." Freddy rubbed his chin. "But she don't know who all you know." He raised his eyebrows. "And what all they into."

"Oh, please."

"People can set you up without you even knowing it," Freddy insisted.

"The same can be said of white people."

"Yeah, but white folks are less likely to go in on a minority. That's why I'd be slow to let a Negro know what I've got. I'll be fifty years old in October and I've never heard of a white boy snatching a black woman's purse. Never!" Freddy pounded the desk.

"I don't know." I sighed. "I just remember when I was growing up in Morgan Park, even though it was still on the South Side of Chicago, it really *was* like a village. When we crossed the railroad tracks into the black section, we felt home. And we felt safe. You could practically sleep out in Ada Park on summer nights. Imagine that, feeling safe when you saw black men at night. It sounds funny now, but that's how it was."

Freddy sat on top of his desk. "I left Mississippi in 1962. I remember on my last day, I went to say good-bye to my best friend, Delmar, out in the cotton fields. For him, it was just another hot, dusty, delta day. For me, it was the beginning of the rest of my life. I bragged that I was going up north to Chicago and find me a good job, buy me a nice car, finish high school, buy me a house and get married and raise a family. Those were my dreams."

"And you accomplished them, didn't you?" At least more or less, I was tempted to add, because of Freddy's modest position. But when I saw the pride shining in his dark eyes, I was glad I'd bitten my tongue.

"Yep, I did." Freddy nodded solemnly, as though he'd invented medicine or at least made partner in a law firm.

"Not everybody can say that," I added, enjoying boosting Freddy's ego.

"That's true," Freddy said, with a faraway look in his eyes. "That day, I asked Delmar what he dreamed about. First, he glanced over his shoulder to make sure the bossman wasn't looking. Then he stopped picking cotton long enough to shade his eyes from the sun. 'I dreams about getting outta this field. That's what I dreams about,' Delmar answered." Freddy sighed. "I remember feeling guilty."

"Why?"

Freddy's voice softened. "I guess, on accounta my dreams was bigger."

"Did Delmar ever get outta that field?"

"Oh yeah!" Freddy exclaimed as he jumped down from the desk. "You can't tell them Negroes nothing now! They living it up down there with them casinos. Your money goes a long way in Mississippi. That's where I plans to retire." Freddy stuck his chest out like he already felt prosperous. "I never thought I'd hear myself say that." He shook his head. "I used to say, 'Mississippi, goddamn.'"

"You and Nina Simone, both. Hey, I can relate. I was born in Alabama, and folks used to call it the meanest state in the union. Probably still do." I glanced at my watch. "Nice talking to you. I had a little extra time to kill, but now I'd better bounce."

"Accident on Sheridan Road," Freddy reported as he opened the door for me. "You headed that way?

I shook my head. "I'm headed out to O'Hare to pick up my friend and her daughter."

"You still stay fifty-some-hundred North Sheridan Road, don't you?"

"Yeah, I'm still in Edgewater."

"Soon, you won't be able to tell the difference between the North Side and the South Side, after your people get through with it. Y'all done already took over Uptown and Rogers Park."

I groaned. Freddy and I had just shared a Kodak moment and now he had to go and spoil it.

"Plenty of black folks keep their property up," I protested. "There are some nice black neighborhoods on the South Side," I added.

"Yeah, but folks still afraid to go outta they doors at night. And the business districts are a mess. You want something tore up, just dial, N-I-G-G-E-R-S. They'll get the job done."

"I don't have time to argue with you, Freddy. You sound ignorant."

It had been like a furnace all day, but by the time I stepped out of the car at the airport, there was something of a breeze. I waved excitedly toward two familiar figures, sporting long braids and pushing luggage carts. It would be great having my best friend home this summer. Our old asses could check out the scene together, take in some blues clubs, maybe even attend a few singles parties. We could support each other in our attempts to find Mr. Right.

"Look at Tyeesha, she's bigger than I am!" Sharon pointed, after we all hugged each other to death. "She can't even steal my clothes anymore," She chuckled as we loaded the car. "Girl, I may as well be taking care of a grown woman."

Tyeesha rolled her eyes before she slumped into the backseat. I could tell that she didn't want to hear it.

"Don't feel bad, T, we can walk the lake together."

"Yeah, look like you've gained, too," Sharon said, glancing at my middle as I slid behind the wheel. "You all make me look skinny."

"Haven't seen your behind in almost a year, and the first thing you wanna do is cap on folks' weight." I tried to sound casual as I started up the car, but I felt sensitive about the pounds that had crept up on me, and figured Tyeesha did, too.

"I'm sorry, girl, you're right. It's good to see you."

"So, what did you want to tell me?" I asked, driving out of the airport.

"I'll tell you after we get settled."

"Yeah, it might cause you to have an accident," Tyeesha warned.

"I can't stand all this suspense! Unless you robbed a bank, or murdered somebody, or blew up a building, just blurt it out."

Tyeesha put on her headphones. "This is an A and B conversation. So I'm gonna C my way out of it."

"Good, Tyeesha, 'cause you've already given me your two cents," Sharon said.

"Well, I'm waiting with bated breath to give you mine," I said.

"Okay, Dee Dee." Sharon cleared her throat. "I'm a lesbian."

"You're a lesbian!" I shouted, slowing down to keep from rear-ending a minivan. "How can you be a lesbian? You've been a heterosexual fool the whole almost thirty years I've known you."

I paused long enough for Sharon to tell me that I hadn't heard her correctly. But she didn't open her mouth.

"Remember, I'm the one who called Reggie Davis to ask him if he liked you. After you begged me to, I might add." I shook my head as I changed lanes to avoid a tailgater. "You have a long rap sheet. Remember us following Michael Green's car to see if he was going over to Paula Benjamin's house?" I whined as if I were recalling fond memories. "Damn near had me hiding in bushes."

I continued trying to sound like a good sport. "And nobody could tell you not to marry..." I caught myself. I didn't want to mention Tyeesha's disappearing-act father. He'd hung around just long enough to see her graduate from kindergarten.

I was thoroughly confused. I'd assumed that Sharon's heterosexuality had been written in stone. I just couldn't understand how she could suddenly do such an about-face. I mean, I never saw any signs. I also felt abandoned. It was like my running buddy had run out on me.

"That was a long time ago," Sharon said. "I was desperate to have everything fit."

"Didn't everything fit?" I asked. "No pun intended, but I don't remember hearing any complaints." I sped up to stay with the flow of traffic.

"Yeah, things fit, so long as I didn't know any better."

"So, now you suddenly woke up and smelled the pussy, so to speak. Is that what you're saying?"

"Dee Dee, please, don't be crude. Remember, Tyeesha's still in the car."

"I'm sorry," I said, glancing into my rearview window. Tyeesha's eyebrows were raised almost to the roof of the car. "Keep those headphones securely over your ears," I ordered.

"Acknowledging my feelings toward women goes beyond sex," Sharon continued. "It's about emotion and intimacy. Things I never got from a man."

"I don't know anybody who has a truly intimate relationship with a man. Although in all fairness, Phil is probably more capable of intimacy than Sarita. But generally speaking, men are from another planet. You can have sex without intimacy," I continued. "And you can have intimacy without sex. But having both is rare. Most women I know get their intimacy needs met from their good girlfriends and female relatives. They're just thankful if they can coexist with a man. I didn't think true intimacy was even a goal these days."

"Well, it is for me. But maybe I just want a little more than most women."

I groaned as I maneuvered around a row of orange construction cones.

"They're always working on the roads here," Tyeesha observed from the backseat.

"Sharon, didn't you say kids on campus don't even get into relationships anymore? That's what you told me. They're ridiculed as Velcro twins if they do. They just go out, drink and pick each other up. There's no intimacy. You said that yourself."

"So, Dee Dee, are you wigging out or what?" Sharon asked.

"No, I'm not wigging out," I said, loosening my tight grip on the steering wheel. "I'm just surprised." I glanced at Sharon. "Have you ever even been with a woman? Have you even kissed a woman?"

"See, Mom, that's the same thing I asked you."

"Go back to your music! Dee Dee, if I had, I would've told you. I wouldn't keep something like that from you."

"You haven't done anything? Then how did you come up with this foolishness?" I asked, changing to the slow lane.

"You are wigging out!"

"No, I'm not," I insisted. But I secretly wished I still had a stick shift to grab on to for support. When I turned forty last year, I decided I was too old to shift gears and bought an automatic.

"I don't appreciate your calling my feelings foolishness!"

I could hear the hurt in Sharon's voice and see Tyeesha's eyes widen in my rearview mirror. My voice softened. "I'm sorry, dear heart. I want to support you. I just wondered how you know you're gay, that's all."

"How do you know you're straight?"

"Because men peel my paint, and women don't. For me, it's always been that simple."

"Well, maybe for some of us, things are a little more complex. I would never have chosen to be gay. But I'm not ashamed of who I am. And I'm not going to beg for anybody else's approval."

"I don't think you should. You have to do what's right for you. It's just a surprise, that's all. I mean, you must've had some inkling all these years. You're forty-two years old, for heaven's sake. Isn't it a little late to be coming out of the closet?"

"Yeah, it's embarrassing. I'm probably too ancient to do anything about it. My dentures might fall out," she said sarcastically.

"You're getting oral now. Remember, T's here."

"I forgot for a minute."

"Speaking of Tyeesha, I would expect it more coming from her." I sighed. "I hate to say it, but it just seems so lame at your age."

"Excuse me?" Tyeesha pulled off her headphones. "Keep my name out of it."

"It's just that you're young, your hormones are raging. Your mother's on the verge of menopause. Her hot days are behind her. She'll be facing hot *flashes* soon," I said.

"Life begins at forty," Sharon declared.

"Well, for the record, I'm strictly dickly," Tyeesha informed me.

"Your virgin behind better hush," Sharon warned.

"Sharon, didn't you have a crush on a teacher or friends or somebody?"

"Yeah, a few times, but I repressed them. Boys showed interest in me and I was relieved. I didn't see being gay as an option."

I hesitated. "You didn't have a crush on me, did you?" I asked, glancing at the rows of chocolate brick apartment buildings above the freeway.

"Yeah, I did."

"Oh, really? When?" I swallowed.

"Way back when we were kids."

"Oh." I breathed a sigh of relief. And let a car cut in front of me. "When we were still back at Morgan Park High?"

"No, even before that, eighth grade, back at Shoop. As soon as I got to know you, it wore off."

"Well thanks; I mean, I'm glad that your attraction was short-lived. But you know you could do worse."

"You can't have it both ways. You're my best friend, but you're just not my type, romantically. That's all."

"So, what *is* your type, romantically? I mean, just out of curiosity."

"I'm not sure. But you're a little too artsy to be my type. Maybe we're too much alike."

"Well, that's a relief."

"So, Dee Dee, tell me quick before I faint. Is we friends or is we ain't?"

"I hope we stay the best of friends," I said, glimpsing the breathtaking downtown skyline. "This doesn't change that as far as I'm concerned." I sighed. "I guess I was partly looking at this from a marketing standpoint. I just like to think of my friends as being on the cutting edge. I mean, lesbian is so passé. Can you at least identify yourself as bisexual? That way you can keep your options open. You should see all the personal ads in the *Sun-Times* from black women who are bi-curious or bisexual. It's damn near an epidemic. Why not ride that wave?"

"Because I'm not interested in being trendy. I'm just interested in being Sharon."

I glanced sideways at Sharon as I exited the freeway. "Girl-friend, I may not understand you, but I accept you."

"Then can I be open with you?"

"Open about what? You haven't done anything. You don't have any firsthand experience." You don't even have a lab coat yet."

"If and when I do, I don't want to feel like I have to repress myself. Like I can't talk about stuff. If the thought of two women making love repulses you, let me know now."

"Ugh," Tyeesha volunteered.

"Grow up, Tyeesha."

"Yeah, grow up Tyeesha," I agreed.

"Mom, you can't have it both ways. I can't grow up *and* stay your little girl."

"Well, try."

"To answer your question," I broke in, "no, I'm not repulsed by the thought of two women being together. I've seen it in movies. I've read about it in books. If there's a good story line, I can share the fantasy. I'm just not interested in doing it myself, that's all."

"Well, that's cool."

"Cool was never the issue. I will continue to be your cool role model," I said.

Sharon and Tyeesha giggled. "I don't have a problem with gay people," I continued. "This is 1996, not 1956. I work with gay people. I even have a gay friend. You remember Randall."

"How could I forget? You cried a river on my shoulder."

"Well, once I got over the shock and the betrayal, Randall and I became closer than we ever were when we called ourselves dating," I admitted. "He confides in me and so can you."

"I was just afraid that you might be more threatened by a lesbian than a gay man."

"Look, I don't feel threatened at all. That was never the issue," I said, running a yellow light. "I'm secure in my sexual identity."

"I'm glad to hear that."

"It just seems like you should've figured yours out twenty years ago. That's my only sticking point."

"Maybe I was in too much denial back then. I was numbing myself with alcohol, remember."

"Sharon, if I *remembered* the seventies, I wouldn't have really been there."

"And if I'd *come out,* back then, I wouldn't have T. Did you ever think of that?'"

"That's right, I would've never been born," a voice protested from the backseat. "And without me, she's nothing."

"Dream on, big ears!" Sharon teased.

"I guess sometimes things happen when they're supposed to happen," I conceded.

"*Sí.*" Sharon nodded as I pulled in front of her South Loop townhouse.

"*No por mucho madrugar amanece más temprano:* Just because you rise very early, doesn't mean daybreak is going to come any sooner."

five

When I first laid eyes on the mediator, I saw that he wasn't fine. Skylar Thompson looked no better than most reasonably attractive brothas in horn-rimmed glasses. But he was still easy on my eyes. Because my eyes weren't looking for fine. They were just scoping for a man that was attractive to *me*. And Skylar's full, kissable lips definitely rang my bells. Not to mention his bunny-shaped nose that made me want to nuzzle it. His satiny smooth skin reminded me of the color and finish of a violin that beckoned to be stroked. I enjoyed finding a man attractive by *my* standards. It was like listening to my own private orchestra.

I wore a dark, loose, African print dress that I hoped camouflaged my weight. I'd been good last night. I'd walked on my treadmill forty minutes and avoided my usual late-night snack. I'd eaten a light breakfast and a vegetarian lunch. Tomorrow night, I'd be taking my first belly dance class. Now, if I could just land this brotha, it would feel like Christmas in July.

Skylar cleared his throat. His eyes were earnest. "I asked for a private meeting, or 'caucus' as we like to call them, with one disputant at a time"—he paused, massaging his chin with his thumb and index finger—"in order to first get a clear idea of your goals and needs."

My goal is to get to know you better, and my need is get to know you better, I thought, gazing accross the conference table. I'd always been a sucker for earnest eyes.

"Mediation is a non-adversarial process," Skylar continued.

I'm a lover, not a fighter, I thought, dreamily supporting my chin with one hand.

"I don't serve as a judge or jury," Skylar explained. "It's not my job to determine right and wrong or to place blame."

I sat up straight. "But don't you ultimately render a decision?" I asked, confused.

Skylar shook his head and clasped his fingers. I gazed at his large hands and couldn't help wondering whether he was well-endowed. I tried to pay attention to what he was saying, but I wished I had X-ray eyes that could see the chest underneath his short-sleeved business shirt and the bulge inside his pants. You have to understand: It had been a long dry season.

"My role is primarily that of facilitator. My only interest is in helping you to resolve your differences and reach a negotiated settlement based on a 'win-win' solution."

"Well, how do we achieve this negotiated settlement that results in a win-win solution?" I asked.

Skylar smiled and adjusted his glasses, like he lived to answer such questions. "By my providing you with a forum to see conflict as an opportunity."

"An opportunity for what?"

"An opportunity to acknowledge and appreciate differences."

"Say what?"

He glanced down at his clipboard. "I facilitate communication by helping disputants describe their feelings, clarify issues, determine their true interests, identify underlying concerns and, where possible, reach agreement. That's my role in a nutshell."

Well, you must be a nut if you think that I have any wish to determine Bill's true interests or identify his underlying concerns, I thought. I had absolutely no desire to explore the reasons why Bill was a jerk. "Where are you from?" I asked.

"Santa Cruz, California. Why?"

No wonder. "With all due respect, I have no interest in acknowledging and appreciating Bill's differences. As far as I'm concerned he's a dog, bow, wow, wow. I let him know that I didn't have any bones for him. And he put his tongue back in his mouth. End of story. So, long as Bill doesn't interfere with my fifty thousand watts of radio power and stays in his little booth, we're cool."

"Daphne. May I call you Daphne?"

I nodded. "Everyone's on a first-name basis here. You can even call me Dee Dee."

"Daphne, may I ask you where *you're* from?"

"I hail from Alabama, but I've lived most of my life here in Chicago." I eyed the framed poster on the wall with the famous slogan CHICAGO AIN'T READY FOR REFORM!

Skylar glanced at the poster. "I've heard that there is such a thing as a Chicago personality. Do you think that's true?"

I nodded. "If you look up 'real' in the dictionary, there should be a picture of a Chicagoan."

Skylar chuckled. "Is that right?"

"Yeah. We tell it like it is. We give it to you straight, no chaser."

"Funny we should be having this conversation, because on the way over here, a cabbie said to me, 'You talk to a Chicagoan for five minutes, and you feel like you've known him your whole life.' He said that I'd quickly learn to love it here, despite the weather. I'd told him I was new, that I was still learning my way around."

"You told a cab driver *that*? I hope he didn't take you on the scenic route."

"I hope not, either," Skylar said sheepishly. "Anyway, the cabbie said some places, you never feel like you ever get to know folks. But here in Chicago, you do."

"That's true," I agreed. "Chicagoans are easy to get to know. And we're loyal. You make friends with a Chicagoan, you got a friend for life. 'Got to Be Real' is our theme song," I added.

"Well, tell me straight up, Ms. Windy City, are you open to mediation or not?" Skylar asked with a twinkle in his eye.

I was tempted to say, "Baby, I'm open to you."

Instead, I answered, "Hey, I'm not advocating that people duke it out in the alleys, but mediation just sounds so textbook and apple pie. I mean, some people are just jerks. And everything is not always equal." I raised my eyebrows. "In some cases, there *is* a right and a wrong."

Skylar stood up and paced in front of me. "We encourage disputants to walk in the other person's shoes, to see things from his or her perspective, and vice versa. Sometimes, it's not what is said, but what is meant. The same communication may have different, even opposite, meanings for different people." He glanced down at me. "For example, a marriage may mean one thing to a wife and something completely different to a husband." He caressed his empty ring finger.

"That's certainly true," I interjected. "At least, that was my experience."

Skylar shot me a sympathetic look. "And a belly dance performance can be a form of artistic, even spiritual expression for one person," he continued, "and arouse prurient interests in another."

I stretched my legs underneath the table. "That person can still keep his prurient interests to himself," I said. "Or at least be willing to take 'no' for an answer."

Skylar stood in front of me with his arms folded. He glanced down at his clipboard. "Mediation permits a disputant to model useful behavior and techniques for avoiding future conflicts."

I made a scornful face. "Bill can avoid future conflicts by not acting like a dog. It's that simple." My tone turned playful. "Some answers are not on your clipboard."

Skylar blushed beneath his brown color. "You referred to Bill as a dog earlier, and you just did it again," he pointed out, sounding like a damn lawyer.

"So?"

"So, mediation permits parties to become human to each other." He smiled. "The conventional negotiating world is controlled by egocentric self-interest. But mediation is controlled by enlightened self-interest." He was reading from his clipboard again.

I felt my shoulders tighten. I was getting pissed. I was tired of this clipboard bullshit. Why were we even having this conversation? Skylar and I should be strolling along the beach, whispering sweet nothings in each other's ears. It wasn't every day that I felt physically attracted to someone. I needed juice, not sawdust. I needed a chocolate Superman, not Clark Kent.

"This is not about enlightened self-interest!" I blurted out. "This is about a creep sneaking up behind me and massaging my shoulders, with his fingers damn near touching my breasts. If I want a massage, I can pay a professional!"

"It sounds to me like your feelings regarding Bill are unresolved."

"I prefer to let sleeping dogs lie."

Skylar sat down across from me and folded his hands. His long, sexy fingers were a turn-on. Ham-hock hands with stubby fingers turned me off.

"One possible solution might be for Bill to hear, from you, what emotional meaning his words and actions had for you," Skylar suggested quietly. "Also, correct me if I'm wrong, but maybe it would be helpful for you to hear from Bill the meaning he ascribes to his actions and comments."

"You're wrong. So, I'm correcting you," I answered with a fake smile. "I have no interest in the meaning Bill ascribes to anything, except radio engineering."

"I can understand why you might've been offended by Bill's behavior," Skylar conceded. "But…"

"But what?"

"But strange as this sounds, he may have intended it to be complimentary."

I stood up and threw my arms in the air. "I don't care what Bill's intent was! And I'm not that hard up for compliments."

"I'm not saying that Bill has acted appropriately," Skylar said almost apologetically. "But what requires mediation is less the conflict between intent and interpretation than between the meanings different parties find in the same terms. Mediation reveals the parties' deeper motivations."

Skylar's gobbledygook was getting on my last nerve. And yet, to my frustration, my undies were still in a bunch. "I don't care about Bill's deeper motivations!" I shouted. "I'm not sure I even care about my own."

"Growth can be scary," Skylar replied.

"I'm already grown," I explained with exasperation. Skylar had severed my last nerve. "Besides, this is not about growth! This is about a jerk saying, 'I like my women, like I like my coffee: hot and black!' This is about a dog saying to me at the watercooler, 'They've only got these small cups. They hold just enough water for my dick!'"

Skylar looked taken aback but not blown away. I was surprised by my outburst. But it felt good to get angry. Maybe Skylar and I could still make mad, passionate love together, even though we pissed each other off.

"Perhaps Bill was just trying to say he had a small dick." Skylar winked.

"Yeah, perhaps," I said, unable to keep from smiling. "I hadn't thought of it that way," I acknowledged. I could feel myself letting go of some of my anger. I liked it that Skylar had finally said something not on his clipboard. Maybe he could actually be fun. I'd love to give it up again to a man with a sense of humor and a twinkle in his eyes. I looked at Skylar and saw possibilities. "Sorry I went ballistic."

"There's no need to apologize," Skylar insisted. "So long as I didn't have to duck." He pretended to move out of the way of a flying object.

"I believe in nonviolence," I assured him.

"That's comforting," Skylar said with an exaggerated sigh of relief. He folded his arms. "So, Dee Dee, do you want to give this process a shot or not?"

I noticed that he had called me Dee Dee. It sounded so sweet coming from his lips. I was definitely feeling open to him again.

"I see the value in mediation," I answered, diplomatically. "I honestly do. In fact, I think it might really be positive for Bill and Jade to go through it, since their conflict is ongoing and unresolved. But I'm content to sit on the sidelines." I shrugged. "Maybe I just wasn't raised to make a mountain out of a mole-hill."

"Do you consider sexual harassment a molehill?" Skylar asked, looking concerned.

"It all depends on the severity of it," I said flatly. "I'm not trying to minimize sexual harassment, because it can be a serious problem. But my situation with Bill was something that I was able to handle on my own. I grew up learning how to fight for myself," I bragged. "At least when my big brother wasn't around. Plus I had to take up for my little sister. Anyway, the focus needs to be on Bill and Jade, not Bill and me."

"There can be more than one focus," Skylar said. "I mean, a few minutes ago, you seemed pretty upset about Bill's behavior. You know these resources are available to you as much as anyone else. The radio station is happy to provide mediation to you free of charge." He paused. "Do you feel like you don't deserve to participate in this process?"

I groaned. "No, I don't feel like I don't deserve to participate in this process," I answered sarcastically. "I just don't believe in sweating the small stuff, that's all."

"I see."

"You ever been through a winter here?" I asked.

"Not really. I just moved here this past April."

"You haven't encountered the Hawk full blast then."

"The Hawk?"

"The wind. It blows off the lake and it takes no prisoners. It cuts through you like a knife."

Skylar's eyes widened. "It's been windy, but I can't say I've had that experience."

"Maybe that's why I can't dwell on every little thing. I've been through too many Chicago winters."

Skylar sighed. "Well, I hope I haven't wasted your time."

"Not at all. When I came in here, I was pretty ignorant on the subject of mediation."

"We're all ignorant about something. Try moving to a strange city. And have everybody tell you how easily laid out it is."

"It is," I insisted, talking with my hands. "The streets here are all numbered and laid out like ladders. The corner of State and Madison, downtown here, is ground zero. State divides North and South. Madison divides East and West. The West Side is west of the Loop. And there is no real East Side, just the Lake. It's very simple and to the point," I said breathlessly.

"Everyone gives you a similar speech." Skylar smiled lazily. "I think I've finally got it." He paused long enough for me to admire the way his lips curled when he smiled. "You know, the pace here is somewhat faster than I'm used to," he admitted. "And I'm accustomed to pedestrians having the right of way.

"And I'm not saying that the people here aren't friendly," he said hesitantly. "But their attitudes seem so cut-and-dried sometimes."

"Chicago is called the city that works," I informed him.

"Everything seems so concrete here. I mean that figuratively more so than literally."

"We may appear tough on the outside, but inside we're like marshmallows," I confided.

"I always have to remind myself not to compare my inside with another person's outside."

"Me too." I nodded. "That's one of the best things I learned in Psychobabble 101."

We both laughed. "You sure I can't interest you in mediation after all?" Skylar asked hopefully.

"Just because I'm passing on this one doesn't mean that I don't see the value in the *process*. After listening to your spiel, I would give mediation a shot if I had a conflict that was ongoing," I conceded.

"Thanks, that's good to hear. I really appreciate that feedback," Skylar said, standing up. "Daphne, I'm glad that I met you."

I offered him my hand. "I'm glad that I met you, too," I answered, appreciating the warmth of Skylar's grip. "You see, it turned out to be a win-win situation after all." I smiled.

"Yeah, but it all happened so quickly," Skylar sighed. "I really enjoy talking to interesting people who are willing to say what's really on their minds."

It was my turn to blush. "Well, you can always listen to my show on the radio. And you can call in if you like."

"What if I don't want your listeners to hear our conversation?"

I felt my knees buckle. "Then you can call me at home." I reached in my purse and wrote my phone number on the back of my card.

"Here, Daphne, would you like my card also?"

"Okay," I replied, nonchalantly, struggling to conceal my excitement. "It's been real." I tucked Skylar's card into my handbag.

"It's been more than real." Skylar smiled. "It's been serendipitous."

I didn't need a dictionary to know what he meant. I couldn't have said it better myself. I felt a glow that I hadn't experienced in a long time. And it sure didn't make me feel middle-aged. It made me feel like riding the daggone Ferris wheel.

six

Belly dancing was harder than I expected. It involved a lot of concentration and muscle control. Although I was the only sista, I was relieved to see that the students came in a variety of shapes and sizes and ages. A few danced with their stomachs exposed but most wore leotards or shorts and T-shirts, like me. Everyone tied something shiny and shimmering around their waists. Jade had a basket of things for students like me, who hadn't yet purchased veils and costumes. By the end of the first class, I'd learned that the most common movement was in the shape of a figure eight. We'd done it with our hips, chest and shoulders. My favorite thing so far was to shimmy, because you could just let your butt go like you didn't have a care in the world. Jade said that some cultures, as well as some individuals, were better at controlled movements, and others were better at letting go. So far, I was better at letting go. Maybe it was cultural, I don't know.

There was so much to learn, like even how to walk, only Jade called it "traveling." And how to make snake arms and do veil work and play with finger cymbals and how to undulate. Jade instructed us to pretend that our chests were dump trucks, scooping and dumping, scooping and dumping. I felt proud when Jade said, in front of the whole class, "Dee Dee, your undulations are beautiful." My size-D cups had finally come in handy.

After class, I bought a veil with a rose-colored background and shiny multicolored stripes. Now I could practice flipping it and throwing it in the air and catching it at home. I also bought a pair of finger cymbals called "zilts." You put one on each thumb and middle finger. In class, we practiced playing, left, right, left. After class, I told Jade, "It's a workout, but I think I'm gonna like belly dance."

Jade hugged me. "You've only just begun to experience the power of belly. If you learn to belly dance, you'll learn to love yourself," she assured me.

Who says I don't already love myself? I thought defensively. "If you learn to belly dance, you'll learn to love yourself," I repeated cynically in my head. Sounded like advanced psychobabble. But a little voice inside me said, *Let's hope Jade's right.*

I had faith that I would hear from Skylar soon. It had only been a few days. If he didn't call after a whole week, I'd give him a call. The hell with *The Rules.* In the meantime, I was getting in shape for love. Tyeesha and I were walking along the Lake today. It would be a good opportunity for us to exercise as well as get current. This was the first time we'd really had a chance to talk since Sharon dropped the bomb on us.

"I'm so glad it finally cooled off," I said to Tyeesha as we power-walked along the water. "It's perfect for walkers now."

"Me, too. I have to get used to this humidity again, after being in Seattle," Tyeesha huffed, pushing her braids out of her face. "You can take ten showers and still not feel refreshed."

"Yeah, but don't you like the warm nights?"

"Yeah. Dee Dee, can I come live with you?"

"Why?" I asked, taken aback.

"'Cause you're my godmother and I don't want a lesbian mother."

"What is a lesbian mother?" I asked sarcastically.

"You know."

"No, I don't know," I insisted, lowering my voice. "I mean, how does a lesbian mother act? What does a lesbian mother do? Does she have sex twenty-four-seven or does she put food on the table, pay bills, do laundry, schlepp her kid around—you know, ordinary stuff?"

"I thought you would understand." Tyeesha pouted.

"I do understand. I know that you're trippin'. And I understand that."

"Then how come you don't act like it?" she whined.

I stopped and pushed Tyeesha's braids away and stroked her face. "Because it's tough all over, that's why. Your mother didn't just wake up one day and decide, 'I think I'll freak everybody out and become a lesbian.' I've known Sharon since jumpstreet. And I know that just like she walked the floor with you as a baby, she walked the floor with this. I imagine her stomach has been in knots and she has searched her soul. And I'm sure that for a long time she put everybody else's feelings ahead of her own."

"It's like I don't even know her anymore," Tyeesha said, shaking her head. "I stop myself from saying, 'Mom, don't you think he's cute?' And when we're watching TV, I put a different weight on it now when she says, 'She's so beautiful,' or, 'I love a certain actress or a certain singer.' It's like there's a wall between us and we're on different sides. I hate to say this, but I feel funny now when she even hugs me."

"Now you're *really* tripping."

"You don't think I'm homophobic, do you?" Tyeesha had a concerned look in her big brown eyes.

"Do chittlins take a long time to cook?" I sneered.

"You do, huh?"

"Yeah, but it's understandable. She's your mother, so it's hard. Change is hard, period, and this is a big one. Your mama is your role model and all of a sudden you're not sure whether you can identify with her."

"Yeah. I just can't understand why she would wanna go that way. I mean, I know it's hard to find a good man at her age."

"All right, baby girl, you're stepping on *my* toes now."

"But I still think she's giving up too easily."

"It's not a question of giving up, it's a matter of going after what she thinks is right for her."

"You can understand her? Don't you think it's whack, too?"

"You know, I don't understand why people like cantaloupe," I answered. "But everybody in my family liked it and for some strange reason, a lot of people I know eat it. But you know what, I've never bought a cantaloupe in my life and I don't intend to, either."

"Well, everybody has their food likes and dislikes." Tyeesha shrugged. "I hate anchovies." She stuck her tongue out. "I'd rather eat dirt."

I slowed down and Tyeesha followed suit. "Anchovies are pretty easy to avoid and so are cantaloupes, for that matter. But you know what? Everybody has their preferences, period. And some preferences are more important than others. Nobody much cares whether we like anchovies or cantaloupes. We get off pretty easy."

"I can't understand how anybody can hate ice cream, fried chicken or pizza or chocolate," Tyeesha said, shaking her head and rolling her eyes.

I patted my stomach. "Unfortunately for my waistline, I agree with you. But the world is a big place; somebody somewhere dislikes every food you mentioned."

"They're crazy."

"Maybe they're just different from you. If Sharon can find a woman who treats her right, more power to her. I'm not gonna knock her. There are plenty of straight people who make romantic choices that I don't understand or agree with. But they're consenting adults, so what can I do about it? Why should gays and lesbians be held to a higher standard?"

Tyeesha stood still. "Because one of them happens to be my mother. That's why."

"Come here, baby girl." I hugged my godchild. "You still got your mama and you still got me and all the other people who love you."

"I just can't talk to her like I could before," Tyeesha whimpered. "Everything's changed."

"Everything hasn't changed. You just need time to adjust, that's all. You are still your mother's heart. And you always will be. But she has a right to have other relationships. Mothers are people, too, you know."

"Let's flip the script," Tyeesha said abruptly. "Enough about her. Dee Dee, I met somebody and I think he's gonna be the one."

I grabbed Tyeesha's shoulders. "The one for what?"

"The one that I'm gonna give it up to."

"Whoa, wait, how long have you known him and how far have you gotten? Let's chill over there on that bench," I said, pointing.

"We've only been choppin' it a few days," Tyeesha said, breathlessly. "But last night, we played the spitting game." She plopped down beside me.

"Okay, so you've been talking for a few days and you kissed last night. Well, take it slow."

"That's hecka slow, I'm fifteen now, remember. And I know about safe sex."

"A little knowledge can be a dangerous thing," I warned.

"Dee Dee, how old were you when you had your first experience?"

"I waited until after I graduated from high school," I answered proudly. "Well, actually I did it for the first time the week before I graduated. But it *was* prom night."

"How old were you, though?"

"Seventeen, almost eighteen."

"Prom night, that's so romantic. Do you still think about it?"

"Hell no!"

"Was it wonderful?"

"It was the first time, it was just okay. I've had a lot better since, believe me. You know the song Sade sings, 'Never As Good As the First Time'? Well, it's never as bad as the first time, would be more accurate. I mean, for women, sex gets better with age and experience."

"Well, if practice makes perfect, I should hurry up and get started."

"You can practice all by yourself."

"Oooh, don't go there, that's nasty."

"No, it's not nasty," I whispered. "Self-love is the safest sex there is. That's what you need to do until you find somebody who's going to love and cherish you for the treasure that you are."

"That could take forever."

"Well, maybe you oughta wait and find out."

"I don't understand. You grew up in the sixties and the seventies and they were anything goes."

"I've learned from my mistakes, too. There are no bargains out here and there are a lot more pitfalls now." I lowered my voice even more. "I advise you to stick a candle in there or a zucchini until you find a man worthy of you. Now, that's my advice."

"Ugh! Gross!"

"Okay," I said, cutting my eyes. "Some people have to learn the hard way."

"How long do you want me to wait?" Tyeesha pouted.

"If you're smart, you'll wait till you've found the right person and you're over twenty-one."

"All kidding aside, Dee Dee, how long do you *really* expect me to wait?"

"Realistically, till you're eighteen, or at least until after you graduate from high school."

"Eighteen! Nobody waits till they're eighteen anymore. People will be calling me a dyke by then!"

"People might be calling you 'Mama' if you don't. Or they might be calling you HIV positive, if you're not careful."

Tyeesha groaned. "When you were fifteen, it was the middle of the sexual revolution. You didn't have to connect sex with disease and dying. It's not fair." She pouted again.

"No, it's not fair. I'm glad that I came along when I did. But I still had to worry about pregnancy."

"Hadn't the Pill been invented?"

"Yeah, but back in the horse and buggy days, getting the Pill required some serious premeditation. And I was a good girl. I didn't wanna plan it. I expected to be seduced. And also, the Pill used to have major side effects. I was scared of it."

"Did you ever have a pregnancy scare?" Tyeesha asked, looking me in the eye.

"Yeah, a few times," I admitted.

"Did you ever get caught?"

"That's personal," I answered, nervously.

"You did, didn't you?" Tyeesha said, narrowing her big eyes.

"Yeah, I did once," I admitted.

"What did you do?" she asked, raising her eyebrows.

"None of your business," I snapped.

"Come on, I need a role model," she whined.

"Do as I say, not as I've done, okay?"

"What did you do after you found out you were pregnant?" Tyeesha asked sympathetically.

"Lower your voice," I said. "Let's sit over there under that tree and get out of this sun."

We moved to the shade and I let my mind go back to something that I'd buried. "I was in college and I had an abortion," I confided with a lump in my throat.

Tyeesha looked at me with compassionate eyes.

"Luckily, abortion had just become legal in the whole country." I sighed. "Otherwise I would've had to scrape up the money to go to New York."

"Did the guy stand by you?"

I groaned. "I was stupid, it was just some dude I went home with after a fraternity party. I didn't even know his real first name, let alone his last name. Everybody called him Hooty. I knew he probably wouldn't give a hoot, either."

"Probably wouldn't," Tyeesha agreed.

"I was careless and I got caught. I was too embarrassed to even tell him. Your mother was the only one I confided in. *She* stood by me. She held my hand through it all."

"Do you regret it?"

"Of course I regret being so stupid. And yeah, sometimes I wonder if I did the right thing. I wonder if the fact that I ended up with fibroids and had to have a hysterectomy was payback. I got rid of the only child I probably ever would've had. But I was young and scared and so ashamed. I felt like I had to choose between being a statistic and getting an education. Abortion just seemed like the best solution."

"Didn't you think about keeping it or putting it up for adoption, even?"

"I thought about everything. I fantasized about having a girl. I fantasized about having a boy. I even had a nightmare about having twins. I just knew that if I carried it, I would keep it. And I didn't want to be another black girl struggling with a baby with no father. Instead, I wanted to see the look on my mother's face when I presented her with my college degree." I paused. "I made my choice and I've had to live with it."

"Fairy godmother, it seems like life is full of problems." Tyeesha sighed, and put her arm around my shoulder.

I turned and hugged her against my chest. "Life is not a problem to be solved, my child. It is a gift to be opened."

seven

"I'm concerned this morning," the preacher declared.
"I said, I'm concerned this morning!"

"Yassuh!"

"I'm concerned this morning, because some of you are going to hell," the pastor said, searching the faces in the congregation. I felt Jason's little body come to attention. He was sitting between Sarita and me. I hoped the preacher wasn't scaring him. But on the other hand, maybe a little fear wasn't the worst thing these days.

"I repeat, some of you are going to hell," the minister said solemnly.

"Lord, have mercy!"

"You can't give the devil a ride," the preacher continued. "I said, you can't give the devil a ride."

"Amen, Reverend!"

"Because if you give the devil a ride, then he's gonna wanna drive." He pretended to be steering.

"Amen, Reverend!"

"Let the church say amen!"

"Amen!!!!"

"And if you let the devil drive, you're gonna end up in a wreck. I said, if you let the devil drive, you're gonna end up having a wreck. And the only insurance that the devil carries is a one-way ticket to hell!"

"Lawd have mercy!"

"Hallelujah!"

The organist started up and a male soloist belted out "I'd Trade a Lifetime for Just One Day in Paradise."

After church, I changed into some old clothes and rode the exercise bike in Sarita's basement. She sorted piles of laundry on the floor nearby.

"Girl, the way you sang out in church this morning, I thought you were gonna outdo the choir," Sarita teased.

"I have a feeling that I'm about to be blessed, so I made a joyful noise." I pedaled steadily.

"I guess if Skylar actually calls you, next thing you know, you'll be speaking in tongues."

"No, I won't go there. I could never speak gibberish in public," I said, pedaling faster.

"If the Holy Ghost gets into you, you have no choice. He speaks through you."

"Why does the Holy Ghost always choose Priscilla Crockett?" I asked. "I know it's wrong to say it, but I wish she would shut up sometimes."

"You're speaking against the Holy Ghost now. That's blasphemy."

"But it's scary, listening to her screaming and crying, like she's been traumatized. And nobody understanding what she's saying. Why is it, that when two people are speaking in tongues, neither one can understand what the other one is saying? Seems like there should be a universal tongue language."

"There are mysteries that we don't understand."

I slowed down on the bike. "I used to spend my summers in Alabama with my grandparents and cousins. And we went to a li'l old frame church perched on top of a hill. There was this woman, Sister Bertha Fullilove. They used to call her Big Bertha behind her back. Anyway, she got *happy* every Sunday, right before they took up collection. That's why she never had to tap the plate. You could almost set your watch by her. Big Bertha would go to shouting and commence to do a Holy Dance. There were others, of course, but Big Bertha got the spirit in a bigger way than most," I said, my pedaling speeding up again.

"So, what was wrong with that? That's what church is for. It's an outlet."

"I agree. Most folks worked as domestics and sharecroppers and whatnot. And they needed a release after a long week of having the white man's or the white woman's foot on their necks. But the problem was Big Bertha would always head for the back door behind the pulpit, which let out on the top of the hill. She'd get a running start and when she got up to the door, she'd yell, 'Hold me back! Hold me back!' And, of course, the deacons would struggle with her, until they got her back to safety," I said, huffing and puffing on the bike.

"But after awhile they got tired of wrestling with Big Bertha," I continued after catching my breath. "And the deacons complained at their monthly meeting that Big Bertha was getting too much for them to handle. They were afraid that one Sunday she would overpower them and head down that hill out of control and hurt herself. The deacons were at wits' end to come up with a solution. My grandfather suggested that the next time Big Bertha headed for the door and shouted, 'Hold me back,' nobody should budge. There were protests of concern, but Grandpa was head of the deacon board, and he promised to take responsibility for the outcome. So, Grandpa prevailed." I stopped pedaling altogether.

"What happened?"

"That next Sunday as usual, Big Bertha got *happy* and headed straight for the door. When she got there, she flung her arms forward like she was fixin' to run a race and shouted, 'Hold me back! Hold me back!' as usual. But this time, nobody got up, not the deacons, not the ushers, not even the nurses. Everybody just sat and looked. Even the Amen Corner was calm as a can of lard. Big Bertha repeated, twice more, 'Hold me back,' but still nobody budged."

"What did she do then?"

"She straightened her floppy hat and went on back to her pew and sat down, she and the Holy Ghost."

"Did she ever get the Spirit again?"

"Oh yeah, but from then on, the Spirit had a better sense of direction."

Phil ducked his head into the basement stairwell.

"Y'all sure y'all don't want to go to the ball game?"

"Lord knows I shouldn't be working this hard on a Sunday. But after I get this wash in, I just wanna be a good girlfriend this afternoon. I'm not interested in sitting out in the ballpark. I need a break from being an overworked mother and a regimented wife."

"Oh, please." Phil groaned.

"Besides, you and Jason need some father-son time," Sarita continued.

"Yeah, plus I get bored right after the seventh inning stretch," I admitted.

Phil joined us in the basement. "I'm glad to see somebody making use of that bike," he said. "It usually just collects dust. And Sarita just *had* to have it."

"So what? Sarita paid for it with Sarita's money," she retorted.

"You hear that, Dee Dee? Her money is her money, but my money is our money. Now, I ask you, is that fair?"

"Life isn't fair," I answered, continuing to pedal. "That's why I'm on this bike."

Sarita walked to the foot of the stairs and shouted, "Jason, stop running over people's heads!"

"Are you going to see the White Sox or the Cubs?" I asked Phil.

"What a question," Phil said, reaching for a Sox baseball cap on the table. "We're Southsiders, what do you think?"

"I guess I wasn't thinking. I'm so used to being closer to Wrigley Field. I forgot where I was."

"You mean you forgot where you came from," Sarita said, going back to her clothes.

I rolled my eyes at her.

"Baby, did you tell Dee Dee that the house across the street is on the market? Maybe she wants to rent out her condo and move back down here with her people," Phil teased.

"You need to get out more," I answered. "Times have changed. My neighborhood is integrated with all kinds of people."

"It still ain't home," Phil replied. "Home is the 'hood."

Sarita shook her head as she loaded laundry into the washing machine.

"It would take a crowbar to pry Dee Dee off the North Side."

"I need to be able to come in and out at night and feel relatively safe," I explained for the hundredth time.

"I don't know why you don't just get a gun and move back home. Most of the people around here are packing," Phil said matter-of-factly.

"Yeah," Sarita agreed. "The only reason we don't own a piece is because I'm wary, having a child around, especially a boy."

"There's nothing happening down here," I protested. "The South Side is dead, except for Hyde Park. All you can do down here is buy a house, raise a family and go to church and…"

"And pray you don't get killed, huh?" Sarita frowned.

"You said it, I didn't. I just said the South Side was dead, no pun intended."

"So, what they giving away on the North Side?" Phil asked sarcastically.

"Nothing, but there are all kinds of restaurants, different cultures, nightspots, art galleries, recreational facilities. I'm not far from most of the blues clubs."

"We don't need to sit up in a club to experience the blues," Phil said. "We got all kinda blues around here. Mama across the street is on the pipe. There's a grandmother trying to raise her daughter and her son's kids. The daughter is sprung and the son is locked up. Several folks have got cancer. We got a boy across the alley who got shot six times and he's in a wheelchair. We got plenty of blues around here. We ain't no strangers to the blues."

"None of us are," I answered. "But what you described is really sad." I sighed and stopped pedaling.

"It's maddening!" Phil said, pulling off his baseball cap. "That's why I'm in Mad Dads. We walk these streets. We try to turn people around. But despite our best efforts, some of them fall through the cracks. I'm taking a couple of boys to the ball game with us today who don't know what a father is. That's the norm now. Maybe I can make a little bit of difference."

"The truth comes out." Sarita winked. "Phil wanted us to be chaperones. Tried to stick us with Bay Bay's kids."

Bay Bay's kids was a black expression for bad-ass ghetto kids. There was a low-budget movie with a single mother named Bay Bay who had kids who were outta control. And even though most people hadn't actually seen the movie, the expression "Bay Bay's kids" had spread across Black America.

"You always got to be negative." Phil groaned. "Did you give Dee Dee her surprise?"

"What surprise?" I asked.

"I forgot," Sarita said apologetically. "Let me get it."

Sarita returned and held up a T-shirt. "It's a belated birthday present from Phil. Don't laugh."

"'I LOVE BLACK MEN'? You all expect me to walk around with a T-shirt proclaiming in big bold letters I LOVE BLACK MEN?"

"What's wrong with that?" Phil asked.

"I'm a little shy, believe it or not."

"Show your love for the brothas."

"People have to earn love," Sarita insisted.

"There you go again, being negative. That's why we in the shape we are today, cause y'all don't know how to support nobody."

"We're in the shape we're in today because the white man gave y'all the load to tote and y'all turned around and put it all on your women," Sarita snapped. "Too many brothas out here only care about their dicks and their bellies, excuse my language on a Sunday, but I'm just telling it the way it is. Being a faithful husband and a responsible father doesn't even cross some of their minds."

"Preach, sista, preach," I said.

"That's not me, though," Phil said. "I'm a strong black man. And I'm a strong family man. I don't run from my responsiblities. And there are plenty like me, but we just don't get the spotlight. You can't tell me I don't do my part."

"You do *a* part, I will grant you that," Sarita said, cutting her eyes. "But you could do more around the house."

"I try and help out. We just have different standards when it comes to cleanliness, that's all."

"Okay, I believe in giving the devil his due," Sarita conceded. "You're a good husband and a good father and a good man."

Phil clapped his hands. "Congratulations. You were able to say all that without choking. Baby, you're on a roll. Now, repeat after me: 'Phil, you're the best thing that ever happened to me! You're the cream in my coffee. You're the sugar in my tea.'"

Sarita cut her eyes again. "Don't make me curse on a Sunday." She threw the I LOVE BLACK MEN T-shirt at Phil.

Phil caught it and said, "Dee Dee, you wear this shirt, and I guarantee you'll get results. Remember, you can attract more flies with honey than with vinegar."

"Maybe she doesn't want to attract flies."

"Negative, negative, negative." Phil draped the T-shirt over the bike's handlebars.

"Maybe I'll sleep in it," I said.

"If you sleep in it, nobody'll see it but your cat."

"How do you know that?" I asked defensively.

"Sarita woulda told me if you were dancing in the sheets."

"Mmm-hmm," I said, glaring at Sarita.

"I don't tell him your business," she cut in quickly.

"You didn't tell him about Skylar, did you?"

"Is that the mediator?" Phil asked.

"Sarita, you have a big mouth!"

Sarita bit back her bottom lip and looked apologetic. "I'm sorry, girl, me and Phil were gettting along for a change and it just sorta slipped out."

Phil gave me a puppy dog look and patted my shoulder. "Dee Dee, you should understand. After all, there's nothing exciting for us to do down here on the South Side. So sometimes we just have to resort to gossip."

eight

I know that diets don't work. I'm not going to pretend to myself that I can stick to a low-fat diet based on willpower alone. That's just not realistic. It doesn't take into account why I eat and what's eating me. Letting go of weight is one of the most complex things you can do. First off, you don't want to *lose* weight. Because then you'll go looking for it. Instead, you want to *release* weight. Scales don't work, because people become obsessed with weighing themselves. When they gain a little weight, they eat to comfort themselves, and when they lose a little weight, they eat to celebrate. I learned all that from reading *Thin Within* by Judy Wardell.

What I'm mainly doing is eating the foods I love, but cutting down on portion sizes and eating only when I'm hungry. I'm also saying no to sugary and high-fat foods most of the time, but not always, because then I'd feel deprived like a person in jail, and I'd want to bust out. I don't eat or drink diet stuff because I don't like substitutes and besides, the only people who eat and drink diet stuff are overweight. The trick to releasing weight is to think and act like a thin person, according to *Thin Within*. My goal is to cut way down on eating for emotional reasons. When I find myself heading for the fridge, especially at night, I will ask myself, "What do you *really* want?" Oftentimes, it isn't food. Sometimes, I'll call a friend or light candles and meditate or listen to music or take an aromatherapy bath or read or spend quality time with my cat. Sometimes I know I'm really hungry for love and none of that stuff totally works. That's when I masturbate, and sometimes it's really beautiful, but often, its just ends with a few intense jolts. That's cool, because I just needed to release some tension. And it's a lot healthier than binging and purging. Of course, I'd rather be hugged up with a man. That goes without saying.

I still hadn't heard from Skylar, and I was trying hard not to call him. I'd dialed his number a few times and hung up before the phone rang. I was seriously tempted to eat for emotional reasons. I was fighting loneliness and the memories of my stepfather that at times threatened to overwhelm me.

I jumped at the chance to go swimming with Sharon at her downtown health club, high atop the Swiss Hotel. It was a healthy diversion and we needed to catch up. But swimming made me hungry. And it felt good to satisfy my hunger, I thought, biting into one of the green apples they gave away at the health club. Only an apple wasn't quite getting it.

"It's funny, but I'm glad that I'm not in your position anymore," Sharon said as we stood in the hotel hallway.

"What position?" I asked, pausing to look at the view while we waited for the talking elevator. The window faced Navy Pier, and I automatically picked out the building that housed my radio station.

"Waiting for some man to call," Sharon said pointedly.

I sighed as the elevator arrived and the mechanical female voice said, "Going down."

Sharon was practically a card-carrying lesbian now. She'd subscribed to the local lesbian rag and had attended a black lesbian conference at Malcolm X College. She was talking regularly to a sista she'd met there named Michelle. They'd gone out for coffee, but hadn't kissed yet.

"I don't have to follow the damn rules," Sharon crowed as we entered the empty elevator. "Why should someone have the power to initiate just because he has a penis?" I was glad that the door didn't open at that moment.

"I mean, what are you, chopped liver?" Sharon continued. "Why can't you call Skylar your damn self?"

The elevator stopped and a couple got on, then people got on every few floors. So I didn't respond until after we each pocketed a few of the sample Swiss chocolate bars in the big goblets in the lobby.

"You know why," I said finally, as we exited.

"Because if he's really interested, he'll call you," Sharon answered in a singsong voice.

"It's true," I insisted.

"It's sad but true."

"Give me credit, though. I'm not sitting by the phone, moping. I've been active, walking, taking belly dance classes, and we just swam. I've been seeing friends and having fun." I savored the warm breeze blowing off the Lake.

"You do have a life, thank goodness. But it's just nice to be able to be yourself, romantically. When I was with men, I always had to calculate and premeditate. It was like I was playing a role. I'm so happy to be able to put down my damn script. Men and women play too many games."

"Don't rub it in."

"What would happen if you were just yourself with Skylar? Just called him because you wanted to. What would happen if you felt just as free to suggest a date as he did? What would happen?"

"The sample would be ample and he'd move on to a real challenge, that's what would happen," I answered quietly, as the doorman offered to hail us a taxi.

"If you can't risk being yourself, what's the point?" Sharon asked.

"That's so retro." I groaned. "We women haven't been able to be ourselves since the seventies. I mean, you could live in T-shirts and jeans and still get a man back then. You could have sex on the first date and he still called you again. So long as you were willing to *continue* to have sex." I chuckled.

"You could even make all the moves," Sharon agreed.

"Then the eighties came and men were men again and girls were girls." I sighed.

"In the fifties, women weren't allowed to say 'yes' and in the sixties and seventies, we weren't allowed to say 'no,'" I added. "Now, we're caught somewhere in the middle. But we're still not liberated. How can you be liberated if there aren't enough good men to go around?"

"Provided that's what you're looking for." Sharon raised her eyebrows.

"Unfortunately, it is," I said. "In some ways I envy you," I added wistfully.

"Has it come to that? A straight woman, envying a lesbian," Sharon whispered as the doorman deposited us into a cab. "Wonders never cease," she chortled.

"I have no desire to be a lesbian," I whispered back. "It's just that a good man is so damn hard to find."

"Dearborn Park," Sharon told the taxi driver.

"Don't look at that spot on the carpet," Sharon ordered as we entered her townhouse.

"Now I *have* to look," I said, staring at the dark spot on the turquoise rug.

"I'm so pissed. My sublettors spilled red wine and I don't know what I'm gonna do. I guess it could've been a lot worse. Aside from that damn spot and using the wall for a dartboard, I got off light. I kept most of their security deposit."

"They didn't really use it for a dartboard, did they?"

"No, but they hung so much shit on the wall, they may as well have."

"Where's T?" I asked, following Sharon into her living room.

"If you don't hear any loud music, that means she's not home. Enjoy the peace." Sharon turned the stereo on to V103, a popular soul station with a nice mix of hits and dusties.

"It seems like yesterday, when our parents were yelling at us to turn down that daggone music," I reminisced as I settled into a stuffed denim chair.

"Yeah, but at least we listened to real music. You can't compare Motown to the mess they call music today. I could make a rap CD myself. You don't even have to be able to carry a tune now," Sharon said, walking toward the open kitchen area.

"Remember, they said that we couldn't compare Motown to Billie Holliday and Louis Armstrong and Nat King Cole and Ella Fitzgerald?"

"Yeah, but *nobody* could've predicted this," Sharon called from the kitchen.

"Some of it's not bad."

"You're not subjected to it as much as I am. "

"Well, what's up with your youth?"

"We got into it." Sharon returned with glasses containing a sparkling fruit drink.

"About what?" I sipped my drink.

"Curfew. She thinks she's all of a sudden grown. Comes in and out when she gets ready." Sharon headed back toward the kitchen.

"How late did she come in?"

"It was after eleven," she said over her shoulder. "And I'm not going to have it. If she makes her bed hard, she's gonna have to lie in it."

"Where have I heard that before?"

"It still holds true," Sharon insisted.

"I never thought the day would come when you would utter such words. Can't this generation of parents, who invented sex, come up with anything new to say?" I shouted.

"Sometimes, the old school is the best school."

"That's so lame. You didn't say that when we were tearing the old school down."

"Everything changes when you become a parent," Sharon said, returning with a tray of cut-up vegetables and cheese and crackers. "Ask anybody who's raised kids. You spend the first twelve years of their lives worried to death that someone may harm them; then you spend the next six wanting to hurt them yourself." Sharon plopped back against the stuffed denim sofa with a stalk of celery between her teeth.

"Before you do anything rash, let's talk," I said, reaching for a broccoli crown on the coffee table. "I counseled Tyeesha last week and she hadn't jumped off the deep end yet. Maybe there's no reason for you to get alarmed."

"Dee Dee, I know she's had sex," Sharon said between celery chomps.

"How do you know that?" I asked through a mouthful of dip.

"I'm her mother. Tyeesha and I have always been close. And the mother-daughter bond can be the most intense relationship in the world. I know my child, I know her energy. I know when it changes. And it has changed. I've lost my baby," Sharon said tearfully.

"Don't even go there. T will always be your baby."

"It'll never be the same, though. She'll never be innocent again."

"Tyeesha's got a long way to go before she knows shit from Shinola. She needs guidance *now*, more than ever."

"Dee Dee, it's hard. It's like something was snatched from me," Sharon said, putting a piece of cheese on a cracker. "I have never even met this boy. He's not even a boy, he's a man. Tyeesha finally admitted that he's eighteen. I should bring charges."

"Now, now," I comforted her. "It's not like he's over twenty-one. Three years' difference isn't that horrible."

Sharon sighed. "She's still a minor and he isn't. And I'd be willing to bet that my baby got the short end of the stick. She probably didn't even enjoy it. He probably just used her. It was just a booty call as far as he was concerned. "

"Well, you're not going to always be there to protect her, now that she's almost grown."

"Remember when she was about four and we used to live down the street from that Chinese restaurant and we'd get take-out? And Tyeesha used to say that when she grew up she was going to own a Chinese restaurant, remember that?"

"Yeah." I nodded. "It was so cute, T was so precious. We'd play with her with the empty white cartons. We pretended to work for her, remember? And she would fire us, saying that we forgot the soy sauce."

"Moments like that slip by and you can never bring them back." Sharon shook her head sadly. "No matter how much money you have, or what you accomplish, you can never bring them back."

"Nobody can bring back the times. That goes for good times as well as bad times. But we always remember the good times, and pretend to forget about the bad ones."

"I still think that T's doing this to get back at me," Sharon said. "She will do anything she can right now to undermine me. Just because I need to be in somebody's arms and hear soft words whispered in my ear. She's determined that I'm not going to be happy. After all the sacrifices I've made."

"She's just tripping."

"I understand why she's upset. I know it's a rude awakening, but she's going to have to realize that the world doesn't revolve around her."

"She's an only child. It's just been the two of you for so long."

"I have needs of my own. Everyone would understand that if I were looking for a man. I haven't even brought anybody home. The way T walks around here pouting, you would think I was getting busy right here on the rug."

"You have a right to a social life. Tyeesha's just feeling threatened. At her age, she's still insecure about her own sexuality. You know how confused folks are at fifteen. They think they have all the answers and they don't even know the questions."

"Dee Dee, in some ways you're lucky not to have kids."

"I'm starting to see it that way myself. Sarita's mother says it was easier for her to raise five kids than for Sarita to raise Jason. Despite all of the advances, it seems like it's harder to raise kids now than ever."

"We were happier with sugar water than they are with gourmet ice cream," Sharon declared.

"Let's face it," I said. "We're baby boomers. We had an authentic childhood. Today childhood has all but disappeared."

"You're right," Sharon agreed. Then her face grew troubled. "I'm afraid that Tyeesha is going to do something stupid to get back at me. I don't want her to drop a bundle on me. I swear to God I don't."

"I'll talk to T again." I sighed. "See if I can reach her."

"I'm glad your godmother duties are kicking in. I don't want to have to go for what I know. I don't want to have to whup her ass at fifteen."

"Now, now, you were never big on corporal punishment."

"Yeah, I spared the rod for the most part. I did the time-outs and I talked and talked and talked. But I feel like I'm losing her. And I don't know what else to do."

"You've got to communicate," I said automatically. But I knew it was easy to say and hard to do.

"They don't feel they have to answer to anybody. The nurse can't give them a Midol at school, but they can get an abortion without your knowing it. Everybody is telling these kids that they're grown," Sharon ranted. "The music industry, the schools, the courts, their friends. They're dealing with shit we didn't have to deal with. T knows girls who have two babies, who've had abortions, kids who are teenage alcoholics and drug addicts. We're not just talking about a little bit of weed. I'm talking about crack, cocaine and heroin. Kids of all races, too, here and on the West Coast. But you spank a child today and they wanna put you in jail. On the other hand, if you're beatin' the hell out of your kid, they keep giving him back to you till you kill him. "

"You have to pray, to make it today," I said quietly.

"I can't deal with just wanting her to make it. I used to have dreams for this girl." Sharon sniffled.

"Don't you still have dreams for her?"

"Yeah, but they used to be bigger. When I looked at her the day she was born, I didn't think, 'I just don't want her to fuck up, that's all.' No, when I looked in my baby girl's eyes I saw an Olympic gold medalist or a Supreme Court judge or even the first black female president of the United States."

"Damn," I said. "Remember, we had our fun. Don't forget that."

"Yeah, but we were older, we didn't really cut loose until we were outta high school. Now, they're doing everything we did and then some at a much younger age."

"Yeah, but these are different times," I pointed out. "Young people could still go to house parties in the seventies and not have to be worried about being sprayed with bullets," I added nostalgically.

"That's true, they were more innocent times," Sharon agreed. "We just wanted to do a little dance, make a little love and get down tonight."

"Yeah, but we were grown. So what if we drank beer and wine and smoked a little weed? You and I pretty much stayed away from the hard stuff. We had a few one-night stands. We made our mistakes. But we didn't have to pay for them with our lives. That's the difference."

"That's a big difference." Sharon sighed. "If I'd known those really were the good times, I would've enjoyed them more."

nine

Jade was in mediation with Bill, and she said it was going okay. I didn't pump her for information about Skylar. I still hadn't seen or heard from him, and it had been over two weeks since he'd asked for my card. Jade would've mentioned it if Skylar's fingers were broken and he couldn't dial a phone. Anyway, I was fantasizing about him less and less. I had a life.

Right now, my mind was on belly dance. I was surprised to learn that so many belly dance movements originated in the spine. When we made snake arms, Jade instructed us to pretend that we had a beach ball underneath each arm. But our arm movements as well as our hip and shoulder movements originated from the base of the spine. I found this fascinating, especially since when most people thought of belly dancing they focused on an exposed belly. In fact, the spine is the backbone of belly.

Jade says you can make the same movements in a temple as in a strip joint. And the former can be spiritual and the latter can be sleazy. It's not the building that is the determining factor, but one's intentions. A dancer's intentions are the very essence of her expression. The belly dancer is an opener of doors. She can take you inside your own soul, or she can wallow with you in the gut-ter. It's not what's in her movements that make the difference, but what's in her intentions and your own. When Jade used the word "intentions," it reminded me of my mediation conversation with Skylar. But after a few seconds, I was able to concentrate on the belly dance class again.

"Do you realize how tenuous all this is?" Jade asked over Chai tea at a coffeehouse after class.

"What?" I asked.

"Everything. I have to act within bounds. It's like a ball in a game that's not supposed to go out of bounds. That's the way my marriage is. I'm required to hit the ball within the bounds."

"I'm glad that you don't feel like you *are* the ball. That would be a lot worse," I said, between sips of tea.

Jade paused thoughtfully. "I know what would drive Yoshi away."

"What?"

"Just being myself for starters. But I was groomed not to be myself."

"How so?"

"I watched my mother as a little girl," Jade said, licking the back of her spoon. "And it was clear to me that she had to choose between being a wife and mother and being herself." Jade's dark eyes narrowed. "Being loved and being herself. Being loved and loving herself." She took a big swallow of tea.

"I want to love a man and be loved by a man and also love myself. That's what I want," I said, inhaling the steam from my tea.

"If I really expressed myself, everything would go, just like that," Jade predicted.

"Not if you have a good lawyer."

"I mean the marriage would go," Jade answered solemnly. "I visited a psychic once and she told me that I was really a man."

I was confused, as Jade was quite feminine in appearance. "I hope you didn't pay her."

"That's one of the reasons I went into belly dance."

"Because you were a man?" I asked skeptically. "Your flier says belly dance is the ultimate in feminine fitness."

"The psychic said that I was a man in my most recent past life,"

Jade explained. "And I was having difficulty in adjusting to being a woman in this life, because the transition had just been too abrupt. I died suddenly."

"Oh. I'm having a little trouble following you, because I don't think I believe in reincarnation," I confessed.

"The psychic said I was a great leader," Jade said, dreamily.

"Wasn't anyone just a peasant in their past life?" I asked, rolling my eyes.

"I'm sure. But anyway, it all made sense. I've always rebelled against the submissive role that my culture tried to saddle me with, at least inwardly. I've always been in conflict."

"Maybe you just didn't want to be a doormat. That doesn't mean you were a man."

"We all have a male and female side. A yin and a yang. I'm talking about energy."

"I know that."

"Anyway, I got into belly dance because it allows me to express my femininity and still feel powerful," Jade said.

"That's a nice combination," I breathed.

I was early for a staff meeting at the radio station the next day, so I hung out for a bit with Freddy. I'd just barely gotten in ahead of the rain.

"We got some falling weather out there," I said against the backdrop of thunder. "It's really coming down now."

Freddy rubbed his shiny bald head. "Rain's good for the grass and it helps keep the crime rate down. If it keeps up like this, many a nigga'll be runnin' for shelter tonight. So, you oughta be okay walking around with that diamond in your ear. But you better not let the sun catch you," he warned.

I fingered the stud in the second hole in my left ear. "This isn't a real diamond. This is nothing but glass," I confided.

"Well, you still better be careful walking around with it," Freddy insisted. "Everybody ain't no diamond expert," he said, raising his eyebrows. "You don't wanna cause some nigga to grab yo' ear for nothin'."

"Freddy, should I just resign myself to the fact that you've become a bigot in your middle age?"

"Maybe I'm just a liberal who's been mugged, as they say."

"Well, they've pumped drugs into our communities." I shook my head. "It's a shame. Drugs and the lack of jobs are what's driving most of this crime. And warehousing folks is not the answer."

"Nobody can make you take a drug," Freddy countered. "Y'all got too many weak-minded individuals, *that's* what's driving this crime. And these crim'nals don't care nothin' 'bout me *or* you if they think we got somethin' they want. A lot of 'em *need* to be warehoused." He sighed. "Everybody's lookin' for a 'scape. They had ten problems and now they only got one problem, a drug problem. You put something bad out there, yo' people will knock each other down tryin' to get to it. You put something positive out there, they don't want no parts of it."

"We don't have enough positive role models," I argued.

Freddy folded his arms and shook his head. "Y'all the only race of people who gotta have role models. Be your own damn role model," he insisted, swatting my arm playfully with the rolled-up sports section

I shrugged. "You know, there was a time, no matter what color you were, if you couldn't use your brain, you could use your brawn, remember?"

Freddy nodded begrudgingly. He couldn't deny his age and he hadn't completely lost his memory.

"My uncle was a steelworker," I added. "I still have a picture in my mind of him in his gray work clothes, carrying his yellow hard hat and metal lunch pail. When we were little and rode past U.S. Steel on the bus," I continued, "we used to point and sing, 'This is Leon's work, this is Leon's work,' so loudly that Mama had to tell us to hush."

Freddy smiled nostalgically.

I sighed. "U.S. Steel has been silent and rusted for years now. We've lost a ton of blue-collar jobs. A lot of people feel useless.

The message they get is, they're in the way." I tapped my foot against the floor. "It's dangerous when people don't feel needed. You shouldn't have to be a rocket scientist to be able to raise a family on one income."

"There's nothing wrong with working on more than one job," Freddy protested. "I work on two jobs and I only have a high-school diploma. A lot of people just don't wanna work," he insisted.

"Because the jobs they qualify for don't pay anything," I shot back.

"They shoulda went to school."

"People need affordable child care and transportation. You can't raise a family on minimum wage," I argued.

"These immigrants do."

"They stick together," I explained. "And their self-esteem is more intact."

"*And,* they get up early in the morning, and bust their cans," Freddy said, nodding his head. "You know how long my wife had to wait outside the beauty-supply store for them to open one time?" he asked.

I hunched my shoulders.

"Almost an hour," Freddy answered. "They came dragging in there whenever they got ready."

"Well, did they have an explanation?"

Freddy groaned. "The clerks said they forgot that the time had changed."

"Well, I can see how that could happen."

Freddy folded his arms and shook his head, "That's the difference between yo' people," he said, pointing to me with the rolled-up newspaper, "and my people," he said, pointing to his chest. "My people, white folks, would've made it *their business* to remember that time had changed. They'd have been there at 8:30." Freddy paused for effect. "Koreans would've been there at dawn."

Just then, two white women breezed through the lobby wearing raincoats and carrying briefcases. Freddy rushed to open the door for them.

The women passed through it without a word of thanks. "You're welcome," Freddy said sarcastically, but not loudly enough to put his job in jeopardy.

"They're not paying you any attention," I said. "They don't even see you, Freddy. They couldn't pick you out in a lineup. I don't know why you call them *your* people."

"Those two were strictly corporate," Freddy pointed out. "It wasn't about color."

"Maybe not. But still, as far as they're concerned, you're just old black Sam."

"Well, next time, I'm gonna let them get their own damn door," Freddy grumbled. "Old black Sam has left the building."

But he had a lost look in his eyes.

We celebrated Rob's turning the big Four-O at the staff meeting with cake and champagne. I indulged somewhat and was feeling pretty amicable when Bill asked me if we could talk. He'd heard that I wasn't interested in mediation, and that was fine. He said he just wanted to touch bases with me for some closure. I said that would be cool with me, partly because it was cutting up outside and I'd forgotten my umbrella. Plus, I didn't have to be at my other job for a couple of hours and I had time to kill downtown. Besides, Jade had rushed to a teeth-cleaning appointment after the staff meeting. So she wasn't around to judge me.

"I guess it's okay for us to talk, since we're not in mediation," I said cautiously after the room had cleared. "But you and Jade are still in it, right?"

Bill adjusted his glasses. He reminded me of the picture of Jack Sprat in the nursery rhyme book.

"Yes, we're in the middle of it. But we can keep that separate."

"Yeah, I don't want to get mixed in with you all's issues."

"Well, I appreciate your being willing to talk to me," Bill said, sounding respectful.

"Sometimes, talking can clear the air."

"I don't know where to start," Bill stammered. "It just seems like things have been blown way out of proportion."

"Depends on who you talk to," I replied.

"I don't mean to minimize anybody's feelings," he said, awkwardly leaning his tall, slender frame back against the folding chair. "And I support mediation," he added halfheartedly. "I really do. I don't want to be defensive or dump on you."

"What *do* you want from me?" I asked, ready to cut to the chase.

"I don't know," Bill answered, straightening his glasses again. "I guess I want to connect on some level."

"What level?"

"I don't know. Just on a human level, for God's sake." Bill sighed miserably. "I mean I know everybody's busy and most people have their two-point-three friends and—"

"Bill, are you trying to be my friend?" I interrupted, feeling awkward.

"I'm not asking you to be my friend or anything." He looked away. "It's not like we're in the sandbox and I'm asking, 'Will you be my friend?'" He sighed again. "It's not like that."

Bill made eye contact. "It's just that people probably see me as the guy that fools with the gadgets and keeps them on the air. And that's okay. I mean that's understandable."

"I'm not sure that I get your point." I saw an unexpected vulnerability in Bill's eyes.

"Everybody has to have a point?" He leaned back in the chair again. "So, let's see, what's my point?" I was concerned that he might tip over. "Maybe I don't have a point," he said finally. "Maybe I had a point yesterday. Or I'll have a point tommorow or in ten minutes. But is it okay for me to not have a point, just for a few minutes?" He looked like a child asking permission.

I narrowed my eyes and looked at Bill like I was trying to make out small print. I was having trouble getting a read on him.

"Maybe I have a point that you don't see," he said, spitting as he talked. "Or you'll see one that I don't have. Anyway, can you just let me get this stuff out?"

"Yeah, go ahead. Just watch your mouthwater."

"Sorry."

"I have some time," I said, begrudgingly. "So long as the conference room continues to remain available."

"It is. Nobody's due in here for awhile, I already checked," Bill said enthusiastically. He looked like he was having to restrain himself from shouting, "Goody, goody, gumdrop!"

I told myself that it would be good practice for me to show Bill a little compassion. After all, I never knew when somebody was going to call me up on the air and say they were feeling blue enough to jump off the Sears Tower or something.

Bill tilted his chair back to the ground. "Anyway, I went to a grief workshop last weekend," he said casually.

"Oh, I'm sorry, I didn't know you lost someone."

"Thanks, but I didn't go to the grief workshop because I lost someone."

"I just assumed that most people would go for that reason."

"Most people did go for that reason, but maybe I'm not most people," Bill said, laying on each word and clasping his fingers.

You're absolutely right, I thought. Most people wouldn't corner someone to tell them about attending a grief workshop when they weren't even grieving. I'd almost dusted the violins off for nothing

"If you didn't go because you lost somebody, why *did* you go?" I asked, confused.

"I went because I was *at* a loss." Bill sighed. "I had nobody to lose."

"Is this all connected to you and Jade?" I asked, warily.

"I don't know where the connection is. I'm just telling my story, just like in AA. Have you been to AA?"

"Yeah, I used to go with a friend of mine." I flashed on Sharon dragging me to those smoky, soul-searching meetings.

"Anyway, I wanted to be around people who were sad," Bill continued. "I wanted to be able to *be* sad."

I wondered if Bill was clinically depressed.

"I think a lot of people are sad, don't you?" Bill asked.

"Yeah." I shrugged. "There are a lot of people on Prozac and Zoloft." Maybe, by this winter, I'd be reaching for St. John's Wort myself. I shuddered.

"But nobody talks about it," Bill said, shaking his head. "They pretend to be happy. But a lot of people are not happy. They're sad. And when you lose somebody or get diagnosed with cancer, then it's all right to act sad."

"So, how was the grief workshop?" I asked. "Did it bring you down more?"

"No," Bill answered firmly.

"That's interesting."

"Oh, it was hard hearing about this one's lover who died of AIDS and that one's sister who was murdered. It was real hard, but it was real real," Bill said quietly. "It was mighty real, as you say on your radio show. Anyway, I could relate to the people who were sad. Because I was sad, too." He paused. "And I discovered compassion for myself." He looked at me, teary-eyed. "I know I've made some stupid remarks and been somewhat of an asshole. And I apologize for that. But I haven't assaulted anyone."

"People are afraid these days," I said softly. "They don't know if you're gonna stalk them or what."

"You're probably right," Bill agreed. "I saw a woman I went to college with waiting for the El. We chatted on the platform for a couple of minutes. I wasn't trying to pick her up or anything, but when we got on the train, I naturally sat next to her. I figured that we'd continue to catch up on old times, right?"

"Right?"

"Bong." He hit his head with his fist like he'd just lost a point on a game show. "You can just pick it up in the body language," he said. "All of a sudden you're pond scum. You're vermin, something that crawled out of a swamp. Did you say anything wrong? Probably not. Do you have bad breath? No. Do you have body odor? No. She's just decided that you're unwelcome, you're unwanted, you're the *other*."

"I have some experience with being the *other* myself," I interjected. "It's called being black in America."

"I'm sure you can relate, then. Anyway, suddenly you're not good enough to sit next to her and continue a fucking conversation."

"People can be cold."

"So, I crawl back into my world of computers and electronics. I hole up in my bachelor's apartment. And I go to work, play computer games, jog just so I can have some release. And then one day, da da!" Bill waved his hands dramatically. "There's a glimmer of hope in the form of a grief workshop. Imagine that." He sighed, making soulful eye contact.

I didn't try to imagine it, but seeing the sadness in Bill's eyes made me sigh, too.

"Dee Dee, do you ever wonder about what's gonna happen to us after we die?"

"You're not suicidal, are you?" I asked nervously.

"No, I just think about death a lot of the time," he said casually, locking his hands behind his head. "It's natural to think about death. We're all gonna die. Every morning we wake up, we're all a day closer to death. It's the one thing that we all have in common. But nobody talks about it." Bill folded his hands in his lap.

"What's there to say?" I asked.

"Do you think about it?"

I shifted in my chair and felt the smooth wood of the conference table with my fingers. I remembered asking when I was a child, "If God made the world, then who made God?" I never got a good answer.

"I used to to think about it when I was little," I said. "And then I stopped. But I think about it again, now that I'm getting older," I admitted. "I just pray that when my time comes, I'll leave everything in order." I paused and added, "You know, I'd hate to die suddenly and the house was a mess. Like I haven't cleaned out the litterbox. Or my important papers weren't in order. And I wonder who would take my cat."

"What would you care? You're dead."

"I still think about my cat and the people I'd leave behind. That's why suicide is so selfish. I hope you realize that. Bill, you have too much to live for."

"I guess you probably figure it's easy being a man, especially being a white man. You probably think I have it made, huh?" Bill narrowed his eyes.

"I think you have certain advantages," I answered, matter-of-factly.

"I see myself as a guy who's pretty much followed the rules and has done okay. Everybody thinks I have the goodies, but you know what? I don't." Bill stretched out his empty hands. "I envy the freedom you have to speak your mind sometimes. As a white guy, I gotta walk on eggshells. I'm under a spotlight."

"Not as far as the police are concerned or the public, for that matter," I argued.

"Okay, I'll buy that. I was referring to the politically correct crowd."

"Well, as a black woman, I feel that I'm at the bottom of the food chain sometimes. "

"I guess what I'm driving at is, you can be this so-called all-powerful white guy who actually leads a pretty empty existence." Bill leaned back casually, but his voice was choked with emotion. "I'm a white guy that basically nobody gives a shit about."

"Somebody must care about you," I insisted, able to muster up a bit of sympathy, although I wasn't ready to throw a pity party for a white man, just yet.

"Name 'em." Bill said.

"What about your family?"

"Dead or don't give a damn."

"People don't hate you here at the station."

"People don't hate me, is that the best that I can hope for? I'm just a fucking robot in a fucking control room. Is that all there is?"

"I don't know. Bill, what do you need from me?"

"I need human contact. I need to know that I'm not fucking invisible. I need to know that I'm more than my fucking job. And I know you're thinking, 'Boy is this guy needy!' People who need people are the neediest people in the world. The worst thing you can do is need somebody in this fucking world."

"You sound like you're really angry."

"You sound like a fucking therapist. I *am* angry. Haven't you heard about angry white men?"

"Are you one of them?"

Bill sighed. "I'm not sure what I am. I know I'm supposed to have it all. Hey, I've got a good job, a nice apartment, a reliable car. I'm a white man. I'm doing okay."

"Yeah, by most standards."

"Bong. No...I can't fucking connect. I listen to you and Jade doing your shows and I feel a connection. It's like you're my friends. I listen to Jade's music and it stirs something inside me. I express that to her and I get shot down. It's like I'm this slimy piece of shit that no one wants to connect with."

"Maybe it's the *way* you express yourself."

"Why is it when a woman does it, it's sensual and beautiful, but a man is always seen as crude and intrusive?"

"You don't intend to be crude?"

"Look, I was socialized as a male. And there was nothing in my indocrination as a male in this society to prepare me to be able to just watch a beautiful, scantily clad woman, gyrating and motioning toward me seductively with her hands. I thought I'd died and gone to heaven, okay?"

"It was all part of Jade's performance. It wasn't personal."

"Everything's a performance these days. Nothing's personal."

"She felt uncomfortable when you approached her. Serious belly dancers don't want to be seen as sex objects."

"I want to respect that. But there was nothing in my training as a man to see belly dancing as anything but sexual. Especially when you throw alcohol into the mix."

"Yeah, when people are drinking, it's hard for them to focus on the spiritual aspects of a belly dance, I will agree."

"It was so seductive. And she was so beckoning," he whined.

"You know Jade's married, don't you?"

"Yeah, but not happily."

"How do you know that?"

"Even though I'm not a woman, I have some intuition. I'm not all nerd."

"You surprise me. I didn't know that you were so emotional."

"Sometimes, I wish I weren't." Bill shrugged. "Then I'd be in less pain."

"I think that we're all in pain on some level," I said quietly. "I used to think you were either happy or you weren't. People used to say, 'I just want you to be happy.' Books used to say, 'And they lived happily ever after.'"

"Who the fuck is happy?" Bill asked.

"Happiness is just a whistle-stop," I said. "It comes and goes. They lived happily ever after. What a crock." I laughed. "I'm happy right now laughing about it, though, I must admit. But it's easier to be happy when you've had some champagne. Anyway, nobody's really happy all the time."

"Did you know that a study showed that half the people in this country would rather shop than have sex?"

"No, I missed that survey."

"There's a name for those people, too." Bill laughed. "Women."

We were both laughing when Jade and Skylar entered the conference room. Everyone spoke hastily. I tried to cover up my disappointment that I hadn't heard from Skylar. Of course, he didn't mention it. He even avoided my glance. But I could see the look of betrayal in Jade's eyes. I knew she was shocked to see me laughing with the enemy. I had some 'splaining to do.

"We're scheduled to have a session now," Skylar said, awkwardly.

"No problem," I answered. "I'm on my way out. Bill, it's been *serendipitous.*"

When I got home, I checked my voice mail. I wasn't at all surprised when I heard Jade's voice. She was still in the city and wanted to drop by and have a word with me after her class. I coaxed

Langston out of his favorite window and petted him in order to relax my nerves. I wasn't in the mood for Jade to get in my face about Bill.

I had to make my own decisions about people. Bill knew he'd messed up, but his actions weren't unforgivable, I said to myself as I answered the doorbell.

Jade looked fit to be tied. She was still wearing her sparkly belly dance costume, but her face told a different story. Langston instinctively kept his distance, immediately disappearing upstairs into the sleeping loft. I offered Jade tea, although I could have really used a glass of wine myself.

"I can't believe that you let Bill manipulate you like that!" Jade shouted, followed me into the kitchen area.

"I don't let anybody manipulate me," I insisted, setting the red enamel tea-kettle down on the stove.

"Why was it *so* important for him to talk to you?"

"He just wanted closure," I said, flicking on the gas burner.

"He set you up is what he did," Jade fumed. "Bill knew we were meeting in that conference room. He timed it perfectly."

I folded my arms and leaned against the kitchen counters. "No, he didn't. We ended up talking longer than either of us expected," I explained, facing Jade. "Nobody could've predicted that Bill and I would hit it off the way that we did."

"Hit it off," Jade echoed accusingly. "So he's your newfound friend? Is that what you're saying?" She narrowed her almond-shaped eyes.

"No, I'm saying that we had *one* decent conversation and it cleared the air. It's probably better for us to be on good terms, if possible," I said, straightening my posture.

"Bill already thinks I'm a raving feminist," Jade said, waving her arms. "Now that you're so cozy with him, I look even more like a lone lunatic. Don't you see that he's only using you to get back at me?" Her eyes pleaded with me to understand. "And what better audience than me and the mediator? It was so perfect." Jade bit her bottom lip and shook her head. "And so inappropriate."

I glanced up at the high ceiling. "Look, Jade, I don't know what

Bill's agenda is or whether he even has one. But I think I know when to trust my own instincts."

"Your instincts should've told you that Bill was a jerk. And besides, your loyalty toward me as a friend should come first."

"I am a very loyal friend," I retorted, feeling defensive.

"Actions speak louder than words!"

"Look!" I shouted. "There's no comparison between my feelings for you and my feelings for Bill. You're a close friend, and he's just a casual acquaintance, at best."

"You and Bill weren't laughing about me?" Jade asked suspiciously.

"Of course not. I'm not going to let anybody put you down. Stop tripping."

Jade sighed and leaned against the refrigerator. "I'm leaving Yoshi."

I turned the kettle off. "You're leaving Yoshi? Wait a minute, how did we make that transition?"

"I'm not in love with Yoshi and I haven't been for a long time," Jade lamented as we sat in the living room nursing glasses of wine. I'd decided that we needed to drink something stronger than tea.

"What's love got to do with it?" I scowled, stretching out in my leather recliner across from Jade on the sofa. "We're talking about a man worth five million bucks," I paused. "I hate to sound like a stereotypical sista. But that kinda money brings out the sista in me. And, don't forget, you've been married for upteen years."

"Sometimes, I wish I *could* forget."

"That moon spoon June shit only lasts for a few years at best," I scoffed. "I mean, is he beating you or what?" I sipped my wine thoughtfully.

"No, nothing like that." Jade frowned. "It's just that Yoshi's always been critical. He's not a joyful person, even with all his money. Yoshi almost never smiles."

"You should be smiling enough for both of you," I said, freshening our drinks. "Is there somebody else?"

"No," Jade answered flatly. "I don't think Yoshi's having an affair. He's too much of a workaholic."

"What about you?" I asked. "Are your eyes wandering?"

Jade sipped her wine thoughtfully and cleared her throat. "Well, I've sort of met someone else."

"Sort of met someone else," I repeated, rolling my eyes. "Are you hugged up with somebody or not?"

"No, not really. It's just an attraction. I mean, I haven't done anything about it yet."

"Yet?"

"I'm not even sure it's mutual. Although I feel it is." Jade looked soulfully into my eyes. "Nothing may ever come of it. It's just reminded me that it can still happen, that's all." She let her head sink back and stretched her arms along the top of the sofa.

"Of course it can still happen," I said. "You're not even forty yet. It's not like you're past fifty."

Jade sat upright. "Age is not the issue. It's just that I put my passion into my belly dance and kids and I thought that was enough. That I could get by." Her voice trailed off.

I thought about the song "We Got By" that Al Jarreau sang. It was one of my all-time favorites. But when Jarreau sang about getting by, about her bringing the beans and him bringing the wine, he wasn't talking about what Jade was talking about. Jarreau was talking about getting by without money. Jade was talking about getting by without passion. They were entirely different matters.

"But I couldn't really get by," Jade continued. "I mean, I almost could until this new musician began performing at Arabian Nights," she added softly.

"Arabian Nights, it sounds so romantic," I murmured after a sip of wine.

Jade's eyes lighted up. "When I dance to this guy's music, it's like making love with my soul mate."

"That's beautiful," I said with a sigh. "Stick to that fantasy.

Because reality would probably only disappoint you. I mean, what else do you know about this guy?"

"I don't need to know anything else about him," Jade protested. "We're in harmony."

I drank a swallow of my wine. "Yeah, but is harmony worth throwing everything away for? I don't think so. Just continue to enjoy things the way they are," I suggested. "Don't rock the house-boat."

"I *am* going to rock the houseboat!" Jade said, jumping up. "This marriage is making me lose faith in myself. The only thing we have in common is our kids. I feel totally devalued and unappreciated," she moaned. "Yoshi thrives on making me look stupid. Last month at a party, he made this big deal in front of people because I thought Brut was a brand of champagne. I didn't realize it meant 'very dry.'"

"Don't feel bad, I just recently learned that myself. I never bought champagnes that much. I just graduated from Korbel to Chandon."

"Yoshi claims that his friends aren't interested in what I have to say. But he doesn't communicate, he lectures. I'm sick of it and so are my sons!" Jade shouted tearfully.

"I understand," I conceded. "I mean, you shouldn't have to be miserable. But maybe you should just pamper yourself. You could take a spa vacation."

"A spa vacation is not a magic bullet, Dee Dee. I've been there, done that and got the T-shirt."

"Well, some women would take Yukihiro Yoshimuri for everything he's got in an effort to find a magic bullet," I pointed out.

"I want more than what Yoshi's *got* and it doesn't have to do with money." Jade sighed. "It has to do with feelings, Dee Dee. Don't you do feelings?" She looked me in the eye.

I swallowed. I felt uncomfortable, like I could break down and cry myself. I felt like maybe something was wrong with me all of a sudden. I considered myself a warm, feeling person. I knew I wasn't perfect. I had my fears and insecurities, but didn't every-body? I might not be the deepest person in the world, but I didn't consider myself shallow, either. I didn't appreciate Jade capping on me, but I wanted to respond to her without sounding defensive.

"Yeah, I do do feelings," I answered. "But I'm no expert. Maybe I'm still in kindergarten."

"We were probably better in touch with our feelings when we *were* back in kindergarten," Jade suggested.

"You got a point," I agreed. "Maybe that's when we *were* experts."

"I'm sorry, Dee Dee. I didn't mean to be so hard on you. I just felt frustrated."

"You were just trying to make it real. I understand. We're cool."

Jade paused and sat back down on the couch. "I just want the artist I fell in love with." She sighed. "Not the working stiff who tells our sons that the nail that sticks out is the one that gets pounded down."

"Who would believe you met Yoshi at an artists' colony?," I marveled.

"Yeah, he was a painter and I was a poet. It seems like another lifetime," Jade added with a faraway gaze. "The first week we were there we went for a walk in the woods and we got lost. I really was frantic, because soon it would be dark and cold and I wasn't sure what wild animals were around." She hugged her knees. "I directed Yoshi in circles, getting scratched by bushes and splashed by mud. Finally, Yoshi said, 'Don't worry, you're with a Buddhist.' I was so impressed with his calmness." Jade exhaled, sinking against my plump leather sofa. "I had nothing left to lose, so I just put my faith in his ability to lead us back to the trail. That was hard because all my life I'd rebelled against the sexism in my family and my culture. But there was something gentle about the way Yoshi took charge. And I told myself, if he finds the way back, I'll marry him, if he'll have me. Anyway, Yoshi led me back to where we originally got lost and we discovered that we hadn't gone far enough to make the turn. We were exhausted and relieved. We've been together ever since."

"It's so romantic."

Jade frowned and sipped her wine. "But we've come to the end of our road now. I hardly write poems anymore and Yoshi hasn't painted in years. Our tantric lovemaking is just a memory."

"I'm sorry that I tried to talk you into settling," I conceded. "Don't tolerate anything less than harmony."

ten

I resigned myself to never hearing from Skylar. I was determined not to contact him. My mother's words rang in my ears: "If a man is interested, he'll let you know." I might never hear from any eligible man again, I told myself. It was possible that I might spend the rest of my life as a cat owner/auntie/godmother/ friend who gave to the needy, fought fat and helped preserve the blues. It wasn't a bad fate. I had a lot to be thankful for, I reassured myself as I wrapped up another shift in the control room.

I paused at Freddy's desk on my way out as usual.

"Why is it black folks suddenly become so wise when they get old?" Freddy asked, reaching for a slice of pizza. I was so tempted to join him in devouring the thick, juicy slices, but I wasn't really hungry. Still, hunger and wanting to eat could be two different things.

"Freddy, you must be a mind reader. I was just thinking about my old age, just a minute ago."

"Well, to be considered wise all you have to do is live long, do little and say even less," Freddy advised solemnly.

"I might be able to manage that." I nodded, leaning against the wall. "My problem is what to do in the meantime."

"In the meantime, you best grab you a piece of this pizza," Freddy pointed. "You don't wanna be saying, 'If I had my life to live over, I wouldn't have let that pizza get cold,' do you?"

"No thanks," I answered, backing away. "I try to only eat when I'm hungry. I'm in between sizes now."

Freddy winked. "The hell with being in between sizes, you need to be in between two sheets. Girl, you need some sugar in your bowl."

"Don't go there," I warned. "Don't *even* tell me what I need."

"Dee Dee, I'm just talking to you as a friend. I just want you to have a reason to glow."

"You can't just reach out and find Mr. Right," I snapped. I didn't want Freddy feeling sorry for me like I was a spinster closing up the library.

"Well, maybe you need to settle for Mr. *All* Right, then," Freddy suggested.

I tensed up. I couldn't bring myself to say, it wasn't like Mr. All Right is busting my door down, either. I felt frustrated. I didn't expect to cause whiplash at age forty-one. I would settle for turning just one head, provided it was the right one.

"Dee Dee, there is nothing wrong with your body." Freddy's soothing tone interrupted my thoughts. "You was never fat, you was just what they call healthy."

"I'm not trying to be skinny," I said, as though thinness were within my reach. "My main goal is to be fit. I just want to feel good in my body."

"Somebody else could feel good in your body, too," Freddy teased.

"Freddy, you're creating a hostile work environment. It could be considered sexual harassment," I added half jokingly.

Freddy looked skeptical. "Anyway, like I was saying, there's no such thing as a dumb, old, black person in a rocking chair," he said, chomping on his pizza.

I swallowed my saliva. My mouth watered for the tangy sensation that Freddy was savoring. But I reminded myself that I wasn't really hungry. "It's true," I agreed, glad to have the subject changed. "I just saw this great movie called *Lone Star*. It had a wise old sista in it, rockin' with purpose and the sheriff hangin' on her every word."

"Y'all can be dumb as doorknobs in y'all's heyday, too," Freddy marveled. "But don't let y'all get old," he added, wiping tomato sauce from the corner of his mouth. "'Cause then evahbody'll think y'all Solomon."

I nodded. *At this point I would settle for a mushroom,* I thought.

"It's like you've caught it all your life," Freddy continued, narrowing his eyes and biting his bottom lip back. "And the darker you are, the more you've caught it. I mean from both black folks and white folks."

I nodded. Freddy reached for a small brown paper bag and took a swallow of beer. "And therefore, the more people want to hear what you gotta say, before you croak." He belched.

"Yeah, because like Langston said, 'A Negro has known rivers. And a Negro's soul has grown deep like the rivers,'" I recited.

"You ain't got a talking cat, do you?" Freddy asked, taking another swallow of beer. "'Cause if you do, then you could really make you some money."

"My cat's named after Langston Hughes, the poet and writer. That's who I was referring to."

"Oh, yeah," Freddy mumbled, trying to play it off. "Anyway, seems like you oughta be able to retire from being black." He yawned. "Oughta get a gold watch or something."

I was driving home the next night from my marketing job. I especially liked my neighborhood on summer nights. It had rained again earlier, but it had stopped as abruptly as it had started. The streets were still wet. The air was warm and clean and breezy like a tropical night. The pleasant weather had brought folks out. It was nice to see children playing under the watchful eyes of parents on their front stoops. Our neighborhood had an eclectic mix of people, different ethnicities, young, old, gay, straight, artists, families and singles, blue collar and professional folks. It was a good balance of trendy and real. For me, Edgewater had become home.

I could smell the breeze off the Lake as I walked toward my building. I planned to light vanilla-scented candles and take a long soak in my bathtub before curling up with my mystery. It was times like these that I appreciated my empty nest. The only responsibility I had was feeding my fur child. A lover would be nice, but tonight I cherished the rare feeling that I was enough all by myself.

"What are you doing here?" I asked, surprised to see Tyeesha in a rain poncho sitting outside my building. I wondered if something had happened.

"Fairy godmother, I need to talk to you," Tyeesha said in a barely audible voice, her head drooping, covered with wet braids.

I felt relieved. Nothing traumatic could have happened, because if it had, Tyeesha would've been too broken up to call me fairy godmother.

"Here, you're young and strong," I said, handing Tyeesha the sack of cat food. "What happened?" I asked as she followed me into the building.

"I'll tell you when we get upstairs," Tyeesha answered mysteriously. Maybe T was still trippin' on Sharon's coming out, I thought. I knew that her mother had begun dating that woman she'd met at the conference at Malcolm X College. Maybe T was having trouble coping with it. Or maybe Tyeesha had gone and done something foolish and it had nothing to do with her mother.

"I did it," Tyeesha announced, after I made her take off her wet poncho and began towel-drying her braids.

"It" had to mean sex. I frowned instinctively. I was feeling so motherly, rubbing her head. "I thought we agreed that you were going to wait," I reminded her.

"Wait for what?" Tyeesha asked, sounding clueless.

"Wait until you were ready," I answered firmly.

"I *was* ready."

I sighed and gave Tyeesha's head one last good rub. "I just hate to see you growing up so fast. I want you to enjoy your teenage years."

"Can't sex be part of enjoying them?" Tyeesha asked, throwing the towel into the hamper.

"I wanted you to be able to enjoy your innocence for as long as possible."

"What's there to enjoy about innocence?"

"Sometimes there's nothing more precious than innocence," I said, flashing on my childhood abuse. My eyes watered. I didn't want to go back to jumpstreet. I paused and took a deep breath. "I just don't want you to be burdened by adult worries like..." My voice trailed off.

"Like what?" Tyeesha asked.

I swallowed. I remembered the shame and worry, the cold instruments, the twinging pain, the sound of the vacuum suction, the nurse telling the doctor that the contents were overflowing, and those contents were what would have become my baby. The memory of my despair would echo forever, all because of one mistake. I felt a wave of protectiveness wash over me. "I just don't want you to have to go through what I went through."

"We practiced safe sex." Tyeesha rattled the words off so automatically that it reminded me that we were living in matter-of-fact times.

"I'm glad you took precautions but nothing is one hundred percent except abstinence," I recited.

"You want me to become a born-again virgin?" Tyeesha asked.

"Yeah, but I'm not naive," I answered. "I know that it's hard to put the genie back in the bottle, once he's gotten out. But remember, when you open the door to sex, you open the door to a whole host of stuff, and it's not all physical," I cautioned.

"Like what?"

"You can go to stupid city. And you can get your heart broken. Because, when you open yourself sexually, you're also making yourself vulnerable emotionally. A man's sexuality is hanging all out there." I motioned with my hands.

Tyeesha covered her mouth and giggled.

"I'm serious," I continued. "Your sexuality is like a buried treasure. And it does make a difference, no matter what anybody says," I added firmly. "Most women can't separate sex from love that easily or that completely. Sex and love are both powerful. That's why it's so important for a woman to love herself. And that often comes with maturity. End of speech."

"I really care about Malik. He's been nice to me," Tyeesha said, goo-goo-eyed.

"That's good—he should be nice to you."

"Everybody tells us how to stay away from boys." Tyeesha shrugged. "But nobody tells us how to *be* with boys."

"Well, my advice to you in dealing with anybody is to ask yourself, 'Is this person good for my self-esteem? Does he make me feel good about Tyeesha?' If he makes you feel bad about yourself, then he's bad for you."

"Malik is sweet to me. He is so sweet," Tyeesha gushed.

"Well, I'm glad to hear that," I said, feeling a little envious of her puppy love. "I won't stand for anybody dogging you. And I *am* thankful that you all used protection."

"Yeah, we did," Tyeesha said, bending down to pet Langston. "At least the first time."

"The first time!" I shouted. "What do you mean the first time?"

"We did it three times," Tyeesha confided, raising her shoulders to her ears like she was afraid of me.

"Three times! Three damn times! In one sitting?" I asked.

"We weren't sitting," Tyeesha protested, confused.

"I mean…you know what I mean." I sighed. "Anyway, you only used a rubber once?"

"Yeah, it sort of came off the second time," Tyeesha explained sheepishly as she followed me, carrying Langston. "And we didn't have another one."

"Then why did you do it a third time?" I asked loudly.

Tyeesha stared down at my Santa Fe tiles. "Malik said, since it came off in the middle of the second time, it was already too late. We may as well do it a third time. "

"Jeepers creepers!" I exclaimed. "Nobody in my day ever did it three times."

"Nobody in my day says, 'jeepers creepers,'" Tyeesha commented.

I rolled my eyes. "We had a first time and that was it," I insisted, setting Langston's food dish on the floor. "That's why they call it the first time," I added, filling Langston's water bowl. "We did it once and we didn't particularly enjoy it, because it was only the first time. It was supposed to get better. Maybe it took three times or ten times to get good. But it didn't get better the same night."

"Maybe the rules have changed," Tyeesha suggested, raising her eyebrows. "Maybe everybody does it more than once now in the same night." She batted the long eyelashes people had been exclaiming over since she was a baby.

"I know I'm not that out of step with the times," I snapped. "My ear isn't that far from the ground."

Tyeesha folded her arms and set her jaw. "I'm glad that we did it three times."

I leaned against the kitchen sink. "How can you say that, when you risked pregnancy and disease, twice?" I asked quietly.

"Because the first time it hurt. And the second time it still hurt. And I was gonna keep trying till it got better. And the third time was like the charm." Tyeesha smiled.

"There's nothing charming about unprotected sex," I warned. I sounded like an old biddy, instead of someone who couldn't remember the seventies because she was there. But in the seventies, we didn't have to worry about AIDS, I reminded myself.

"Can't you be happy for me because I had a good time?" Tyeesha's big brown eyes pleaded with me. "Can't you just be my friend, right now?"

What a concept. I never expected my mother to be happy that I had a good time. My generation, despite all the press, still pretty much had to sneak and creep.

"Baby girl, I *am* your friend," I said. "And I *am* glad you had a good time." Tyeesha gave me a hug. "But I'd rather you hold off having another good time until you're around twenty-one," I said, ruining our Hallmark moment.

"Twenty-one, that's whack!" Tyeesha cried, pulling away from me and rolling her eyes.

"Okay, eighteen, and I just wish you'd taken more precautions. When is your period due?" I asked with concern.

"In a couple of weeks," Tyeesha answered casually.

"A couple of weeks!" I screamed. "You're smack-dab in the middle of your cycle! You really like living on the edge, don't you!"

"We used a rubber."

"Yeah, once."

"We didn't plan to do it more than once. It just happened."

"It just happened!" I mimicked her. "Well, AIDS just happens and herpes just happens and pregnancy just happens, too!" I shouted.

"If I'd known you were going to go off like this, I would've never told you!" Tyeesha sucked her teeth and moved away from me. "You've forgotten what it feels like to be in love and to want to have a good time!" she blurted out at what she probably thought was a safe distance.

Tyeesha had a way of making me feel as old as a fossil. Of course I hadn't forgotten what it felt like to be in love and to want to have a good time. I *still* wanted to have a good time. I was only forty-one, not dead. I was in my sexual prime, after all.

I remembered a substitute teacher who said in frustration once, to our unruly third-grade class, "One day you're going to want to try to teach someone something, and then you'll know how it feels to not be listened to." And I thought, *I'll never be that old.* At eight years old, I couldn't imagine wanting to teach someone something, any more than I could fathom paying a mortgage or saving for retirement.

"Truth be told," I finally answered, "I want you to have more than *a* good time. I want you to have many good times. And to have good times, you have to make the right choices." I patted myself on the back for sounding like such a good role model.

"You sound like my mom."

"I take that as a compliment. 'Cause your mother is dead in your corner. Where is she, anyway?"

Tyeesha rolled her eyes. "Out with what's-her-name."

"Michelle, right?"

"Yeah."

"Have you met her?"

"Yeah."

"Is she nice?"

Tyeesha shrugged. "She seems okay. But she's a woman. And Mom's a woman."

"I know that. That's etched in stone. So?"

"So"—Tyeesha shrugged her shoulders—"I still have to get used to it, you know."

"Just give yourself time."

"I don't want Mom to know about me having sex, okay?" Tyeesha narrowed her eyes. "Don't rat me out."

"Why not? It would be the perfect way to get back at her," I said with fake enthusiasm. "And if it turns out that you're pregnant or have a disease, that would really stick it to her, wouldn't it?"

"That's whack," Tyeesha said, scowling.

"You do want to hurt her, don't you?" I asked, raising my eyebrows. "Wasn't that the plan?"

"I don't want to hurt her," Tyeesha said, groaning. "And there *was* no plan."

"That's right." I slapped my forehead. "If you'd been planning, you'd have brought along three condoms."

Tyeesha cut her eyes at me. "I thought you said you were my friend."

"I am your friend, but I'm not one of your peers. That's the difference."

"Anyway, it's not about her," Tyeesha insisted. "You think everything is about her."

"Well, at least if you get pregnant, nobody will think you're like her," I said, twisting my mouth and head to one side.

"I'm not like her, whether I get pregnant or not," Tyeesha said coldly. "I'll never be like her!" She put her hands on her hips. "I'll never be a dyke *or* a dried-up spinster, either!"

She covered her mouth like she hadn't meant to blurt that out, but it was too late.

I swallowed. "Who's the dried-up spinster that you're talking about?"

Tyeesha remained silent. I pointed my finger in her face. "I'll have you know that I'm not dried up." I sniffed as Tyeesha backed away. "And, in case you've forgotten, I'm not a spinster. I've been married."

"I didn't call any names." Tyeesha pouted.

"And, by the way," I continued, "there are worst fates than being gay or being a dried-up spinster. And if you're not careful, you're going to find that out."

eleven

Several days later, I was on the radio, closing out the set. "I'm going home this evening," I declared into the microphone. "I said, I'm going back to the South Side, do you hear me? Naw, I'm going all the way back to the West Side. Naw, I'm pulling out all the stops tonight. I'm goin' clear back to Crackville, Alabama. But we ain't praying for Sheetrock, y'all. We praying for good lovin'. And I got me a witness outta Memphis, Tennessee.

"I'm talking 'bout a sista who left her back door open all night long. Hoping her man would come on back home. But instead, jus' 'fo day, here come the blues to shut her do'." I paused and sucked my bottom lip. "I know some of y'all can relate," I said, shaking my head. "Not to leaving your back door open, 'cause it's too danger-ous for that now. But you can relate to wanting somebody to feel the need in you." I lowered my voice, causing it to sound husky. "This sista is talking 'bout her nature tonight. She's talkin' 'bout the sho' 'nuff blues. And I'm talking 'bout the Hoo Doo Lady herself, Memphis Minnie McCoy, doing the 'Moanin' Blues.' Give it up, y'all!"

A light was blinking. I had a caller. It was Reverend Johnson, a reg-ular.

"Dee Dee, I know you're not running a religious program. But, speaking of back doors, I wanna see if I can sneak God in through the back door tonight after all that moanin' that we just heard."

"Go 'head, Reverend Johnson, I left my back door open."

"You know, I'm so thankful now that when we were growing up we were so poor, we didn't have nothin' but God."

"You've got a big prosperous church today, Reverend Johnson."

"Yeah, but when I started, I only had a handful of folk and half of them were talking about leaving. 'Cause they couldn't deal with me. But I kept right on glorifying God. Dee Dee, tell your listeners to let go and let God."

"You just told 'em. Now what can I play for you?"

"'God Bless the Child.'"

"Okay, Lady Day is coming right up."

"God bless you, Dee Dee. God is using you through me."

My first thought when I saw Phil waiting for me outside the control room was that something bad had happened.

"Is everything all right?" I asked, raising my eyebrows.

"Everything's fine," Phil assured me. He looked professional in his sport coat and slacks. I wondered where he was coming from. "I just came from a focus group at your company," he said, as if he were reading my mind. "I finally got called."

"Oh, good, what was the product?" I asked.

"Ice cream," he said, clearing his throat. "I make most of the ice-cream-buying decisions in our household."

"Oh, yeah, they're trying to market a new brand to people who don't usually buy gourmet," I said.

"I figured as much." Phil balled up his fists and stretched his arms out like he had sat too long. "We chose ice-cream names, logos and designs. We did everything but eat it. I don't think I'll ever look at ice cream again in the same way. Anyway, thanks for hooking me up."

"Thank you. Marketing is a two-way street, you know."

"Well, it was an easy fifty bucks. Jason needs shoes," Phil informed me. "The boy's feet are almost on the ground."

"So, what made you stop by?" I asked as we walked through the reception area.

"I'm so seldom downtown," Phil explained. "I said to myself, 'Dee Dee is live, why not holler at her?' I caught the tail end of your show in the car."

"Oh, it was a little racy tonight," I said, feeling a little vulnerable.

"The sho' 'nuff blues always have been." Phil winked. "I've never even seen the studio before. Ain't nothing funky about this place."

"No," I agreed. "It's state of the art."

"You know, when you think of the blues, you think of a hole in the wall."

"Well, we do a variety of music here, but the set never changes. Imagination is a wonderful thing," I added.

"So, you got any big plans tonight?" Phil asked, making eye contact.

"Not really," I answered, looking away. "Langston is waiting for his snack, but that's about it."

"Cool. It's a nice night, let's just say we chill for a bit."

"What did you have in mind?" I asked cautiously. I felt a little awkward because Phil and I didn't hang out alone. Not that there was anything technically wrong with it. I mean, I did consider Phil a friend.

"I just thought we could grab a couple of beers down here, have a little conversation, you know," Phil answered casually.

"How are Sarita and Jason doing?" I asked as we rode alone in the elevator.

"They're fine," Phil answered matter-of-factly, but his terse tone made me wonder if things were really okay between him and Sarita.

"Hi, Freddy, this is Phil, a friend of mine," I said entering the lobby. "Freddy is my ace here at work." Phil extended his hand and Freddy shook it enthusiastically. I could tell that Freddy liked that I'd referred to him as my ace. But I also figured that he was disappointed that I wouldn't be able to linger tonight, especially since he was about to go on his vacation and we wouldn't see each other for a while. Freddy shot me a look that asked, "Who is this dude? I want the dirt."

"Freddy and his wife are about to go on a Caribbean cruise," I said. "Isn't that nice?"

"Yeah, my wife and I are talking about doing that," Phil said. That was news to me. Sarita hadn't mentioned anything to me about any cruise. She'd gotten seasick on a boat ride on Lake Michigan.

Freddy gave me a can't-believe-you-messing-with-a-married-man look.

I cleared my throat. "Phil is the husband of one of my best friends."

Now Freddy's eyes seemed to say, "Stabbing a friend in the back makes it worse."

"Bon voyage," I said, giving Freddy a quick hug. "Have fun."

"You take care."

"Nice meeting you, brotha."

"Same here," Freddy said, graciously accepting the brotherly acknowledgment, even though he insisted that he wasn't one of us.

"Tell me if this sounds crazy," Phil said, as we walked into the warm night air, out onto the pier.

"Okay," I agreed, wondering what Phil was going to say.

"Let's say we ride the Ferris wheel," he suggested, pointing to the neon-lighted ride. "I haven't ridden one since I was a kid."

The Ferris wheel looked so innocent and yet so enticing.

"It doesn't sound crazy…"

"Well then, let's do it!" Phil said, gazing up at the colorful ride.

"But…"

"But what?"

"But, but I don't know if would be a good idea," I stammered.

"Why not? Look, there's even a full moon," he pointed out.

"It's a paper moon." I swallowed. I couldn't help but drop my jaw in appreciation. But now I was even more hesitant about climbing up on the Ferris wheel with somebody else's husband. It was just too damn romantic.

"Dee Dee, I almost never get down here," Phil whined. "You have the opportunity to ride the Ferris wheel all the time. You work right here."

"Yeah, but I've never ridden it. I've thought about it, but I've never actually ridden it," I said, watching the colorful wheel turn slowly against the darkening sky.

"Well then, stop putting it off. Tonight can be the night."

"Phil, it just seems like you should want to ride the Ferris wheel with Sarita or Jason. You can't go home saying that you did it with me," I said, regretting my choice of words. "They might feel cheated."

"I don't have to tell them everything," Phil said quietly.

"Then it would be like a secret," I protested. "It would be like we had something to hide. And we don't. We have no reason to keep a secret."

"Okay, forget it," Phil said tersely. "Look at the line, anyway. I'll ride the Ferris wheel some other time. Maybe I'll go on it with Jason or even by myself. I doubt that Sarita has a desire to ride a Ferris wheel. I really doubt that very seriously."

Phil and I sat down at the far end of the pier, facing the dark water. I could've used a beer, but I sipped a ginger ale instead. I wanted to have command of all of my faculties. Alcohol loosens your inhibitions, and I couldn't have that happening.

"I know I give you a hard time, sometimes," Phil said, smiling shyly in the moonlight as his long legs dangled above the water.

"About what?" I asked.

"You know, about living on the North Side and stuff."

"Oh, that. I don't take that personally," I assured him. "I realize that people on the South Side don't have many recreational options and therefore some fall back on signifying," I teased.

"Dee Dee, that's cold, especially coming from a former Southsider," Phil said after a swallow of beer. "I called myself trying to declare a truce."

I sipped my ginger ale. "Okay, I accept your apology for giving me a hard time. It shows growth that you can admit that your dogging me about living on the North Side has been wrong."

"All kidding aside, there's a part of me that wants something different," Phil admitted, staring at the dark body of water.

"What do you mean?" I asked nervously. I hoped that Phil wasn't referring to his marriage. "Are you trying to say that you want to move to the North Side?"

Phil took another swallow of beer. "No, it's too hard to find a parking space on the North Side. I've just been contemplating some things lately, that's all."

"Contemplating? You're sounding a bit avant-garde for your 'hood, wouldn't you say?"

"Dee Dee, you're not on the air anymore. Stop performing and let's get real!"

I was taken aback by Phil's intensity. "Let's get real about what?" I asked defensively. "I thought we were just chillin'."

"Let's just come out of our boxes for a minute," Phil said. "Pretend we're on the Internet. There's no North Side or South Side. We're just human beings."

"Phil what is up with you tonight? Are you going through a midlife crisis?"

"Maybe so. I'm looking at my life in a way I never have before," he answered quietly. "I can't talk to Sarita about certain things. I don't feel that I can really get that deep with her, you know what I'm saying?"

"She's your wife. You've been married for over twenty years," I reminded him. I hoped that Phil wasn't trying to dust off that lame-ass, classic, my-wife-just-doesn't-understand-me bullshit.

"So, that doesn't mean I can get deep with her," Phil protested. "Don't get me wrong, I love Sarita and I would do anything for her. And she would do anything for me."

"But?"

"But, she and I have a certain *kind* of relationship."

"What kind is that?"

"Sarita's not the kind of woman I would choose to marry now," Phil said bluntly.

I gulped. Phil was talking about my friend. They were like family to me. I didn't know what to say. I felt shaky inside.

"I'm not the same person at forty-two that I was at twenty-two or even thirty-two," Phil continued.

"I'm sure Sarita's not the same person she was back then, either."

"Sarita's still basically the same," Phil insisted. "She still has her good points. She still goes out of her way for other people."

"Yeah," I agreed. I remembered Sarita spending a whole weekend teaching me how to do the splits. If it hadn't been for her, I never would've made the pep squad. I have to give credit where credit is due.

"Sarita is just not the type of woman who wants her man to get weepy on her."

"I never saw you as the crybaby type."

"What I'm trying to say is, Sarita can only go so deep." Phil paused as a warm breeze blew in off the Lake. "For a lot of years, that was okay. But sometimes, after awhile, you want more, you want to go deeper. And there's nowhere deeper to go." He threw up his hands. "I don't know why I'm telling you all this."

"Maybe you should be talking to Sarita instead."

"I just told you, I can't talk to Sarita on this level."

"Have you tried?"

"When you've been married for over twenty years, you've tried everything. You know what works and what doesn't."

"What attracted you to each other in the first place?" I asked. "You need to get back in touch with that," I said, hoping this marriage could be saved.

Phil let his lip curl into a cross between a smile and a smirk. "I was the best slam-dunker on the basketball team and Sarita was head of the pep squad. We both looked cute in our uniforms. That's probably what attracted us to each other in the first place. Neither of us can fit into our uniforms anymore." He sighed.

"Have you considered couples' counseling?"

"Sarita wouldn't go for that." Phil frowned. "We don't have any problems, so far as she's concerned. So long as our marriage functions."

"Maybe that *is* the problem," I said. "Your marriage just functions. Is that what you're trying to say?" I felt uncomfortable getting so involved in Sarita and Phil's private business. I didn't want him to go back and say, "Dee Dee said this" or "Dee Dee said that." Then I'd probably end up falling out with both of them.

"You hit it!" Phil exclaimed. "Sometimes, I just wanna come into a different house or see different furniture or eat different food or something. Just something different," he added glumly.

"Sounds like you think you're in a rut."

"I know I'm in a rut," he admitted. "At times, I envy somebody like you. You've got independence. You don't have to consider anybody but yourself."

"Sometimes, *I* envy people like *you*, who have somebody they can always count on," I said, as a laughing couple strolled by. I was nobody to envy, I thought sadly. I envied people like *them*. Life was sweet for people in love. If they rode the merry-go-round or the Ferris wheel, they wouldn't be able to tell the difference when they got off. I knew the feeling. I just wondered if I would ever feel it again.

"Sarita's on Prozac," Phil said, as the couple's happy voices trailed off.

"I didn't know that," I answered, surprised. "And I'm supposed to be one of her best friends."

"I'm supposed to be her husband. And *I* didn't know, till I saw the pills." Phil shook his manicured head. "When I confronted Sarita she said her depression had nothing to do with me."

"You can be depressed all by yourself." I finished off my drink. "I can testify to that."

"Yeah, but how can you be depressed in a marriage and it have nothing to do with the person you're married to?" Phil pondered. "I mean, that is, if every other area of your life is humming along. There's something wrong with that picture."

"We all have our pain, and some of it goes way back," I said.

Phil stood up and stared at the seemingly endless water. "What's the point of being together, if we're alone with our pain?"

I stood alongside of him. "Maybe, it beats being alone and *still* being alone with your pain," I suggested.

"Sometimes you can feel lonelier *with* somebody, than being alone." Phil sighed.

"I need to remember that."

"Dee Dee, I guess I just needed to talk." He kicked at the ground with the toe of his business shoe. "Maybe I can go on another twenty-odd years now without saying squat." Phil faced me and made eye contact in the moonlight. "Dee Dee, can you just give me a hug, let me know that you're there?"

"You need to hug Sarita." I folded my arms against the breeze. "That's who you need to be hugging on."

"Sarita don't come from a hugging set of people," he said, taking off his sport coat and draping it around my shoulders. I felt like I was back in high school and a boy had offered me his school sweater.

"I need a *real* hug," Phil said decisively. "Not the kind of half-assed hug Sarita would give."

"Okay," I finally consented. After all, I prided myself on my ability to give hugs. I hadn't always been good at them. But after participating in a few Black Women's Health Project workshops, I'd gotten good at hugging. I actually felt warm and secure, embracing Phil on the edge of the darkened pier. But then Phil's lips covered mine. Our tongues met for a tantalizing split second, before I pushed him away. Phil apologized, but I knew that I could've pushed him away sooner. And that disturbed me more than anything. I insisted on walking alone to my car.

I drove silently, without even the radio on, north along the outer drive and then Sheridan Road. Soon, I would be safe at home with my cat.

I wished Phil had never come to see me tonight. I wished he'd kept his feelings to himself. I wished he'd kept his lips and especially his tongue to himself. And most of all, I wished I hadn't enjoyed it for a fleeting second. My body had betrayed me. I could never let that happen again.

I remembered that I used to be able to leave my body when my stepfather came into my room at night and mess with me. I would watch what was going on like I was on the ceiling looking down. Learning how to leave my body had been a good trick to know when there was no place to go. Much of that time period was a blur; it was roughly during the months that my mother was pregnant with my baby sister.

It was like one day, I was a kindergartner skipping along, and the next day, I was living my life in a daze. My new stepfather told me to climb in his lap and tell him about my first day at school. What stood out most in my mind was that the bathroom walls were covered with the word "pussy." I didn't know what that word meant. But I recognized it from the nursery-rhyme book that Mama was teaching me to read. In that book, "pussy" had referred to a cat. But I figured that it must mean something else on accounta it was scrawled on the bathroom walls.

"Daddy Sherman, what does the word P-U-S-S-Y mean?" I asked innocently. I was proud of myself for being able to spell it by heart. I was glad that Mama had taught me my ABCs.

At first, my stepfather didn't answer, and I wondered if I should've asked Mama or my brother instead. But I'd figured that my stepfather knew more about the world than they did. It wasn't like a word from the dictionary. If anybody knew what a word on the bathroom wall meant, it should be him. After all, he drove a truck for a living and went lots of places. And besides, Mama said we should let our stepfather get to know us. She'd smiled when she passed by us a minute ago on her way to the kitchen. I knew she was glad to see me up in Daddy Sherman's lap.

"Daddy Sherman, P-U-S-S-Y was written on the bathroom walls at school. What does it mean?" I asked impatiently. "Are they talking about a cat?"

My stepfather shook his head. "Naw, they ain't talking 'bout no cat. It's a bad word. They talking 'bout what's in between a girl's legs," he said quietly. I noticed a glazed look in Daddy Sherman's eyes. I got an icky feeling inside and something told me that there was something wrong with what was between my legs. Daddy Sherman had said pussy was a bad word and it was what was between a girl's legs. I was a girl. That was a fact. I had something bad between my legs, therefore a part of me was bad, too.

I began to feel something growing hard underneath my thigh. I jumped down from Daddy Sherman's lap instinctively. I left him with a drunk look on his face and a bulge inside his pants.

My brother rushed into the room and asked, "Dee Dee, wanna play marbles?"

"Boy, you quit that running!" Daddy Sherman yelled before I could answer.

He took his belt off and started whipping Wayne. My brother's screams got my mother's attention. She came into the living room and asked what was going on.

Daddy Sherman said, "I'm gonna break this boy from running, if it's the last thing I do."

Mama tried to calm everybody down. She tried to smooth everything over, but it was too late. She was caught up in the daze.

I raided the refrigerator when I got home. I needed to eat badly.

After I stuffed myself, I went to the bathroom and threw up. I just needed to get some things out. And to feel in control again. I needed a fresh start.

twelve

On Sunday, I was in church with Phil, Sarita and Jason, just like old times. Everything was cool. It was like what happened between Phil and me had been a dream. After church I hung out with Sarita and Jace, while Phil went over to visit his mother.

I crossed my fists and held them out in front of Jason. Sarita stood nearby washing the dishes. "Which one has the rock?" I asked.

Jason tapped my left fist and was surprised to see that it revealed a rolled-up dollar bill. "Here," I said, "you get to keep the dollar. I didn't have a rock."

"What do you say, Jason?" his mother prompted.

"Thank you, Aunt Dee Dee."

"You're welcome."

"Now, I want you to put that dollar in church next week," Sarita said.

Jason's smile was quickly replaced by a scowl. "In church!" he protested.

"Yes, in church."

"But, Mama, I wanna buy something."

"Sarita, I didn't put any strings on it," I pointed out.

"Jason doesn't need to buy anything." Sarita frowned. "He needs to learn the meaning of giving. It's time for him to make a few sacrifices."

"But I wanna buy something," Jason pleaded tearfully. Just then the music from the ice-cream truck sounded.

"I didn't know they still came around," I said.

"I wanna buy ice-cream!" Jason shouted and bolted for the front door.

"Boy, you better not darken that door!" Sarita warned.

But Jason kept going, like he hadn't heard a word out of his mother's mouth. Sarita looked stunned. She shouted, "Jason, come back here!"

"He's gone," I said matter-of-factly.

"I don't know what to do." Sarita sighed. "No child of mine has openly defied me like that." Suddenly, she looked tired to me. I noticed the wrinkle lines on her forehead.

"I know it's hard raising kids," I said, sympathetically.

"I'm actually quivering, Dee Dee," Sarita said, stretching her hand out in front of her. I nodded. Her hand did look a little bit shaky. "Jason's crossed a line that has never been crossed before." She leaned against the stove for support. "Is this the beginning of the end?" She folded her arms tightly as if she were cold. "Now, I'm scared of what I might do."

"Jason's probably scared, too." I said. Damn, I was beginning to feel scared, myself. "I'm sorry I gave him that dollar now. I had no idea it would cause all this mess. Sarita, try not to be too hard on him."

"Humph," Sarita said, cutting her eyes at me. "I'm never too hard on him. Jason's lucky," she insisted. "If either of us had pulled a stunt like that, our mamas would've chased us down and whupped our tails right out there in the street. Not just my mama or your mama, but Black Mama U.S.A., period." Sarita put her hand on her hip and let her backbone slip.

"That might be true," I conceded. "But when you know better, you can do better." I hesitated. "With all due respect, I think you coulda said, 'Jason, you can put fifty cents in church and spend fifty cents.' You could've compromised." I fingered the bumpy glass of the salt and pepper shakers.

"But I didn't." Sarita glared at me. She straightened herself and stood over me with her arms folded. "I said what I said," she continued. "Why do I have to be perfect? Why can't parents make mistakes anymore? I remember all kinds of arbitrary things my mother said. 'You can't wear this. You can't do this. You can't do that.' Sometimes she had a good reason, and sometimes she didn't. And you know what?" Sarita leaned forward and raised her eyebrows. "Sometimes she was wrong. But she was still my mama." Sarita snapped her fingers. "So, why do I have to second-guess myself now?"

"Don't you remember how it felt, though, not to have a say in things?"

"A child can't have a say in everything," Sarita said firmly. "Sometimes, a parent has to say, 'Because I said so, and that's the end of it.'"

"You know Jason is going to be afraid to come back in here now."

"I'm afraid for him to come back in here, too," Sarita confessed, biting her bottom lip.

"What are you going to do?"

"Dee Dee, girl, I know you haven't raised nothing but a cat. But you've read a lot and observed things. So, let me ask you something." Sarita sat across from me at the kitchen table. She folded her hands in front of her like we used to do at our desks back in grade school. "If I go for what I know, you know I'm gonna tear Jason's butt up, and that's just a fact."

"Yeah, that would be my guess," I said, rolling my eyes. "Now, tell me something I don't already know."

"Okay." Sarita nodded, sucking her bottom lip. "I'm willing to consider other options. I'm not so rigid that I can't grow. But I will not have a child that I can't do anything with. I'd sooner have you pack his bags now."

"What if he stays outside too long?" I asked nervously. "Somethin' could happen to him. It's not like when we ran the streets," I reminded Sarita. "He might be too scared to come home." I remembered the frightened feelings I'd grown up with. Anticipating a whipping was often worse than actually getting one.

"The longer he stays away, the worse it's gonna be for him," Sarita warned. "He knows that."

"Yeah, but he might stay away just long enough to give you time to cool off."

"He'd better come back when he's eighteen, then," Sarita said, wiping up the salt and pepper that I'd spilled onto the table.

I fingered the smooth glass sugar bowl.

"In some ways you're just like a child, Dee Dee," she continued. "You're always touching stuff. No wonder you can relate to kids so well."

"I'm not hurting your sugar bowl, so hush. Anyway, I try to look at my life in terms of what the real bottom-line need is. In this case, I think the real need is for Jason to be safe. If he stays outside because of fear, anything could happen to him out there in the streets. These are serious times."

"*My* bottom line is Jason did wrong, and I can't overlook that."

"Maybe I should go out there and get him to make sure he's safe," I offered. "You should just pack him a little bag and I can take him straight over to my house. That could be his punishment."

"Dee Dee, you oughta quit. That's no kind of punishment. Jason would love that."

"For some reason you're hesitant about giving him a whipping, though. I think you should pay attention to that."

"That's only because I'm afraid that if I whup him this time, I'll really hurt him," Sarita confided. "Neither of my girls ever defied me to my face." She paused and traced a wrinkle near her mouth. "I don't know how I will react. I might just go off. And nowadays, you gotta be careful." She lowered her voice. "You can't beat kids the way you used to and get away with it. You have to be very careful not to leave marks. It's not like the old days."

I flashed on the welts my stepfather's belt often left on my brother. "You shouldn't leave marks," I protested. "If you do, you're hitting too hard. You know I don't condone whippings. An occasional hand spanking, okay, but not whippings."

"You haven't raised kids." Sarita groaned. "Besides, I couldn't get through to Jason with a hand spanking at this late date. I would hurt my hand trying."

"Why don't you put him on some kind of punishment?"

"He might rather get a whupping and get it over with."

"Make sure the punishment fits the crime, though. I mean, Jason was wrong to defy you. But I can also understand where he was coming from."

"There's no excuse for what he did," Sarita replied angrily.

"I gave him that money with no strings attached," I pointed out. "Sometimes, you have to see things from a child's perspective," I insisted. "Once you said he had to put the dollar in church, it was the same as taking it away from him."

Sarita folded her arms and tilted her head. "Okay, so I'm a rotten person because I suggested that Jason give the money to the Lord."

"No, you meant well," I assured her. "But, with all due respect, I think you should've taken Jason's feelings into account, that's all."

Sarita sucked her teeth. "Being a parent isn't always about psychoanalyzing everything before you make a decision. My mother raised five kids, mostly by herself, and she made her mistakes, believe me. But none of us are in jail or on drugs or on the corner. And I've tried to not be as hard on my kids as she was on us, Lord knows I've tried." Sarita sighed. "But I don't wanna throw the baby out with the bathwater. I didn't bring a child in this world to end up whupping me."

I was startled and relieved to hear the doorbell. I knew instinctively that it was Jason, despite the timid ring. He usually laid on the bell. At least he'd come home. Better for him to have to deal with Sarita than some drug dealers.

"Let me get it," I volunteered. "You need to take a deep breath and count to ten. Make that twenty," I added, rushing toward the door.

I saw Jason's ice-cream–smeared face through the door's glass window. He was such a messy boy. I kept wondering when he'd get old enough to eat without getting food all over himself. When I took him out to lunch last year, I had to roll his sleeves up to his elbows first. He practically needed a bib.

Jason looked relieved to see me, with Sarita nowhere in sight.

I wondered what his strategy was. He must fear that Sarita was about to pounce on him at any moment. I even feared it. But, before I could say anything, Jason barreled past me. I assumed he was headed for his bedroom or perhaps to lock himself in the bathroom. But to my horror, Jason headed straight for the kitchen, toward Sarita. I followed him and watched as he wrapped his arms tightly around Sarita and pleaded, "Mama, I'm sorry! Mama, I'm sorry!"

Sarita grabbed her son's chin and said angrily, "Sorry didn't do it."

I couldn't believe she'd fallen back on a line we used as kids. I was concerned that Jason's disarming strategy might backfire. But I couldn't help but admire his willingness to run into the arms of the enemy. The longer he held onto Sarita physically, the more the anger seemed to drain from her body.

"Get off of me!" Sarita ordered. "I don't want you in my face right now." She sounded more tired than angry.

"Maaamaa," Jason whined, refusing to let go.

"Don't 'Mama' me. Now you wanna be lovey-dovey. You didn't care nothing about me before." Sarita pouted. "All you cared about was some daggone ice cream. You didn't care nothin' about me. Showing out in front of Dee Dee like that."

"Mama, I *do* care about you."

"Boy, get off of me. It's too hot for this." Sarita made a half-hearted attempt to push Jason away. "Leave me alone. I can't even move," she fussed. "Boy, you make me sick!"

Jason continued to cling. Finally, Sarita picked up her nine-year-old son and held his chin in her hand. "You pull a stunt like that again, and you're gonna get a spanking, you understand? Dee Dee says I shouldn't hit you with a belt, so I'm gonna hit you with my hand, okay?"

Jason nodded, and shot me an appreciative look.

"He's always been like this, crazy about ice cream and crazy about his mama," Sarita bragged. "Remember that first time you kept Jason when he was a baby? Remember how he hollered the whole time I was gone?"

"Yeah, I remember."

"He's always been so attached to me," she said, momentarily cuddling her son. "Now, boy, go'n get outta my face, so grownfolks can talk," she ordered, successfully pushing Jason away. For the first time in a long time, I envied the closeness between Sarita and her son.

"I can't even get the door open good before you start," I fussed at my cat the next night. "You would think you were being mistreated. I wish I had somebody to take care of me. I've created a monster." Langston rubbed against my leg. "I will feed you after I check my mail and my messages, if you don't mind."

Langston continued to meow, like he hadn't heard what I said. I bent down and picked him up. "I'm sorry for being so grouchy. I'm gonna give you your food."

I was playing with Langston, dangling his rubber mouse on a stick, when the phone rang.

"Hello," I said, plopping down into the leather recliner with Langston in tow.

"Hi, is this Daphne?"

It was a male voice. So far, so good. He hadn't asked for Dee Dee.

"Yes, who is this?"

"I don't know if you remember me, but this is Skylar, the mediator."

"Oh, yeah," I answered, like I hadn't been fantasizing about him day and night, a couple of weeks back.

"Well, you said it would be all right if I called. Is this an okay time? I hope I'm not interrupting anything."

"No," I gulped. "Just quality time with my cat." I had to bite my tongue to keep from saying, "I'm really surprised to hear from you."

"You have a cat? Of course you have a cat, or you wouldn't have said that, right?"

"Right. He's in my lap right now."

"Sounds cozy. Well, how was your day?"

"How was my day? Let's see," I stammered. I wasn't used to talking to anyone with romantic potential. I felt a little rusty. "I led two focus groups on coffee drinkers."

"Focus groups?"

"My other job is consumer research for advertisers."

"Oh, go ahead, finish telling me."

"Our clients are introducing a new brand of coffee." I cradled the phone. "You sure you want to hear this?"

"Yeah, please."

"Anyway, one group was comprised of some pretty hard-core coffee drinkers. They sifted through the beans, smelling the aroma, judging the color and the freshness, and coming up with names for drinks."

"They were serious, huh?"

"As a heart attack. They were not one of your more laid-back groups. I felt like I'd had about six cups of coffee just being around them."

"Sort of like a contact high?"

"You got it. And at the end of the group tonight, one of the most high-strung ones asked me, 'What do we do with our name cards?' See, they had long cards with their first names on them that were placed in front of them."

"Sort of like a game show."

"Right. So, it's finally the end of a long workday, and I can afford to be nice.

"So I answer, 'You can take it home with you, if you like.' Would you believe this woman cops an attitude?"

"No."

"Yeah. She says, 'I don't need this. *I* know who *I* am!'"

"Why did she ask you about them in the first place?"

"I don't know, maybe she wanted to put it in the right pile or something. A place for everything and everything in its place."

"Maybe she's just a control freak."

"Probably. Anyway, enough about me. I must be boring you with these mundane details."

"No, I'm enjoying this."

"You're not just trying to be polite?" I asked shyly. I knew that it was tricky being regular with men. You didn't want them to feel too relaxed. Men didn't want to feel comfortable, they wanted to feel excited. I didn't want to remind Skylar of a pair of old baggy pants or favorite house slippers. Because then I'd be taken for granted. There would be no suspense, no challenge, no chase. It wasn't Sunday dinner at Mom's and he was asking for another helping of mashed potatoes.

"I'm not being polite," Skylar insisted. "I like listening to you. And I like talking to you."

I swallowed. I felt touched, but was afraid to read too much into Skylar's remarks. "I guess off the top of my head I couldn't think of anything real exciting to say," I confided. "It's been a pretty routine day. At least up until now." I was glad that Skylar couldn't see me over the phone because I blushed.

"That's very sweet of you to say that. I mean, what have *I* said that's so exciting?" Skylar asked.

I almost said, "Hearing your voice is exciting." But instead, I said, "You have a point."

"Anybody can hold somebody's attention when they have something exciting to say," he continued. "But it takes a special person to capture your attention with the flypaper of life."

"Now that's sweet of *you* to say. But I guess I feel a little awkward because I wonder if you're finally calling now because we ran into each other last week in the conference room. That happened completely by accident."

"I gathered that."

"And I don't want you to feel obligated."

"I don't feel obligated. I wanted to call you before."

"You did?" I exhaled and petted my cat.

"Yes, I wanted to ask you if you'd be up to having dinner with me. But I just didn't feel like I would be good company until now, 'cause I was dealing with something."

"Oh." I swallowed. "You sure know how to put a nice spin on things. I almost believe you."

"I'm telling the truth. As archaic as it sounds, trust me."

"Let me check my calendar," I said, throwing Langston to the floor. "I'll see if I can fit you in." I savored the opportunity to play hard to get for a minute. It had been a long time coming. I felt like purring like a kitty.

thirteen

I was kickin' it with Sharon before getting ready for my first date with Skylar. We were sitting on opposite corners of my mattress in my upstairs loft bed. Sharon thumbed through a magazine while I polished my fingernails. Sunshine filtered through the skylight and Langston lay stretched out in the middle of the bed, soaking it up like royalty. But my cat wasn't the only thing between us.

What I couldn't blab to Sharon was that Tyeesha was afraid that she might be pregnant. I'd promised not to rat on her, but I felt torn between allegiance to my goddaughter and loyalty to my best friend.

I'd agreed to let T take a home-pregnancy test at my house next week if she still hadn't gotten her period. I felt guilty about keeping all this from Sharon, but I hoped I was ultimately giving her a gift by being a confidante to her daughter.

Sharon had gotten rid of her braids and was wearing her hair in a short, stylish 'fro. Girlfriend hadn't looked like a lesbian to the trained or untrained eye before her haircut. But now, Sharon told me, she noticed that the trained eye was definitely checking her out. Funny how hair can have a lot to do with who's zooming who.

Generally speaking, black men don't go for women with short hair, especially short, nappy hair. But Sharon predicted that short

Afros on women were about to have a rebirth. And soon, provincial black folks would stop deriding them as "men heads."

I understood Sharon's logic. If you weren't out there trying to catch a conventional brotha, why not choose a short, carefree cut? Besides, Sharon was all hugged up with Michelle these days, and Michelle thought Sharon's haircut was the bomb.

Sharon looked up from my latest *Essence*.

"Don't you just really hate first dates?" she asked, frowning.

"Yeah, but I hate *no* dates even more," I answered, carefully applying rose-colored polish to my toenails.

"How can you even enjoy a first date?"

"You mean because on first dates your bowels won't leave you alone, and your hands are like ice water? Your stomach is like a butter churner. It's worse than a job interview."

Sharon nodded.

"You don't have to enjoy a first date," I explained. "You just have to get through it."

"Sorta like losing your virginity?"

"Precisely."

I fretted over what to wear tonight. It used to be simply a matter of what I could get into. Now I could fit into two of the three sizes in my closet and even have breathing room left over.

"I still think you should just chuck *The Rules* and be yourself," Sharon muttered, setting the magazine aside.

I smiled. "There will be plenty of time to be myself after the honeymoon."

Sharon shook her head. "You've been reading the wrong books. The key to finding Mr. Right—or Ms. Right"—she pointed a finger at herself—"for women who are more creatively inclined, is to bet on yourself."

"Sharon, when are you going to get your own talk show?"

"What's not to like about Oprah? Anyway, there must be a man somewhere on the face of the earth who wants to love and cherish the real Daphne Joy Dupree in all her splendor."

"Tyeesha has wondered the same thing about you."

Sharon sighed and rolled her eyes as though she were weary from having to explain herself. "I got tired of looking for a needle in a haystack," she said. "I'm not anti-men. I'll leave that to you heterosexual women." She smiled.

I gave her a fake grin. "Thanks for your generosity."

Sharon shook her head. "I don't doubt that there are some wonderful souls out there, disguised in men's bodies. Maybe you'll get lucky and Skylar will turn out to be one of them. So I would advise you to be receptive." Her laughing eyes shone in the sunlight.

I adjusted the small fan so it would blow on my wet toenails. "Are you giving me advice on how to land a man now?"

"Why not? The auto insurance people say you can learn a lot from dummies. Just imagine what you can learn from lesbians." Sharon rolled up the magazine and pointed it toward her chest.

"You can learn something from anybody," I conceded. "But go easy on my magazine. I haven't finished reading it."

"Sorry," Sharon mumbled. "You know, I have a couple of male buddies who can talk to me much more easily than with the straight women they date."

"Maybe because you don't have to deal with their shit," I teased.

"This might sound strange," she confided, "but I feel closer to men now than I ever did when I was trying to be involved with them."

"That's interesting. Remember in the movie *Tootsie*, Dustin Hoffman impersonated a woman to get an acting job?"

"Yeah, of course."

"Well, he basically concluded that he was better with women as a woman than he'd ever been as a man."

Sharon paused and wrinkled her face. "How are you relating that to me?"

"Maybe you're getting in touch with your male side now that you're with a woman. And therefore you're able to relate more to the male perspective."

"I don't think so, girlfriend," she protested. "I think it's because I no longer want anything *from* men. And therefore I can be more real."

Now I was left with something to chew on.

"I'm basically shy," Skylar confided. He dipped his bread into a small plate of olive oil.

He *looked* shy in his baby blue dress shirt, sitting across from me in the candlelight. But I'd learned to take what men said on first dates with a grain of salt. Sometimes, when a man tells you he's shy, he's really hoping you'll nurture him right into the bedroom. Or maybe he's decided that you're not *all that*, and shy just means "not interested." Then, when he doesn't make a move on you, he hopes you'll tell yourself, he's just shy. But the truth is he doesn't want you.

I glanced across the table again. Skylar wasn't wearing his glasses. He looked better without them. Maybe he had on contacts. Anyway, Skylar's narrow dark eyes looked earnest in the candle's glow.

"I guess I wanted to cop to being shy right away," he continued after chewing on his bread, "because experience has taught me that women either like shy men or they don't."

Let's say a man truly is shy, just for the sake of argument. And he happens to confide it while I'm savoring a Chardonnay with a smoky aftertaste in a room painted with Italian street scenes and lighted by old-fashioned street lamps. I just might want to help him out. So I answered, "I'm one of those women who likes shy men. I find them charming."

Skylar sipped his wine. "I have a confession to make. I'm only shy in the beginning."

"It's natural to be shy in the beginning," I said. "I feel a little bit shy myself."

"Sounds like we're on the same page then."

"It depends on how you define the beginning," I said.

"You should've been a politician," Skylar teased.

"I don't have the stomach for politics."

"So, how did you end up playing the blues?"

"Well, I've always loved music," I replied.

"Same here."

"I was the entertainment critic for my college newspaper," I elaborated.

"That must've been interesting."

"It was. I interviewed B.B. King once. He told me that it hurt his heart that so many young black people had turned their backs on the blues. I promised him that I would do my best to keep the blues alive."

"You've certainly kept your promise," Skylar said, smiling.

"Yeah, and I've never regretted it. But, enough about me. What kind of music are you into?"

"I like all kinds of music."

"What don't you like?"

"I'm not wild about country or bluegrass."

"Me, either. I like some opera, but I'm not crazy about it."

"I like it when I'm in the mood," Skylar admitted. "Sometimes I'm in the mood for classical."

"Yeah, me too. I like a little rap occasionally, and disco to dance to."

"I'm into blues and reggae, but I'm really a big jazz fan."

"We have a lot in common musically." I smiled, feeling that maybe I'd met a man after my own heart.

Skylar nodded. "This is the first year in a long time that I've had to miss the Monterey Jazz Festival."

"You were really nearby, in Santa Cruz, huh?"

Skylar nodded.

"The closest I ever got to the Monterey Jazz Festival was when I saw *Play Misty for Me* with Clint Eastwood."

"That movie made Roberta Flack a star," Skylar reminded me.

"Yeah, people who saw it kept talking about that song, 'The First Time Ever I Saw Your Face.'"

"Do you have it in your collection?"

"Yeah."

"Will you play it for me sometime?"

"Sure." I sighed, recalling the sensuousness of Roberta Flack's rendition. I gazed momentarily into Skylar's sexy, dark eyes. "I was into jazz big time during the seventies," I related. "I guess you would actually call it jazz fusion. You know, the Crusaders, Bob James, Al Jarreau, Patrice Rushen, Dee Dee Bridgewater, Grover Washington, Jr., Randy Crawford and Pat Metheny."

"Wow, you've said a mouthful. But, girl, you were half-steppin'," Skylar teased. "What about jazz legends like Monk, Coltrane, Bird, Sarah Vaughan, Ella Fitzgerald, and of course, Betty Carter?"

"I dipped and dabbed a bit in them."

"Well, I dipped and dabbed a bit in fusion," he confessed. "I must admit, I wouldn't mind hearing Randy Crawford sing 'Street Life' again."

"Well, that can be arranged."

Skylar's lips curved in a sexy smile. "It's a date I won't wanna miss."

I was swimming inside Skylar's bedroom eyes when the waiter appeared with our spinach salads.

"I may as well put my cards on the table," Skylar said as we dove into our pasta dishes.

I felt a sense of trepidation. I hoped Skylar wasn't about to throw me a curveball. Things had been going so smoothly; I really felt attracted to this guy.

"I'm happily picking up the tab for this dinner," he continued. "But I don't have money to burn or anything."

"*I'm* not 'panning for gold,' if that's what you're worried about."

"I make a decent living, doing mediation and legal aid work," Skylar added between forkfuls of pasta, as if he hadn't heard me. "I have a law degree, but I don't do much practicing. I'm a single father."

He rushed through the sentence as if he wanted to slip it by me unnoticed, but I noticed and I called him on it.

"Oh! I didn't realize that you were a parent. You really buried the lead."

"Well, it's just a first date. I didn't want to wear my fatherhood on my sleeve."

And scare away a potential mother, I thought.

"I admire a man who's takes responsibility for his children."

"Being a single parent is pretty stressful."

"How many children do you have?"

"One. I started to say, only one. But, hey, one is a handful."

"Girl or boy?"

"An eight-year-old girl."

"That's a nice age. What's her name? Do you have a picture?"

"Brianna. And, no I don't have a picture with me," Skylar said, almost apologetically.

"You're a single father and you don't carry pictures," I marveled.

"I have a couple in my other wallet. Besides, I didn't plan to bore you all evening, talking about my kid."

"I wouldn't be bored. I love kids."

"Do you have any?"

"No, that's why I love 'em."

"I hear you. You think you'll ever have any?" Skylar asked.

I felt a pang of guilt as I flashed on my abortion. I looked away, sipped my wine and paused thoughtfully. "I've thought about adopting, but I don't think I want to raise a child alone. But if I happened to…"

"If you happened to what?"

"You know…"

"If you happened to meet someone who had a child or children already, you'd be open to it?"

"Well, yeah, maybe I'd be open to it," I answered cautiously. "But I'm not really looking for instant family."

Skylar cleared his throat. "Well, I'm not shopping for a mother for my child, if that's what you think." He sounded defensive.

"I didn't mean to make it appear like I thought you were," I stammered.

"I'm just looking for some connection. I'm not trying to put my daughter off on anybody. I want to make that clear."

"I didn't feel that you were. In fact, I find it appealing that you have a child," I admitted to myself as much as to Skylar.

"Well, you should be aware that there's a downside."

"There's a downside to almost everything," I said, and sipped my wine.

Skylar gulped his water. "I can't always do things at the drop of a hat. I have to arrange child care. And sometimes my daughter is sick, or she has to go to an activitiy. It can be complicated."

"I bet. But I'm sure it's worth all the hassle. Your daughter's probably a daddy's girl."

"I wouldn't say so. I was happy to have a girl, but I didn't want a daddy's girl. I have a good friend like that. I mean, her father spoiled her rotten. She followed three boys, so you can imagine. But in the end I think it was detrimental to Lisa. In fact, it crippled her. She lacks a certain confidence and inner strength that I think is important to have out here in the world. And she has consistently picked the wrong men. None of them can measure up to Daddy. I'm trying to raise my daughter to be able to stand on her own two feet. But it's really hard when you're trying to do it all by yourself." Skylar paused. "I mean it's the hardest thing I've ever done, including passing the California bar exam."

I nodded sympathetically, but underneath I felt disappointed. Feeling sorry for my date just wasn't my idea of a romantic evening. I wanted to first get to know Skylar the romantic lover. Later for Skylar the overwhelmed single father. Besides, when did parenting become the hardest job in the world? When I was growing up, it just seemed like something people did, almost on automatic pilot. Nobody talked about parenting being so hard back in the sixties. Not even mothers, who had the brunt of it. I remembered relatives remarking about how easy Mrs. So-and-So had it because she only had one child. "Imagine only having to take care of one child?" they marveled. Nowadays, even people with one child can feel totally whupped.

"Isn't being a parent rewarding, though?" I asked, feeling like I was playing devil's advocate.

"Absolutely," Skylar said. He licked tomato sauce off his lips. "It's the most rewarding thing I've ever done. Brianna's a great kid. But she deserves two involved parents."

Hint, hint, I couldn't help but think. The hell if he's not shopping around for a mama. "Where's Brianna's mother?"

"In Indianapolis, living with *her* mother. That's why we're in
Chicago. I wanted Brianna to be closer to Allison, but so far it
hasn't made much difference."

"Doesn't Brianna see her mother?"

"Not enough."

"Why's that?"

"Her mother loves her in her own way." Skylar sighed. "But
she's got some problems. Allison's life is pretty untogether right
now. She got injured in a car accident. She's almost recovered now,
but she lost her job, got depressed and fell in love with painkillers.
It's another story."

"Oh, I'm sorry to hear that. That's sad."

"Yep, it's really sad for Brianna. Allison's not there for her the
way she should be."

"Well, I'm glad that Brianna has you."

"I never thought I'd end up having to play Mr. Mom." He
sighed again. "Anyway, I didn't plan to spin a tale of woe tonight. I
really *did* want us to have a nice, relaxing, candlelight dinner."

"Well, we almost did," I said, smiling ruefully.

Skylar and I had definite chemistry going for us. A couple of days
later, I was still vibing on the good-night kiss that he laid on my lips
after we parted at the restaurant. But I managed to get behind a
mike and get down with the blues, same as if nobody had paid me
or my lips any recent attention.

"I'm playing some blues that y'all can use tonight. I tell you,
folks scared of the blues. They think the blues'll bring 'em down.
But the truth is, sometimes you can be so far down that only the
blues can bring you up. I know when I'm depressed I wanna hear
'bout somebody worse off than I am. So I turn to the blues. And if
I listen long enough, I guarantee you I'll hear 'bout somebody
more pitiful than me. And I get to feeling that my burden ain't so
heavy after all." *You're good,* I told myself.

"The blues are 'bout sucking the marrow out the bone," I continued. "See, the blues ain't 'bout being proper. I know some folks done got too proper for the blues. They're afraid they might sweat their heads out. Well, that's what the blues are about. The sho' 'nuff blues are guaranteed to sho' 'nuff sweat your head out!

"Don't let me get to preachin', y'all. Don't let me start. The blues ain't nothin' but a pain in yo' heart." I leaned closer to the mike and spoke in an intimate tone. "There was a time not long ago when people didn't need all these pills. Nobody talked about being depressed. Sistas were too busy to have nervous breakdowns. It's amazing how we used to cope. We turned to the church and we turned to the blues. Some of those same folks that were in the juke joints on Friday and Saturday nights were in the Amen Corner on Sunday mornings. Now some folk have gotten too proper to shout, 'Laud have mercy on your chile.' But you know what? Folks weren't running to a therapist back then, paying a hundred dollars an hour, and they weren't poppin' Prozac and Zoloft and St. John's Wort. The blues used to be the best medicine. The blues used to cure what ailed you."

I backed off the mike and raised my voice a little. "The blues are about self-expression. The blues are about confession. The blues are about telling it like it is and letting the chips fall where they may. I'm talkin' 'bout the sho' 'nuff blues today. And that's what I'm fixin' to play. 'Meet Me With Yo' Black Drawers On,' by Sweet Baby Jai, a favorite diva outta L.A."

My shift had ended. I hadn't had a chance to holler at Freddy on my way up to the control room. I'd been rushing. But I had noticed that he was a couple of shades darker from his days in the Caribbean sun. I was eager to get back up in his face again and hear what was up.

"Thanks, Freddy," I said, accepting a colorful, beaded change purse. "That's so thoughtful of you to bring me back a souvenir."

"Now that ain't for everybody's eyes," Freddy warned. "I couldn't afford to pass out gifts to the whole building."

"I understand. I'm flattered. So, did you and your wife have a good time on your cruise?"

"Had the time of our lives!" Freddy wiped his bald head and the back of his neck. He patted his stomach. "They really feed you good, too. We shoulda swam back, as much as we ate." He pretended to do the front crawl.

"Vacations can be hard on relations," I said, sounding like I was still rhyming on the air. I teased, "You and your wife are still speaking and everything?"

"We got along like two dumplings in a pot of stew."

"Freddy, you're happily married, huh?"

"It was twenty-five years in June. And I would do it all over again."

"What's the secret to a happy marriage?" I leaned against the lobby wall.

Freddy cleared his throat and answered solemnly. "Don't expect to *stay* in love."

"Are you serious?"

"Look, you can love a person without being *in* love with 'em."

I whispered, "So, you're not in love with your wife anymore?"

"After twenty-five years, hell no," Freddy said, wrinkling his forehead. "And don't wanna be, neither. I've had that *in love* experience several times in my life. I've been on the roller coaster of love. And I enjoyed it. But now I prefer a mellower ride."

"So, that's your secret? Don't expect to stay in love?"

"Right, and don't look for everything in one person."

"How do you mean that exactly?" I asked, raising my eyebrows.

"Now, don't take this the wrong way. I've been a faithful husband. But what I'm trying to say is, no one person can be all things to anybody. For example, my wife ain't big on conversation. So I don't look her up when I'm in the mood for a big debate. I talk to you or my sister or my buddy."

"Are you saying that everyone has limitations?"

"Exactly." Freddy nodded. "And you have to learn to work within those limitations. You don't try to get gold from no silver mine. The main thing is to have an understanding," he continued. "Know each other's bottom line. It's just like in business. For example, my wife's bottom line is fidelity. So I'd think long and hard before I would cheat on Grace."

"That makes sense. What's your bottom line?"

"I need to spell relief, at least a couple times a week." Freddy winked.

"I take it that you don't spell relief with an antacid?"

"Not at those particular times, I don't."

"I saw a man wearing a T-shirt one time that said, ONCE A WEEK IS NOT ENOUGH!" I smiled.

"I second that emotion," Freddy said, stretching his palm out for me to give him five. I slapped his hand. "Anyway," he continued, "my wife needs to hear me tell her that I love her about twice a week. So it works out pretty well."

"Yeah, sounds like you two are pretty compatible."

"Yeah. Another one of my bottom lines is knowing where the remote control is at all times. So Grace has bought me three of 'em." Freddy paused and waved to a man in a trench coat leaving the building. "I'll give you another example. I love home cooking, and most days my wife obliges."

"That's nice of her."

"Well, it's a two-way street. Grace ain't crazy 'bout doing laundry or cleaning floors. Ever since our kids moved out, I've taken over most of the housework."

"Wow, I had no idea that you were so supportive."

"Girl, I don't know what you talking about. I've got dishpan hands," Freddy said, displaying his stubby fingers.

"Don't worry, your secret's safe with me. But you do need to check out Palmolive," I teased.

Freddy walked with me toward my car. "Yeah, we hated to leave paradise."

He sighed in the stale, humid, underground air. "It took me awhile to adjust to being back. But you know when I really knew I was back?"

"When?"

"When I heard Bay Bay's kids carryin' on at the bus stop. That's when I really knew I was back."

"Oh."

"It was a damn disgrace, too," Freddy said, letting out an exasperated sigh. "And it's so unnecessary for y'all to be so loud and ignorant."

I swallowed. "Don't give me that y'all stuff. I wasn't there."

"It was yo' people. Anyway, you can't say nothing to 'em, 'cause they're liable to pull out a gun and shoot you." Freddy sighed again. "At least cuss you out." He shook his head. "Some of the girls are worse than the boys."

We stood in front of my car. "Maybe you should try to help out some of these kids who need direction," I suggested.

Freddy shook his head. "I've helped raise my own kids. I've even got a grandbaby to help look out for now. I can't take responsibility for other folks' kids who don't have respect for nobody."

"Maybe we need to see them all as our kids," I said, folding my arms and leaning against my car.

"I'll leave that to you. Maybe that's your calling." Freddy paused. "Now that I've traveled, it's been proven to me that black children don't have to be loud and ignorant. That was really my point."

I rolled my eyes.

"You should've seen how orderly and disciplined the kids were on those islands. I ain't heard no loud cussing and carrying on whatsoever. Those Caribbean kids in their starched and ironed school uniforms made me feel proud to be of African descent. It was a good feeling, too."

"Sounds like it was worth the price of a ticket for that experience alone," I commented.

"Have you ever done a home-pregnancy test before?" Tyeesha asked. We stood over the vials waiting for the results.

I shook my head. "Back in *the day*, you had to go to a clinic. We didn't have all these modern conveniences in the sixties and seventies."

"Dee Dee, when's the last time you had sex?" Tyeesha asked, following me outside the bathroom.

"Sometime back in the seventies," I teased. "I don't remember the exact year."

"Come on, Dee Dee, be for real! Has it been hecka long?"

"Never mind," I said.

"Why won't you tell me?" Tyeesha persisted, plopping down on the hallway floor. She looked up at me attentively, like she was about to hear my business.

"We're not going there," I said firmly. I leaned back against the wall across from Tyeesha and folded my arms.

"If I *am* pregnant, you think it will make Malik come back to me?" T asked after a pause.

Malik had gone back to his girlfriend, Rheema, who'd been in St. Louis for the summer. He'd told Tyeesha that it was over between him and Rheema. But I suspected it had just been a case of absence making the heart go yonder.

"I'm not thinking about Malik. And you don't need to be, either," I said, standing over Tyeesha. "The hell with him." I folded my arms tighter.

"I was just thinking that maybe that it would be good, you know, if I *were* pregnant," Tyeesha said, looking at me with her lost brown eyes. "Because then Malik might come back to me."

"Whoa! Have you lost your mind?"

"It might matter to him, you know, if I was having a baby for him."

"Girl, you better come back to your senses. You need a whole new mind-set." I sat down across from her and held her chin in my hand. "First of all, if this pregnancy test comes up negative, you need to consider yourself having just gotten out of the way of a speeding train. You're not ready to raise a child, with or without Malik. You are only fifteen years old. You still need to find out who Tyeesha is." I released her face.

"Did you know that in many societies it's accepted for fifteen-year-olds to be mothers? It's considered normal," Tyeesha said.

"Well, you don't live in *many* societies," I reminded Tyeesha. "You live in this society. And in *this* society it's hard to raise a child at any age, let alone at a young one. You need a reality check, girl. We don't have the extended families that we had, even thirty years ago. And you need an education and a half to make it today. A high-school diploma or a G.E.D. isn't gonna get it."

"You still haven't answered my question about Malik coming back to me if I'm carrying his baby."

I sighed. "Malik probably planned to go back to Rheema from the get-go. Think logically, T, she was away for the summer. Haven't you heard that when the cat's away, the mice will play?"

"Malik said they were broken up."

"Malik said." I rolled my eyes.

"Are you trying to say he was lying?"

"If a boy wants to get in your pants he'll tell you a lot of things." I groaned. "Mainly, he'll tell you what he thinks you want to hear."

"You act like I should never trust a man."

"At your age, maybe you shouldn't. They say it takes a fool to learn that love don't love nobody."

"You act like you never needed a man's touch."

I bristled. "You know that's not true. I need a man's touch, all right, but without *self*-love, it ain't much. You hear me? It ain't much."

"Do you think Malik is a bad person?"

"I don't know. I didn't say he was."

"If he used me and then kicked me to the curb, he *is* a bad person."

"Maybe he's just a teenage boy with raging hormones who did a bad thing. If he didn't force you, I wouldn't say he was necessarily a bad person. T, I love you and I want you to feel safe, strong and free. I don't want to be worried about you getting pregnant or contracting AIDS or gettin' beat up or anything like that. I just wish you could cherish these years and be a carefree teenager."

"A carefree teenager?" Tyeesha smiled ruefully and stood up and headed back into the bathroom.

"Yeah," I said, standing up. "But I guess that's an oxymoron these days," I called to her. "If you're smart, it won't be."

"Look, Dee Dee!" Tyeesha exclaimed, from inside the bathroom. "It didn't turn blue!"

"Huh?" I said, leaning my head inside the door.

"Don't you know what that means?"

"You're not pregnant!" I shouted. "Yea! Yea!" I yelled, raising my fist in the air and running into the living room. "You just got another crack at being a kid."

"You still think I'm some kinda moron?" Tyeesha asked with a concerned look on her face.

"I never called you a moron," I protested.

"What does oxymoron mean, then?"

fourteen

Skylar and I watched from our small table as the last belly dancer took her bow. We clapped as she let her shiny, rainbow-colored veil drape across the performance space floor. After a few weeks, three dates and several hot kisses, Skylar and I had become an item. Sitting close to his tall, firm body was in and of itself a turn-on, and I found his musky cologne very enticing.

"Belly dancing is beautiful," Skylar mumbled. "I'm glad you twisted my arm."

"Yeah, right," I teased, rolling my eyes. "It wasn't much of a twist. But anyway, thanks for coming to Arabian Nights with me. It helps me to improve my technique by going to performances."

"Hey, I'm glad to be of service." Skylar smiled. "I have absolutely no problem watching women show off their techniques."

"It's almost mesmerizing, huh, the music, the costumes…" I said.

"Yeah, especially when you throw the women into the mix."

"It's really downright haunting." I sighed.

"Very haunting," Skylar agreed mischieviously. "I felt quite haunted; in fact, it was a hauntatious experience."

"Hauntatious is not a word," I challenged.

"Well, belly dancing defies description. Bill was right, it *can* stir something inside of you."

"You're bad. Don't tell me you've sunk to Bill's level."

"No, I just appreciate women. And I appreciate them even more, after this experience."

I sipped my Chai tea and made playful eye contact with Skylar. "I just hope that the spiritual aspect of belly dancing wasn't lost on you."

Skylar gave me a look. "I don't think I missed anything. But I'd be glad to keep coming back, just in case."

"This is not AA."

"You mean because they say, 'Keep coming back, it works.'"

"Yeah. Look, here comes Jade."

"Athena, you were fantastic," Jade yelled over her shoulder to a departing performer.

"Thanks, so were you."

"Jade, I should take lessons from you," a belly dancer said as she passed by our table. "Your veil work was great."

"Thanks, Xochil, you're doing fine. Sign up for my advanced class."

Jade greeted me with a hug and offered Skylar her hand. She was still in full makeup and wearing her costume.

"You were in rare form tonight," I gushed. "I mean, you're always great, but tonight was special. I've never seen you perform with live music before."

"Jade, you were really quite wonderful," Skylar agreed.

"Thanks, I'm so glad that you got a chance to experience first-hand what I've been talking about."

"I definitely felt a spiritual connection here tonight. There's no doubt about it."

I couldn't help wondering if Skylar were being sincere or if he were being funny. But what I really wanted to know was which of the musicians Jade had a crush on. Although I still didn't want her to do anything foolish, like run off with him.

"Jade, the musicians were hot. By the way, which one was the one you were telling me about?" I winked.

"The one with long wavy, dark hair, and olive skin. He had his shirt off," Jade whispered. "He was playing the oud."

"What's an oud?" Skylar asked.

"It's like a large mandolin. But it's much more ancient," Jade explained.

"He was the one that did all the moaning, too?" I asked.

Jade nodded, her eyes twinkling.

"He has a nice voice and a nice chest," I said.

Skylar cleared his throat. "Dee Dee, I thought you came here to work on your belly dancing technique."

"I did. Jade just happens to have a *spiritual connection* with one of the musicians. And now that she's pointed him out, I'm simply giving her my assessment."

"Oh."

"Anyway, what are you two planning to do afterwards?" Jade asked.

"We're kinda limited," Skylar said. "I have to relieve the babysitter, so we're just about ready to call it a night. Why?"

"Well, I'm always keyed up after these performances. I thought we might all hang out, maybe have a snack at Soul Kitchen over in Wicker Park."

"I live South," Skylar said.

"Are you in Hyde Park?" Jade asked.

"Yeah."

"Jade's way out in the north suburbs, in Lake Forest," I said.

"If you didn't have your daughter, you guys could come out there," Jade offered. "I could put you up. You could go for a walk on the Prairie tomorrow."

"Jade has a nice spread. And I don't mean bedspread. She lives near Ragdale, the artist colony."

"I have to take a rain check. I hate to be a party pooper, but I *do* have my daughter."

"You could bring your daughter along," Jade suggested. "I've got plenty of room. Yoshi's away on business. And both my sons have gone back to school."

"They're in New Hampshire in boarding school," I informed Skylar.

"Brianna hasn't even met Dee Dee yet," Skylar said awkwardly. "And I don't want her to wake up in a strange house. She's been through a lot of changes lately."

"I understand," Jade replied. The coffeehouse emptied out.

"But thanks anyway."

"Yeah, maybe some other time," I added regretfully. I felt a little irritated that Skylar couldn't go with the flow and hang out. Why couldn't he imagine that it would be an adventure for his daughter to wake up in a mansion?

"Dee Dee, don't let me cramp your style," Skylar said.

"What do you mean?"

"Just because I'm stuck with a kid doesn't mean you can't continue to have fun. Jade's all keyed up and going home to an empty house."

"Well, Jade, we could hang for awhile," I offered.

"Cool."

"Skylar, you sure you don't want a lift?" I asked.

"No, that's miles out of your way. I can hail a taxi."

"Don't tell 'em you wanna go South," I instructed. "Tell 'em you wanna go to *Hyde Park*. That is, if you can get anyone to stop," I added. "It's hard for a black person, especially a man, to hail a taxi at night."

"Yeah, sometimes it's been difficult." Skylar sighed.

"I could hail the taxi, and you could jump in," Jade suggested.

I nodded. "Jade stands the best chance of being picked up, with or without her belly dancing costume on."

"Actually, I'm gonna change out of it. I'll be right back."

"I would really like to hang with you ladies tonight," Skylar said ruefully. "I don't relish being in this position. My father was a good provider, but he still used to put his hat on, and simply say, 'I'm gone' or 'I'm going out.' And that was it. Women were tied down, men weren't." He shrugged. "I know it wasn't fair, but that's the way it was in our household."

"Mine, too," I agreed. "And, you're right, it wasn't fair."

"I'd really like to be free to do a lot of things with you. I wish we had the whole weekend together." Skylar caressed my hand with his long fingers.

"I appreciate the thought," I said. "But I do understand. You're a single parent."

Skylar twisted his face like he was sucking on something sour. "Sometimes I cringe when I hear those words."

"What words?" I asked.

"'Single parent.' I know it's true, I *am* a single parent. I suppose a man just doesn't grow up expecting that label to ever apply to him."

"A friend of mine has a button that says 'Mom is not my real name.' You need one that says 'Daddy is not my real name.'"

"Yeah, I do need one," Skylar said, stifling a yawn. "But a single parent by any other name is probably just as whupped."

"I'll take your word for it." I patted him affectionately on the shoulder.

"Right now, I'm reminding myself that when I stand over Brianna's bed tonight and watch my little angel sleeping, I won't want to trade places with anybody else in the world."

"That's got to be the bomb, watching your child sleeping."

"Yeah, it doesn't get much better than that," Skylar agreed.

"Just think, tonight you'll get to have this cosmic experience watching your baby sleep, and Jade and I'll just be two chicks sitting around talking."

Jade hailed a taxi and Skylar jumped in and was on his way. I didn't even have a chance to kiss him good-bye properly. I missed him already.

Jade and I settled into one of the cavernous booths at Soul Kitchen. The trendy, dimly lighted restaurant always reminded me of Halloween, with its Gothic decor. The food was geared to appeal to health-conscious souls. They didn't cook it to death and it wasn't swimming in grease.

After we placed our orders, I gazed out of the picture windows facing a revitalized Milwaukee Avenue. Jade and I made the usual remarks about how Wicker Park had changed in the last ten years. It had gone from a working class, predominantly Hispanic area, to up-and-coming, and, finally, to the yuppie place to be. Everyone regretted not buying property here ten or fifteen years ago, including me. The average person couldn't even afford a condo in Wicker Park now. *What a difference a decade makes,* I thought.

"So, it seems to be going well between you and Skylar," Jade said, sipping her beer.

"Yeah, so far, so, good," I answered cautiously. "Tonight was our fourth date. We haven't gotten hot and heavy yet. I'm still taking Skylar with a grain of salt, just to be safe."

"You sound like you're waiting for the other shoe to drop."

"Not really; it's just that after you reach a certain age, you're more aware that there *is* another shoe. I mean, I realize that everyone has baggage. I'm not some giddy teenager."

"You don't have to be a teenager to be giddy," Jade insisted. "This is the spring of your relationship. It's a magical time. Enjoy it while you can, before you two really get to know each other." Jade helped herself to the basket of tasty breads.

"Yeah, you're right. I will confess, I have let myself feel hopeful lately."

"That's good."

"But sometimes I wonder if I'm being foolish. Haven't you heard that saying, 'I felt much better once I gave up hope'?"

Jade nodded. "Hope was the last thing to come out of Pandora's box," she reminded me.

"Yeah, but sometimes I've wondered if hope is really a good thing."

"That's why it was in Pandora's box."

"There's nothing worse than dashed hopes." I pouted.

"So, are you advocating hopelessness?"

"I don't know," I said, nibbling a piece of organic corn bread. "But I'm toying with it. Many a life has been ruined by great expectations. Blessed is she who has no expectations, because then she won't be disappointed."

"Yeah, but the greatest risk in life is not to risk anything," Jade said, with a faraway look in her dark eyes.

"Jade, don't get optimistic on me now. I always thought I could depend on you to be pessimistic in a crunch."

"I've always tried to maintain a balanced outlook," Jade protested. "Besides, you're not in a crunch. You're falling in love!"

"I am not falling in love."

She shook her head and smiled.

"You think I'm falling in love?"

"Yeah, your eyes look brighter. Your whole being is more radiant. And your voice even has a more vibrant quality."

"Is that all? You're jumping to conclusions," I insisted.

"I could be wrong, but you appear to be a woman under the influence to me."

Suddenly, I felt giddy and I knew it was true. I was actually falling in love, like it or not. Sometimes when I was with Skylar, I imagined that we were the only two people in the world. It was like I was floating. My whole body felt tingly. My face felt like it wanted to smile forever, and everything looked brighter. Just thinking about Skylar made me feel one with the neon lights outside the restaurant windows.

"Maybe you're right." I was unable to keep my mouth from breaking into a grin.

Jade smiled and nodded approvingly. I could tell she had a good feeling about Skylar. That was reassuring. I put a certain amount of stock in her opinions.

"I don't want to jump into anything," I added, forcing myself to frown. "But I'm willing to take a calculated risk."

"Well, you know I'm a great believer in balance," Jade pointed out. "Yin and yang. And, speaking of balance, you may have noticed that we focused on you first for a change."

"Yeah." I smiled. "Wonders never cease. I never thought I'd say this, but, enough about me, what about you, Jade?"

Jade cocked her head to one side. "I definitely do have some news. But I will tell you later tonight when we're hanging out at your place. I'd like a little more privacy," she said, glancing around the crowded restaraunt, just as the waitress appeared with our orders.

"Well, spit it out," I commanded Jade, once we were holed up in my living room. I handed her a mug of tea. "Don't keep me in suspense any longer."

Jade blew on the steaming cup, kicked her sandals off and settled back against my leather sofa. She held my cat in her lap with one hand. "Okay. In a nutshell, Yoshi wants to be spanked."

"Spanked," I repeated with disbelief, as I spun around in the recliner. Even Langston's ears perked up. I wasn't shocked, because I don't shock that easily. But I was surprised. I quickly tried to equate the quiet, reserved, almost rigid person that I knew to be Jade's husband with someone who wanted to be spanked.

I gulped. "Yoshi wants to be spanked? You're kidding."

"I was surprised, too," Jade acknowledged, petting Langston. "But then, when I thought about it, it made sense. I mean, he's a CEO, he has a lot of power. And with that comes a lot of pressure." She sipped her tea. "Secretly he wants to have less control. Spanking is a way for him to escape all of that pressure and responsibility. It's a relief for him to turn the reins over to someone else."

"You're right," I agreed. "It does make sense. It's funny, all this time you've been frustrated, and all your husband needed was a good butt whupping." I laughed. "I'd like to see them present your story in that women's magazine in that section called 'Can This Marriage Be Saved?' And the answer would be, yes, the husband just needs his behind beaten."

"Yoshi doesn't want to be whipped or beaten, just a hand spanking." Jade rocked my cat like a baby. "Thank goodness he's not into anything heavy."

"I don't think I want anybody whipping my butt," I said. "I hated it when I was a child. A hand spanking is a little more understandable, though," I conceded. "In fact, I wish my parents *had* spanked me. Shoot, that would've been an act of love compared to getting whipped."

"Well, anyway, I think it's worth it to save my marriage, don't you?"

"Yes, I think so. It's a small price to pay when you consider Yoshi's portfolio. But you've really done an about-face. You were ready to run off with that musician from Arabian Nights."

"That was before Yoshi shared his feelings with me. Now we have a truly intimate relationship. Some people would call it weird, but I don't give a damn what anybody else thinks about our marriage."

"What goes on between two consenting adults is nobody else's business."

"Yoshi would be so humiliated if he knew I was telling anybody this," Jade said, covering her face with her hand like an embarrassed schoolgirl. "He'd probably want to kill himself," she added. "His image means everything, you know. Shame is worse than death in some cultures."

"Yeah, I know. I'm surprised Yoshi even told *you*."

"I'm sure it was out of desperation. I told Yoshi that I was leaving him because we didn't have any real communication. I said that he'd become like a stranger, and that he never shared his feelings with me. And that's when he just blurted it out to me, that he had this need to be spanked. It was a very powerful moment. Yoshi started crying. He told me he's even paid a dominatrix to spank him a few times."

"Wow! How did you react?"

"Of course, like I said, I was surprised," Jade said, shrugging. "Because I had no idea. But I also felt relieved. It was like, maybe there was hope for our relationship after all." She sighed, sipping her tea. "Actually, I felt closer to Yoshi than I had in a long time. So I just decided to be open."

"I can understand. You have a lot invested."

"And to be honest, in a way, it made Yoshi more interesting, less uptight, you know?"

"Yeah, you would never think of him as kinky before."

"And I'd rather do it to him than have him pay some domina-trix to do it. Yoshi feels the same way. It's not like I'm so into spank-ing, personally, but…"

"I knew I felt a butt coming on."

"It's not like I *can't* get into it, when I'm in a certain mood," Jade confided.

"Yeah, on a slow night, I could see how a hot spanking could put a little spice into your marriage. Well, whatever floats your boat."

"It has allowed Yoshi to release a lot of pent-up energy," Jade said.

"I can imagine."

"And I have to admit that it is a turn-on for me when we're in the middle of making love and Yoshi's naked butt is up in the air and I give it a few sound slaps and…"

"He pumps it good, like you wish he would?" I added, finishing Jade's sentence.

"Yes, definitely," she answered with a mischievous smile. "He pumps it real good."

"Damn, Jade, I'll never look at Yoshi the same way again."

"Remember, he would rather die than have you know," she cautioned. She held Langston playfully in the air.

"I won't breathe a word," I promised, pressing my index finger against my lips. "But you know I'll be really temped to say, 'Yoshi, you better be a good boy or else you're gonna get a spanking.'"

fifteen

"My phone line is hot. 'Cause it's Big Mama Dot. What can I do for you?"

"Play me some blues that I can use while I cook my pot of beans. But, before you do that, lemme say a few words. All this talk 'bout folks being depressed ain't nothin but the blues."

"Right, Big Mama Dot. They just in a lonesome mood, huh?"

"The blues is just a woman gone bad. You don't need no Krozac."

"Prozac."

"None of that—you don't even need St. Jim's Wort."

"St. John's Wort."

"Whatever they call that mess. It's just like a snakebite. You need a serum, and what's the serum made outta?"

"Snake venom."

"That's right. The good news is, the blues can cure the blues."

"You're speakin' the truth, Ruth. And all of you who keep the blues alive. I love it when y'all call. 'Cause otherwise I'd be sittin' up in here lonely as the Maytag repairman."

"Dee Dee, I ain't think the day would come when I would say this. But you'd be surprised what you can do with frozen black-eyed peas."

"Get outta town! I know you didn't say *frozen* black-eyed peas."

"I know you've seen 'em in the store."

"If I have, I haven't paid them any attention."

"You better be careful putting down a food on the air. You don't want them frozen black-eyed peas folks coming after you."

"Okay, I'm giving them a forum. So, here's your chance to change some minds."

"Okay, you cut up some onion and garlic and green pepper."

"Green pepper?"

"Yeah, and you sauté everything in a little oil."

"You heard her, a *little* oil. That's right, we're watching our cholesterol."

"Yeah, I can't eat the way I used to. I never thought the day would come when I would cook black-eyed peas without any meat in 'em."

"Black-eyed peas with no fatback or salt pork! Dang! Well, the truth be told, Big Mama Dot, I've had to make some changes myself."

"I know you've changed. You say you stay over on the North Side now."

"Yeah, but I get around. So, back to your beans with no meat in 'em."

"I'll be honest with you. Come New Year's, I'm still gonna use dry beans and sneak a piece of salt pork or fatback in 'em."

"Yeah, you don't wanna mess with tradition."

"I need all the good luck I can get, chile. Anyway, with the frozen beans, instead of water, I use chicken broth. I don't even put meat in my greens no more. I just use chicken broth."

"Get outta Dodge! Are you serious?"

"I'm serious as the heart attack I'm trying to keep from having."

"I hear you. Okay, I hope I'm back in good with the frozen food people now. You've won me over. I'm gonna send you a T-shirt. And next time I'm at the grocery store, I'll pick up some frozen black-eyed peas, and do 'em just like you said."

"Don't forget the chicken broth. It comes in the big boxes now."

"Oh, maybe the chicken broth people'll send me a case."

"Put on Alberta Hunter, baby, 'Remember My Name.'"

"I won't forget."

"...And we opened the set with the legendary Katie Webster, doing 'Too Much Sugar for a Dime.' That was by special request from Amy, who's pissed because her boyfriend left her for a man."

"I've got a caller now. Caller, you're on the air."

"Hi, Dee Dee. I'm a little nervous."

"That's okay, just take your time."

"I'm a first-time caller...but a long-time listener."

"Glad to hear from you."

"My name is Jim. I love your show."

"Thanks, Jim, welcome to the program."

"You can probably tell by my voice. I'm a white boy," the caller said timidly.

"You can't always tell one hundred percent. Anyway, I wasn't trippin' on it. You know I have a lot of white listeners calling the program."

"You still might ask yourself, what does a white boy really know about the blues?"

"I wasn't asking myself anything. Plenty of white people follow the blues. Jim, what would you like to hear?"

"Do you know what black people can teach white people?"

"What?"

"Black people can teach white people how to have a free spirit. That's what black people can teach white people."

"Y'all heard it here first."

"When black people sing, don't tell me that they don't sing from the depths of their souls," Jim said in a shaky voice.

"Okay."

"You know what white people do? Opera. And that ain't it."

"You said it, I didn't."

"All I know is that I was raised to be so uptight."

"Some black people were raised to be uptight, too, Jim. Be careful generalizing."

"I don't know, maybe. I only know my experience, understand that. I only know what it is to be me."

"That's true."

"I'm just speaking from my heart, okay?" Jim said, his voice seemingly choked with emotion.

"Okay."

"I look at our planet and our country and what I see is separation and division. Is that not true?"

"Sometimes."

"At least that's the appearance. But in the depths of our souls, color means nothing."

"I hear you."

"At the core of our beings, color means nothing."

"That's true."

"All we all want is to be loved and to give love. That's all we all want, black or white, gay or straight, Jew or gentile. That's all we all want."

"I hear you, Jim."

"Why can't we be free to live from our souls? And why should color be a factor?"

"You tell me, Jim."

"I spent most of my life doing what I was supposed to do, you know, conforming to what others thought I should be."

"I think I know what you're saying."

"And you know what it brought me?"

"What?"

"Unhappiness, that's what it brought me, unhappiness."

"Jim, I feel your pain. What can I play for you?"

"Thanks. Could you play that woman who sings about leaving her back door open all night long? I don't remember her name or what it's called. I just know that she left her back door open all night long."

"Memphis Minnie McCoy, the Hoo Doo Lady herself, doing the 'Moanin' Blues.'"

"That's it. She sings that song with such feeling. She sings from the core of her being. She's in pain, but she's still hopeful that her man will come walking through that door. I'm in pain, too, but I'm still hopeful after all these years that we can heal as a nation. I'm still hopeful that the entire planet can be transformed."

"Jim, thanks for calling. Stay true and stay blue."

On Friday night, Skylar moved in slow motion toward my sofa while I lighted various candles. He'd arranged a sleepover for his daughter so that we didn't have to make an early evening of it. I knew what he had in mind. I had the same thing in mind. It was our sixth date, and we'd already discussed protection. I even had condoms in case Skylar had forgotten them. I was ready to end my long, dry season. I popped my fingers. The Isley Brothers were playing on the box.

Anything other than candlelight would appear harsh, I thought as I stifled a yawn. This was bad, I told myself. This was really bad. Mexican food had been a mistake—or maybe it was the margaritas, I thought, bleary-eyed. I felt tired and Skylar looked tired. My first chance in many moons to dance in the sheets, and I felt as heavy as the lard they'd put in the refried beans. But I didn't care how lethargic I felt, I had to pull it off. We had the entire night to ourselves. Who knew when we'd have another chance like this? We couldn't afford to blow it, no matter how tired we were. Overnight child care was too precious to waste.

I joined Skylar on the couch and we looked at each other like a couple on their wedding night who knew they had to do it, but weren't sure they could pull it off.

I put my lips within kissing distance of Skylar's. After a moment, we wrapped our arms around each other, partly for moral support. The kisses were comfortable—sweet, yet sexy, too. But my closed eyes couldn't mask my fatigue. Our lips stayed smashed into each other, not moving until Skylar pulled away and yawned. And before I could admonish him for it, I yawned, too.

Skylar asked out of the blue, "Do you watch *Politically Incorrect*?"

Don't tell me he wants to watch TV, I said to myself. *Don't tell me he'd rather watch a television program than be with me.*

"Yeah, sometimes." I yawned again.

Skylar glanced at his watch. "It's almost about to come on."

"I thought we could do something a little more romantic."

"I'm kinda tired." Skylar sighed. "I'm sorry I suggested Mexican food. I didn't realize that it was so heavy this late at night."

"Yeah," I agreed.

"I've been running since early this morning," he continued. "I had to consult with clients, do my usual stuff with Brianna and pack all of her stuff for her sleepover and walk her over there. Fridays are hectic enough as it is, and those margaritas have a way of sneaking up on you."

"Yeah, and alcohol is a depressant."

"Maybe we should just take the pressure off ourselves. What do you say we take off all of our clothes and crawl into bed together." Skylar winked.

I smiled. It sounded sexy and sweet at the same time. "Sounds good to me. I like to cuddle."

For once, I felt relieved to be middle-aged. It was so grown-up to accept that you were too tired to perform, but not too fatigued to experience the delicious closeness of each other's bodies. And wise enough to have a condom close by, just in case.

I turned away from Skylar and undressed quickly in the dim light. I felt a little self-conscious about him seeing my voluptuous body, even though he had assured me that he didn't want a stick. He said he preferred women with meat on their bones. But I still felt a little bit shy. After all, it was our first time being naked together.

Skylar and I slipped into bed and lightly touched our nude bodies together in the candlelight. I felt his rubbery tootsie roll bounce against my thigh, and it breathed life into my tired body. I gathered him close to me and we kissed and rocked in each other's arms. I stroked his firm back. He nibbled my ear and I sighed. I knew Skylar was tired and I didn't want to pressure him. But when I felt his tongue inside my ear, my whole body tingled and I moaned for more. And Skylar gave it to me, licking my neck, sucking my breasts and finally rubbing his hard penis up and down my thighs.

"Do you wanna be on top?" Skylar whispered.

"Sure." I nodded.

"I better get the rubber."

I found energy that I didn't know I had. I sucked Skylar's nipples and stroked his chest and caressed his penis. Then I gave his hard joystick a playful tug before slipping the condom on it. I rubbed Skylar's penis against my clitoris, before sliding it into my wet, juicy vagina.

Skylar's fingers played with my clitoris while I moved up and down and all around.

"Dee Dee, you feel too beautiful for words!" Skylar moaned. "You feel too beautiful for words."

Then shut up, I was almost tempted to tease. But instead, I basked in the glow of Skylar's praise. It wasn't my first rodeo. I'd been out of the saddle for a long time, but it felt great to be back.

sixteen

Labor Day meant the winding down of summer, although today it was hotter than July. After checking out my brother and his family, I ended up at a barbecue with Sharon and T at Sharon's aunt's house. I could've invited Skylar, but I didn't want to flaunt my heterosexual privelege. After all, Sharon didn't feel comfortable bringing Michelle to family gatherings yet. She'd recently come out to her aunt and mother and sister. They'd all had similar responses. They loved the sinner, but hated the sin. I felt like it was more important to show my support for Sharon by hanging out with her around her family than put Skylar in everyone's face.

Sharon and I huddled alone in the family room of the finished basement, eating from plates of food on snack trays.

"I don't know how to even put this," Sharon said, sucking on a chicken wing. "But anyway, when I came out to you, you took it almost okay."

"It was just a surprise at first," I said, defending myself through a mouthful of potato salad. "It wasn't like a new hairstyle. Besides, I think I've been reasonably supportive after I got over the initial shock."

"I guess that's what I'm saying. You didn't say, 'You go, girl,' and on the other hand you didn't say, 'Go to hell.'"

"That's true."

"I know as a societal outcast I'm supposed to be grateful that you're still speaking to me," Sharon continued. "I'm supposed to be thankful for the crumbs."

"What do you want from me?"

"Don't be defensive."

"I'm not. I'm just asking what you want, because I feel I've been pretty accepting."

"That's my point—you've been reasonably supportive and pretty accepting. Well, at the risk of sounding like Oliver Twist, I want more." Sharon looked at me earnestly with her normally laughing eyes. "You see, Dee Dee, like any courtship, Michelle and I have our ups and downs."

"And I'm open to hearing about them," I said, rearranging myself in the folding chair.

"I need to really feel accepted by somebody here," Sharon said plaintively. "Most of my support is long distance. When you're in a relationship with a man, people go, rah rah. Well, I need a cheering section, too. And I have a harder row to hoe. I need at least one person in Chicago to actually be excited for me. Is that too much to ask?"

I realized that I just took for granted that people would be excited about my dating Skylar. And they were.

"No, it isn't too much to ask, especially from a best friend," I assured her.

Sharon looked relieved and touched that I was still calling her my best friend. I was surprised to feel a lump in my throat. Sharon was still my ace.

"Dee Dee, I know you're ahead of most people in your thinking."

"Thanks."

"Well, you are. My family expects me to be grateful just to be tolerated. And of course they think, 'How could she do this to Tyeesha?'"

"I'm sure they do."

"I'm lucky that I don't have to hide on my job." Sharon sipped her lemonade. "I can be out at Columbia. Thank goodness, I teach at the most progressive college in Chicago. It's one of the few islands of real acceptance in this city. Poor Michelle teaches in the public schools."

"You told me. Sixth grade, right?"

"Yeah, and she'll be walking on eggshells soon. Heaven forbid that she should let something about our relationship slip out. I'm not talking about being explicit, I'm talking about just everyday things."

"I know what you mean."

"Like even telling a fellow teacher where she went for the weekend."

"I get your drift. And I admit that it's a privilege that straight people take for granted."

"To top things off"—Sharon raised her voice as if encouraged by my show of support—"Michelle came out to her son and he pitched a fit."

"Oh no! He's ten, isn't he?"

"Yeah. He asked Michelle about me, and she came out to him. Maybe it was too soon, but sometimes you get tired of living a lie."

"Especially in your own house," I agreed.

"It's like at some point you feel like you're going to explode."

"I can understand that."

Sharon shook her head and stood up. "Now Michelle is worried that her ex-husband will find out and fight her for custody." She sighed and looked worried.

"That's a lot of pressure."

"Yeah, and Michelle is a devoted mother. But all of that could be brushed aside simply because she's a lesbian. There are judges in this country who would sooner give a child to a murderer or even a child molester than to a lesbian mother. It has nothing to do with the best interests of the child."

"That's true."

"If people really gave a damn about the children, they would work to change society so gay and lesbian families would feel accepted. I mean, couldn't an argument be made that children with attractive parents fare better?—or wealthy or educated or thin, for that matter? I mean, where do you draw the line? Why not take children away from parents who don't go to church, or to the right church?"

Sharon's Aunt Ivy walked into the room with Tyeesha. I figured they'd heard the tail end of Sharon's sermon. Sharon's aunt was a petite, brown-skinned woman with a neatly coifed perm. She was carrying a pitcher of lemonade.

"You people are holed up in here where it's nice and cool," Ivy said, freshening our drinks.

Tyeesha announced, "They're serving the homemade ice cream now!"

"We'll get some in awhile," Sharon answered.

"I saved room for it," I said.

"Dee Dee, you've really lost weight."

"Just about five pounds," I replied. When people made so much over a modest weight loss, they made it seem like you were a beached whale before.

"Five pounds is nothing to sneeze at," Ivy insisted. "You can really see it in your face."

"I've lost three pounds," Tyeesha said proudly. "We've been walking."

"Go easy on that ice cream, if you wanna keep it off," Ivy cautioned before turning her attention toward Sharon. "You were always good at making speeches. I always wanted you to take up the law. You would've been a terrific lawyer."

"You heard our conversation, huh?"

"I couldn't help but hear it, the way your voice was carrying."

"Oh, we didn't mean to disturb the peace," I said.

"This isn't a tea party, there's no peace being disturbed," Ivy assured me. "Sharon, I have something I want to say to you."

"I'll go check out the ice cream," I volunteered.

"Me, too," T said. "But I'll just have a couple of scoops."

"No, Dee Dee, you stay in here," Ivy insisted. "As far as I'm concerned, you're like family. Tyeesha, I want you to hear this, too. There will be plenty of ice cream left.

"I'm from the South, so bear with me," Ivy began as she and T pulled up a couple of chairs. "Dee Dee, I know you know what I'm talking about, because you're a Southerner."

"I left Alabama when I was almost four," I pointed out.

"Yeah, but you spent summers there, didn't you?"

"Yes."

"Okay, then. Once a Southerner, always a Southerner."

I thought of myself as a Chicagoan, but I didn't argue with Ivy. It would go against my Southern hospitality.

"I wanna tell y'all a story. It's a true story," Ivy continued, clasping her hands in front of her. "It happened to me. It's nothing fantastic or worth writing down, but maybe it'll mean somethin' to y'all."

And maybe it won't, I thought. *You said yourself, it's nothing fantastic or worth writing down. And when you get finished telling us your uneventful story, all of the homemade ice cream might even be gone.* But I listened politely anyway.

"I used to be an X-ray technician," Ivy began. "T, do you remember that? Remember when you were growing up and I used to wear a white uniform and white stockings and shoes?"

"Oh, yeah. They were always so clean and starched."

"When I started out as a technician, it was before the days of spray starch. You used to buy a box of rock starch. Sharon and Dee Dee, y'all remember that."

"Yeah." Sharon nodded. "Argo Starch in that blue and white box."

"Kids used to like to suck on starch," I added.

"And chew on it," Sharon said.

"We didn't have all the modern gadgets they have now," I said in response to T's bewildered expression.

"When I was a little girl, our toys were mostly sticks and rocks," Ivy added, causing T's jaw to drop even furthur. "Anyway, back to my story. I was a young woman in February 1967. It was a hopeful time. Progress was being made, the world was changing. Despite the fact that we were in the grip of a fierce Chicago winter. But, it was still a hopeful time. I don't remember whether the groundhog had seen his shadow or not that year," Ivy rambled. "Six weeks never made any sense, noway. Any Chicagoan knows that an early spring means the season ticket holders don't have to dust snow off their seats on baseball's opening day."

"I heard that." I smiled.

"Anyway, like I said, the times were hopeful," Ivy continued. "And I was hopeful. People were just beginning to drop the words 'colored' and 'Negro' by the wayside, and we were becoming black."

"Those really were the olden days, huh?" T asked.

I chuckled. I was unaccustomed to thinking of my youth being referred to as the olden days.

"I had a secure job at a big white hospital on the near North Side," Ivy continued. "I was bringing home a decent wage. And, although I was yet to meet the man of my dreams, I was content with the pride that my family and even the neighbors took in seeing me stepping out in my white uniform."

"It was a different time, all right," I said for T's benefit. "We had a sense of community then," I explained. "Neighbors knew who you were."

"And they cared who you were," Sharon added.

"They were hecka nosey, huh?" T frowned.

"Yeah, but they still cared about you," Sharon insisted. "Whatever you did reflected on the whole community, back then."

"The entire race," I added.

"Well, they pretty much referred to me as a nurse," Ivy continued. "It was no point in always trying to explain to folks that I was just an X-ray technician. I once corrected my neighbor, Mrs. Lyle, who stayed up on her front porch during the summer months. After she told me how proud she was of me for becoming a nurse, I tried to tell her my job title. But she said they let me wear the nurse's uniform, so I was a nurse. From then on I was referred to by her as an X-ray nurse."

"It's funny, all the years I worked at a black hospital on the South Side, there was nothing even resembling a psychiatry department. Some folks used to read the *Defender* just to find out how many Negroes got killed over the weekend. And don't let it be a holiday weekend. Anyway, no matter how many folks got shot or stabbed or got a faceful of hot grease or scalded by grits, they never even had a psychologist on duty."

"That's ironic," Sharon mumbled.

"Well, I got over there to the near North Side with the rich white folks, and lo and behold, didn't they have a whole psych wing? Just goes to show you." Ivy took a drink from her lemonade.

"In those days, black women were too busy coping to have nervous breakdowns," I said.

"And brothas didn't consider suicide over a lost job or a bad business decison," Sharon pointed out.

"I just wanted to give you all a little background about that cold, clear morning that I rode the El like any other morning."

"Okay, the suspense is killing me," Sharon teased.

Yeah, cut to the chase, I started to say. But then I remembered that you can't rush a Southerner.

"It was early, the 6:38 A.M. train, the third car," Ivy drawled on. "I've never ridden the 6:38 A.M. train and the third car since that day," she said solemnly. "Never."

We listened patiently, giving Ivy her propers, showing respect for our elder.

"Anyway, I sat down next to a man in an aisle seat. That time of morning the train was carrying a lot of domestics and factory workers. All of a sudden, out of nowhere, a man came up from behind me and hit me with his fist as hard as he could."

Sharon, T and I gasped and sighed in reaction, as Ivy continued her story.

"I slumped over toward the man sitting next to me and said with disbelief, 'That man hit me.' The man sitting next to me looked at me like I was dirt."

"Didn't anybody come to your aid?" I asked.

"I heard a woman's voice say, 'I don't know why he hit her,'" Ivy replied. "You know how people are, especially black people," she added. "If something bad happens to a woman, they usually find a way to twist it around and make it the woman's fault."

"Yeah," Sharon agreed. "As if there's ever an excuse for abuse."

I sighed. "They probably figured he was your man, and he whupped you. And they didn't want to get involved."

"Deep down, a lot of people hate victims," Sharon said, narrowing her eyes. "Believe it or not, it's easier for them to identify with the perpetrator."

Yeah, that's why so many incest victims are so reluctant to come forward, I thought. T*hat's why so many of us are alone with our pain.*

"But you would think somebody would've shown a little compassion," T said, her voice choked with emotion.

"No one even asked, 'Dog, how do you feel?'" Ivy said, shaking her head. "Anyway, the next stop was mine, and I managed to stumble off the train. I thought for a minute that maybe it hadn't really happened. I didn't really feel anything. I just felt numb. But then I felt the pain. By the time I got to work, my face had swelled up like a melon. I told my immediate supervisor what had happened, and she was very sympathetic. Nancy was white, but she was sweet toward everyone."

"Thank goodness, somebody showed you some compassion," T said, sounding a little relieved.

"Just goes to show you, good and bad come in all colors," Sharon pointed out.

"When Nancy told the big boss what had happened to me, can you believe what he said?"

"What did he say?"

"He said, 'Maybe if she does some work, she'll feel better.' He said that right in earshot of me."

"He was cold," I said.

"He was hecka cold," Tyeesha added.

"You know how cold people can be, especially white people," Sharon's aunt said matter-of-factly.

"Yeah, definitely, back then," I agreed. "Attitudes were just beginning to change."

"Your boss was worse than the people on the train," Sharon said angrily. "In fact, he was as bad as the man who hit you. He didn't show you one ounce of compassion."

"He should've asked you if you wanted to lie down and rest," T said.

"They should've offered you treatment," I added. "There you were in a hospital."

"Nancy did give me an ice pack to use during my break. But otherwise I had to put in my eight hours, just like nothing happened."

"Your boss treated you like a slave," Sharon muttered.

"I had to ride the El home that night. I didn't have money for a taxi. And I had to ride the train the next morning. But I never rode the third car of the 6:38 A.M. train again, and it's been almost thirty years. Mama comforted me when I got home, but nothing could erase the trauma entirely. We concluded that it was just one of those random acts of violence. I will probably go to my grave not knowing why that man attacked me."

"It makes me hecka sad," Tyeesha said.

"Yeah," Sharon and I agreed.

"I didn't mean to bring y'all down," Ivy said softly. "I never talk about that story, but Sharon, after you opened up to me about yourself, I got to studyin' on a lot of things. I remembered my experience on the El and to my surprise I could relate it to your situation."

"My situation?" Sharon looked puzzled.

"Yeah, your taking up with women."

"I'm only dating one woman, Aunt Ivy."

"Dee Dee, you know what I mean. You're from the South."

"She just means that you're a lesbian," I told Sharon.

"I was trying to find a pretty way of saying it. You didn't have to be so blunt," Ivy protested. "Anyway," she continued, "I haven't finished having my say about this lesbian business, if that's what y'all wanna call it."

The room got real quiet. We were hanging on every word. Suddenly, the outside chatter of the others sounded like it was coming from a distant yard. The air had changed also. I could feel the increased humidity, even in the cool basement. My head began to sweat and I noticed the odor of barbecue lingering on my greasy fingers.

"I know how alone I felt on the El train that morning when that man hit me and nobody showed any feeling for me," Ivy continued, staring at the three of us. "I knew all of y'all would have empathy for me if I told you my story." She swallowed. "Doubt didn't even cross my mind. And I asked myself, would I have empathy for someone that happened to if it hadda been a man? And the answer was, yes. I asked myself, would I have empathy if that had happened to a white person? And the answer was, yes. I asked myself, would I have had empathy if that had happened to a gay person? And the answer was, also, yes. What I'm trying to say is, baby, I don't ever want you to feel isolated with your pain." Ivy swallowed. "And whatever adjustments I have to make to accept you, I'm going to go ahead and make 'em," she added, choking back tears.

Sharon hugged Ivy, and there wasn't a dry eye among us.

"Auntie, you remind me of Forrest Gump in the movie," Tyeesha said.

"What do you mean?" Ivy asked.

"You know, the part when Forrest Gump says, 'I may not be a smart man, but I know what love is.'"

seventeen

Sharon was all up in arms several days later because while doing the laundry, she'd found cigarettes in Tyeesha's pocket. I couldn't blame Sharon for hitting the ceiling. Even though she and I had both tried cigarettes in high school and had been occasional smokers in college, neither of us had ever gotten hooked. We were both eternally grateful for that.

Sharon asked me to give her some backup around this smoking, and I did. I got as serious as lung cancer when I got up in T's face.

"Dee Dee, I only smoked a few cigarettes," Tyeesha protested as I backed her into a corner in her cluttered bedroom. "You and Mom act like I have a two-pack-a-day habit."

"We're nipping this mess in the bud before you *do* have a two-pack-a-day habit," I shouted, popping my fingers in Tyeesha's face. "Cigarette smoking is not an option for you. There's nothing to discuss. We don't need to have a dialogue. Do you understand?" I towered over T like a drill sergeant.

"You make it sound so bad," Tyeesha whined.

"It *is* bad," I said emphatically. "Smoking can kill you."

"Everybody who smokes doesn't get cancer."

"I don't like the odds. And I told you, I'm not going to argue with you about this, Tyeesha. I'm drawing my line in the sand. And if you cross it," I threatened, "you're no longer my godchild. That's the real deal, okay?" I said, narrowing my eyes. I knew I was selling woof tickets, but I just hoped that T would buy them. I didn't know what else to do.

Tyeesha's mouth flew open and she gave me a pained look.

I hoped that my pronouncement had rendered her speechless. She'd never known a time when she didn't have me in her life.

"Dee Dee, I thought you would be my godmother until the world blew up," Tyeesha said in a shaky voice, her lips quivering.

I was touched by her show of emotion. But I knew that I still had to stand firm. "I really hate putting my godmothership on the line," I said, solemnly, "but baby girl, I'd rather do that than for you to die a slow, painful death from lung cancer. Now you can make your choice. I've said my piece."

"Dee Dee, I'm not into cigarettes," Tyeesha protested. "I just tried them, that's all, but I know it was whack. I never thought you all would jump in my Kool-Aid like this about smoking."

"Well, now you know. We consider cigarettes a big *no no*."

Tyeesha rolled her eyes. "I'm playing soccer at school now. I'd look stupid having a cigarette jones and calling myself an athlete, now wouldn't I?"

"Yeah," I said, "hecka stupid."

I was startled by the doorbell a couple of nights later. "Langston, who could that be coming to see us this late? It's after eleven o'clock." The orange and white mass of fur straightened itself out as if suddenly on duty. I knew that nobody was collecting for some charity this late at night.

"Who is it?" I shouted into the intercom, trying to sound tough.

"Dee Dee, it's me."

The male voice sounded familiar and he knew my name. But I wasn't certain of its origin. "It's me, who?" I asked.

"Phil."

"Phil! What are you doing over here? Is everything all right with Sarita and Jason?"

"They're okay, sort of. Buzz me up so I can tell you what happened."

"What do you mean, sort of?" I raised my voice.

"Just let me in. Don't make me talk about my business out here in the street."

Phil better not be coming over here trying to get over. Things could get ugly. I wasn't sure if letting him in was the right thing to do. But then again, it wasn't like he was some kind of monster. I mean, we went way back. I pressed the buzzer. Something must've happened, I told myself. Phil wouldn't be over here after eleven at night for nothing. But what could've happened? Was Sarita or Jason in the hospital? Had Jason had an asthma attack? I opened the door to a sullen-faced Phil.

"I'm glad you're still up," Phil said, glancing at me in my yellow terry-cloth bathrobe and my hair standing all over my head.

"Yeah," I answered, feeling a little self-conscious. "I just took my braids out. I'm getting my hair redone tomorrow. So, anyway, tell me what happened?"

"Sarita and I had it out," Phil reported, with almost a hint of relief in his voice.

"What do you mean, had it out?"

He sighed as he folded his tall frame into my leather recliner. Langston had already scooted upstairs. He was one of those cats that didn't take to men.

Nervously, I asked, "It didn't come to blows, did it?"

"Not quite."

"Not quite? What do you mean, not quite?"

"It came close, but no punches were actually thrown."

"Where was Jason?"

"Up in his room, probably pretending to be asleep. But nobody could've slept through all that glass breaking."

"Glass breaking! What got broken?"

"Just a set of cheap dishes."

Sarita always kept a set of cheap dishes, just in case she went off. They must've finally come in handy.

Suddenly, the phone rang loudly, startling me. I still had the ringer up as high as it would go because I was hoping to hear from Skylar. But I doubted that he would call this late.

I felt my body tense up. "What if that's Sarita?" I asked, my eyes wide open.

Phil looked like if he hadn't seen a ghost, he'd at least seen a rat.

"Don't answer it," he ordered.

"She's my friend, I can't betray her."

"You're not betraying her," Phil insisted. "Just pretend you're not home."

"The voice mail has picked up now," I said. "Maybe I should check to see who it was. Maybe it wasn't Sarita. Maybe it was somebody else." I picked up the phone. "They didn't leave a message," I reported. "It probably *was* Sarita; she figured I wasn't home, and didn't want to leave a message. She doesn't know you're here, does she?"

"No, of course not. She'll think I went over to my mother's."

"Why *didn't* you go there?"

"Because I wanted to talk to *you.*"

"I don't want to be drawn into the middle of you and Sarita's mess," I said, holding my hands up in a defensive posture.

"You would listen to *her,* if she were here."

"We've been friends since MP High."

"You and I go all the way back to Morgan Park, too."

"But Sarita and I are good girlfriends. And you're not coming between us," I added, pointing my finger. "So don't *even* go there."

Phil held his head in his hands. He took a deep breath and blew it out. "All I want is someone to talk to, Dee Dee. I don't want anything else from you."

"Don't you have any male friends?"

Phil groaned. "I can't just call up a buddy."

"Why not?"

"'Cause the conversation would last about two minutes max. Men don't listen to other men's problems unless they owe them money. You're the only one I can really open up to."

"I just hate being in the middle, that's all," I said, folding my arms and letting out a frustrated sigh.

Phil took another deep breath and puffed out his cheeks like he was playing a trumphet.

Easing down on the couch, I reluctantly asked, "So, what was the argument about?"

Phil turned the recliner in my direction. He leaned forward hopefully, like I was a hotshot lawyer who'd just agreed to take his case.

"It started off pretty lame. It wasn't like I wasn't used to being nagged." He shook his head. "But something in me just snapped. I saw myself in the prime of my life, day in and day out living with a nag and not gettin' none most of the time on top of it."

"Sex?"

"Yeah, she's always too tired or not in the mood, lately."

"Maybe what you two need is a vacation."

"I need a vacation, all right. A long vacation *away* from her."

"I can't help you, then." I yawned. "You oughta head back home. Sarita might be worried."

"If she is, she can just stay worried, as far as I'm concerned. I don't want her up in my face talking more foolishness tonight. I need a good night's sleep. Dee Dee, doesn't your couch pull out?"

"Yeah, it's a sofa bed. But you can't sleep here."

"Why not? I thought we were friends."

"We are. And if you want us to stay friends, you better bounce."

"We're not *real* friends then," Phil grumbled.

"We *are* real friends," I insisted.

"No, we ain't. If you were *really* my friend, you would understand that I need a change of scene. You would understand how bored I am with my life. You would understand why I just need to chill out for a minute."

"I do understand. I'm just not letting you chill out over here. You know I have an allegiance to Sarita."

"Allegiance is something that you pledge to the flag. It's just some words that you mouth. It really doesn't mean that much."

"Well, I'll make it plain then. I'm not going to mess around with anybody's husband, let alone one of my closest friend's husband."

"Fine, I respect you for that. I'm not asking you to mess around with me. I'm simply asking you to open your couch to me as a friend, in my own right." Phil sounded sincere, with pleading puppy dog eyes.

"I'm not sure I can do that without jeopardizing my friendship with Sarita."

"Dee Dee, as much as I joke about it, it did me good to drive over here to the North Side." Phil stood up and began to pace with his arms folded. He paused at one of my warehouse windows. "I might not want to live over here, but it's a nice place to visit," he conceded, continuing to pace. "It's just nice to be out, seeing something different. Being in your condo, checking out your magazines and books, the art and CDs, sitting on different furniture, looking at a different view. Wondering where your cat's hiding at." He streched his neck in the direction of my upstairs level.

It's come to that, I thought. Your life has become so humdrum, that even wondering where Langston is hiding breaks the monotomy. Phil's quest for variety was almost endearing.

"Don't you understand?" he asked. "Everybody needs to get out sometimes. Everybody needs a change. You know what I mean?"

"I'm not sure. It's one thing to take a drive; it's another to bail out of a twenty-two-year marriage."

"Look, I want to keep my family together. Lord knows I wanna do that. But I don't think I can stick it out for the sake of the kid anymore."

I stood up and faced Phil. "It would be hard on Sarita if you left. You know that. But it would be really hard on Jason. He looks up to you. And Jason still has to face the teenage years."

"Yeah, I know." Phil sighed. "I wanted to be different. I didn't want my kids growing up without a male role model, especially my son. Nine outta ten black boys who become athletes give all the credit to Mama when they get on TV."

"Jason's at a critical age, Phil. He could go either way. He needs your guidance."

"I'm not planning to skip town." He looked around the room restlessly. "I'm not going out for a pack of cigarettes and not come back."

"You don't even smoke."

"Okay, ice cream or a newspaper. You know what I mean. I would still be a part of Jason's life, no matter what."

"I know, but it wouldn't be the same as having you in the house."

"Having me in the house? You make me sound like a potted plant."

"Phil, it's more than a notion to get a child safely through the teenage years, these days."

"So, what are you saying, I should sacrifice everything for my son? I should put my needs on hold till I'm past fifty?"

"I don't know what you should do. I don't have all the answers."

Phil sat down and held his head. "Well, it makes a difference having someone to ask the questions to, at least. Maybe that's half the battle. Just having someone to talk to."

"I'll send you my bill in the morning."

"Dee Dee." Phil paused. "Are you afraid that you could feel closer to me than Sarita? Is that what you're really afraid of deep down?"

I gulped. "I don't think so."

"Maybe unconsciously?"

"I guess anything's possible," I said, with a nervous laugh.

"I saw a bumper sticker on my way over here," Phil continued. "It said, 'Be Fearless, Choose Love.'"

"Well, sometimes, love means saying good night," I said firmly.

"What do you think of stripping?" Tyeesha asked me a few days later as we power-walked past hotels, restaurants and stores along downtown Chicago's Magnificent Mile.

"Stripping what? The paint off of something?" I visualized antique furniture as we hurried along bustling Michigan Avenue.

"No, you know, like 'take it off baby.'" T said, pausing just long enough to pop her fingers and wiggle her hips, and yet not be trampled by the continuous onslaught of foot traffic on the busy sidewalk. "Stripping," she repeated.

"What do I think of it?" I asked.

"Yeah."

"I think it's cheap and degrading toward women. That's what I think."

"Isn't that hypocritical?"

"How?"

"Your friend Jade is a belly dancer and *you* take belly dancing classes."

"That's different. Belly dancing is spiritual."

"Are you saying that men watching belly dancers are trying to get closer to God?"

"If we're going to have a conversation, let's get away from all these people," I said, pulling Tyeesha toward the water tower nearby. It would give us a little privacy and a chance to catch our breaths.

"Maybe the spirituality is lost on some people, but belly dancing is very different from stripping," I panted. "Its purpose is not to appeal to prurient interests." We stood below the tall, old, yellowstone structure.

"Well, I don't think a lot of people see a big difference," Tyeesha said, rolling her eyes. "And if you're going to be close-minded about strippping, you should be able to understand why people are close-minded about belly dancing."

"As far as I'm concerned, there is no relation between my taking a belly dance class for fitness and well-being and somebody taking her clothes off to turn somebody on."

"Your friend Jade performs."

"She doesn't perform nude."

"She probably has half her stomach out."

"Anyway, why are we discussing stripping?"

"Because I was thinking about checking it out," Tyeesha said, having the nerve to look me in the eye.

"Checking it out, how? You just got out of the way of a speeding train and now you wanna throw yourself in front of a Mack truck. Have you lost your mind?"

"Me and Katyana were going to go to Amateur Night. They say you can make hecka money."

"Where?"

"At the Admiral Theater."

"That place over on West Lawrence?"

"Yeah, have you been there?"

"Of course not." I groaned. "I've just driven past it. Wait a minute—first of all, you're under age. Have you forgotten that you're a minor?"

"Katyana's cousin can get us some fake IDs. With makeup, we can both pass for over eighteen."

"What would possess you to want to take your clothes off in front of a bunch of horny strangers? I mean, you couldn't be that hard up for money."

"I could use some cash. There are lots of things that I wanna buy," Tyeesha said, pointing toward a store window.

"There are *some* things that money *can't* buy. Self-esteem is one of them. And your reputation is another. No amount of money can buy back your reputation.

"A handful of dollars may seem like a lot now, but it's really nothing."

"Gimme plenty of nothing, then."

"Your values are screwed up, T," I said, leaning against the water tower. "It has to go beyond money. You're not doing without. I would give you a hundred dollars, if you were desperate. It couldn't be about the money."

"It's exciting to get paid a bunch of cash for a few minutes of your time. But it's not just the money. I think it would be tight to have all these guys looking at me, wanting me, giving me tips. All eyes on me. I'm only gonna be young once," Tyeesha said mournfully. She folded her arms and leaned against the building.

"That's why I hate to see you waste it."

"Well, when I get to be your age, it'll be all over. I'll just have memories."

I swallowed. "It gets better with age."

Tyeesha cut her eyes like she didn't believe me. "I just thought it would be fun to be able to look back and know that for one night at least, I was really wanted." Her voice was wistful. "That I was truly hot."

I stood up straight. "You need to stop looking for somebody else to make you feel good about yourself."

Tyeesha folded her arms again and faced me. "How am I 'sposed to make myself feel good about myself? Don't tell me about those zucchinis again," she whispered.

"I don't know. It's like we're all looking for the Wizard of Oz. But what we're looking for is inside of us. The Wizard or anybody else can't give it to us. The Wizard has his own problems. He's trying to get home himself. You think some drunk, horny man can make you feel special? Do you really think that?"

"I'm afraid that I'll end up like a lot of women that I see. In my forties and unmarried or being with another woman because I can't find a good man."

"Like me and your mother?"

"At least you finally found a boyfriend. Dee Dee, you act like it's so horrible to get pregnant when you're a teenager. But what difference does it make? I mean, I don't want to be one of those women who forgets to have kids. And there's no guarantee I'll ever find Mr. Right and have a family and the white picket fence. Everybody tells black girls there's not much out here for us when it comes to men. So why are you so surprised when we start believing it? The way I figure it, we have a small window of opportunity. And it's getting smaller and smaller. My friend Katyana's sister is in college, and she says that a lot of the sistas are holding up the walls or dancing with each other at their sorority dances. Katyana says a sista can go through four years of college without a single date. I feel like what I have going for me is that I'm young and cute. But every year there's more and more competition. I don't want to be twenty-seven and not know where my next date is coming from."

"Twenty-seven?" I asked, surprised. "It's come to that."

"Yeah."

"Well, it's still a mistake to treat men like they're a scarce commodity, because you can't do that without devaluing yourself."

"What's the answer, then? That's what girls like me want to know. What's the answer if you want love in your life? Tell me at fifteen and save me a lot of heartache and pain."

"The answer is to love yourself first."

"But what if you want someone else to love you, too?"

"Ask yourself, does this person make me feel good about myself? Do I feel safe, strong and free with this person? Those are the questions you need to ask."

"But what about being seduced and surrendering? I thought a woman was supposed to feel weak, not strong."

"That's Hollywood. You have to be strong to truly be open."

"But what if men no longer think a woman is tight? Like she used to be considered fly, but she's gained weight and has gotten older and nobody's saying, 'Man, she's flossy.' What does a woman do then? How can she still feel good about herself?" Tyeesha asked, with a perplexed expression.

I sighed. "That's what I'm working on myself."

"Have you found the answer yet?"

"It's a work in progess. But I heard an expert say on tv recently, 'If you go within, you'll never go without.'"

A few days later, after a staff meeting, Bill asked, "Dee Dee, howdja like to grab a coupla sandwiches and go up on the roof?"

I turned toward Jade, hoping for an out. I'd rather hang with her this afternoon, than Bill. She and Bill had recently completed their mediation, and it had been declared a success. Jade had told me she doubted she would ever be bosom buddies with Bill, but she didn't dislike him anymore. I thought that represented a major victory for Skylar *and* Bill. But Bill was still moping around as usual.

"Dee Dee, you go ahead, I've got a few errands to run. Besides, I think it's good that Bill has you to talk to," Jade twisted her lips to say.

"That's what I'm concerned about. Bill strikes me as being kinda depressed lately. You think it's safe?" I swallowed, trailing Jade out of the conference room. I whispered, half jokingly, "Bill's not gonna try and jump off the roof or anything, is he?"

"Oh no, I think Bill's okay. He might even be entering his manic phase right now. It's such a beautiful view up there, and it's not too windy for a change. Dee Dee, you should take advantage of these last warm days."

I rolled my eyes before heading back toward Bill.

Bill and I walked out onto the flat rooftop, carrying our lunches. We gazed at the Lakefront and the tall buildings in the Loop.

"Wow, look at the view!" I exclaimed. "Chicago probably has the best-looking downtown in the country."

Bill shrugged. "Last night I had a transformation, Dee Dee." He bit into his pastrami sandwich.

"You had a transformation," I repeated. "So, what exactly happened?"

"I was masturbating," Bill said, between bites of food.

I frowned. "I don't want to hear this shit! Bill, you haven't changed. I do not want to hear about you masturbating. I want to eat my pastrami sandwich, without hearing about your dick."

Bill squinted and straightened his glasses. "I was just giving you the background, that's all. I wasn't going to get graphic."

I rolled my eyes. "Okay then, so how were you transformed?"

"I was having one of my usual fantasies."

"Fantasies! I don't want to hear about your fantasies. Can't you talk about the weather or the presidential race or something?"

"Okay, it's a nice day and I think Clinton's gonna get reelected. How's that?"

"Never mind, go ahead. Just try not to be too explicit." I took a swallow of ginger ale.

"I don't know why you're feeling threatened. My fantasies don't involve you."

"Good."

"I've had the same ones for years." Bill chewed thoughtfully as he leaned against a corner of the roof. "I'm always in control," he said, looking over at me. "Women are like my sex slaves."

I cut my eyes at Bill.

"Sometimes, I even feel sorry for them," he added, with a far-away look in his eyes. "I've often been disturbed by my fantasies."

I groaned. "I should've become a therapist. I should get a hundred dollars an hour to listen to people like you."

Bill picked at his sandwich. "I even wrote to a sex advice columnist about my fantasies, once. And she said that they were just harmless ways for me to feel powerful. So long as I didn't force them on unwilling people, I shouldn't worry."

I felt uncomfortable. Words like "force" and "unwilling" when connected to sex made me flash on my own experience of sexual abuse. But, maybe feeling the uncomfortable feeling was somehow therapeutic.

"Wouldn't you rather feel true intimacy than feel powerful?" I asked.

"Yeah, sure, on some level." Bill shrugged. "It's just that feeling powerful gives me such an adrenaline rush. But finally the sense of emptiness got to me, the lack of real pleasure. And I sorta hit bottom. I realized that I was just like a junkie with a monkey on his back. I'm thirty-nine years old and I got sick of doing the same thing over and over and getting the same empty results. I was like the rat going down the maze, over and over, even though they took the cheese out a long time ago."

"Real rats aren't that dumb," I said.

"Yeah, I was a dumb rat." Bill paused. "I used to be a scrawny kid who got made fun of a lot. But then I became a guy fantasizing about having sex slaves to feel good about myself. I don't need to do that anymore."

"That's good, but even if you backslide every once in awhile, it doesn't make you a bad person." I asked warily, "You've never gone out and attacked anybody, have you?"

"No," Bill assured me. "I've just been your garden-variety asshole."

I felt like I was a therapist to everyone but myself. "Bill, I gotta go."

"Why?"

"I just need to think my own thoughts right now."

eighteen

Listening to Bill talk about his sexual fantasies had reminded me of my own sexual history. I'd gone years without thinking much about it, but nowadays my memories refused to stay dormant. It was like my unconscious had developed a mind of its own. I could've gone and bought some dessert on the pier and come home and raided the refrigerator and then thrown up. That's what the old me would've done. But something had changed inside of me.

I went home and cried into my cat's soft fur, for the little girl who was made to feel dirty and low and ashamed, but covered it up with good grades and party dresses and a sense of humor. No matter how hard I had prayed, God had never jumped down from the sky to save me. No matter how good I had been or how disobedient, no one had ever noticed the source of my pain.

When I woke from nightmares, my screams had fallen upon deaf ears. When my parents had criticized my clumsiness and the way I grasped a fork or a pencil, I wished I could've explained that awkwardness was understandable in a child forced to handle a man's penis.

I knew of one other girl sorta like me. I heard about her on the playground. Girls whispered that Portia's older brothers were freakin' with her. She was afraid to go home after school. Portia wore wrinkled, dirty clothes and had a worn-out expression on her face. Most kids didn't want anything to do with her; they said she had the cooties. I pretty much stayed away from Portia also. She was a reminder of my own pain.

Girls said that Portia even told her mother about the molestation, but her mother hadn't believed her. She'd told Portia to get away from her with that mess. And Portia obeyed. She still had a home to go to. She still had a mother who would cuss a teacher out on her behalf. And she still had two big brothers who would kick anybody's ass who messed with her, except them.

I tried to tell my mother in indirect ways. I tried to tell her by going to the bathroom in my bed. Lying in my own excrement felt cleaner than I felt when my stepfather came into my room. But Mama dismissed my accident. She explained that children sometimes regress when a new baby's in the house. I didn't know what "regress" meant, but I knew that was the end of the discussion. I remember once my mother was putting a hem in my dress, and my stepfather sat nearby, reminding me of the wolf in *Little Red Riding Hood*. I told my mother that I wanted my hem as long as she could make it. My baffled mother set the hem just above my knees, despite my desire to have it long enough to hide my whole body. Maybe then I'd be invisible, I thought, and he would leave me alone. Perhaps in the same way, women hide inside their fat. Maybe they think if they get fat enough, they can disappear.

Even after thinking about all this, I didn't binge and purge today. I knew it was not the answer. It never had been. This was a big personal win for me. It is so important for us to acknowlege our wins. Little by little, maybe I was gaining the courage to deal with the sewer inside me. I was a victim, but I was also a survivor. I didn't deserve what happened to me, despite the fact that nobody helped me, not even God. I used to think it was my fault. What else would a child think? I used to think that there was something dirty about me. When I was growing up, it was common for kids to be told, "You brought it all on yourself." Parents had the power to punish you, and if they did anything bad to you, it was because you deserved it. Not only was I bad, but I was worthless. When my step-father used me, I felt like a piece of dirty, slimy trash. When I left my body and watched from the ceiling, I saw that the person he was rubbing against had ceased to exist. She'd been rubbed out like a mistake was rubbed out with a dirty eraser. She was just a smudge that could never come clean again.

I went through a promiscuous phase during young adulthood. I felt that all I had to offer men was sex. However, a handful of one-night stands during the seventies didn't raise many eyebrows. In fact, my behavior was considered normal. But it had nothing to do with sex. It had to do with sleeping with someone so I wouldn't feel so alone. I was completely passive, like a child, waiting for men to undress me and do their business. I never really enjoyed the act itself much. I was just an object to be acted upon. But I felt that in order for me to be deemed worthwhile, I needed a man to want me. I was taught at an early age that sex was my greatest value. And I figured that was all I was worth.

I can understand why my marriage failed. It wasn't anyone's fault. The real truth is, I drove my husband into another woman's arms. I didn't want him to whisper sweet nothings in my ear, Instead, I asked him to tell me how low and ugly and dirty and worthless I was while we were having sex. He refused, with tears in his eyes. I drove my husband into another woman's arms, because he couldn't bear to debase me. He couldn't save me; and he chose to save himself.

No one who's abused is going to just waltz through life. In many ways, I've been lucky. I've only stolen a candy bar, even though a lot more was stolen from me. Children who are abused are going to have problems with their sexuality and with relation-ships and even life in general. Mental hospitals used to be filled with incest survivors. Incest has been this country's dirty little secret.

As far as my sexuality is concerned, I've come a long way. Occa-sionally I've gotten headaches or had flashbacks while having sex. At age forty-one, I can truly say that I've learned to have a satisfying sex life. But, it wasn't always like that. I lighted candles, took long bubble baths, got massages, and wrote affirmations. And slowly I began to heal. I was determined that the man who caused me so much pain, would not rob me of a lifetime of pleasure also.

It wasn't even that I'd hated Daddy Sherman all my life. On the surface, I came from a normal, dysfunctional family. I had hardworking parents that kept it together. My stepfather wasn't a monster; he was respected on the job, at church and in our community. He'd married a widow with two kids and saved them from living in the projects. He had a hearty laugh and encouraged me to love music. Daddy Sherman gave me my first harmonica and taught me how to play. I often wondered how a person can do monstrous things and yet not be a monster. He can even have admirable qualities. In some ways, that makes it even harder for the victim. That's why it was easier for me to blame myself and even convince myself for a time that the abuse never even occurred. It would've been harder to deny if the abuse had been ongoing. My stepfather molested me during the months before and after my mother's pregnancy with my baby sister. It all happened when I was in kindergarten. But the scars might last forever.

It's easier to deny when on the surface your clothes are clean, everyone says grace at the dinner table, you attend church regularly, you pile into the car and go visit relatives on summer vacations and your parents bug you to do your homework. It's pretty easy to convince yourself that yours is a normal family. I buried the molestation, pretty much until I was a young adult. I always had a reasonably amicable relationship with my stepfather, by all appearances. He died without ever witnessing my rage bubble to the surface. Ironically, my mother and I had more occasional volatility, although we still had a pretty good mother-daughter relationship.

But, despite the picture we showed the world, I always had a haunting sense that something bad had happened to me. The anxiety surfaced when I did a paper on child abuse in college and I had this weird feeling that I was writing about myself.

And then, little by little, I began to remember. I read books about sexual abuse and I was able to identify. It had happened to me. And it was still affecting my life.

I was ready to let go of my crutch. I knew that I wasn't going to be an occasional bulimic anymore. I would face my fears if I had to. I was willing to experience the hunger. I refused to swallow any more shame.

nineteen

"I've heard that it's not wise for parents to introduce their child to a date too quickly, but I can't wait to meet Brianna," I said, wrapped up in Skylar's arms with my feet hanging off my sofa, later that evening.

He'd brought over a stack of CDs and called himself hipping me to straight-ahead jazz. Of course, fusion was more romantic.

"Your daughter sounds so cute on the phone," I continued. I tugged playfully at Skylar's soft naps.

Langston stared disapprovingly at a safe distance from his favorite window.sill. He actually tolerated Skylar and his spacey music better than I'd anticipated. I'd expected him to go somewhere and hide.

"I've thought about introducing you to Brianna," Skylar answered. "I just don't know how she'll react."

"I understand, it might be too soon. We've only really been seeing each other three months."

"Who's counting?" Skylar asked, gently stroking my face.

"I hope you mean that in a good way."

He pulled me closer to him. "I mean that in the best way."

We kissed and hugged. Being in his arms reminded me of the warmth of the sun and the earthiness of a riverbank.

I sighed happily.

"Do you feel like a teenager?" Skylar asked.

"Better."

"Yeah, it's not being wasted." Skylar smiled. "I could utter all kinds of stuff, but I'm afraid it would all sound so clichéd."

"Try me."

"I'm not good at lines. The truth is, I just feel privileged to be able to spend time with you."

"That's very sweet of you to say," I breathed. "Are you sure you don't have a rap?"

"It's just the way I feel. I haven't told you much about my past. I don't want you to throw me a pity party or anything."

"I want to be your friend as well as your lover."

"Thanks. You know I was a foster child, and to be honest, I don't really have anybody."

"What do you mean?" I asked, giving Skylar a hug.

"I have a few close friends in California and my daughter, but I don't really have an extended family to fall back on."

"I understand what you mean."

"There are a lot worse stories than mine, believe me. I was actually pretty lucky. I'm still in touch with my foster parents. I even get together with them sometimes at holidays."

"That's good. So you do have your foster parents. At least you have some extended family."

"Yeah, but it's different being a foster child," Skylar said, massaging my shoulders. "You don't ever really feel secure."

"I can imagine." Although you don't have to be a foster child to never *really* feel secure, I reminded myself. But I still thought I knew what Skylar meant. Being a foster child had to be a somewhat unique experience.

"My foster parents were great people," Skylar continued. "I mean, they still are. I don't fault them in any way. They're this interracial Santa Cruz couple who took in a bunch of kids of different races. Some were disabled. They really couldn't afford to adopt all of us. It was like Grand Central Station. I learned from my white foster mom and my black foster dad that love comes in all colors, shapes and sizes. Some people live their whole lives and never understand that, or even know what love is.

"Mom and Dad are still there for me, if I need them. And they're crazy about Brianna," Skylar continued.

"So it's not like I want you to feel sorry for me or anything."

"I didn't think you did. I just thought you were sharing."

"Yeah, I am." Skylar settled deeper into my embrace. "Even though I have a family connection," he continued, "it's not the same as having a traditional family. I was just one of many. It's like there have been so many somebody elses in my room, I can't keep track. They might've painted my room pink by now." He smiled wryly.

"I admire people like your foster parents," I said. "It takes a special calling to do what they're doing."

"Yeah, I know they made the difference for me. I was so angry and what do they call it…shut down, when they took me. I was almost ten years old and had been in a bunch of different homes. I was given up as a toddler; my mother just couldn't take care of me. I don't even remember her. I just remember being told that my mother couldn't take care of me, ever since I can remember." Skylar swallowed.

I lovingly massaged his head as he leaned against me.

"I came close to being adopted a few times, but it always fell through. Talk about feeling unwanted." Skylar sighed.

"What were the other foster homes like?"

"There was a range, everything from a foster mother from hell to foster parents who were basically just doing a job. They kept me clean and fed, but you could tell that it was just a job. It wasn't until I got with the Washingtons that I felt loved."

"What was the foster mother from hell like?" I wanted to give Skylar an opportunity to open up to me if he chose.

"Well, for example, one morning about six o'clock, she woke me up whipping me with an extension cord. I'd been in a dead sleep, so it was kinda traumatic. I kept asking, 'What did I do, what did I do?' She said, 'I'm whuppin' you for what you might do today.' She was evil—she was into insurance whuppins."

"Some people have no business dealing with kids," I said angrily. "It's like they've totally forgotten how it feels to be a child."

"They were probably treated the same way or worse," Skylar replied matter-of-factly.

"That's still no excuse. Get the help you need and do better."

"I agree; that's why I've read books and tried to get information so that I can be a good parent to my daughter."

"Come here, baby," I said, hugging Skylar and stroking his face.

I held him against my breast. "Lemme make it up to you," I mumured as I rocked Skylar inside my arms.

"I don't know if I want to share you with Brianna," Skylar mumbled. "I just might wanna keep you all to myself."

I was surprised when Skylar informed me that his daughter liked sushi, and suggested that the three of us meet Wednesday at a Japanese restaraunt for our first visit. I asked myself why I felt nervous going to dinner with an eight-year-old, but I knew that if I hit it off with Brianna, we could become one happy family. I cautioned myself not to push too hard. I wasn't sure how she would take to me, because she was still missing her mother. Skylar said he'd told Brianna that I was a new friend. He wasn't sure whether Brianna would resent a date: She'd never seen him romantically linked to a woman except her mother.

I fell for Brianna hook, line and sinker. The cherub-faced darling with a mass of red curls almost walked into my arms on our first meeting. Skylar and I took Brianna to her favorite all-you-can-eat sushi place. I was still trying to digest the idea of a child being into sushi. I reminded myself that Brianna was from California. We spoke Spanish to each other and translated for Skylar. When Brianna asked her father if she could invite a playdate to church, Skylar reminded her that Ariel was Jewish and her parents might not want her to attend a Christian church. Brianna promptly answered, "I go there and I'm not a Christian."

"What are you?" Skylar asked.

"I'm biracial," Brianna responded.

"In some circles in the Bay Area, it's almost a religion." Skylar chuckled.

"Is biracial the opposite of Christian?" Brianna wanted to know.

"Biracial is not a religion," Skylar explained. "It means that you…"

"I know what it means," Brianna interrupted. "Mom's bi and you're racial. And I'm biracial." She giggled.

"Out of the mouths of babes," Skylar said rolling his eyes.

"This evening went well," I commented to Skylar as we walked out of the restaurant.

"That's because I was here," Brianna chirped. "I'm a superstar!" she bragged, and skipped ahead.

"When your daughter pats herself on the back, she doesn't use a feather." I laughed.

"I've read that girls at her age have a lot of confidence," Skylar said sheepishly.

"Let's hope she doesn't lose too much of it."

When I said good-bye to Skylar with a friendly hug, I was touched that Brianna hugged me also.

Our first meeting had been a success. I fantasized about becoming part of an "us" with them. Maybe I was being selfish, but I thought it might be for the best if Brianna's mother stayed in the background. I could easily visualize myself playing mother to this precocious child.

The next week, I accompanied Skylar to Brianna's school play. She wasn't the star, but I found myself hanging onto her every word and watching her every movement.

I glanced over at Skylar. His eyes were shining with pride. At intermission I told Skylar about his glow. He insisted that it wasn't just pride; that it was partly relief.

"I was nervous as a cat," Skylar confided as we stood sipping punch next to the snack table. "I was just so thankful that Bri didn't forget her lines."

We were able to see Brianna for a moment backstage during intermission. I was chewing gum and Bri asked me for a piece. I told her that it wouldn't be a good idea for her to come out on the stage chewing gum. Brianna assured me that she didn't have to do anything in the second half. I didn't want her to think I was like a wicked stepmother, so I gave the child a piece of sugarless gum and cautioned her to be discreet. I wondered if Brianna knew what the word "discreet" meant as Skylar and I made our way back to our seats.

To my horror, a few minutes later, I looked up to see Brianna onstage, chewing like a cow. She was upstage in a group scene, and she wasn't speaking lines, but it still didn't look good. Skylar immediately came to attention, motioning to her from the audience. I felt sweat creeping down my neck and then my back. Brianna continued to chew, and Skylar continued to motion to her. Several people around us were focusing on Skylar instead of the play. Finally, he managed to get Brianna's attention. But instead of swallowing her gum, she asked loudly, "What, Daddy?"

There were a few snickers as Skylar motioned for Brianna to get rid of the gum. She swallowed it and the show went on. I felt an empathetic lump in my throat. I felt like I was becoming part of a family.

Sarita called me the next day. She was beside herself because Phil hadn't come home last night. She'd contacted the usual suspects: his mother, sister, drinking buddy, the other two barbers in his shop. No one had seen or heard from him, including me. I grilled Sarita to make sure that an argument hadn't preceded Phil's disappearance. When she assured me that one hadn't, I became quite concerned. Phil was not the type of man to just up and disappear for more than a few hours. In the back of our minds lurked the possibility of foul play. Almost every other day you read or heard about some horror story in the news. Crime was much more common than rare. I had to put my being in love on the back burner. I had an uneasy feeling this brisk autumn day.

Sarita had contacted the police and they'd told her to wait twenty-four hours before filing a missing person report. I told

Sarita if she didn't hear from Phil by tonight, I'd come over and sit with her.

Later that evening, Sarita called to tell me that she still hadn't heard anything from Phil, but she wanted me to stay put, just the same.

"It's no point in your blundering out here tonight. There's too much crime going on out here in these streets. It's not safe out here for man or beast, much less for a woman alone."

"I want to lend you moral support."

"I appreciate that. I really do. And you're giving me that by being concerned and talking with me on the phone, and remembering me in your prayers."

"You've checked the hospitals? He might've had a car accident."

"I've checked the major ones. Besides, they would've notified me by now. Phil always carries ID. We're even listed in the phone book."

"He could've lost his ID. He could've been robbed. You check the jails?"

"The jails?" Sarita sounded defensive.

"He could've been arrested for jaywalking or just driving, *while black*."

"I checked with the police station. I've even checked with the morgue," Sarita said softly.

"Well, the fact that he wasn't there is promising."

"Dee Dee, I just don't know what I'll do if something has happened to Phil," Sarita said in anguish. "He's always been a good husband and a wonderful father. I could kick myself for all the times I got on him about little or nothing."

"This is no time to beat yourself up. Let's just try and stay hopeful."

"This just isn't like Phil. I just know something bad happened. I don't want to think like that, but what else can I think? Phil just wouldn't walk off like this. He had customers waiting for haircuts."

"How is Jason weathering all of this?"

"He's worried sick, of course. My daughters are both nervous wrecks; they're talking about flying home. I've tried not to let Jason see me crying, but I've broken down a few times. Lord knows I'm trying to be strong, but sometimes I just can't," Sarita said, sniffing.

"That's understandable. Crying isn't a sign of weakness."

"Well, Jason and I have both cried together. I called my pastor and he came by earlier and prayed with us. Some of the ladies from the church offered to come sit with me tonight. But I told them that I was gonna call my good girlfriend, and take some melatonin and go lie down. If I stay up all night, I'll worry myself sick. I have to turn it over to God now."

"Well, call me any hour of the night or day if there's anything that I can do. I'm always here for you."

"Thanks, Dee Dee, but just pray for us. It's in God's hands now."

Doing my radio show the next day helped me take my mind off my worries. It was as if when I disappeared behind the glass door of the control room, I entered another world.

"That was Larry Davis doing his rendition of 'As the Years Go Passing By.' Ahead of him was Howling Wolf, with 'Howlin' for My Darlin.' Before that was Smokey Wilson's rendition of Elmore James' 'Something Inside Me.' And I opened the stampede with my homie, Wilson Pickett, doing 'Mustang Sally.'"

"I hear you can get down with a harmonica," the leather-faced bluesman seated next to me said into the mike.

"Wait a minute, listeners, did I ask anybody anything? I mean, who's conducting this interview, me or you?" I teased.

"Excuse the hell outta me," the brotha said in a Mississippi-molasses drawl.

"For those of you just joining us, I'm chillin' with Fatback Brown, one of the baddest bluesmen around."

"That's right, and I got money in my pocket and I'm rarin' to clown! So meet me with your black drawers on."

"Fatback's just kiddin'. He's not a player. He's been married to the same woman for twenty-something years. And she don't take no stuff."

"That's true, I've been married to the same bowlegged woman, built like a fiddle with plenty of room in the middle, for twenty-nine years."

"And I wish you twenty-nine more," I said.

"So, Dee Dee, heard you mixed it up the other night with J.J. Malone and his Backroads Blues Band."

"Yeah, I was on harmonica for a minute. Jill Baxter took a break. That white girl sho can blow, huh?"

"I hear you wasn't too shabby yourself."

"I did okay, I wasn't too rusty. I got a little practice a while back, sitting in with a few of the bands during an event they have here every August over at B.L.U.E.S. on North Halsted."

"Across the street from Kingston Mines?"

"Yeah, two blues clubs on one block. You know, Chicago is the home of the blues. Anyway, the event is called 31 Bands in 31 Days, all Chicago Bands. It was pretty tight."

"Don't forget to plug my gig tonight, now, while you naming the rest of 'em."

"I got you covered. Will you trust me to do my own show, here?"

"G'one, I'll hush, then."

"Speaking of the Home of the Blues, the legendary Checker Board Lounge on the mighty South Side will be boiling over with the blues tonight. Because they are hosting the sizzling Fatback Brown and his Black-Eyed Peas. "

"That's right, we gonna blow the roof off the sucker."

"Fatback, we're gonna chew the fat a little while longer, then I'm gonna play some of your music so our listeners can get a taste of your pot likker blues."

"Okay. First, did you hear about the judge asking the man why he hit his wife upside the head with a chair?"

"No."

"The man say, ''Cause, Judge, I couldn't lift that couch to save my life.'"

"That's cold. Now after I've just given you a nice plug, you wanna come on here and act a fool. The phones are gonna be ringing, folks will be callin' my show sexist. They'll be saying I'm promoting domestic violence."

"We just havin' a little fun."

"But you know I'm somewhat of a feminist. I like women as well as men."

"Now, I ain't gonna touch that."

"I don't mean it that way. I ain't trying women unless the world runs outta men, y'all hear me?"

"Whatever. Fatback is sophisticated. He can go with the flow. Anyway, I ain't really no sexist. Ask my wife."

"You've never raised your hand to her, right?"

"You know I'm proud to say I haven't," Fatback said, making eye contact.

"That's good."

"I've wanted to, 'cause sometimes she likes to give me a lotta lip. You know how sometimes women are just beggin' for a whup-pin.'"

"You're diggin' your ditch again. The phone lines are starting to light up."

"Anyway, I've always been strong enough to walk away and wait till my wife comes to her senses."

"A truly strong man doesn't have to hit," I said.

"That's right, even if a woman deserves a good whuppin'."

"Women don't deserve to be hit, period."

"You gotta be careful, too, 'cause some of them women hit back. You could end up with a face full of hot grits like Al Green. Or wake up missing something important like that guy, John Wayne Bobbitt. Or you might just have a woman who'll hit you upside the head with one of them heavy pots. Then your head'll be all wrapped up like a Hindu. Your buddies'll be asking you, man what happened to you, man? You be saying, I slipped and fell."

"I've got several phone lines blinkin' now. The views expressed here are strictly those of the guest. Joan, please screen my calls. I don't want to get into it about domestic violence or Hinduism. I contribute to battered women's shelters and I have a wide range of friends."

At that moment, an intern came into the control room with a message slip. I could see Sarita's name on the top of it. I gathered up my courage before I opened it.

It said, "Phil is home safe!"

I felt so relieved. Thank the Lord! I would get the details later. I put on Fatback's music, but I really felt like playing "Oh Happy Day."

"What do you mean, your ex-wife has shown up?" I asked Skylar over the phone the next night. "Shown up how?" I struggled to keep from shouting.

"Allison was at our doorstep when we got home this evening. She didn't call or anything. We weren't expecting to see her until next month."

"So she just came for a visit," I suggested hopefully.

"Well, not exactly. Allison told Brianna she wants to try to live in Chicago."

"Live in Chicago! Why?" I asked, trying to sound neutral.

"I imagine that she wants to be closer to her daughter. Maybe she's gonna try to be a mother to her again. Maybe Allison will clean up her act and we can even work out joint custody or something. Then I could have more time to spend with you," Skylar added seductively.

I felt touched that I was part of the equation, and softened my tone. "Where does Allison plan to stay?"

"She's staying at a hotel on the lakefront. It's right over here in Hyde Park."

"How long can she afford to stay *there*?"

"I didn't ask her a lot of questions. We don't have a real communicative relationship. I'm not involved in her life. The only thing we have in common at this point is Brianna."

"That's a lot," I said.

"Yeah, it's a whole lot, but that's it."

"How is Brianna taking this?"

"She's always glad to see her mother."

"Well, keep me posted."

After I hung up the phone, I started for the refrigerator, but then turned around. I realized that food would just be a distraction from my apprehension. I took a hot bubble bath instead.

Sitting in the lavender-scented water, I inhaled the vanilla fragrance of my lighted candle and let Skylar's words echo through my mind. "Then I could have more time to spend with you."

A few days later, Skylar and I were sipping Chardonnay at a waterfront restaurant during happy hour. I was beginning to almost appreciate his ex-wife's return, as she was our babysitter this evening. Skylar swore up and down that it was over between him and Allison. She wasn't even sleeping over there. I decided to take him at his word.

"I never told you the details about what happened to my friend Sarita's husband, Phil."

"You told me that he turned up safe and sound."

"Yeah, but I didn't get to tell you what actually happened to him."

"What happened to him? Was he abducted by aliens?"

I gulped my wine. "Almost. He was kidnapped by bounty hunters."

"Bounty hunters!" Skylar exclaimed, wide-eyed.

"Yeah."

"I've read about how they can abuse their powers."

"They arrested Phil coming out of his barber shop. He was taking out the trash in the back. They pretty much ambushed him. They thought he was some other guy, a convict with the same name. Phil kept trying to tell them that they had the wrong person, but they wouldn't listen."

"That's terrible."

"They put him in a van, handcuffed and bound," I said, holding my wrists together.

"Damn!"

"Yeah, and they drove him away. He couldn't even make a phone call to a lawyer or his wife. They kept him prisoner."

"And this is supposed to be the land of the free and the home of the brave." Skylar groaned.

"Yeah, right. Phil says they picked up other people along the way. They barely fed him or let him go to the bathroom."

"How did he get away?"

"They delivered him to their headquarters in Kentucky. He finally convinced them that they had the wrong man."

"How?"

"He didn't look like the picture of the guy they were looking for. And his fingerprints didn't match, so they released him. The bounty hunters told Phil that if he wanted to sue, he could, but no one had won a case so far."

"There should be some recourse for that kind of treatment," Skylar said, shaking his head. "It's ridiculous! Something's gotta be done! Bounty hunters are like the secret police."

"Something *is* gonna be done," I assured him. "I have a few media connections. There's a TV reporter I know, Lupe Hernandez from the six-o'clock news."

"I've seen her. She's sharp."

"She's in my Women in Media group. I've put in a call to her. Lupe's good people. She'll be dead on the case."

"All right!"

"Excuse my French, but this shit is not gonna fly!"

"I hear you, sista!"

"A lot of people have been affected by the bounty hunters' gestapo tactics," I continued. "Phil's family was worried sick. And I was almost a wreck myself."

"I can understand why. Tell Phil if he wants to pursue any legal channels, I'd be happy to work with him, pro bono."

"Thanks, I'll pass that on. Excuse me for a minute. I've got to go to the ladies' room."

"Sure. I better put in a call home. Allison needs to get to her twelve-step meeting, and I need to let her know I'll be back soon."

After exiting the bathroom, I recognized Skylar's back in front of one of the pay phones in the hallway. I wasn't trying to snoop, but I couldn't help overhearing a snatch of his conversation.

"Yeah, I've just finished presenting these briefs to my client. Everything appears to be in order. We're about to wrap up. I'll be home in less than an hour."

I scooted past Skylar and beat him back to our cocktail table. I was somewhat perturbed that he'd lied about his whereabouts to his ex-wife. I mean, they *were* divorced. Skylar didn't have to throw our dating relationship up in Allison's face, but he shouldn't have to hide it, either, unless there were still some embers burning in their relationship that he wasn't copping to. I couldn't help but feel a little suspicious. For all I knew, Skylar could be lying when he said it was over between him and Allison. If that was the case, I'd rather him be honest about it. Skylar obviously wasn't being honest with Allison, so how could I trust that he was being honest with me?

"Everything's fine, Brianna's doing her homework. I told Allison I'd be back in time for her to make her meeting," Skylar reported nonchalantly.

But I was ready for him. "I'm glad that everything is fine," I answered sweetly. "How about if I drop by later, after Brianna has gone to bed, if you're up for some company. Baby, isn't it time that I saw your digs and peeked at your daughter while she's sleeping?"

"Ahh, I'm-I'm not really set up for company," Skylar stammered. "I'd have to straighten up." I'd clearly caught him off guard.

"You didn't straighten up for Allison, did you?" I challenged.

"Well, she's not exactly company," Skylar said, clearing his throat.

"I wouldn't be coming in to do a white glove test. I just thought we could hang out a little. I wouldn't be coming over there to judge."

"I've got to deal with getting Brianna ready for bed," Skylar said, shaking his head.

I kept pushing. "I said I can come over after Brianna goes to sleep."

But Skylar wasn't going to go for it. "It's just not gonna work, Dee Dee. I want things to be right when you come over. I want to have a chance to clean up and set a mood. Tonight's just not the right night. It's too hectic."

"Okay." I sighed. Sherlock Holmes couldn't tell for sure if Skylar was covering something up. I still had to do more detective work. "How about if I give you a call later and we just have a cozy, intimate chat on the phone?" I suggested.

"Sure, let's do that. I'll be waiting to hear from you."

I called Sharon from my car phone to run my concerns about Skylar by her. She told me to come on over to her townhouse.

"I can see why you would feel threatened," Sharon said, sitting across from me on her her plump denim couch. "I mean, they do have a child together. He still has a connection with that woman."

"Did I tell you she was white?" I asked, sinking into the generous chair cushion.

"His ex-wife?"

"Yeah."

"No, you didn't tell me, but I'm not surprised. The Bay Area is the Interracial Dating Capital of America."

"Brianna has green eyes and red hair. She's a light caramel color."

"Is she cute?"

"Yeah, really cute."

"That's good. I hate to say it, but if you're gonna be biracial, you should at least be cute. People expect you to be cute. It's a disappointment if you're not."

"You sound like old-timey folks now. You're bordering on callin' somebody yellow wasted, if they're not cute."

"I don't think like that," Sharon protested. "I just meant it's hard enough being caught between two worlds. You may as well have looks going for you."

I nodded.

"Anyway, so did it bother you when you found out that Skylar's ex-wife is white?"

"Maybe, a little, but not that much. Skylar isn't your typical brotha. He's such an individual. I told you he was mostly raised by a white woman. So I wasn't that surprised. I'm not really tripping on Allison's race. People have a right to date and marrry whomever they choose. What concerns me is, if Allison is trying to get back with Skylar, he might fall for the bait. She's already got one foot in the door now. She doesn't seem to have any solid plans. She's staying at a hotel, but I don't think she has money to burn. Supposedly she's in recovery. She's at a twelve-step meeting as we speak. I just wish I knew what her real agenda was."

"It's impossible for you to know, unless she tips her hand. She might even be confused herself. But, more importantly, you need to know what Skylar's agenda is."

"He claims he's through with her; he's just being cordial for Brianna's sake. Skylar says that he's glad that Allison is showing more interest in their daughter, since he wants them to have a good relationship. He even says that if Allison cleans up her act, he wouldn't object to joint custody. Then he could spend more time with me."

"Look at it this way: If she's in the picture, you've got a regular babysitter. Who knows, one day you and Skylar might even be able to spend a whole weekend together."

"Yeah." I smiled, imagining Skylar and me waking up together in a quaint bed and breakfast in a little antiquey town. "So, how's it going with you and Michelle?" I asked. "How is her son handling your relationship?"

"Thanks for asking. As a matter of fact, we're doing pretty well. The boy has made a one-hundred-and eighty-degree turn!"

"That's great, Sharon."

"Now Ryan constantly wants to know when I'm coming over. It makes you mad when you think about how these heterosexist oppressors have used kids against us. Children have always been used as the hammer to beat us down. It's always been 'the kids can't handle it,'" Sharon said sarcastically. "Kids can handle it just fine. It's the adults that have the problem."

"Yeah, Professor, sho' you right. Kids are very flexible. What kids need most has nothing to do with who you sleep with or how you cross your legs."

"I heard that."

"Now, teenagers are different. They've already been indoctrinated. What's T up to?"

"She's at the computer. She's got a big paper due. She waited till the last minute. Luckily she can get a lot of information off the Internet."

I decided to call Skylar from Sharon's place. It had gotten a little late, and also I might need Sharon for moral support.

"I can't believe it. I dialed the number twice and there's still no answer," I said a few minutes later, staring at the receiver as if it could explain.

Sharon looked up from the pile of clean laundry she was sorting on the couch. "Did you check the number?"

"I know it by heart," I said, "but let me verify it in my book." I reached for my purse. "The number's right. I can't believe Skylar would step out after ten o'clock. It's an hour past Brianna's bedtime. And he knew I was gonna call."

"Maybe he's got the phone unplugged, or something happened and he just can't deal with the phone right now. It doesn't have to be serious; his daughter could just have a tummyache. You know a single parent's work is never done." Sharon continued to fold clothes.

"I'm surprised he's not letting the machine pick up, though."

"Maybe he forgot to turn it on."

"I let it ring a bunch of times."

"Dee Dee, stop trippin'. There's probably a logical explanation."

"They say God sends you a pebble before he sends you a brick."

"Don't get paranoid," Sharon cautioned as she folded a towel. "Now, maybe this is a red flag, and maybe it isn't. Why not have a 'wait and see' attitude?"

"Wait until I see what?" I jumped to my feet. "A red flag as big as that beach towel?" I pointed.

"No, of course not. I just don't want you to act too hastily. I think this relationship might have potential. Maybe Skylar is a good guy," Sharon said, setting the towel atop a stack of folded clothes.

"Well, a part of me has hope and another part of me hears, 'All men lie and only a fool would put her trust in a man' echoing in my memory."

"Well, maybe it's time for you to go beyond that thinking," Sharon suggested. "Maybe it's time for you to learn that it is possible to find a man that you *can* trust."

I looked at Sharon incredulously. "Easy for you to say, now that you don't deal with them." I folded my arms. "You know, I really resent the fact that now that you've become a lesbian, you wanna always give men the benefit of the doubt."

"How ironic." Sharon laughed, placing her hands on her hips. "Well, at least you're not calling me a man-hater. I have to give you points for originality."

"I don't know why I ever got my hopes up about Skylar in the first place," I said, throwing my hands up in the air and beginning to pace. "Let's get real. What are the chances of an overweight, over forty, black woman meeting Mr. Right? Come on," I challenged Sharon, "what are the chances? Statistics say I have a better chance of being struck by lightning," I said, pounding my chest.

Sharon shrugged. "So you're slightly overweight, and so you're slightly over forty," she said, squaring off with me. "Dee Dee, you're an attractive, dynamic, intelligent, warm, caring, witty woman, and anyone would be lucky to get you. Now, that's the real deal."

"You really mean that? You're not just saying that 'cause you're trying to hit on me?" I asked, half teasingly.

Sharon rolled her eyes. "Just take it in. Dee Dee, don't try to diminish yourself by insinuating that I have an ulterior motive. Everything I said is true, just accept it."

"Sharon, I never thought I would say this, but I'm glad you're who you are."

"Come again?" Sharon had a puzzled look.

"I mean, some straight sistas are so competitive with each

other. When they give another woman a compliment, it's a gift. The praise doesn't flow out like water. But you can say I'm all that and it doesn't take anything away from you."

"Why should it?" Sharon hunched her shoulders. "Your being all that, doesn't keep me from being all that, too. Why can't we all be all that and a bag of chips?"

"When you first came out to me as a lesbian, I thought I'd lost something," I said, feeling a catch in my throat. "But now I realize that I gained something."

"We both did," Sharon said, giving me a hug.

"Lemme try the number again."

"Yeah, maybe Skylar was just taking a long shower and didn't hear the phone ring."

But there was still no answer. "Still in the shower," I quipped. I paused. "I hope his ex-wife left. If not, anything could be going on."

"Yeah, they could be making love. They could be making war. They could be making popcorn. We don't know," Sharon said.

I pictured Skylar arguing with an imaginary strawberry blonde and then I pictured them having sex together. I much preferred the former image.

"I just want to know the truth," I said firmly. "I'm not in too deep at this point to walk."

"That's good," Sharon said. "That sounds healthy."

"It would be painful, but I'd rather know the truth."

"You wanna check your voice mail? Maybe he left you a message."

"Yeah, good idea." I called in to hear my messages.

"Nothing," I reported, hanging up the phone.

"Are you gonna try calling Skylar from your car phone?"

"No, because I don't want to act obsessed."

When I got home, I did have a message from Skylar. It was ten minutes old. He'd been waiting to hear from me, he said, but he was going to go ahead and turn in now. "Not yet, you aren't," I said aloud. "You got some 'splaining to do."

Skylar's voice sounded calm on my voice mail. Obviously, no calamity had occurred. It was like he'd been expecting to hear from me, but for some reason I just hadn't called and therefore he was just going to go to bed.

My heart was pounding when I dialed his number. I wasn't sure if he would answer, but he did.

"Hi, Dee Dee, I thought I would've heard from you earlier," Skylar said, sounding puzzled.

"I called your number a few times." I was ashamed to admit that I'd dialed four times and let the phone ring almost a total of forty times.

"What do you mean? The phone hasn't rung all night."

"Are you sure it was plugged in?" I asked, trying to speak in an even tone.

"Yeah, I'm sure."

"Maybe you were using it. Do you have call waiting?"

"No, I don't. And I haven't used the phone at all tonight. I've been sitting right next to it all evening while working on a legal brief."

When I heard the words legal brief, I saw red. "Skylar, is that the same legal brief you told Allison that you presented to a client while we were having dinner?"

"What do you mean?" Skylar stammered.

I mean you're stone cold busted, I thought. "I just happened to overhear your phone conversation," I said. "I heard you lie."

Skylar sighed into the phone. I felt nervous, but I'd rather get down to the real nitty-gritty than to pretend.

"Dee Dee, I told Allison that just to keep the peace. I really don't want her in my business. And the more I say to her, the more I *have* to say to her. You don't understand. Technically, I have joint custody. Allison could run with Brianna at any time. I can't afford to rock the boat. That's why I'm walking on eggshells with her."

"You were right next to the phone and you never heard it ring tonight?"

"Not once."

"By the way, where's Allison now?"

"Allison?"

"Yeah, Allison, your ex-wife, remember?"

"What's Allison have to do with anything?"

"Where is she? Did she go to her meeting?"

"As a matter of fact, she got the days mixed up. That meeting is a different night."

"Oh, those things happen. Well, did she leave?"

"The phone didn't ring, Dee Dee, okay?"

"Where is Allison now?"

"She's sleeping on the couch, if you must know."

"I thought she had a hotel room."

"She checked out this afternoon."

"Is she going back to Indianapolis tommorrow?"

"I told you, she said she was going to try to get established here in Chicago."

"Look, Skylar, I wasn't born on April First. If you want to get back with your ex-wife, just say so. That is, if she *is* your *ex*-wife."

"She is definitely my ex-wife," Skylar snapped. "The only reason she's here is because of Brianna. Allison and I are cordial at best."

"When was your cordial divorce final?"

"At the end of May. Do you wanna see a copy of my divorce paper? I will be glad to fax it to you tomorrow or mail you a hard copy."

"Mail me a hard copy."

"Okay, no problem."

"I still have a problem. In fact, *we* still have a problem. I need to know how long Allison is going to stay there. I need to know what your agenda is. I just want you to be straight with me. I do not have time to play games."

"I'm not playing games with you. I *am* being straight with you. I just couldn't put Allison out in the street tonight. She *is* my daughter's mother. But she knows that she'll have to make other arrangements pretty soon."

"Is pretty soon a day or a month?"

"In one way, it doesn't really matter, because there's nothing going on between us."

"It matters to me."

"Allison will not be here a month, believe me, or even a week. I want her to leave as soon as possible."

"Skylar, I wanna believe you, but I have to protect myself. I'll be honest with you. If I find out you're lying to me, I swear to you I'll walk."

"Dee Dee, don't you threaten me. I don't need this shit. Stop jammin' me. I told you that the only thing between me and that woman is the little angel sleeping in the next room. So, please, don't threaten me."

"Skylar, it wasn't a threat. It was a promise."

twenty

Halloween had come and gone and Thanksgiving was fast approaching. They were already playing Christmas music in one of the department stores. I was in love, and therefore happy to be in the holiday spirit. Skylar had recently sent me a dozen red roses and a copy of his divorce paper.

However, all was not bliss. Skylar's ex-wife was wreaking havoc on our lives. She'd been sleeping on his couch for almost a week now. Allison had promised to be out by this coming Saturday, and I was counting the days. The only silver lining was that she was our babysitter and we were therefore able to wake up on this cold, overcast Sunday morning in each others' arms. We had shared a night of exquisite lovemaking. The afterglow had really been the bomb for me. It was one of those times when you're just in awe and you want to utter, "So this is what life is all about." But instead you have sense enough to just let your mouth hang open.

"I didn't want to tell you what she did, yesterday. I didn't want to spoil our evening," Skylar said, nuzzling my neck.

I automatically knew who "she" was. I gave Skylar a concerned look. I wanted him to feel comfortable sharing his problems with me. I wanted to be supportive. "What did Allison do now?" I sighed. I was tempted to use the word "bitch," but I restrained myself.

"It was really emotional abuse," Skylar said, sitting up and jamming the pillow behind his head.

"What happened?"

"*I* can handle her foolishness, but what really got my goat is that she dragged Brianna into it."

"Tell me about it."

Skylar sighed and gave me a pained look. "Allison told Brianna some private things about our relationship, very private."

"Like what?"

"She told Brianna that I talked her into having an abortion a few years ago. That was totally inappropriate."

I gulped. Abortion was still a painful topic for me. I had never completely forgiven myself for having one. Yet I steadfastly believed in a woman's right to choose. "It was definitely inappropriate for Allison to tell Brianna about the abortion," I agreed. "Even if you did pressure her to have one."

"I didn't pressure her," Skylar said defensively. "I just gave her my opinion."

"Regardless, she shouldn't have told Brianna," I said, gently stroking Skylar's face. "Baby, I'm not judging you. I'm agreeing with you. What Allison did was horrible."

"We weren't getting along at the time," Skylar said with a faraway look in his eyes. "Brianna had just started school. I didn't think that we were equipped to begin all over again with another child. But I didn't force Allison to have an abortion." He frowned, creating deep creases in his forehead.

"It's not like I even threatened to leave or anything."

"It's an agonizing decision to have to make, especially for a woman," I mumbled. "I've never really forgiven myself for having an abortion, even though I felt it was the best decison for me at that time."

Skylar sighed. "Don't beat yourself up. I'm sure you did what you thought was best under the circumstances. If men had to go through what women have to go through as a result of sex, this would be a different world."

"Yeah, there would be a lot less sex and a lot fewer people."

"When it comes to their bodies, women definitely have a harder row to hoe," Skylar said. He held me closely and I felt snug inside his embrace.

"How did Brianna react to hearing about all this?"

"She was upset." Skylar shook his head. "She cried herself to sleep. She asked me why I made Mommy kill her little sister."

"That's heavy."

"Yeah, tell me about it," he said in a beleaguered tone. "I really gave Allison a piece of my mind."

"What did she say?"

"She claims it just came out." Skylar rolled his eyes. "And she needed to let Brianna know that she loved her and that she wasn't always the bad guy and that she'd been in a lot of emotional pain during our marriage."

"It was still inappropriate."

"Thank you," Skylar said, wrapping the sheet around himself. "I hate even leaving Brianna with her. But I don't think she'll do any further damage."

"Let's hope not. Can you give me some of the sheet?"

"Sure. I wanted to be with you so much. I've missed everything about you."

I pressed my softness against Skylar's hardness in the manner we'd become accustomed to.

Sharon called me the following evening and informed me that she'd overheard Tyeesha planning with her friend to strip at a club. I felt a little guilty because I'd failed to warn Sharon that T had mentioned stripping to me. But I'd been under the illusion that I'd talked T out of it. I was royally pissed at her for not following my advice. I didn't appreciate flapping my lips for nothing.

Sharon said that she had half a mind to let Tyeesha go on with her plan, and half a mind to beat the shit outta her. I thought that two heads might be better than one, and said, "I'm on my way over."

I expected to hear shouting as I neared Sharon's door, but it was almost eerily quiet. Maybe I was already too late to prevent a murder-suicide, I joked to myself. Sharon answered the door wearing the long face of a mother of a rebellious teenager. At least one of them was still alive, I thought.

"Where's T?" was the first thing that came outta my mouth.

"I decided to let her live at least until you got here. Come in and sit down."

I plopped down in a comfortable chair. "Is she up in her room?"

Sharon nodded and began to pace. "Dee Dee, I feel like telling her, go on out there and make your bed hard if you want to. You're the one who's gonna have to lie in it."

"Yeah, but she's underage. The law still holds you responsible for her. You better try and communicate."

"You try communicating with a fifteen-year-old if you're her mother."

"You know, I've tried to steer her the right way," I said, without admitting that I knew anything about this.

"I appreciate what all you've done. But let's get down to brass tacks. I can absolutely forbid Tyeesha to strip, but, let's face it, she might do it behind my back anyway."

My eyes followed Sharon as she continued to pace with her arms folded. "You could contact the strip club and threaten their license."

"There's no guarantee that Tyeesha wouldn't go to some other club. She claims her friend's getting them fake IDs."

"We could both try to talk some sense into T," I suggested.

"Have you ever tried talking some sense into that girl?"

"Yeah, and sometimes it's worked." Just not in this case, I thought.

"We've both talked up a blue streak to Tyeesha aka Taurus the Bull lately," Sharon said wearily. "And, to be honest with you, Dee Dee, I'm tired of her *bull* shit. Tyeesha's pulling this mess to get back at me for being with a woman. That's what's at the root of everything she's pulled lately."

"Maybe so. Maybe Tyeesha's trying to prove that she's not a lesbian. But you have to understand, she's at an insecure age. Her own sexual identity is still somewhat fluid. I can understand why she would feel threatened."

"Is it my fault that we live in a homophobic society?" Sharon asked defensively. "Am I supposed to be the scapegoat because of it?"

"No, I'm just saying that because we *do* live in a homophobic society, you should cut T a little slack. You should be able to understand why she's not jumping for joy because her mother's a lesbian."

"Now she's saying that she wants to go live with her father."

"That's just talk. T's just saying that to upset you. She knows she can't rely on her daddy."

"Well, in all fairness, he always paid child support, even if it wasn't always exactly on time. And he's never missed her birthday or Christmas."

"Yeah, but you're the one who's been there, twenty-four-seven, three hundred sixty-five days a year. There's no comparison."

"That's true," Sharon agreed, slouching down in the other plump chair. "But now that T's older, I have half a mind to let her go to New York and live with her daddy, if he'll take her. Let him share some of the load. And it might be good for T. Sometimes you don't realize what you have until you get away from it."

"Yeah, but Tyeesha still needs the protectiveness that only you can give her as a mother. You really don't know what kind of father Victor would be at this point."

"That's true, but a part of me would like to teach T a lesson by lettting her find out."

"I think I hear her coming down the stairs."

Tyeesha walked into the living room with her mouth poked out. "I don't appreciate you all talking about me behind my back."

"Good, now I can say it to your face," Sharon said, rising and squaring off with her daughter. "Tyeesha, I am sick of your bullshit! Excuse my choice of words, but I can't think of a better way to put it."

"Well, I'm sick of yours, too."

"What are you sick of, T?" Sharon demanded with her hands on her hips. "Let's go on and get real! What are you *really* sick of?"

"Your bullshit."

"What is my bullshit? And don't you use that language with me. I'm still your mother."

"You used that language with *me*," T protested, folding her arms.

"The girl has a point."

"Dee Dee, nobody asked you. This is all about my being with a woman, isn't it, Tyeesha?" T glared back in silence. "But you know what, T, I'm not going to grovel for your approval. I'm not going to even go there. I have paid my dues. I carried you for nine months. I went through a long hard labor and that was just the beginning. I've been there for you when you were sick. I put food in your mouth and clothes on your back. I have sacrificed to keep you in good schools. I've put your needs ahead of my own. You haven't wanted for anything."

"Nobody asked you to do all that. You could've gotten an abortion or put me up for adoption."

"But I didn't!" Sharon shouted. I admired her restraint. I'd known parents to slap a child for saying less. "I married your damn father, who I wasn't really all that in love with, if you really wanna know the damn truth, just so I could give the baby I was carrying a daddy."

"Well, it didn't work out anyway."

"I'm sure you blame that on me, too. Well, let me refresh your memory. I never walked out on your father. He walked out on me."

"You mean *us*."

"He didn't leave you, he left me."

"Either way, I was still *left* without a father. All the time I've been growing up, I've wished Daddy would come back or you'd get me a new father," Tyeesha confided. "Now that you're a lesbian, I'll never have a chance to grow up with a father. I've run out of time. At least before you came out, I had a shot at having a father. Now I don't even have hope."

I noticed Sharon's face soften. "I'm sorry that I dashed your hopes. In fact, I didn't even know what your hopes were. I was willing to try and make the marriage work, for your sake. But Victor's the one who said that because you were a girl, you'd be okay without a father. You didn't have to have a male role model."

"Well, I'm gonna tell my dad, that's whack. There were times I could've really used a dad," Tyeesha added softly.

"T, did you figure that you might as well hurry and grow up now and get it over with, since your hopes were never gonna be realized?" I asked gently. "So that you could put your disappointment behind you?"

"Yeah, I s'pose," T nodded. She slumped down onto the couch, as if the wind had been taken out of her sails.

"I know the feeling," Sharon said quietly.

"You know *what* feeling?" T asked.

"I know what it feels like to rush through the motions of a marriage, without really feeling what you're doing. I guess I'm what they call a late bloomer."

"Mom, it's not that I don't want you to be happy," Tyeesha said with a hint of compassion in her voice. "It's just that it's been hecka hard with us both blooming at the same time."

"I'm sorry it's been hard for you," Sharon said, her voice choked with emotion. "I never wanted to cause you pain. Tyeesha, you will always be my heart."

T sighed. "I don't wanna strip anymore," she mumbled.

"I know I should quit while I'm ahead," Sharon said, cautiously. "But I'll ask anyway. Why not?"

"Because it doesn't really make sense to me anymore."

"How come?" I pushed.

"I guess because it's too superficial. And, even though in a way I hate to admit it, I am a pretty deep person. I mean I have a superficial side. But let's face it, I've got it going on in the brain department."

Sharon and I nodded and smiled.

"It just seems to me that it's smarter to keep my clothes on at this point," T continued. "Even when I had sex with Malik, looking back, I don't feel that it was really that meaningful. So, why would taking my clothes off in front of a bunch of horny strangers amount to anything?"

"That's my heart talking," Sharon said proudly through her tears.

The next week, I arrived early enough to my belly dance class to stake out a central spot on the dance floor. I carefully laid out my veil and brass finger cymbals before checking my stance in the wall mirror. I practiced rotating my hips and shoulders in a figure eight while the other students drifted in.

"We have a new student," Jade announced from the back as I made snake arms. "This is Tyeesha."

I spun around in disbelief. It was T! She was wearing a black leotard with a shiny purple sarong tied around her waist. She flashed me a big grin.

"Dee Dee already knows Tyeesha quite well." Jade winked.

"Yeah, I most certainly do."

"Is she your daughter?" a petite young woman asked.

"She's my goddaughter."

"How nice." An older woman smiled.

"Mom and I wanted to surprise you." T beamed. "She dropped me off and gave me the money to take the class."

"Well, you really did surprise me. I had no idea, whatsoever."

"Well, welcome to the world of belly," the older woman proclaimed. "It's encouraging to see a young person take an interest in such an ancient dance form."

"I think you'll like belly dancing," a large, pleasant woman joined in. "Even if you never perform, it's a good workout. It's called the ultimate in feminine fitness."

"I definitely plan to perform," Tyeesha announced, placing a hand on her hip and walking toward me. "I'm not like Dee Dee. I'm gonna strut my stuff."

"Class, let's face the front mirrors and get grounded," Jade instructed. "I'm going to say this especially for the benefit of our new student, but also as a reminder to everyone. We all need to be mindful that belly dancers are not posers. The belly dancer's body is simply a vehicle for her spiritual expression. We don't strut our stuff so much as we reveal our souls. Like I often say, you can make the same movements in a temple as in a strip joint. It's a dancer's intentions that make all the difference."

I caught T's eye and winked.

There was something indeed touching about Tyeesha's first awkward attempts to rotate her weight from foot to foot and isolate the large muscles of her hips. She reminded me of myself when I was new. I cringed a bit when I heard T struggling to play a smooth left, right, left pattern with her finger cymbals. It brought back memories. I half expected T to burst into tears after getting swallowed by her veil a few times. I remembered my early frustration, trying to toreador my own. I felt proud that T's undulations appeared natural and fluid on her first try. And the girl could shimmy almost as good as her godmother.

I was spending Thanksgiving with Sharon. I knew that Sarita always had my name in the pot, but I felt like I owed it to Sharon to spend this Thanksgiving with her. I would've spent the holiday with Skylar, but he hemmed and hawed. He finally said spending Thanksgiving with me might be too much, too soon for Brianna. Allison had gotten a room at a Hyde Park bed and breakfast. I called my sister and brother and wished them and their families a Happy Thanksgiving. I'd see them all at Christmas at my brother's.

Sharon's girlfriend Michelle and her son Ryan and Aunt Ivy also had places at the table. Michelle and Ryan planned to call it an early night because they were attending a late dinner in nearby Evanston with her parents. I was glad that Michelle was leaving early and dropping Sharon's aunt off on her way. I would be able to hang out with my best friend without feeling like I was intruding.

Thanksgiving dinner with lesbians was no big deal for me, of course. I was worldly. However, I knew it was somewhat of a step for Aunt Ivy. But she'd invited herself, and she knew the deal.

Sharon thought that it would be good for me to be there to provide balance, anyway. I promised to do my heterosexual best.

Tyeesha was spending Thanksgiving with her father and his family in New York for her yearly visit. T was particularly close to her grandmother and a couple of her cousins.

Michelle was an attractive, fortyish, brown-skinned woman with a stylishly cut perm. She was full-figured in a womanly way. Michelle struck me as warm, and I liked her from the get-go. She immediately gave me a look that said, "I hope we hit it off." I didn't interpret it as needy. I felt flattered. I thought it was an acknowledgment that Michelle and I both cared a lot about Sharon, and it would be nice if we liked each other.

Michelle's outgoing son looked like she'd spit him out. They definitely favored each other, except his body type was more slender. Ryan sported a recent haircut, a missing front tooth, big brown eyes and a devilish smile.

He stood in the center of the room and held court. Sharon was in the kitchen, and the rest of us adults were sitting on the denim living room furniture. Ryan excitedly showed us a couple of bullet casings he'd gotten from a friend who found them near a shooting range.

Michelle fussed, "Can you believe he traded his ski cap for them?"

"Uhmp," Aunt Ivy, said, shaking her head disapprovingly and folding her arms against her tailored dark suit. "As cold as it's been lately."

"I know you were fit to be tied," I said.

"You got that right," Michelle replied.

"He's lucky. Some mothers would've torn his tail up," Aunt Ivy said, raising her eyebrows.

Ryan shot his mother a worried look.

"He's getting that cap back after the holidays, or else it's coming out of his allowance."

"Boy, you better be thankful that your mama didn't say, 'Or else it's coming outta his behind,'" Aunt Ivy said, sternly.

Ryan blew through the bullet casing again. The piercing sound was about to get on my next to last nerve when his mother told him to stop.

"I never even let Ryan play with guns," Michelle said. "But I've discovered that he can make a gun out of anything—an umbrella, a banana, you name it. I took him to see the *Nutcracker* last year and I asked him which he liked most, the beautiful music, or scenery, or costumes or dancing."

"What did he say?" I asked.

"Tell them what you said, son."

Ryan smiled, as if he'd been called on to answer this question before. "I said, the part when they shot the gun," he said, slapping his hand against his chest dramatically and crumpling to the floor.

"I didn't even remember them shooting a gun in the *Nutcracker*," Michelle acknowledged. "But I guess boys will be boys, as they say." She drew her son close to her and affectionately ruffled his hair.

"Well, at least he's *all boy*," Ivy declared. "You don't have to worry about him being a sissy."

There was a minute of awkward silence. Then Michelle said she'd better go help Sharon with the turkey.

I couldn't think of anything diplomatic to say, so I asked Ryan to let me hold the bullet casings. At least it prevented him from blowing through them again.

Sharon and Michelle returned with drinks and appetizers.

"Here," Sharon said, handing Ryan a glass of juice. "Don't spill anything, boy, or you'll have to answer to Triple V," she teased.

"Triple V stands for Triple Virgo," Ryan explained.

"I know what Virgo is, but I don't know what triple Virgo is," Ivy confessed.

"It means that her sun, moon and rising sign are all in Virgo," I said.

"Yeah," Sharon added. "You can't leave a crumb around with Michelle. Virgos think it's their job to tidy up the world."

"The world needs more of us." Michelle pouted.

"Is Triple Virgo the highest?" Ryan asked.

"That's cute." I smiled. "He's thinks it's like a deck of cards."

"Yes, son, triple Virgo is the highest." Michelle smiled.

"No, it isn't," Sharon countered. "Capricorn is the highest, because we climb to the highest point."

"I'm a Capricorn, so I'm number one, too!" Ryan announced proudly. "Right, funky goat?"

"Right, funky goat! " Sharon said, clinking his glass.

"It's nice that they've bonded." I smiled.

Ivy asked, raising an eyebrow, "You let him call you a funky goat?"

"Yeah," Sharon answered nonchalantly. "One day we were at a restaurant and 'Midnight Train to Georgia' came on. Ryan and I started using the utensils for microphones."

"I hope it wasn't a nice restaurant," Ivy said.

"Oh, Aunt Ivy, it wasn't the Ritz."

"They thought they were the Pips." Michelle smiled.

"Michelle even joined in with us."

"It was contagious," Michelle said. "Besides, I was the only one who could really sing."

"You were no Gladys Knight."

"And you all were no Pips."

"Sharon doesn't have a bad singing voice," Aunt Ivy countered. "She soloed once in the junior choir."

"Anyway," Sharon said hastily, as if in an effort to keep the peace, "Ryan said that we needed to have a name, and Michelle named us Triple Virgo and the Funky Goats. Ryan and I are both Capricorns."

"He could get out in public and call you a funky goat." Aunt Ivy sniffed like she was smelling something bad. "People will think he's trying to say that you stink."

I gulped my wine. I just wanted everthing to be pleasant.

Michelle cleared her throat. "I called them funky goats because they were soulful, not because they stank," she said sheepishly.

"You just got finished saying they couldn't sing," Aunt Ivy reminded her.

"You can be soulful without being able to sing," I suggested diplomatically.

"Not if you can't carry a tune," Aunt Ivy argued.

"Remember, Michelle, that night after Ryan took a bath, he came running out the bathroom shouting, 'Now I'm a clean goat!'" Sharon said, inadvertently adding fuel to the fire.

"See, he thought you meant they were funky, too," Aunt Ivy said, facing Michelle. "That proves my point."

Sharon shot Michelle a look that said, "I didn't mean to dig you deeper into the hole."

"I really just meant *soulful*," Michelle pleaded.

Just then, the telephone rang, and I almost said, "Saved by the bell." I was surprised when Sharon returned to the living room and handed me the cordless phone.

"Hello," I said, hoping it was my man.

It was.

"Happy Thanksgiving," Skylar answered.

"Happy Thanksgiving to you," I murmured. "I'll take it upstairs," I said over my shoulder.

"Go in T's room, if you the want the most privacy."

"It's so nice to hear your voice," I said, pushing T's half open door.

I decided that I didn't want to be surrounded by clutter and the aroma of old banana peels, so I went into Sharon's room instead.

"Well, Allison has gone and had surgery," Skylar informed me.

"Gone and had surgery?" I asked, cradling the phone. "How do you *go* and have surgery?"

"She's still dealing with the aftermath of the car accident. She had the pins taken out of her ankle."

"On Thanksgiving?"

"It was actually yesterday. I just found out today. The hospital wants to release her, but somebody has to pick her up."

"Where does she plan to stay?"

"That's just it. She plans to go back to Indianapolis tomorrow. She just wants to stay here tonight. Her mother's boyfriend says he'll come and get her."

I felt myself getting tense. I'd been patient, but now I was through being patient. I was afraid that once Allison got holed up in Skylar's apartment, he would never be able to get her out. "Why is it that I'm starting to feel like a guest on the Jerry Springer show?" I said.

"What to you mean?"

"You say it's over between you and Allison, right?"

"It is."

"So, let it be over."

"She only wants to stay here one night."

"That's what she says now. Once she gets her foot in the door, no pun intended, you can't just put her out in the street, especially in her condition."

"I told you, her mother's boyfriend will come and get her tomorrow. He's pretty dependable, when he's sober."

I sighed. I didn't have time for any bullshit. I chose not to go into social work for a reason. "Skylar, you're setting yourself up."

"How?" he asked innocently.

"Why would Allison's mother's boyfriend run here to get her, especially during the holidays? He might take his own sweet time. She's not an asset, she's a liability. They were probably glad to unload her."

"They know she can't stay here indefinitely."

"Why not? She's with her family. Brianna is her own flesh and blood. The woman is almost forty years old. She's not a child, she's already been raised. They probably figure the two of you will get back together. Why would they break their necks to interfere with that?"

"I just hate to turn my back on Allison in this condition. She *is* my daughter's mother."

"Why is it your responsibility? Why not let the hospital take responsibility? And why can't her mother's boyfriend come here today? The roads are not closed."

"It *is* Thanksgiving."

"Tomorrow, it will be something else," I predicted. "It will be raining or snowing, or the car will break down, or he'll be sick or have to work. They could make excuses from now until Easter. You are just enabling Allison," I charged. "Once they release her to you, she'll be your responsibility, period."

"No, she won't," Skylar replied weakly.

"Just mark my words," I said, firmly. "Allison must have known she was having surgery when she came back to Chicago. How was she going to get established, knowing that she had to recover from that?"

"You do have a point."

"You damn straight, I have a point."

"Dee Dee, I just need to meditate on this," Skylar pleaded, wearily.

"Well, go ahead and meditate. You have to do what you think is right for you.

"But I've given you my opinion. And it's only fair for me to inform you that your actions will have consequences."

"I can understand that."

"If you open your door to Allison tonight, and she's not out of there tomorrow, then I will have to meditate on what's right for me."

I walked through Sharon's bedroom into the master bathroom, still carrying the portable phone. After freshening up in the mirror, I noticed a lavender-colored statue of a goddess on the vanity. I picked it up and rubbed my fingers across its smooth surface. I thought it was odd for a statue to be made out of a rubbery substance. I heard voices coming toward me. It was Sharon and Michelle.

"I can't believe we're actually alone. I've wanted to kiss you so badly."

"Me too, oh me too," Sharon moaned.

I was about to reveal myself before they went too far when I realized that the statue I was fondling was actually a dildo. I froze. Feeling awkward, I was debating whether to wash my hands, or the figurine or both, when I heard the bedroom door shut. I felt trapped. There was no way that I could make a graceful exit at this point. What if Sharon remembered that she'd left the dildo out and felt embarrassed that I'd seen it? Michelle and I didn't know each other *that* well.

I glanced through the slit in the partially open bathroom door. Sharon and Michelle were kissing all over each other's faces and necks. I quietly set the dildo back on the vanity to wait it out.

"I fantasized about spreading mashed potatoes and gravy all over your breasts and then nibbling those giblets," Sharon said playfully.

"Oh, you are sooo hot!" Michelle exclaimed.

"Then I would take that whipped cream you brought for the sweet potato pie and squirt it between your thighs and lick it off. Mmm, mmm." Sharon stuck her tongue way out and continued to make exaggerated sounds.

"You're really turning me on!" Michelle cooed. "Baby, I'm on fire!"

I was beginning to feel a little warm in the peanut gallery myself.

"Can you believe how naughty we're being right now?" Michelle giggled. "Our guests have no idea what we're up to. That makes it an even bigger turn-on. I wonder what Miss Manners would say."

"You think we have time for a quickie?" Sharon asked mischievously, thrusting her pelvis playfully against Michelle's and cupping her backside.

I almost flushed the toilet in protest.

"The lavender goddess is in the bathroom," Sharon added seductively.

I cringed.

"I much prefer the goddess that's in my arms," Michelle said, to my relief. She planted little kisses on Sharon's puckered lips. "Too bad I have to go to my parents' place tonight," she lamented. "At least you get to visit with Dee Dee. I like her, she seems nice."

I couldn't help but smile.

"Dee Dee is a great friend, but you know I'd much rather be with you."

I couldn't help but frown.

"Baby, we'll get together soon," Michelle murmured.

"Yeah, we'd better get back downstairs. It can only take so long to find some pictures. Thank goodness Aunt Ivy and Dee Dee are both long-winded."

I bit my tongue to keep from defending myself.

"Aunt Ivy is probably still telling Ryan one of her stories."

"Yeah, but Dee Dee might be off the phone soon."

"She might've gone back downstairs, but I think she's still in Tyeesha's room."

"Okay, one more long, juicy, uhm, uhmm, uhmm, kiss."

"Sharon, you awaken feelings in me that I never knew I had."

"Ditto."

"I'll never look at mashed potatoes and gravy the same way again. Not to mention whipped cream," Michelle added breathlessly.

My undies were slightly in a bunch when I left the room after Sharon and Michelle departed. And it was really hard for me to keep a straight face when Sharon ladled the gravy over Michelle's mashed potatoes at the dinner table with a wink.

Sharon and I rinsed the last of the dishes and packed them into the dishwasher. Everyone else had said their good-byes. Aunt Ivy had survived her first Thanksgiving with lesbians, and so had I.

I waddled into the living room and stretched out across a chair, feeling as stuffed as the furniture. Sharon and I continued our kitchen conversation about Skylar.

"Girl, people do what they wanna do. You can't change Skylar or anybody else. And if he's co-dependent, you sure as hell can't rescue him. Rescue animals, not people."

"I'm not trying to rescue Skylar. I just hate ambiguity, that's all. I hate not knowing the real deal."

Sharon raised her eyebrows. "Maybe you know it, but you just don't want to see it."

"Everything is not black and white, Sharon. The envelope keeps being pushed, the line keeps moving. First, Allison was gonna stay in a hotel, then one night at Skylar's place turned into almost two weeks. Skylar finally put his foot down. I thought it was settled, but now she's trying to weasel her way back in. And of course, now Allison's needier than ever and only Skylar can save her," I said in a mocking tone.

"You don't need this mess, do you?"

"Of course not. I'm not a drama queen. But I love Skylar, and my heart tells me to just hang tough."

"What does your head tell you?"

I paused and closed my eyes. "That Skylar is a decent guy, he's just been presented with a curveball. I really want to believe him when he says it's over between them. I really do." I bit my bottom lip. "I don't want to go through my whole life not ever trusting a man," I said plaintively.

Sharon gave me a sympathetic look. "I can understand that, but I just hope that he's worthy of your trust. I just hope you're not ignoring the red flags."

"I'm not ignoring them. I'm monitoring them," I insisted. "Hey, I thought you were in Skylar's corner."

"Dee Dee, I'm in *your* corner. I only know Skylar through you. And, based on what I've heard, I'm still willing to give him the benefit of the doubt."

"By the way, I like Michelle."

Sharon smiled. "I thought you two would hit it off. She likes you, too. Dee Dee, she's really been good for me. And Ryan and I have really gotten tight."

"I'm glad."

"He's like the son I never had. I always wanted a boy and a girl."

"Yeah, me, too. But it just might not have been meant to be for me."

"You do have Langston," Sharon reminded me.

"Yeah." I shrugged. "Well, I better get home and feed my boy."

"Girl, take some of this food home with you," Sharon said as the phone rang.

I fixed a plate, while Sharon chatted with Tyeesha.

"T's having a ball," she reported after settting down the cordless phone. "She says she's stuffed. She told me to tell you hi, and she'll see you at belly dance class." Sharon smiled.

"I'm glad she's having a good time."

"Chile, she says her grandma and aunts really cooked up a storm. T said her daddy's been parked in front of the TV watching football most of the time. But T says they're getting along fine."

"You think T will tell Victor about your being a lesbian?" I almost whispered for no reason.

"No. But the truth be told, once back in the seventies, Victor and I got high on some weed and he suggested that we do a three-some with another woman," Sharon divulged. "He even brought your name up."

"No, he didn't!" I protested. "Girl, you need to quit."

"Yes, he did, too. If I'm lying, I'm flying."

"Victor was wasting his breath," I said.

"*I* was the one who wasn't interested." Sharon giggled. "Victor was ready."

"It sounds like he can't protest too much if T does tell him about you, then."

Sharon shook her head. "Girl, Victor doesn't have a leg to stand on."

We hugged good-bye and I thanked Sharon for a great dinner. I reminded myself that I had a lot to be thankful for, even though in the back of my mind I was worried about Skylar and Allison.

When I walked in the door, the phone was ringing and Langston was meowing. It was Skylar on the phone. I threw Langston a piece of turkey to shut him up.

"I told Allison she couldn't stay with us," Skylar said firmly, after we exchanged greetings.

"How did she take it?" I asked, feeling relieved.

"It didn't go over too well. Allison kept insisting that it would be for only one night. I told her that I was sorry, but I just couldn't take her at her word. She'd broken too many promises before. The hospital people even got involved. A nurse asked me if there was any way possible that Allison could stay here just for tonight. I felt like Scrooge."

"What's she going to do now?" I asked, balancing the phone in one hand and feeding Langston another pinch of turkey with the other.

"I didn't know that you were concerned for her."

"I have compassion for anybody in her situation," I replied, fingering my cat's head. "I don't want to see Allison on the street. I just don't want to see her move in with you."

"Well, as it turns out, Allison's not going to be on the street."

"That's good," I said, carrying the phone into the living room area and settling into the recliner.

"She's staying here with me and Brianna."

"I thought you just said that you told Allison that she couldn't stay there!" I shouted.

"You didn't let me finish. Like I said, the hospital people got involved and I felt like Scrooge. The nurse asked how could I not take my daughter's mother in under these circumstances?"

I felt my body stiffen. "I don't believe that the hospital would've put Allison out in the cold," I said tersely.

"You don't know that," Skylar insisted. "Hospitals can be pretty cold these days."

"What about a hotel? It might've been cheaper in the long run to cough up some money."

"Allison was afraid to be alone. The woman just had surgery. Her foot's in a cast."

"Okay, so her mother's boyfriend is coming to get her tomorrow, right?"

"I'm gonna be honest with you, Dee Dee."

"Please do."

"I can't say one hundred percent when Allison's mother's boyfriend is going to get here. He might come tomorrow and he might come in a week. Let's be realistic—you know how people are."

"Yes, my reasoning exactly. I already told you that," I reminded Skylar. "I just don't feel comfortable with this situation, Skylar. I really don't."

"I'm not crazy about it, either. But I was between a rock and a hard place. Brianna wants her mother here and I do have compassion for Allison. She's not a bad person. And, anybody can be in need. You *need* to trust me. It's over between me and Allison, period."

"It's not that I don't trust you, Skylar. It's that I don't trust the situation."

"Well, you need to have faith in me."

"Stop telling me what I need to do," I snapped. "I feel like I need to back out now, because otherwise I could really get hurt. If I don't protect myself, no one else will."

"Back out of what?"

I swallowed. "Our relationship," I answered firmly, despite feeling shaky inside.

"Are you planning to end our relationship just because I gave my daughter's mother a place to heal from surgery?" Skylar asked in a raised voice. "Is that what you're planning to do?"

"I need to back off and regroup."

"Regroup for how long—a few days, a week, a month?" I deserve to have information," Skylar demanded.

"I don't know how long."

"You don't have any papers on me, Dee Dee. You can't just expect me to sit around twiddling my thumbs, until you decide you've regrouped!"

"I have no control over what you do, Skylar. You've proven that."

"I love you and I want to be with you, Dee Dee," he said, softening his tone.

"You went against my feelings," I reminded him.

"I had to do what I thought was right in my own heart."

"Well, now I have to do what I feel is right in my own heart."

"Dee Dee, If you walk away now, there's no guarantee that I'll be waiting for you, when and if you decide to come back," Skylar warned.

"That's just the chance I'll have to take, isn't it?" I said as a chill went through my body.

"This is really turning out to be a sad Thanksgiving." Skylar sighed.

"Tell me about it," I retorted.

"Brianna asks about you," Skylar added. "I can tell that she really likes you."

"I really like her, too," I said, as tears welled up in my eyes. I realized I was putting my hopes for becoming a family on the line. But better to experience disappointment now, I counseled myself, than devastation later. If Skylar was going to go back to Allison, let it happen before I became too attached to Brianna, so that it wasn't such a double whammy. "I was looking forward to getting to know your daughter," I confided softly. "Your child really touches my heart."

"What about me?"

"I love you, Skylar. But right now, I have to step back, even if it means losing you. I need to look inside myself for answers."

"If Allison leaves tomorrow, will you come back then?"

"I can't say how I'm gonna feel tomorrow. I can't even say how I'm gonna get through tonight."

twenty-one

Last night, after talking to Skylar, I'd attempted to lose myself in the haunting sounds of belly dance music while I ate my Thanksgiving leftovers. I'd binged, but I hadn't purged. Progress, not perfection, I reminded myself. I'd finally taken a melatonin tablet so that I could fall asleep.

By the next night, I still hadn't heard from Skylar. All day, I'd half expected him to call and announce that Allison had departed for Indianapolis. And yes, I would take him back. But I never got the call. So, I figured Allison was probably still there. And yes, I felt sad; and yes, I was trying not to overeat. And yes, I'd cleaned the house like a maniac. I'd finally dug out my harmonica and played the blues.

I couldn't believe that I might've let Skylar slip through my fingers and might spend the rest of my life waking up alone. Maybe I should call Skylar and beg him to take me back. Even if he were involved romantically with Allison, it didn't have to be the end of our world. Why couldn't I just look the other way like a lot of women? Why couldn't I just take Skylar at his word? Why couldn't I trust him? Even if Skylar was seeing Allison and I caught them in the act, I could still choose between believing Skylar and believing my lying eyes.

Listen to yourself, the other side of me admonished, you sound like a woman who's asking to be used. You deserve to have an honest, loving relationship with a man that you can trust. And how can you trust any man in this situation? It's smart of you to step back and see if Skylar still carries a torch for Allison. Because if he does, you're the one who stands to get burned. It's painful enough to walk away now, but it could be devastating later. If Skylar is meant for you, it will happen.

I was counting on the blues to cheer me up tomorrow. My radio show should be a good distraction. Sunday, I'd listen to church on the radio and sing and shout as loud as Langston would allow. That would help take my mind off Skylar also. I decided to throw myself into my advertising job, starting on Monday. I vowed to bring new exuberance to leading my upcoming focus groups on frozen ravioli dinners, greeting cards and sport utility vans.

I had a meeting scheduled Tuesday with Phil and Lupe Hernandez from the *Tribune Magazine*. Phil had passed on Skylar's offer to try to take legal action against the bounty hunters. He never gave a coherent reason; he just said he didn't want to deal with the courts. I was in no mood to argue with Phil, since Skylar and I hadn't spoken in almost a week. I was heartbroken, because I figured that Allison was still there and Skylar couldn't bring himself to tell me that.

Anyway, Lupe said she was certain that her editors would jump at the chance to publish Phil's riveting tale. Phil told me that because he'd never been interviewed before, he'd like me to be there for moral support. Lupe said it was cool with her; it would be nice to see me outside of our Women in Media meetings. I told her, "Ditto," and everything was set. The three of us were scheduled to meet for a late lunch tomorrow at Heaven on Seven, a popular Creole restaurant downtown on the seventh floor of the Plymouth building.

The doorbell rang, startling both Langston and me. It was somewhat late, almost time for the ten o'clock news. I fantasized that it was Skylar, coming on bended knee, carrying a white flag and two dozen roses. But unfortunately, we heard Phil's voice on the intercom. My cat gave me a bored look, as if to say, "Not that joker again."

As I buzzed Phil in, I wondered if he'd gotten cold feet about the interview tomorrow. Maybe he was concerned about possible ramifications. He might be afraid that the bounty hunters would come after him if his story got out. It was understandable that he would be afraid after what they put him through.

"You're looking fit these days," Phil said, after entering my condo.

"Thanks, I just got off the treadmill a little while ago. Don't get too close," I cautioned. "I still gotta take a bath."

"I can't smell you."

"Anyway, enough about me. You just happened to be in the neighborhood? I mean, what's up with this surprise visit?"

"Your phone was busy," Phil answered, nonchalantly.

"I must've been dialing Sharon's number." I'd turned to her for moral support.

"You don't have call waiting."

"People complained about being interrupted," I said. "Now I have voice mail."

"Well, I'm not here to sell you phone services," Phil said, sitting down in the recliner.

"What's up, then? You didn't get into it with Sarita again, did you?"

Phil shrugged. "We're cool. We're back to our usual miserable selves."

"Are you worried about tomorrow?"

"You could say that." Phil sighed, his eyes looking red and tired. "You got any brew?"

"Thanks," he said, after I handed him a beer. "Where's your cat? How come I never see your cat?" He twisted around in the recliner.

"He's hiding. He doesn't warm up to men that easily."

"Well, I'm glad that you don't feel that way. I couldn't help but notice that you're wearing your I LOVE BLACK MEN T-shirt." Phil smiled.

I smiled back. "Oh, yeah, I forgot I had it on. You won't believe it, but this is the first time I've worn it. And you show up. What a coincidence."

"I wish you would wear it out in public, show it to the world."

"Maybe I will. Anyway, don't worry about tomorrow. You're doing the right thing. And I don't think those bounty hunters will come after you. Not with you in the spotlight. They wouldn't risk it."

"I wasn't kidnapped," Phil said matter-of- factly.

"What?"

"I wasn't kidnapped by no bounty hunters."

"You *weren't* kidnapped by bounty hunters? It never happened?"

"That's right." Phil hung his head. "I made it all up."

"Let me sit down," I said, settling into the couch. "Let me sit *way* the hell down." I wished I was in the recliner instead of Phil. If he weren't looking so pitiful right now, I'd make him get up. I folded my arms and stared at Phil's bowed head in the lamplight. "Do you mean to tell me that you've been living a lie?"

He sighed and nodded.

"This is deep," I said, shaking my head.

"Dee Dee, I never asked you to make a big deal out of this," Phil whined.

"It *is* a big deal to me when somebody is snatched off the street and stripped of all his civil rights. I *thought* I was fighting an injustice."

"I'm sorry."

"Maybe the truth will also make a good story," I said, sarcastically.

"No, it won't, unless I wanna be sitting up on one of those talk shows."

"Well, what *really* happened?" I groaned.

"I was up with another woman."

"You had an affair!" I cut my eyes and sucked my teeth. "Phil, how could you be so messy? I mean, why did you have to disappear for beaucoup days? Whatever happened to afternoon delight? Or meeting every day at the same café at six-thirty? Or noticing the time and having to go, 'cause it's way past nine?"

"It would still be adultery," Phil said solemnly.

"Yeah, but you wouldn't have had to invent high drama."

"One thing just led to another." He shrugged.

I groaned. "Why do people always say that?"

Phil cleared his throat. "We just met that afternoon. The lady came into my shop to get her hair cut. We hit it off, one thing led to another."

I rolled my eyes. "Can you be more specific?"

"You know what I mean," Phil said sheepishly. "We felt it was a once-in-a-lifetime opportunity. Her husband was away on business for a few days. It reminded me of that movie Sarita dragged me to see, *Bridges of Madison County*. I planned to tell Sarita that I was at my mother's. And when I remembered that Mama was at a revival and Sarita's sister was with her, it was too late. I just went with the flow. But I had to think quickly. And I came up with the idea of being kidnapped by bounty hunters. I'd seen a front-page story about them on a stack of old newspapers at Kim's place. I decided to come up with that story."

"Clever," I said sarcastically.

"I fooled you and a bunch of other people and I probably could've fooled that reporter."

I asked, dryly, "So, are you going to come clean with Sarita now?"

Phil shook his head. "We got too many knives in the house."

"It's just such a betrayal, Phil. And now you've got me drawn into it. Tell me this is just a bad dream."

"You don't have to say nothing to nobody."

I hunched forward, resting my elbows on my thighs and holding my head in my hands. "It will be brought up for the next hundred years. And I will have to pretend, just like you."

"Pretending is a lot safer than getting killed. Besides, it's over between me and Kim. It was just a one-time fling. We don't talk anymore. So why not let sleeping dogs lie?'"

"I just can't live inside a web of lies."

Phil sighed and rested his elbows on his thighs also. "What would you do at this point? If you were me?" He faced me and cupped his chin with his hands.

"I don't know. I'd probably go into couples counseling."

"I do need counseling, living with Sarita."

"You need to consider Jason, too. How can you lie to your son and still look at him in the face?"

"How can I lie to him?" Phil asked, widening his eyes. "The question should be how can I tell him the truth, without going from a hero to a zero?"

"You do have a point."

Phil groaned. "I'm just gonna get the hell outta this marriage. It's all over but the leaving, anyway. No, I know what I'm gonna do," he said decisively. "I'm gonna give Sarita a choice. I'm gonna either get me a computer and get on line and talk to women on the Internet, or else me and Sarita can go into counseling . She can choose whichever one she wants. Now, you don't have to say squat. I got it all figured out."

"It's not my place to say anything, except I do have to tell Lupe the truth. But you're just a name to her."

"I'm sorry if I put you in a bad light with your reporter friend."

"She'll be pissed off, but she'll get over it. I'll leave a message on her voice mail tonight."

"Thanks, Dee Dee. So, me and you are cool, then, right?"

"Nobody's cool," I answered, "but we gotta live with it."

"Can I check out the news before I bounce? I wanna catch the sports."

"There's the remote. I've gotta run to the bathroom."

"Dee Dee, come quick," Phil shouted as I washed my hands.

"What is it?" I asked.

"Ain't that the security guard I met at your radio station that time?"

"Freddy?" I asked, wiping my wet hands on my sweatpants. I glimpsed the familiar moon face before they cut to a commercial. "Yeah, it's definitely him," I confirmed.

"He's coming up on the next segment."

"What happened to him?"

"He rescued a lady who had a heart attack and crashed into the shoulder on the Dan Ryan," Phil informed me. "Freddy drove across two lanes of traffic to help her. His call to 911 saved her life!"

"Wow, our Freddy!" I marveled.

"The lady was driving a van with kids from D.C.F.S."

"Were any of the children hurt?"

"No, not seriously. A young brotha pulled over and helped Freddy calm the kids down. I heard about it earlier on the radio, but I didn't have a face to connect it with. I didn't realize."

"Be quiet," I interrupted. "I want to hear what he says."

I watched as Freddy looked solemnly at us from the TV.

"I done what any decent person would've done. I was raised to treat people the way you wanna be treated. It was just that simple. I ain't nobody's hero."

"A lot of people would disagree," the blonde reporter cut in.

"I'm just somebody who done the right thing," Freddy insisted.

"What about the young man who helped you?"

"DeAndre is a wonderful example of African-American youth. He's renewed my faith in young black people."

"Well, I'll be black," I commented to Phil. "I can't believe Freddy said that."

"DeAndre and I got to talking. He's never had a father to take him even to a Bulls game. And he lives a stone's throw away from the United Center. Maybe I can take him and all the kids that was in the van to a game," our Freddy added.

"I don't think Freddy Johnson is going to have much trouble getting a bunch of complimentary tickets to a Bulls game, do you? This is Katelyn Meyers reporting live from the South Side. Back to you, Paul."

"No," the news anchor agreed. "And, I'm happy to report that the woman's condition has been upgraded from critical to stable. The doctors say she's expected to make a full recovery and that she wouldn't have made it if it weren't for the efforts of a couple of good Samaritans. By the way, none of the kids who were in the van was seriously injured."

With a puzzled expression, Phil said, "I thought you said Freddy didn't consider himself black?"

"He doesn't. Or at least, he *didn't*...just yesterday, when I left the station, Freddy still thought the white man's ice was colder."

When I returned to the radio station on Saturday, Freddy was bursting with pride. My happiness for him momentarily distracted me from my broken heart. A banner reading FREDDY JOHNSON OUR HERO was on the wall above his desk. He showed me a plaque he'd received from the Department of Children and Family Services.

"Congratulations. I'm so proud of you. I saw you on TV; you said some good things."

Freddy shrugged. "I really wasn't looking for the spotlight. I just wanted to help that poor woman."

"How's she doing now?" I asked. "Any update?"

"Thank God, it looks like she might make a full recovery. They've taken her out of intensive care. They've upgraded her to stable condition. I just talked to one of her nurses this morning."

"I'm glad to hear that she's doing better."

"Yeah, that's what's important."

"Freddy, with all the press you're receiving, I don't think you'll be working here much longer. I'll miss you, but I'll understand."

Freddy rubbed his bald head and gave me a quizzical look. "Why is that? I didn't say I was going nowhere. It ain't like I won the lottery or something. Now, if I hit the jackpot, then I'm outta here. And the last Negro can turn out the lights." He smiled.

"Yeah, but you've been on the news. With all this publicity, the job offers can't be too far behind." I sniffed. "I smell change in the air. Mark my words, but don't quit your day job just yet, brothaman," I cautioned. "You are a brotha again, right?" I winked.

Freddy tilted his head back and twisted his mouth like he was figuring out a chess move. "Yeah," he finally answered, begrudgingly. "I'm gon' go 'head and give y'all another shot."

"Good," I said. "We need all the heroes we can get these days."

Freddy's face flushed with pride. "I caught some of them trashy talk shows recently, and it really opened my eyes to just how many ignorant white people there are in America," Freddy said, shaking his head. "I was shocked. I believe a lot of eyes have been opened. You and I both knew how ignorant black folks can be."

"*Some* black folks," I interjected.

"Anyway, you expect *us* to come out there and clown. But I had no idea that there were that many trifling white folks willing to show their drawers on national TV," Freddy marveled.

"They're gladiator shows." I groaned.

"Well, they made me ashamed to call myself white." He sighed, shaking his head again. "And these white folks on these talk shows might just be the tip of the iceberg. No telling how many ignorant white folks are really out there. I decided that the only safe thing for me to do was to distance myself from white folks. I've had to disown them."

"I'm sure you'll be sorely missed." I chuckled. "But a brotha's gotta do what a brotha's gotta do."

"Plus, after that black kid came through the way he done and helped me save that poor woman's life, I decided I just might as well go back to being black," he explained.

I teased, "You're not gonna become Korean?"

"Naa, they get up too early in the morning for me. I'm a night owl."

"Well, you're a credit to the race," I said, patting Freddy's shoulder before heading up to the control room.

"You've been listening to Jesse Mae Hemphill, also known as the She-Wolf," I informed my listeners. "Those were some of her early recordings from 1979 and 1980. The She-Wolf is a very special blues artist, and this set was by special request from my friend, Dianne, a blue-eyed soul sister who knows that when you make dressing or stuffing or whatever you wanna call it, you gotta use corn bread. It's as simple as that.

"And I don't have anything against pumpkins, so I don't wanna hear nothing from the pumpkin patch. But when it comes to pies during the holiday season, if it ain't sweet potato, you're committin' treason.

"Hold on. I've got a caller. Hope it's not a pumpkin eater. Go ahead, caller."

"Hi, I'm a little nervous."

"There's no reason to be nervous, what's your name."

"Skylar."

It was *my* Skylar! *I take that back. There is a reason for you to be nervous,* I thought. *Me and you both.*

"Skylar, what can I play for you?"

"I've got the blues."

"Why is that?"

"The usual. My woman up and left me."

"If you wanna do-right woman, you gotta be a do-right man."

"I never dogged her. We just had a misunderstanding. She thought I was sneaking behind her back with my ex. But I just did a favor for my ex because I was being a good Samaritan."

"There was no hanky-panky involved?"

"None whatsoever."

"Is that the only reason that you did this favor for your ex? Because you wanted to be a good Samaritan?"

"Maybe not totally. I guess, to be honest, I was also scared."

"Scared of what?"

"I was scared of the depth of my feelings for my girlfriend."

"So, on some level you might've wanted to push her away."

"Maybe. I was afraid of things moving too fast. I just came out of a failed marriage, you have to understand."

"It's natural to be afraid. But love is letting go of fear. Jane Fonda says courage is fear that's said its prayers."

"You should've been a therapist."

"Thank you, but I'm happy doing what I'm doing."

"I realize now that I'm less afraid of my love for my girlfriend

than the emptiness I feel without her. I guess I needed time to be sure of what I really wanted."

"Sounds like you care a lot about this woman."

"I do. I love her very much."

"I think this woman is gonna take you back."

"You think so?"

"Yes, I feel it in my soul. How about if I play 'At Last' by the one and only Etta James for you and your one and only."

"Thanks."

My lonely days were over, I thought. My love had come around.

twenty-two

Later that night on the phone, Skylar confirmed that Allison had finally returned to Indianapolis the day before. He said that he was glad to have his life back. We couldn't wait to see each other. We were back in love again.

The next day, I took Sarita out to Sunday brunch to celebrate her forty-first birthday. Phil was hanging out at home with Jason, so Sarita had the whole day off from her wifely and motherly duties.

Sarita and I carried our plates of brunch food to our corner table. The Retreat was a restored Victorian on the far South Side that was an "in" place for about-something black folks looking for good food and charming surroundings, especially after church. The restaurant was festively decorated in celebration of the holiday season.

"People tend to overlook your birthday when it's close to Christmas," Sarita said, between bites of food. "But you have always remembered my birthday. That means a whole lot to me, because all my life I've been shortchanged." Sarita eyed her beautifully wrapped present that contained luxuries for the bath.

"I understand. My mother's birthday would've been tomorrow," I recalled with emotion. "She trained me to remember."

Sarita gave me a caring look. "Now, I didn't come here to see how much I could eat," she said, reaching for a biscuit. "So at some point, help me push away from the table."

"Girl, just enjoy yourself."

Sarita giggled. "Easy for you to say, you look like you can fit nicely into a fourteen now."

I shrugged. "This dress is a size fourteen."

"How much have you lost?"

"I don't deal with scales. I just go by how I fit into my clothes. But I would guess I've released about ten pounds."

"Released?" Sarita raised her eyebrows.

"Yeah, when you lose something, you tend to go looking for it. It's a different mind-set."

"Well, what are you doing, in a nutshell, to *release* weight?"

"You can borrow my book, *Thin Within*. But basically, you eat only when you're hungry, eat the foods you love and quit before you're full."

"Wait a minute, now you know our people don't like to experience hunger. It's a carryover from slavery."

"Yeah, but hunger can feel okay when you know you can satisfy it."

"And are you saying that if I love macaroni and cheese and biscuits and pound cake and fried chicken, I can just knock myself out?"

"Yeah, if you're hungry and you stop eating before you're even nearly full. You can't stuff yourself. The idea is if you eat enough chocolate chip cookies, sooner or later you'll be cravin' broccoli."

"That's deep."

"It's a comprehensive program. You work on delivering honest communications and acknowledging your daily successes in life. And you set and meet goals. Weight is just the outer manifestation of your inner situation."

"Preach, Dee Dee, preach. Is this infomercial one of my birthday gifts?"

"Sure, I'm in a generous mood."

"I'm gonna try to release weight today at this buffet."

"When you're eating, eat slowly, pay attention to your food and savor every bite," I instructed.

"I thought we were having a visit," Sarita protested.

"You go back and forth, eating and talking. You rotate, paying attention to me and paying attention to your food."

"But you can't let yourself get full?" she asked with a worried expression.

"No—in fact, you're supposed to leave food on your plate."

"Leave food on your plate! We were raised never to waste food!" she exclaimed.

"It's already on your plate. It's not like it's gonna save starving children, whether you eat it or not," I reasoned.

"I think I wanna start this program tomorrow. Can we just eat like normal people today, since it *is* my birthday?"

"Sure, I just wanted to offer you the tools to weight mastery, as they call them."

"I'll borrow the book one day and learn all about weight mastery, but today I just wanna be a slave to my taste buds."

"I hear you." I laughed.

"It's just so nice to be able to eat food that you didn't have to cook and don't have to worry about fixin' somebody else's plate and cleaning up afterwards." Sarita polished off a piece of catfish. "I'm so glad you helped me to escape for a few hours. I don't have to hear Mama this and Mama that, and I don't have to hear Phil asking, have you seen this or where did you put that?"

"You deserve a break."

"Did I tell you that the school tried to get me to put Jason on drugs?"

"On drugs?" I asked through a mouthful of macaroni and cheese.

"You know, Ritalin or Prozac, something. It's big business, now, to fill these kids up with drugs, especially boys."

"Have you looked at diet? Are you cutting down on his sugar and caffeine?"

"I'm trying to go that route." Sarita lowered her voice. "They made me agree to take a parenting class, since I refused to put Jason on drugs."

I sipped my mimosa. "Something good can come out of a parenting class. Anybody could probably learn to become a better parent," I said.

"That's true."

"They say being a good parent is the hardest job in the world."

"It's funny, because you know, it didn't used to be. Marriage seems harder, too." Sarita sighed. "It's better in some ways and worse in others. Would you believe Phil wants us to go into counseling?"

"You thinking about doing it?"

"We don't have money to give to a counselor. We can put that money into a computer."

I remembered Phil's threat to enter the chat rooms and talk to women on-line. I almost choked on my greens, and reached for my water. "Is it just a question of money?" I asked. "Because there's inexpensive counseling available."

Sarita sighed again, and I noticed the lines in her made-up face and the bags under her eyes. "I guess when you get right down to it," she said, "I'm just not the therapy type. Not to say that I don't have problems and that I don't ever get the blues. Shoot, I took Prozac for a minute. Now I'm on St. John's Wort and I'm drug-free. It's natural, it's an herb," she added proudly.

"It's good that it's natural."

Sarita paused and took a swallow of her mimosa. "There's no point in me and Phil paying somebody to listen to why we get on each other's nerves."

"Maybe counseling could bring you two closer together, though. Maybe you could work through stuff, improve your communication, understand each other's feelings better."

"Now you sound like a shrink. Look, girl, I don't want to understand Phil's feelings. I'll be honest with you, Dee Dee, I'm not big on probing things. I don't even want to probe my own feelings, let alone somebody else's. And as far as I'm concerned, Phil and I can either stand each other's ways or we can't. It's that simple.

"Remember how some women used to say they just wanted a man who had sense enough to work?" Sarita continued.

I nodded.

"Well, the truth be told, I can relate," she confided.

I shook my head. "I want a man who has a lot more than just sense enough to work." I paused. "I want intimacy. Not just sex; I mean *intimacy.*"

"Sounds complicated. Sounds like a lot to ask for from a man. Is that what you have with Skylar?" Sarita seemed skeptical.

"We're developing it."

"Well, I'm so glad y'all got back together. Phil caught your show yesterday at the barber shop. He said it was really touching. Phil said if he hadn't known who Skylar was, you could've fooled him. I sure wish I'd heard it. But I was out shopping in River Oaks."

"I'll send you a tape."

"Why don't you bring Skylar by the house during the holidays, him and his little girl. The kids can play together."

"Thanks, but can I take a rain check? Brianna's spending the holidays in Indianapolis with her mother and Skylar's going to be in California."

"Okay, then, sometime after the first of the year."

"I think you'll like Skylar. He's really a good brotha."

"Did you ever find out why he didn't answer the phone that time?"

"Funny you should ask. It remained an unsolved mystery until last night. A phone installer remarked to Skylar outside his building that they were working on the phone lines again. Skylar asked when they'd had problems on the line before. The installer told him a couple of months ago. Skylar figured out that's what happened when I tried to reach him that time."

"And you believe Skylar?"

"Yeah, I do. It sounds like a logical explanation to me. They sometimes have trouble on the phone lines. I was married to a telephone installer, remember?"

"I forgot Wendell was a telephone installer, but I never forgot how he dogged you."

"Well, I love myself a lot more now. It's hard to love someone who doesn't love herself. Anyway, I think I've found a man that I might be able to trust."

"You're being gullible if you ask me. I put a question mark after anything a man tells me," Sarita insisted.

You didn't put a question mark after Phil telling you that he was kidnapped by bounty hunters, did you? I said to myself.

"Let me tell you something funny Brianna said," I interjected in a effort to change the subject. "Skylar took her ice-skating last week and she didn't want to leave when he needed her to. She started boo-hoo-ing and copped an attitude. Skylar called her on it and read her a little bit. And Brianna said, 'Daddy, you judged me.' Wasn't that cute?"

"Uhmph, you judged me," Sarita repeated, rolling her eyes. "I wish Jason *would* tell me I *judged* him. I'd say, boy, you're lucky your butt can still sit down."

"Those words would never come outta Jason's mouth," I said. "Jason is a homeboy."

"What planet is Brianna from?"

"Santa Cruz." I smiled. "That little girl is a stone Northern Californian."

"Sounds like you've really taken to that little mixed rascal."

Did I detect a hint of jealousy in Sarita's voice? I tried to sound less gung ho. "We seemed to have hit it off." I shrugged. "But it's really too early to tell. At this point, Brianna just thinks of me as her daddy's friend. I haven't spent the night yet. She hasn't even seen us kiss. So far, I don't seem to be a threat. But the jury is still out. I'd say I'm cautiously optimistic."

"I think you're more optimistic than cautious. And from what I heard about how you and Skylar carried on yesterday on the radio, I'd say it's all over but the shouting."

"I wouldn't go that far. Ultimately, it's a package deal. And Brianna's and my relationship hasn't really been tested yet. But it's about to be. Skylar's babysitter moved out of the area. So we're going to have to include Brianna in some of our dates out of necessity. I'm even going to start spending the night."

Sarita raised her eyebrows. "Where do you plan to sleep?"

"I'm gonna start out on the couch."

"Well, so long as you avoid the appearance of evil," Sarita advised, "I do think that sneaky is the way to go."

"Brianna's gonna figure out sooner or later that I'm more than just her daddy's friend, anyway. I might even suddenly feel like a threat to her."

"Well, whatever happens, don't totally neglect Jason. He's still your play nephew, remember."

"Don't worry, Jason is still my boy. And I *do* appreciate the invite."

"Well, keep me posted about this intimacy stuff. I am curious about it, although, personally, I don't think it would work for me."

"Don't you want to be open to new possibilities?" I smiled.

Sarita frowned. "I don't want to get too close to my husband. I don't want to understand everything about him. If the bills are paid and the grass is cut and I don't have to shovel snow or worry about putting gas in my car or taking out the garbage, and he's Dr. Feelgood when I wanna feel good, I don't have a lot of complaints. The fact that we might fuss, so what?" Sarita paused and sipped her mimosa. "Phil and I are lucky. Not everybody finds somebody that they can be happy being miserable with."

January first came and went and I let out a sigh of relief. I'd survived the holidays. I hadn't binged or purged, despite the tasty temptations. Skylar had called me several times from the West Coast where he was visiting his foster parents. He'd sent me a beautiful floral arrangement. I bought him a photo book of jazz legends for his coffee table. I missed Skylar terribly. I was also looking forward to getting to know his precious little girl. I longed to make that child my own.

Spending time with my sister and brother and their families during the holidays had been pleasant enough. Nothing introspective, nothing deep, just a good time. I had fun playing with their kids. We all had a lot to be thankful for. Everyone was in good health and gainfully employed. My siblings were glad to hear that I had a new love.

I'd spent New Year's Day with Sarita, Phil and all three of their children. Their daughters were home from college for the holidays. Sarita had served the traditional black-eyed peas for luck. She'd stunk up the house with a big, steaming pot of chitterlings. I'd sneaked and lifted the lid off the pot a couple of times and inhaled their pungent aroma. Most people hated the smell of chitterlings, but I secretly savored their odor while they were cooking. It was just one of my quirks. By the way, I don't eat just anybody's chitterlings. I almost have to watch you clean them. But I trusted Sarita's cleanliness standards even more than my own.

twenty-three

My relationship with Skylar was humming along a week
or so later. Life was pretty much sweet, I thought as I sat in my
recliner, watching Skylar build a fire.

"You're gettin' pretty good at lightin' my fire," I teased.

"I'm no stranger to a fireplace." Skylar smiled. "I'm just not
used to freezing half to death several months outta the year. If it
weren't for your warmth, I swear, I'd take my daughter and leave
this godforsaken climate."

"Look at it this way. A cold winter really makes you appreciate
spring."

"Yes, dear," Skylar said with a fake smile. He lit the kindling and
began stoking the fire.

"Anyway, speaking of cold," he continued, "yesterday I was
walking down the street with a client and the Hawk was kicking our
asses. We were being slapped mercilessly with wind mixed with
snow. I was wondering if my nearly frozen fingers and toes would
have to be amputated, when my client pointed to the temperature
displayed outside the bank and remarked, 'It's really warmed up
nicely. Look, it's eighteen degrees.'"

"I couldn't utter a word of protest without sounding like a
wimp," Skylar added. "Especially since I was all bundled up in layers

plus had on a hat, scarf and gloves and the other guy was bare-headed, and wearing a trench coat."

"You're not a wimp," I assured him. "You're just a Californian."

"Well, thanks for letting me *share*," he said with mock sweetness.

A few days later, Dr. King's birthday ushered in a cold snap that got the attention of even the most jaded Chicagoans. Flights were canceled and thousands of people were snowbound. I was at Skylar's high-rise apartment the night the weather got ugly. He and I were sitting in his retro-style living room on an upscale beanbag loveseat when we decided that the roads were too snowy to navigate and it was best for me to stay put. We'd been planning for me to spend the night at some point soon anyway, and decided tonight would be ideal. I had an excuse.

Brianna and I were getting along well. When she was told that I would be sleeping on the couch, she appeared nonchalant. Of course, the plan was for me to start out on the couch and then "visit" Skylar's bed after Brianna was soundly asleep. I would return to the sofa in the wee hours of the morning and Brianna would be none the wiser. Or, so we thought.

Skylar and I stood over Brianna, watching her as she slept. I inhaled her preciousness. She'd hugged me good night and it had raised my hopes. Maybe it wasn't too late for me to be a mother after all. Maybe, despite having had an abortion and a hysterectomy, I would get another chance. And, if I was good at it, maybe I could finally forgive myself. I fantasized that I'd found the "we" of me that the heroine in *Member of the Wedding* longed for.

The alarm didn't awaken me: Brianna did. Skylar had unlocked the bedroom door after we'd finished making love. Brianna came dragging into the bedroom before dawn. Luckily, I'd changed into my flannel p.j.'s in the middle of the night. I wasn't sure whether I should hide further under the covers or sheepishly reveal myself. It was too late to slide into the space between the wall and the bed.

Maybe if I just remained still, Brianna wouldn't notice me in the dark.

"Daddy, my tummy aches," Brianna whined.

Skylar sat up in the queen-size bed. "You're not going to throw up, are you?"

"I don't know, Daddy, I might," Brianna warned.

Skylar leapt out of the bed, grabbed his daughter and ushered her toward the bathroom.

I almost shouted, "Skylar, you're naked, put some clothes on!"

"I gave her some Pepto-Bismol, and put her back to bed. She'll be all right." Skylar yawned, as he snuggled in beside me.

I sat up against the pine headboard. "Did she say anything about me?"

"No," Skylar answered, burying his face in a pillow.

"Do you think she saw me?" I asked suspiciously.

"I don't think so," he mumbled. "She didn't say anything. She probably ate too much junk yesterday. She'll be okay." He yawned again. "There's no school today anyway because of the snow," he added. "They said that on the news."

Tummyache, my ass, I thought. That little girl wasn't fooling me. Brianna thought she was slick. And here I'd believed she was so sweet. She knew what was up with me and her father. I was hipped to her game.

"I think you should've put on some clothes," I admonished Skylar as he tried to go back to sleep.

"Huh?"

"Do you realize that you ran outta here buck naked?" I said, shaking him.

He turned over and frowned. "I was concerned about Brianna."

"Maybe you should be *concerned* about being more modest."

"I don't make a habit out of walking around with no clothes on." Skylar yawned. "But Allison and I didn't raise our daughter to see nudity as some big taboo."

I cringed at the mention of Allison's name and the phrase, "our daughter." In my fantasies, Allison didn't exist. "Our daughter" meant me and Skylar's child.

"I was just raised differently, that's all," I replied. "I never saw my stepfather naked," I snapped. And then I remembered that wasn't completely true. But the times that I *had* experienced my stepfather's nakedness, I wanted to forget.

A week or so later, Skylar and I fell back on being sneaky. We'd included Brianna on our dinner date at a Thai restaraunt. Everything had gone well and our little sugar plum was snug in her bed. And we were cuddling in ours.

In the middle of the night, we had another snowstorm. This time, the howling wind, blowing off the nearby lake, awakened me instead of the alarm. The Hawk was raging, causing the windows of Skylar's high-rise apartment building to rattle. Realizing that children and scary weather didn't mix well, I figured we might have a little visitor soon.

I took the wind's next howl as my cue to retreat to the couch. But before I could make a serious move, Brianna stumbled into the bedroom. Skylar had insisted on leaving the door unlocked, in case of an emergency. I rolled over toward the wall in my plaid flannel gown. I hoped I was invisible in the dark.

"Daddy, the lights are out," Brianna announced in a distressed voice. She shook her father. "Daddy, I'm scared!"

Skylar sat up in the bed and mumbled, "Huh? What's wrong?"

"We're having a snowstorm," I explained. "Don't you hear that wind? The power must've gone out."

"Daddy, why is she in your bed?" Brianna demanded.

I was momentarily speechless. I felt like Goldilocks being discovered by Baby Bear.

"Come here, sweetie," Skylar said soothingly. Brianna walked gingerly toward her father. Skylar sat up and hugged his daughter. "You don't have to be scared. Daddy's here's now. He'll protect you."

"Can I get in the bed with you, Daddy?" she whimpered.

"I don't think that's such a good idea."

"Why not?"

Because your father doesn't have any clothes on, I almost blurted out.

"I wanna sleep with you, Daddy! I wanna sleep with you, Daddy!" Brianna shouted.

"Don't act like that, Brianna," Skylar scolded. "You're a big girl now, remember. You're too big to sleep with Daddy."

"Why's Dee Dee in your bed, then?" Brianna challenged. "She's a bigger girl. How come you let her sleep with you and you won't let me sleep with you?"

"It's different, honey. Dee Dee's a grown woman."

"Mommy's a grown woman and you didn't sleep with her."

"Your mother and I are divorced."

"Even when you weren't divorced, you didn't sleep with Mommy. You didn't sleep with Mommy!" Brianna repeated.

"Huh," I said aloud.

"The last year of our marriage, Allison and I slept apart," Skylar explained. "You know how that is."

I nodded.

"I want my mommy!" Brianna cried. "I want my mommy!"

"You can call her on the phone, a little later," Skylar said, gently. "You know she's not a morning person."

I felt awkward, like suddenly I didn't belong anywhere. Skylar reached for the flashlight on the nearby nightstand. "Brianna, I'm going to carry you back to your bed now. If you're afraid, I'll sit with you until you fall asleep.

"Dee Dee, would you please hand me my robe?" he asked, shining the flashlight on it.

I had a feeling that the honeymoon was over as I watched the two shadowy figures exit the room.

I became the enemy overnight. Brianna gave me dirty looks at the breakfast table. Her scowling face was crushing my dreams. I almost felt comforted by the howling wind.

After breakfast, I stood outside the bathroom door waiting for Brianna to emerge and resume watching her Saturday morning cartoons. I was anxious to collect my cosmetic bag and head for the radio station to do my afternoon show.

Skylar sneaked up behind me and wrapped his arms around

me. "She'll adjust," he whispered softly. "She's been through a lot, just give her a little time."

"Okay," I agreed. I pulled away from Skylar when I heard the door open. Brianna came out the bathroom wearing her nightie and with my red lipstick smeared all over her face.

She flung her arms open wide and shouted, passionately, "Kiss me all over! Kiss me all over!"

Skylar and I stood aghast.

"You shouldn't have gone into Dee Dee's lipstick!" Skylar finally said sternly. "You knew better than that."

"It's okay, I have another tube of red," I responded diplomatically. "I left the cosmetic bag open anyway."

"That's not the issue."

No, the issue is your daughter saying "Kiss me all over," I thought. Your child is troubled. She has a problem with our relationship. And therefore we have a problem.

"Daddy, I heard screaming last night," Brianna interjected, before making a face at me.

Now I was starting to get pissed. Brianna was lying her ass off.

She hadn't heard any damn screaming.

"Screaming, what are you talking about?" Skylar asked, looking concerned.

"In your room last night," Brianna answered matter-of-factly.

"What kind of screaming?" I demanded skeptically.

"Ahh . . . ahhha . . . ahhhh!" Brianna shouted, imitating a movie orgasm.

I felt a chill run down my spine. To think I'd imagined that Brianna was so sweet. Okay, fine, she wasn't going to be the daughter of my dreams. But was she going to wreck our relationship to boot?

Skylar and I had taken pains to conceal our love life. We'd waited until late into the night to have sex, and we'd been discreet. I'd even covered my mouth during our lovemaking. Neither of us had cried out, even when we came. We'd sneaked around like criminals, but now we'd gotten caught in Brianna's childish trap.

Even though I knew Brianna hadn't heard screaming, I couldn't help but feel guilty. Were we being selfish? I wondered. I didn't believe that our sleeping together was wrong. But maybe we were wrong for exposing Brianna to the truth of our relationship. But because we weren't married, did that make having sex a cardinal sin? I'd spent a lot of years working to get to the place where I felt good about my sexuality. And now an eight-year-old manipulator was trying to undermine my efforts.

"Brianna, there wasn't any screaming," Skylar said firmly.

"That's right, there wasn't any screaming," I echoed.

"Yes there was, too!" Brianna insisted. "I heard it." She pointed accusingly. "It was her!"

"You didn't hear anything," I protested. "You never heard my mouth," I added, struggling to keep my cool. I'd never liked a liar. And this child was starting to remind me of the bad seed.

"Nobody was doing any screaming in here last night," Skylar said decisively. "Brianna, you're just making that up. I don't want to hear another word from you about it, do you hear me?"

Brianna nodded.

"Brianna, you're just trying to upset us," I said, feeling calmer now that Skylar had put his foot down. "If you want to talk to us about your feelings about your father and me being together, I'd be happy to do that. Right now, I have to go to the radio station and do my show. But we can set up a time."

Brianna responded by making a face at me.

"I saw that face," Skylar warned. "You're pushing your luck, Miss Brianna. You'd better straighten up."

We decided that I would continue to "officially" sleep on the couch. We agreed that I should exit the bedroom earlier, to lessen the chances of being caught. This proved to be a winning strategy. The next weekend, I got fewer dirty looks from Brianna and I almost began to hope again.

On Valentine's Day, a dozen red roses were waiting for me at my desk when I arrived at my marketing job. Of course they were from Skylar. I really felt loved. Too bad we didn't have a babysitter tonight. When I called Skylar to thank him for the flowers, I insisted on treating him and Brianna to dinner that evening.

During our dinner date, Skylar and I kept the mushy stuff to a minimum. Everything had gone smoothly during the meal and now Brianna was skipping ahead of us in the cold night air, clutching her minature box of chocolates. Skylar had given us little identical boxes of candy. He was so sweet.

"You are my sunshine," Skylar whispered in my ear as we hurried against the wind.

"I can't breathe," Brianna panted a few minutes later, as I drove south on the outer drive.

"Dee Dee, open the windows!" Skylar shouted in alarm.

"It's freezing outside," I answered, a little taken aback by the intensity in his voice.

"That doesn't matter, hurry up, press the button!"

I lowered Brianna's window.

"Brianna has asthma," Skylar informed me. He leaned over his seat and observed his daughter.

"I didn't know that," I exclaimed.

"I still can't get enough air!" Brianna gasped.

"Do you want me to go a hospital?" I asked. "We're almost at U. of C."

"Are you getting more air now?" Skylar asked.

"A little bit."

"I'd be happy to take her to a hospital," I reiterated.

"No. I think we'll be okay."

"Are you sure?"

"Yeah, I think the worst is over."

"Doesn't she have an inhaler?"

"No. I should've gotten her one just to be safe," Skyar answered remorsefully.

"I can't believe she doesn't have an inhaler," I said in astonishment. "My friends' son is asthmatic. But Jason doesn't go anywhere without his inhaler."

"Brianna's only had two attacks in her entire life," Skylar explained. "This is the first one she's had since we moved to Chicago. It's sort of a shock."

"Daddy, you promised to get me an inhaler!" Brianna huffed and puffed. "Daddy, you promised! How can you ever expect me to trust you again?"

"Brianna take it easy, don't upset yourself. Daddy's sorry. Daddy thought you'd outgrown your asthma. But I'll get you an inhaler first thing tomorrow morning. I promise."

When we reached their apartment, Brianna was doing better, but she was still struggling to breathe. She and Skylar crouched on the bathroom floor while hot water streamed from the shower and cold air rushed in through the open window.

"How's she doing?" I asked, peering into the bathroom.

"I think we're out of the woods now." Skylar sighed. He looked down at his resting child. "Her breathing has almost returned to normal."

"That's good," I said, feeling relieved. I gazed down at Skylar in his wrinkled pinstriped suit, as he cradled his little girl. I'd never loved him more.

On Saturday night I sat in a denim-covered beanbag chair in Skylar's living room while he tucked Brianna into bed.

"I don't want *her* to spend the night!" Brianna shouted. "I don't want *her* to spend the night!"

I heard Skylar say, "Brianna, calm down. You just had an attack a few days ago. You don't need to upset yourself."

"I want Dee Dee to leave us alone!" she yelled. "Why can't she go home to her cat!"

At that moment, I longed for Langston's soft fur. I was almost ready to throw the towel in here. I was afraid that I was fighting a losing battle. Skylar and Brianna were a package deal. And part of the package wasn't sold on me. Maybe it was just time to call it quits.

"You have a right to your feelings," Skylar said, loudly enough for me to hear. "But I have a right to be in a relationship."

"I want my mommy back!" Brianna yelled. "I don't want her to be my mommy!"

I could take a hint.

"I want my mommy back!" Brianna shouted again, only this time, she began panting as if struggling to breathe.

I listened intently to her wheezing.

"Here, use your inhaler!" Skylar ordered.

"No!" Brianna yelled. "I don't want it."

"Then stop it. You're trying to make yourself have an asthma attack!"

Alarmed, I rushed to the doorway.

"I think my being here is upsetting her," I said. "I just don't think this is going to work." I glanced warily at Brianna. She was sitting up in her bed, covered by blankets and surrounded by Beannie Babies.

"No. What she's pulling is what's not going to work," Skylar insisted. He sounded drained.

Brianna continued to pant.

"Brianna, stop it, I said," Skylar pleaded. He glanced in my direction. "People can make themselves have an asthma attack. That's what she's trying to do."

"Asthma is nothing to play with," I said solemnly. "I need to back off from this situation, Skylar. Your daughter has to come first. I can't win here."

I noticed that Brianna had stopped huffing and puffing. She appeared to be hanging on our every word.

"Kids test you, Dee Dee," Skylar said wearily.

"Well, I do feel tested. But I'm not sure I can pass."

"If you let her win, we'll all be losers," Skylar added soberly.

"If she's gonna come around, I have to let her do it at her own pace," I said firmly. "The ball's in Brianna's court now. Skylar, we'll talk in the morning, but tonight, I'm going home to my cat."

twenty-four

Things were at a stalemate with Brianna. I hadn't seen her since that fateful night, two weeks ago. I knew that Brianna was the deal-breaker. Skylar and I couldn't become a family without her. I was struggling to resign myself to the fact that she might never come around. And that I might never find the "we" of me.

March came in like a lion, as expected. But unexpectedly, we had precious child care. Tyeesha had called the day before, crying broke and offering to babysit Brianna for a nominal fee. Skylar and I had a whole Saturday afternoon and evening to ourselves. We decided to take full advantage of it.

Skylar and I nibbled and kissed and caressed and giggled and rubbed and sucked and proceeded to ride each other's needs into the sunset. Then it happened. It began with a slow dull ache in the back of my head, which I tried to ignore. And then it escalated to sharp shooting pains that jabbed me in my temples. But I still continued to suffer in silence. I only got these headaches during sex once every blue moon. I could count on one hand the number of times they'd occurred in my entire life. I thought I'd gotten over them.

Besides, what man would want to deal with a woman with incest flashbacks in the middle of hot sex? I thought as I struggled to conceal my pain. I didn't want to make Skylar feel guilty or icky or disappointed. Even a compassionate man might head for the door if he knew the deal.

279

But when the nausea began and Skylar's hands suddenly felt like my stepfather's heavy, clammy fingers, I wanted to disappear. I could no longer contain myself. I was afraid that I was going to vomit right there in the bed.

I pushed Skylar's heavy weight off of me.

"I can't do this right now," I gasped.

"What's wrong, baby?" Skylar's voice sounded concerned. "Are you sick? I thought you were just about to come."

"I'm sorry, but I have a migraine," I said, holding my throbbing head. "I'm really sorry."

"You don't have to be sorry. I'm the one who's sorry. Did I do something wrong?" His swollen penis shrank before my eyes.

"No, you did everything right," I assured him. "It wasn't you." I couldn't bring myself to tell Skylar that his hands felt clammy and reminded me of being molested by my stepfather.

"I didn't mean to be selfish," he said apologetically.

"It's not your fault."

"I didn't realize that you were suffering in silence. You should've said something sooner."

"I didn't know it was going to be so bad," I replied, massaging my temple with my thumb.

"Baby, can I get you something? Let me get you some aspirin, okay?"

"Okay, thanks."

After I took the aspirin, Skylar wrapped his arms around me, but I didn't feel like being close. Being close made my skin crawl.

I pulled away from him and rolled over into the fetal position.

"Dee Dee, I just wanted to make you feel better."

"I know, you're really sweet. But you don't understand. Right now I can't be close to anyone, not even you."

"Why not?"

I should tell Skylar the deal. I had been robbed of my innocence. I'd been made to feel like a dirty rag, and I couldn't wish it away. If Skylar was going to bolt, he might as well leave now. We might as well get it over with. But I didn't tell Skylar what was up with me.

Instead, I traced the raised pattern on the balled-up comforter over and over again with my finger. It reminded me of my old-fashioned pink bedspread from my childhood. It had raised tufts that were like tiny spitballs. I used to roll them around in my fingers over and over again. I used to pretend like I didn't have a care in the world.

Skylar's voice was full of concern. "Dee Dee, what's wrong?"

I didn't respond. I felt far away. I'd already disappeared. I didn't travel to the ceiling and look down like I did as a child. Maybe only children can fly. But I was still gone, just the same.

I heard a far-away voice pleading, "Dee Dee, are you gonna be okay? Do you want me to call somebody? Please say something."

Suddenly I felt the bed shake. I heard my cat purring and felt him rubbing against my neck. Langston usually shied away from Skylar, so I was surprised by his appearance.

"Is the cat okay up on the bed?"

"He's fine," I said, petting Langston. Being close to my cat gave me a secure feeling.

"Is your headache better?"

"It's a little better," I answered weakly.

"Dee Dee, what do you want me to do?"

I looked at Skylar blankly. I felt safe with Langston and I felt safe stroking my comforter. That's all I felt I could handle right now. "I'll be okay, you can go," I mumbled.

"I'm gonna give you some space," Skylar said. "But I'm not leaving the premises. I'll be downstairs if you need anything."

I needed to be alone. I wasn't totally alone, because Langston was by my side.

After Skylar left the room, I began fantasizing about blowing my stepfather up into a jillion pieces. And cutting him up into a jillion more. And beating him with bats and pipes and shooting him with automatic weapons and drowning him and setting him on fire. Finally, I grew exhausted from killing a man over and over again who was already dead.

I felt like a fountain of sludge was shooting out of my mouth and hands. I couldn't hold it back, even if I wanted to. I had no choice, the need to release it was so powerful. I felt that it represented the shame I'd carried with me most of my life. I knew that I needed a safe place to continue to heal. A place where people would understand what I was going through. I was lucky that I had close friends to turn to and that Skylar might be supportive. But I knew that neither my friends nor my boyfriend nor even I could handle the brunt of my pain without my getting professional help.

A few minutes later, Skylar came back upstairs to check on me.

"Dee Dee, I called Tyeesha and arranged for her to keep Brianna overnight. I don't want to leave you alone."

"Skylar, I'm an incest survivor," I said in a clear voice.

"I knew it had to be something big." He sighed. "Dee Dee, I'm really sorry that happened to you. Do you feel like talking about it?"

I shook my head. "Not right now."

"Dee Dee, I want to be supportive. Just let me know what I can do, okay?" Skylar asked with caring eyes.

"Skylar, that's nice of you to say, but you know you don't have to travel this road with me. If you wanna bolt, there's the door." I pointed. "In fact, I will understand. This is no easy walk."

"Dee Dee, what's the point of being on an easy walk, if I'm not on the path with the woman I love?"

A couple of days later, I was still tripping on my flashbacks. Yesterday, I'd spaced out and cut a couple of my fingers while washing a sharp knife. And today, I'd already burned my arm on an oven rack, while removing a pizza.

It was time to face my pain. I called my HMO about getting into a survivors' support group. Dr. Hamilton chastized me for not ringing her back sooner.

"It's already March again," she reminded me. "It's been a year since we've spoken." Dr. Hamilton said they'd been inundated with calls from people during the holidays, but the good news was, she could offer me a spot in a brand-new group that was starting in two weeks. It fit with my schedule, and I felt relieved.

"I've burned myself and cut myself, lately," I confided over the phone. "Not deliberately," I quickly assured the doctor. "I've just had a couple of accidents."

"It's common for abuse survivors to be accident-prone when repressed memories start to surface and they begin to address them," Dr. Hamilton informed me. "I'm glad to hear that you're not injuring yourself deliberately."

"I would never do that," I answered truthfully. "But I understand why women cut themselves, so the outside matches the pain they're feeling on the inside. I guess they're trying to cut through all the denial around them, too."

"I think that's a pretty good analysis. Well, be careful and be gentle with yourself. If you think you might be suicidal, though, ring me up right away."

"Don't worry, I'm not suicidal, I'm homicidal."

"You are aware that if you threaten to harm yourself *or* harm anyone else, I am required by law to act on that information, aren't you?"

"I was only kidding. My perpetrator is already dead."

"That's right, you told me your stepfather passed away over a year ago."

"Yeah."

"Well, Daphne, I'm looking forward to having you in the group. I'm going to transfer you to the receptionist now; she'll enroll you. You've taken an important step today."

"I know, but the thought of actually facing what happened to me makes me feel so vulnerable," I confided.

"This time you won't be alone with your vulnerability, dear. Everyone in your group will feel vulnerable also. Vulnerability is the core of strength."

Skylar commended me for enrolling in the sexual abuse survivors' group during our phone conversation that evening. I warned him that I would be going through some emotional changes. There would be times when I was going to need his support. Sometimes, I would just probably need time alone. Skylar assured me that he would support me in any way that he could.

Then I wound up agreeing to babysit for Brianna. She'd been sent home from school with a cold this afternoon. Skylar said that she was getting over it, but he'd like to keep her home tomorrow, just in case. I was free until my evening focus groups, so I agreed to pitch in. After all, we were a team. Even if we were still missing an important member.

I loaded up on garlic tablets, vitamin C and echinacea and golden seal after I got off the phone. Brianna might be contagious. I wanted to have a strong immune system when I faced that child tomorrow.

"You still have a slight temperature," I reported, after pulling the thermometer out of Brianna's mouth the following day. I glanced down at her puffy, reddish face. She was sitting up in bed, surrounded by her Beanie Babies.

"You only ate a little of your lunch," I continued. "I'm glad you drank most of your orange juice. I'm going to bring you some hot tea."

"What did you mean by 'the ball's in Brianna's court'?" she asked before I could leave the room.

"You mean why did I say that the last time I was here?"

Brianna nodded.

"You have a good memory. Well, I meant like in tennis," I explained. "Do you know who Venus Williams is?"

Brianna nodded again. "She has all those beads in her hair." She coughed and added, "She's cool."

"I'm glad you remembered to cover your mouth. Anyway, when Venus hits the ball over the net, it's in the other player's court, right?"

"Right?"

"And it's up to her to hit it back over, right?"

"*Sí.*"

"So, what I'm saying is, I've tried to be your friend, but I can't be your friend unless you try back."

Brianna paused and looked like she was pondering this concept. "How would you like it if your cat got a cat girlfriend and she was always over at your house, meowing. And nobody ever asked you if you wanted her there or not?"

"I guess I would want to have a say in it," I conceded. "Do you think I'm over here too much?" I asked softly.

Brianna wrinkled her forehead. "How about if you come over once a week."

"Do I get to spend the night?"

Brianna nodded.

Damn straight, I'm spending the night, you little control freak, I thought.

"Okay, that sounds reasonable," I said, diplomatically.

"How would you feel if your daddy talked your mommy into having an abortion?" Brianna blurted out.

I was momentarily speechless. My heart went out to Brianna. It was like I could feel her pain. "Your father just wanted to be a great daddy and he wanted your mother to be a great mommy. And he wasn't sure that they could give a child everything he or she deserved. But your mother had to make the final decision."

Brianna wrinkled her forehead again as if in deep thought. She sat up and hugged her knees. "Okay, then." She sighed. "How would you like it if when your mother was pregnant with you, your father was ambivalent?" Brianna asked quizzically.

"Do you know what ambivalent means?" I asked.

"Yeah, Mommy says it's when you have mixed feelings. My daddy had mixed feelings about me."

"Well, if he ever did, it was before you were born. Your daddy fell in love with you the instant he laid eyes on you. He told me that."

"He did?" Brianna asked with a smile.

"Yes. Your father loves you more than anybody in this world."

"Even you?"

"Yes, of course. Your father definitely puts you first. And I'm sure your mother feels the same way about you. Brianna, you're number one."

Brianna stood up on the bed. "I'm number one!" she bragged, holding up a finger. She bounced up and down on her bed and chanted, "I'm number one! I'm number one!"

"Girl, you'd better sit your butt back down in that bed," I scolded playfully. "You're supposed to be sick, remember."

"I'm glad that they let me be born," Brianna said, sitting down and hugging a couple of Beanie Babies.

"A lot of people are glad that you were born, Brianna," I heard myself say. "And I'm one of them."

"You are?"

"Yes," I said, suddenly feeling a flood of maternal feelings. I sat down on part of Brianna's bed. "I've never said this to you before. But Brianna, I love you."

Brianna looked up at me with her liquid green eyes and answered, solemnly, "I recognize that."

No hug, no "I love you, too," just, "I recognize that." Spoken like a true Californian, I thought to myself, as I wiped away a joyful tear.

On Sunday morning, I woke up to a blanket of fresh snow. Skylar had invited me to attend church with him and Brianna. I swung by and picked them up after digging my car out. Brianna was excited by the sudden, late winter wonderland. It was the first time in over a week she'd really had enough snow to play in. Later this afternoon, she planned to make a snowman.

The church that Skylar and Brianna attended was a progressive, predominantly black church that billed itself more as a spiritual center than as a religious institution.

The three of us were lucky to find seats. The pews were packed with people and their heavy winter wraps. I felt touched when Brianna announced that she wanted to sit between Skylar and me.

I felt uncomfortable when I noticed in the program that the title of the sermon was forgiveness. I wasn't in the mood to have anybody preaching forgiveness at me just yet. I still had a high degree of pissosity in my system toward my stepfather. But I good-naturedly joined the choir in singing "This Joy That I Have."

"We're partying for the Lord twenty-four-seven, three hundred and sixty-five days a year," the regally dressed woman minister declared after we finished singing. "I woke up this mornin' with my mind stayed on spirit," Reverend Cassandra Taylor added. "And I wanna talk about forgiveness this mornin.'"

Well, I'm not sure I want to hear about it, I thought, folding my arms and readying my defenses.

"Last week, I had to go to court and face the boys who gave my grandson the alcohol at the fraternity party that killed him," the minister continued, her voice choked with emotion. "I prayed to God to give me the strength to see past my own grief and be able to forgive. I asked the Lord to let me find it in my heart to forgive these boys. That's not to say that I didn't want them to receive some form of punishment. But I didn't want to continue carrying hatred in my heart for them." Reverend Taylor paused. She was a commanding figure. Even Brianna's eyes were fixed on her.

"While I was praying for the strength to forgive those boys," Reverend Taylor continued, "all of a sudden I saw in my mind the face of this man who had wronged me several years ago. Now I could forgive the boys who gave my grandson the alcohol, because although they acted recklessly, they did not purposely kill my grandson. But I had no intention of forgiving this other man. What he'd done was purposeful. He'd done my daughter dirty." She paused and narrowed her eyes and raised her right arm. "You know, there's a group over here that you can kind of smooth over what they did and forgive them, but then there's another group over here that you can't." She raised her left arm. "When I saw that other man's face in my prayers, that man I had no intention of forgiving, I said, God, I ain't ask you nothing about forgiving this man. I asked you about forgiving these boys. Lord, now you meddling."

Many people in the congregation laughed, including me. But my smile quickly changed to a serious expression as I pondered whether I would ever be able to forgive my stepfather in my heart for what he'd done to me. I could forgive my mother for not knowing and not sensing, because she was in denial. But I wasn't sure I could've forgiven Daddy Sherman even if he'd begged me on his deathbed. Although I would've liked to have seen him do it.

The pastor's words interrupted my thoughts. "I read once that when I forgave someone, I set a prisoner free—and the prisoner was myself. I said, and that prisoner was myself.

"Forgiveness can be a powerful thing," Reverend Taylor continued. "It can be a truly liberating experience."

You have to be *ready* to forgive, I was tempted to shout out. And only you have the right to make that decision.

"But forgiveness ultimately has to be a choice," the minister added firmly, as if she were reading my mind. "We often make kids kiss and make up, but sometimes life isn't like that." She shook her head. "Sometimes we're not ready to forgive. Sometimes it takes time. And maybe for some things, we're never ready.

"Some people are unable to forgive until after the person dies. I've heard of people going to someone's grave site and forgiving them. Some people even write a letter to a deceased person. It's more powerful if you can forgive a person when they're alive, but it's never really too late to forgive. Because whenever you forgive, you're ultimately doing it for yourself.

"Please stand and repeat after me," the minister instructed.

I reluctantly stood, prepared to mouth whatever I was commanded to say. I rarely felt comfortable with people putting words in my mouth. I expected that I might end up feeling like a robot.

"God is the only power in my life," Reverend Taylor pronounced decisively. The congregation, including me, repeated her words in unison. The pastor stretched her arms high above her head.

I knew that God was the highest power in my life, but I wasn't sure that God was the *only* power in my life, I thought skeptically.

"Nothing from without can touch the perfect life of God within me," the minister continued.

That's a nice concept, I conceded.

"No past experience has power over me."

I wish, I thought cynically.

"I am a perfect child of God."

I like the sound of that, I acknowledged.

"And nothing that anyone has ever done or said can interfere with my divine inheritance."

That's reassuring, I thought.

"The power of God is greater than any circumstance in my life."

That is *empowering,* I agreed.

"The strength of God is mine to use."

That's comforting, I admitted.

"Turning away from all feelings of inadequacy, I discover that all I need is within me right now."

That's good to remember, I told myself.

"As I forgive the past I find that I have nothing to atone for and nothing to run away from."

I sighed, feeling compassion for myself.

"Casting off the old me, I discovered my true self."

I took a deep breath. I felt a sense of hope.

"I take dominion in my life."

I planted my feet more firmly on the floor and nodded in agreement.

"Old habits have no power over me," the minister continued.

"Conditions have no power over me.

"Personalities have no power over me.

"I take dominion.

"I'm whole.

"I'm free.

"I'm complete.

"Now and forever more.

"And so it is!

"Say yes!"

"Yes!!!!" I shouted with the enthusiastic congregation. My voice sounded vibrant. I had indeed been inspired.

"Hallelujah!"

"I'm whole! I'm perfect and I'm free!"

"Now and forever more!"

"And so it is!" the minister proclaimed jubilantly. A tenor soloist stepped forward from the choir and sang "I Believe I Can Fly."

The congregation joined in, still on its feet. My voice rang out clear and strong.

Brianna clutched Skylar's and my hands and swung them in time with the music.

I could picture the three of us riding the Ferris wheel together in the spring.